"IN ITS NARRATIVE FORCE, IT IS MORE THAN A LITTLE LIKE *ROBINSON CRUSOE*, AND IT HAS THE SAME KIND OF FASCINATION."
—*The New York Times*

"THE BOOK HAS MORE THOUGHT-CHALLENGING ELEMENTS THAN A SHELFFUL OF ORDINARY NOVELS."   —*Christian Science Monitor*

The FIRST choice of the Science Fiction Book Club

The FIRST choice of the International Fantasy Award

Among George R. Stewart's many works are Storm, Fire, Ordeal by Hunger, *and* Names on the Land, *all of which have dealt with the subject of man against the background of his environment.*

Earth Abides

by George R. Stewart

FAWCETT CREST • NEW YORK

Men go and come, but earth abides
ECCLESIASTES, I, 4

to Jill

Contents

1 World Without End   7

2 The Year 22   139

3 The Last American   291

World Without End

> *If a killing type of virus strain should suddenly arise by mutation . . . it could, because of the rapid transportation in which we indulge nowadays, be carried to the far corners of the earth and cause the deaths of millions of people.*
> —W. M. Stanley, in *Chemical and Engineering News*, Dec. 22, 1947.

Chapter 1

. . . and the government of the United States of America is herewith suspended, except in the District of Columbia, as of the emergency. Federal officers, including those of the Armed Forces, will put themselves under the orders of the governors of the various states or of any other functioning local authority. By order of the Acting President. God save the people of the United States. . . .

Here is an announcement which has just come in from the Bay Area Emergency Council. The West Oakland Hospitalization Center has been abandoned. Its functions, including burials at sea, are now concentrated at the Berkeley Center. That is all. . . .

Keep tuned to this Station, which is the only one now in operation in northern California. We shall inform you of developments, as long as it is possible.

Just as he pulled himself up to the rock-ledge, he heard a sudden rattle, and felt a prick of fangs. Automatically he jerked back his right hand; turning his head, he saw the snake, coiled and menacing. It was not a large one, he noted, even at the moment when he raised his hand to his lips and sucked hard at the base of the index-finger, where a little drop of blood was oozing out.

"Don't waste time by killing the snake!" he remembered.

He slid down from the ledge, still sucking. At the bottom he saw the hammer lying where he had left it. For a moment he thought he would go on and leave it there. That seemed like panic; so he stooped and picked it up with his left hand, and went on down the rough trail.

He did not hurry. He knew better than that. Hurry only speeded up a man's heart, and made the venom circulate faster. Yet his heart was pounding so rapidly from excitement or fear that hurrying or not hurrying, it seemed, should make no difference. After he had come to some trees, he took his handkerchief and bound it around his right wrist. With the aid of a twig he twisted the handkerchief into a crude tourniquet.

Walking on, he felt himself recovering from his panic. His heart was slowing down. As he considered the situation, he was not greatly afraid. He was a young man, vigorous and healthy. Such a bite would hardly be fatal, even though he was by himself and without good means of treatment.

Now he saw the cabin ahead of him. His hand felt stiff. Just before he got to the cabin, he stopped and loosened the tourniquet, as he had read should be done, and let the blood circulate in the hand. Then he tightened it again.

He pushed open the door, dropping the hammer on the floor as he did so. It fell, handle up, on its heavy head, rocked back and forth for a moment, and then stood still, handle in the air.

He looked into the drawer of the table, and found his snake-bite outfit, which he should have been carrying with him on this day of all days. Quickly he followed the directions, slicing with the razor-blade a neat little criss-cross over the mark of the fangs, applying the rubber suction-pump. Then he lay on his bunk watching the rubber bulb slowly expand, as it sucked the blood out.

He felt no premonitions of death. Rather, the whole matter still seemed to him just a nuisance. People had kept telling him that he should not go into the mountains by himself— "Without even a dog!" they used to add. He had always laughed at them. A dog was constant trouble, getting mixed up with porcupines or skunks, and he was not fond of dogs anyway. Now all those people would say, "Well, we warned you!"

Tossing about half-feverishly, he now seemed to himself to be composing a defense. "Perhaps," he would say, "the very danger in it appealed to me!" (That had a touch of the heroic in it.) More truthfully he might say, "I like to be alone at times, really need to escape from all the problems of dealing with people." His best defense, however, would merely be that, at least during the last year, he had gone into the mountains alone as a matter of business. As a gradutae student, he was working on a thesis: *The Ecology of the Black Creek Area*. He had to investigate the relationships, past and present, of men and plants and animals in this region. Obviously he could not wait until just the right companion came along. In any case, he could never see that there was any great danger. Although nobody lived within five miles of his cabin, during the summer hardly a day passed without some fisherman coming by, driving his car up the rocky road or merely following the stream.

Yet, come to think of it, when had he last seen a fisherman? Not in the past week certainly. He could not actually remember whether he had seen one in the two weeks that he had been living by himself in the cabin. There was that car he had heard go by after dark one night. He thought it strange that any car would be going up that road in the darkness, and could hardly see the necessity, for ordinarily people camped down below for the night and went up in the morning. But perhaps, he thought, they wanted to get up to their favorite stream, to go out for some early fishing.

No, actually, he had not exchanged a word with anyone in the last two weeks, and he could not even remember that he had seen anyone.

A throb of pain brought him back to what was happening at the moment. The hand was beginning to swell. He loosened the tourniquet to let the blood circulate again.

Yes, as he returned to his thoughts, he realized that he was out of touch with things entirely. He had no radio. Therefore, as far as he was concerned, there might have been a crash of the stockmarket or another Pearl Harbor; something like that would account for so few fishermen going by. At any rate, there was very little chance apparently that anyone would come to help him. He would have to work his own way out.

Yet even that prospect did not alarm him. At worst, he considered, he would lie up in his cabin, with plenty of food and water for two or three days, until the swelling in his hand subsided and he could drive his car down to Johnson's, the first ranch.

The afternoon wore on. He did not feel like eating anything when it came toward supper-time, but he made himself a pot of coffee on the gasoline stove, and drank several cups. He was in much pain, but in spite of the pain and in spite of the coffee he became sleepy. . . .

He woke suddenly in half-light, and realized that someone had pushed open the cabin door. He felt a sudden relief to know that he had help. Two men in city clothes were standing there, very decent-looking men, although staring around strangely, as if in fright. "I'm sick!" he said from his bunk, and suddenly he saw the fright on their faces change to sheer panic. They turned suddenly without even shutting the door, and ran. A moment later came the sound of a starting motor. It faded out as the car went up the road.

Appalled now for the first time, he raised himself from the bunk, and looked through the window. The car had already vanished around the curve. He could not understand. Why had they suddenly disappeared in panic, without even offering to help?

He got up. The light was in the east; so he had slept until dawn the next morning. His right hand was swollen and acutely painful. Otherwise he did not feel very ill. He warmed up the pot of coffee, made himself some oatmeal, and lay down in his bunk again, in the hope that after a while he would feel well enough to risk driving down to Johnson's—that is, of course, if no one came along in the meantime who would stop and help him and not like those others, who must be crazy, run away at the sight of a sick man.

Soon, however, he felt much worse, and realized that he must be suffering some kind of relapse. By the middle of the afternoon he was really frightened. Lying in his bunk, he composed a note, thinking that he should leave a record of what had happened. It would not be very long of course before someone would find him; his parents would certainly telephone Johnson's in a few days now, if they did not hear anything. Scrawling with his left hand, he managed to get the words onto paper. He signed merely *Ish*. It was too much work to write out his full name of Isherwood Williams, and everybody knew him by his nickname.

At noon, feeling himself like the ship-wrecked mariner who from his raft sees the steamer cross along the horizon, he heard the sound of cars, two of them, coming up the steep road. They approached, and then went on, without stopping. He called to them, but by now he was weak, and his voice, he was sure, did not carry the hundred yards to the turn-off where the cars were passing.

Even so, before dusk he struggled to his feet, and lighted the kerosene lamp. He did not want to be left in the dark.

Apprehensively he bent his lanky body down to peer into the little mirror, set too low for him because of the sloping roof of the cabin. His long face was thin always, and scarcely seemed thinner now, but a reddish flush showed through the sun-tan of his cheeks. His big blue eyes were blood-shot, and stared back at him wildly with the glare of fever. His light brown hair, unruly always, now stuck out in all directions, completing the mirror-portrait of a very sick young man.

He got back into his bunk, feeling no great sense of fear, although now he more than half expected that he was dying. Soon a violent chill struck him; from that he passed into a fever. The lamp burned steadily on the table, and he could see around the cabin. The hammer which he had dropped on the floor still stood there, handle pointed stiffly upwards, precariously balanced. Being right before his eyes, the hammer occupied an unduly large part of his consciousness—he thought about it a little disorderedly, as if he were making his will, an old-fashioned will in which he described the chattels he was leaving. "One hammer, called a *single-jack*, weight of head four pounds, handle one foot long, slightly cracked, injured by exposure to weather, head of hammer somewhat rusted, still serviceable." He had been extraordinarily pleased when he had found the hammer, appreciating that actual link with the past. It had been used by some miner in the old days when rock-drills were driven home in a low tunnel with a man swinging a hammer in one hand; four pounds was about the weight a man could handle in that way, and it was called a single-jack because it was managed one-handedly. He thought, feverishly, that he might even include a picture of the hammer as an illustration in his thesis.

Most of those hours of darkness he passed in little better than a nightmare, racked by coughing, choking frequently, shaking with the chill and then burning with the fever. A pink measles-like rash broke out on him.

At daybreak he felt himself again sinking into a deep sleep.

"It has never happened!" cannot be construed to mean, "It can never happen!"—as well say, "Because I have never broken my leg, my leg is unbreakable," or "Because I've never died, I am immortal." One thinks first of some great plague of insects—locusts or grasshoppers—when the species suddenly increases out of all proportion, and then just as dramatically sinks to a tiny fraction of what it has recently been. The higher animals also fluctuate. The lemmings work upon their cycle. The snowshoe-rabbits build up through a period of years until they reach a climax when they seem to be everywhere; then with dramatic suddenness their pestilence falls upon them. Some zoologists have even suggested a biological law: that the number of individuals in a species never remains constant, but always rises and falls—the higher the animal and the slower its breeding-rate, the longer its period of fluctuation.

During most of the nineteenth century the African buffalo was a common creature on the veldt. It was a powerful beast with few natural enemies, and if its census could have been taken by decades, it would have proved to be increasing steadily. Then toward the century's end it reached its climax, and was suddenly struck by a plague of rinderpest. Afterwards the buffalo was almost a curiosity, extinct in many

*parts of its range. In the last fifty years it has again slowly
built up its numbers.*

*As for man, there is little reason to think that he can in the
long run escape the fate of other creatures, and if there is a
biological law of flux and reflux, his situation is now a highly
perilous one. During ten thousand years his numbers have
been on the upgrade in spite of wars, pestilences, and famines.
This increase in population has become more and more rapid.
Biologically, man has for too long a time been rolling an
uninterrupted run of sevens.*

When he awoke in the middle of the morning, he felt a
sudden sense of pleasure. He had feared he would be sicker
than ever, but he felt much better. He was not choking any
more, and also his hand felt cooler. The swelling had gone
down. On the preceding day he had felt so bad, from whatever other trouble had struck him, that he had had no time
to think about the hand. Now both the hand and the illness
seemed better, as if the one had stopped the other and they
had both receded. By noon he was feeling clear-headed and
not even particularly weak.

He ate some lunch, and decided that he could make it
down to Johnson's. He did not bother to pack up everything.
He took his precious notebooks and his camera. At the last
moment also, as if by some kind of compulsion, he picked
up the hammer, carried it to the car, and threw it in on the
floor by his feet. He drove off slowly, using his right hand as
little as possible.

At Johnson's everything was quiet. He let the car roll to a
stop at the gasoline-pump. Nobody came out to fill his tank,
but that was not peculiar, because the Johnson pump, like so
many in the mountains, was tended on a haphazard basis. He
blew the horn, and waited again. After another minute he
got out, and went up the rickety steps which led to the room
serving as an informal store where campers could pick up
cigarettes and canned goods. He went in, but there was nobody there.

He had a certain sense of surprise. As often, when he had
been by himself for a while, he was not exactly sure what
day it might be. Wednesday, he thought. But it might be
Tuesday or Thursday. Yet he was certain that it was somewhere in the middle of the week, not a Sunday. On a Sunday, or even for a whole weekend, the Johnsons might possibly shut up the store and go somewhere on a trip of their
own. They were easy-going, and did not believe too strongly

in letting business interfere with pleasure. Yet they were really dependent to a large extent upon the sales which the store made during the fishing season; they could hardly afford to go away very long. And if they had gone on a vacation, they would have locked the door. Still you never could tell about these mountain people. The incident might even be worth a paragraph in his thesis. In any case, his tank was nearly empty. The pump was unlocked, and so he helped himself to ten gallons of gas and with difficulty scrawled a check which he left on the counter along with a note: "Found you all away. Took 10 gal. Ish."

As he drove down the road, he had suddenly a slight sense of uneasiness—the Johnsons gone on a weekday, the door unlocked, no fishermen, a car going by in the night, and (most of all) those men who had run away when they had seen another man lying sick in his bunk in a lonely mountain cabin. Yet the day was bright, and his hand was not paining him much; moreover, he seemed to be cured of that other strange infection, if it was something else and not the snakebite. He felt almost back to normal again. Now the road wound down restfully between open groves of pine trees along a little rushing stream. By the time he came to Black Creek Power-house, he felt normal in his mind again also.

At the power-house everything looked as usual. He heard the whir of the big generators, and saw the streams of foaming water still bursting out from beneath. A light was burning on the bridge. He thought to himself, "I suppose nobody bothers ever to turn that out. They have so much electricity that they don't need to economize."

He considered going across the bridge to the power-house, just to see somebody and allay the strange fears which he had begun to feel. But the sight and sound of everything running normally were reassuring, signs that after all the power-house was working as usual, even though he saw no people. There was nothing remarkable about not seeing people. The process was so nearly automatic that only a few men were employed there, and they kept indoors mostly.

Just as he was leaving the power-house behind, a large collie ran out from behind one of the buildings. From the other side of the creek, it barked loudly and violently at Ish. It ran back and forth excitedly.

"Fool dog!" he thought. "What's it so excited about? Is it trying to tell me not to steal the power-house?" People certainly tended to overestimate the intelligence of dogs!

Rounding the curve, he left the sound of barking behind.

But the sight of the dog had been another evidence of normality. Ish began to whistle contentedly. It was ten miles now until he came to the first town, a little place called Hutsonville.

Consider the case of Captain Maclear's rat. This interesting rodent inhabited Christmas Island, a small bit of tropical verdure some two hundred miles south of Java. The species was first described for science in 1887, the skull being noted as large and strongly built, with beaded supra-orbital edges and the anterior edge of the zygomatic plate projecting forward conspicuously.

A naturalist observed the rats as populating the island "in swarms," feeding upon fruit and young shoots. To the rats the island was as a whole world, an earthly paradise. The observer noted: "They seem to breed all the year round." Yet such was the luxuriance of the tropical growth that the rats had not attained such numbers as to provide competition among members of the species. The individual rats were extremely well nourished, and even unduly fat.

In 1903 some new disease sprang up. Because of their crowding, and also probably because of the softened condition of the individuals, the rats proved universally susceptible, and soon were dying by thousands. In spite of great numbers, in spite of an abundant supply of food, in spite of a very rapid breeding rate, the species is extinct.

He came over the rise, and saw Hutsonville a mile away. Just as he started to slide down the grade, out of the corner of his eye, he caught sight of something which turned him inwardly cold. Automatically he tramped hard on the brake. He walked back, scarcely believing that he had really seen it. Just there at the side of the road, in full view, lay the body of a fully clothed man; ants were crawling over the face. The body must have lain there a day or two at least. Why had it not been seen? He did not look closely or long, obviously the thing to do was to get into Hutsonville, and tell the Coroner as soon as possible. He hurried back to the car.

Yet as he started again, he had a deep feeling inside him somewhere, strangely, that this was not a case for the Coroner, and that possibly there would even be no Coroner. He had seen no one at the Johnson's or at the power-house, and he had not met a single car on the road. The only things that seemed real from all the old life had been the light burning at the power-house and the quiet hum of the great generators at their work.

Then, as he came to the first houses, he suddenly breathed more easily, for there on a vacant lot a hen was quietly scratching in the dust, a half-dozen chicks beside her, and a little farther on, a black-and-white cat wandered across the sidewalk as unconcernedly as it would have done upon any other June day.

The heat of the afternoon lay heavy on the street, and he saw no one. "Bad as a Mexican town," he thought, "everyone taking a siesta." Then suddenly he realized that he had said it as a man whistles to keep up his courage. He came to the business center, stopped the car by the curb, and got out. There was nobody.

He tried the door of a little restaurant. It was open. He went in.

"Hi!" he yelled.

Nobody came. Not even an echo spoke back to reassure him.

The door of the bank was locked, although the hour was well before closing time, and he was sure (the more he thought of it) that the day must be Tuesday or Wednesday or possibly Thursday. "What am I anyway?" he thought. "Rip van Winkle?" Even so, Rip van Winkle, though he had slept twenty years, had come back to a village that was still full of people.

The door of the hardware store beyond the bank was open. He went in, and again he called, and again there was not even an echo coming back for answer. He looked in at the bakery; this time there was only a tiny noise such as a scuttling mouse could make.

Had the people all gone to a baseball game? Even so, they would have closed the stores. He went back to his car, got into the seat, and looked around. Was he himself delirious, still lying on his bunk, really? He was half inclined merely to drive on; panic was rising up inside him. Now he noticed that several cars were parked along the street, just as they might be on any not too busy afternoon. He could not merely drive on, he decided, because he must report the dead man. So he pushed upon the horn-rig, and the great blatant squawk resounded obscenely along the deserted street through the quiet of the afternoon. He blew twice, waited, and blew twice again. Again and again, in rising panic, he pressed down. As he pressed, he looked around, hoping to see somebody come popping out from a door or at least a head at a

16

window. He paused, and again there was only silence, except that somewhere far off he heard the strident cackling of a hen. "Must have scared an egg out of her!" he thought.

A fat dog came waddling around the corner and down the sidewalk, the kind of dog you see along Main Street in any small town. Ish got out of the car, and confronted the dog. "You haven't been missing any meals, anyway," he said. (Then he had a sudden feeling of tightness in the throat when he thought of things the dog might be eating.) The dog was not friendly; it skirted him, keeping distance; then it went on down the street. He made no effort to call it closer or to follow it; after all, the dog could not tell him.

"I could play detective by going into some of these stores and looking around," he thought. Then he had a better idea.

Across the street was a little pool-room where he had often stopped to buy a newspaper. He went over to it. The door was locked. He looked through the window, and saw newspapers on the rack. He stared hard against the reflection of the light in the window, and suddenly he saw that there were headlines as large as for Pearl Harbor. He read:

CRISIS ACUTE

What crisis? With sudden determination he strode back to the car, and picked up the hammer. A moment later he stood with the heavy head poised in front of the door.

Then suddenly all the restraints of habit stopped him. Civilization moved in, and held his arm, almost physically. You couldn't do this! You didn't break into a store this way—you, a law-abiding citizen! He glanced up and down the street, as if a policeman or a posse might be bearing down upon him.

But the empty street brought him back again, and panic overbore the restraints. "Hell," he thought, "I can pay for the door if I have to!"

With a wild feeling of burning his bridges, of leaving civilization behind, he swung the heavy hammer-head with all his force against the door-lock. The wood splintered, the door flew open, he stepped in.

His first shock came when he picked up the newspaper. *The Chronicle,* the one he remembered, was thick—twenty or thirty pages at least. The newspaper he picked up was like a little country weekly, a single folded sheet. It was dated Wednesday of the preceding week.

The headlines told him what was most essential. The United States from coast to coast was overwhelmed by the attack of some new and unknown disease of unparalleled rapidity of spread, and fatality. Estimates for various cities, admittedly little more than guesses, indicated that between 25 percent and 35 percent of the population had already died. No reports, he read, were available for Boston, Atlanta, and New Orleans, indicating that the news-services in those cities had already broken down. Rapidly scanning the rest of the paper, he gained a variety of impressions—a hodge-podge which he could scarcely put together in any logical order. In its symptoms the disease was like a kind of super-measles. No one was sure in what part of the world it had originated; aided by airplane travel, it had sprung up almost simultaneously in every center of civilization, outrunning all attempts at quarantine.

In an interview a notable bacteriologist indicated that the emergence of some new disease had always been a possibility which had worried the more far-thinking epidemiologists. He mentioned in the past such curious though minor outbreaks as the English sweat and Q-fever. As for its origin, he offered three possibilities. It might have emerged from some animal reservoir of disease; it might be caused by some new micro-organism, most likely a virus, produced by mutation; it might be an escape, possibly even a vindictive release, from some laboratory of bacteriological warfare. The last was apparently the popular idea. The disease was assumed to be airborne, possibly upon particles of dust. A curious feature was that the isolation of the individual seemed to be of no avail.

In an interview conducted by trans-Atlantic telephone, a crusty old British sage had commented, "Man has been growing more stupid for several thousand years; I myself shall waste no tears at his demise." On the other hand an equally crusty American critic had got religion: "Only faith can save us now; I am praying hourly."

A certain amount of looting, particularly of liquor stores was reported. On the whole, however, order had been well preserved, possibly through fear. Louisville and Spokane reported conflagrations, out of control because of decimated fire-departments.

Even in what they must have suspected to be their last issue, the gentlemen of the press, however, had not neglected to include a few of their beloved items of curiosity. In Omaha a religious fanatic had run naked through the streets, calling out the end of the world and the opening of the Seventh Seal. In Sacramento a crazed woman had opened the cages of a circus menagerie for fear that the animals might starve to death, and had been mauled by a lioness. Of more scientific interest, the Director of the San Diego zoo reported his apes and monkeys to be dying off rapidly, the other animals unaffected.

As he read, Ish felt himself growing weak with the cumulative piling up of horror and an overwhelming sense of solitude. Yet he still read on, fascinated.

Civilization, the human race—at least, it seemed to have gone down gallantly. Many people were reported as escaping from the cities, but those remaining had suffered, as far as he could make out from the newspaper a week old, no disgraceful panic. Civilization had retreated, but it had carried its wounded along, and had faced the foe. Doctors and nurses had stayed at their posts, and thousands more had enlisted as helpers. Whole areas of cities had been designated as hospital zones and points of concentration. All ordinary business had ceased, but food was still handled on an emergency basis. Even with a third of the population dead, telephone service along with water, light, and power still remained in most cities. In order to avoid intolerable conditions which might lead to a total breakdown of morale, the authorities were enforcing strict regulations for immediate mass burials.

He read the paper, and then read it through again more carefully. There was obviously nothing else he needed to do. When he had finished it a second time, he went out and sat in his car. There was no particular reason, he realized, why he should sit in his own car rather than in some other. There was no more question of property right, and yet he felt more comfortable being where he had been before. (The fat dog walked along the street again, but he did not call to the dog.) He sat there a long time, thinking; rather, he scarcely thought, but his mind seemed merely turning over without getting anywhere.

The sun was nearly down when he roused himself. He started the engine, and drove the car down the street, stopping now and then to blow a blast upon the horn. He turned off into a side street, and made the rounds of the town, blowing the horn methodically. The town was small, and in a quarter of an hour he was back where he had started. He had seen no one, and heard no answer. He had observed four dogs, several cats, a considerable number of scattered hens, one cow grazing in a vacant lot with a bit of broken rope dangling from her neck. Nosing along the doorway of a very decent-looking house, there had been a large rat.

He did not stop in the business district again, but drove on and came to what he now knew to be the best house in town. He got out of the car, carrying the hammer with him. This time he did not hesitate before the locked door; he struck it hard, three times, and it crashed inwards. As he had supposed, there was a large radio in the living-room.

He made a quick round of inspection, downstairs and up. "There's nobody!" he decided. Then the grim suggestion of the word itself struck him: *Nobody—no body!"*

Feeling the two meanings already coalescing in his mind, he returned to the living-room. He snapped the radio on, and saw that the electricity was still working. He let the tubes warm up, and then searched carefully. Only faint crackles of static impinged on his alerted ear-drums; there was no program. He shifted to the short-wave, but it too was silent. Methodically he searched both bands again. Of course, he thought, some stations might still be operating; they would probably not be on a twenty-four-hour schedule.

He left the radio tuned to a wave-length which was—or had been—that of a powerful station. If it came on at any time, he would hear it. He went and lay on the davenport.

In spite of the horror of the situation he felt a curious spectator's sense about it all, as if he were watching the last act of a great drama. This, he realized, was characteristic of his personality. He was—had been—was (well, no matter) —a student, an incipient scholar, and such a one was necessarily oriented to observe, rather than to participate.

Thus observing, he even gained a momentary ironic satisfaction by contemplating the catastrophe as a demonstration of a dictum which he had heard an economics professor once propound—"The trouble you're expecting never happens; it's always something that sneaks up the other way." Mankind had been trembling about destruction through war, and had been having bad dreams of cities blown to pieces along with their inhabitants, of animals killed too, and of the very vegetation blighted off the face of the earth. But actually mankind seemed merely to have been removed rather neatly, with a minimum of disturbance. This, he thought vaguely, would offer interesting conditions of life to the survivors, if eventually there were any.

He lay comfortably on the davenport; the evening was warm. Physically he was exhausted from his illness, and he was equally spent emotionally. Soon he was sleeping.

High overhead, moon and planets and stars swung in their long smooth curves. They had no eyes, and they saw not; yet from the time when man's fancy first formed within him, he has imagined that they looked down upon the earth.

And if so we may still imagine, and if they looked down upon the earth that night, what did they see?

Then we must say that they saw no change. Though smoke from stacks and chimneys and campfires no longer rose to dim the atmosphere, yet still smoke rose from volcanos and from forest-fires. Seen even from the moon, the planet that night must have shown only with its accustomed splendor— no brighter, no dimmer.

He awoke in the full light. Flexing his hand, he found that the pain of the snake-bite had shrunk back to local soreness. His head felt clear too, and he realized that the other illness, if it had been another illness and not an effect of the snake-bite, had also grown better. Then suddenly he started, and was aware of something which he had not considered before. The obvious explanation was that he had actually had this new disease, and that it had combatted with the snake-venom in his blood, the one neutralizing the other. That at least offered the simplest explanation of why he was still alive.

As he lay there quietly on the davenport, he was very calm. The isolated bits of the puzzle were now beginning to fit into their places. The men who had fled in panic at seeing someone lying sick in the cabin—they had merely been some poor fugitives, afraid that the pestilence had already preceded them. The car that had gone up the road in the darkness had carried other fugitives, possibly even the Johnsons. The excited collie had been trying to tell him that strange things had happened at the power-house.

But as he lay there, he was not greatly perturbed even at the thought that he might be the only person left in the world. Possibly that was because he had not seen many people for some time, so that the shock of the new realization could not come to him as strongly as to one who had seen his fellow-creatures dying on all sides. At the same time he could not really believe, and he had no reason to believe, that he alone was left upon the earth. The last report in the paper indicated that the population had merely shrunk by perhaps a third. The evacuation of a small town like Hutsonville showed merely that the population had scattered or withdrawn to some other center. Before he shed any tears over the destruction of civilization and the death of man, he

21

should discover whether civilization was destroyed and whether man was dead. Obviously the first call was for him to return to the house where his parents had lived—or, he hoped, might still be living. Having thus laid out for himself a definite plan for the day, he felt the quiet satisfaction which always came to him when confusion of mind yielded even to temporary certainty.

Getting up, he searched both radio bands again, and again without result.

He went into the kitchen; throwing open the door of the refrigerator, he found that it was still working. On the shelves was a fair assortment of food, though not as much as might have been expected. Apparently supplies had failed a little before the house had been abandoned, and the larder was comparatively scant. Nevertheless there were half a dozen eggs, most of a pound of butter, and some bacon, along with several heads of lettuce, a little celery, and a few odds and ends. Looking into a cupboard, he found a can of grapefruit-juice; in a bread-drawer there was a loaf of bread, dry but not impossible. He estimated that it might have been there for five days, and so he had a better idea than before of the time at which the town might have been abandoned. With such materials at hand he was enough of a camper to have built a fire outdoors and contrived an excellent meal, but he snapped the switches of the electric stove and felt the heat begin to radiate. He cooked himself a hearty breakfast, managing even to make the bread into acceptable toast. As always when he came out of the mountains, he was hungry for fresh green stuff, and so to his conventional breakfast of bacon, eggs and coffee, he added a generous head-lettuce salad.

Returning to the davenport, he helped himself from a red lacquer box on the nearby table, and smoked an after-breakfast cigarette. As yet, he reflected, the maintenance of life offered no problem.

The cigarette was not even yet badly dried out. With a good breakfast and a good cigarette, he did not feel himself worrying. Actually he had put worry in abeyance, and had decided that he would not indulge in it until he had really found out just how much need there was.

When he had finished the cigarette, he reflected that there was really no need even to wash the dishes, but since he was naturally careful, he went to the kitchen and made sure that he had left the refrigerator closed and had turned off the burners on the stove. Then he picked up the hammer, which had already proved so useful, and went out by the shattered front door. He got into his car, and started for home.

A half mile beyond the town, he caught sight of the cemetery. He realized that he had not thought of it on the preceding day. Without getting out of the car, he noticed a long row of new individual graves, and also a bull-dozer near a large heap of earth. Probably, he decided, there had not really been many people left to abandon Hutsonville at the end.

Beyond the cemetery the road sloped down through flattening terrain. At all the emptiness, depression settled down on him again; he longed even for a single clattering truck suddenly to come across the rise ahead, but there was no truck.

Some steers stood in a field and some horses with them. They switched their tails at the flies, as they might on any hot summer morning. Above them the spokes of the windmill revolved slowly in the breeze, and below the watering-trough there was a little patch of green and trampled muddy ground, as there always was—and that was all.

Yet this road below Hutsonville never carried much traffic, and on any morning he might have driven several miles without seeing anyone. It was different when he came to the highway. The lights were still burning at the junction, and automatically he pulled to a stop because they were red.

But where trucks and buses and cars should have been streaming by, crowding the four lanes, there was only emptiness. After he had paused just a moment at the red lights, he drove on through them, even though feeling a slight sense of wrongdoing as he did so.

Beyond that, on the highway with all the four lanes to himself, everything was more ghostlike than before. He seemed to drive half in a daze, and only now and then some special scene brought him out, and fixed itself in his consciousness. . . .

Something was loping along the inner lane ahead of him. He drew up on it fast from behind. A dog? No, he saw the sharp ears and the light lean legs, gray shading into yellow. That was no farm dog. It was a coyote, calmly loping along the highway in broad daylight. Strange how soon it had known that the world had changed, and that it could take new freedoms! He drew up close and honked his horn, and the beast quickened its pace a little and swung over into the other lane and off across the fields, seemingly not much alarmed. . . .

23

The two cars lay sprawled at crazy angles blocking both lanes. It had been a bad accident. He pulled out onto the shoulder and stopped. A man's body lay crushed beneath one car. He got out to look. There was no other body although the pavement was spotted with blood. Even if he had seen any particular reason to try, he could not have raised the car from the man's body to give it burial. He drove on. . . .

His mind did not even bother to register the name of the town where he stopped for gasoline, though it was a large one. The electricity was still working; he took down the nozzle from the gas-pump at a large station and filled the tank. Since his car had been so long in the mountains, he checked the radiator and battery, and put in a quart of oil. He saw that one tire needed more air, and as he pressed the air-hose against the valve, he heard the motor suddenly start to build up the pressure again in the tank. Yes, man had gone, but so recently that all his well-contrived automatic processes were still carrying on without his care. . . .

At the main street of some other town he stopped, and blew a long blast on the horn. He had no real expectation that he would have any reply, but there was something about the look of this street which seemed more normal than those of other towns. Many cars were parked at the meters where each one showed the red flag of a violation. It might have been some Sunday morning with many cars parked overnight and the stores not yet open or people beginning to circulate. But it was not early morning, for now the sun was almost overhead. Then he saw what had made him pause, and what gave the place an illusion of animation. In front of a restaurant called *The Derby* a neon sign was still in full activity—a little horse galloping hard, its legs still going as actively as ever. In the full sunlight the faint pink glow was scarcely visible except for its motion. He looked, and as he looked, he caught the rhythm,—*one, two, three.* (And at *three* the feet of the little horse were close tucked up under its body as if it were clear in the air.) *Four*—they came back to the half position, and the legs stretched out as if the body were low along the ground. *One, two, three, four,* it went. *One, two, three, four.* It galloped in a frenzy of activity still, and yet in all its galloping it arrived nowhere, and now even for most of its time it galloped with no eye to observe. As he looked, it seemed to him a gallant little horse, though a futile and a foolish one. The horse, suddenly he thought, was like that civilization of which man had been so proud, galloping so hard and yet never arriving any-where; and sometime destined, when once the power failed, to grow still forever. . . .

He saw smoke rising against the sky. His heart leaped up, and he turned quickly off on a side road, and drove toward the smoke. But even before he reached it, he knew that he would find no one there, and his spirit fell again. He drove up to the smoke, and saw then that it was a small farmhouse quietly beginning to burn up. There were many reasons, he decided, why a fire might start thus without people. A pile of greasy rags might ignite spontaneously, or some electric apparatus might have been left on, or a motor in a refrigera-tor might jam and begin to burn. The little house was ob-viously doomed. There was nothing he could do, and no special reason why he should do it if he could. He turned around, and headed back to the highway. . . .

He did not drive fast, and he stopped often to investigate, rather half-heartedly. Here and there he saw bodies, but in general he found only emptiness. Apparently the onset of the disease had been slow enough so that people were not usually struck down in the streets. Once he passed through a town where the smell of corpses was thick in the air. He remem-bered what he had read in the newspaper; apparently there had been concentrations at the last upon certain areas, and in these the corpses were now to be found most thickly. There was all too much evidence of death in that town and none of life. He saw no reason to stop to investigate. Surely no one would linger there longer than necessary.

In the late afternoon he came across the crest of the hills, and saw the Bay lie bright beneath the westering sun. Smokes rose here and there from the vast expanse of city, but they did not look like smokes rising from chimneys. He drove on toward the house where he had lived with his parents. He had no hope. Miracle enough it was that he himself had survived—miracle upon miracle if the plague had also spared the others of his own family!

From the boulevard he turned into San Lupo Drive. Ev-erything looked much the same, although the sidewalks were not as well swept as the standard of San Lupo Drive re-quired. It had always been a street of eminent respectability, and even yet, he reflected, it preserved decorum. No corpse lay on the street; that would be unthinkable in San Lupo Drive. He saw the Hatfields' old gray cat sleeping on their porch-step in the sun, as he had seen her a hundred times before. Aroused by the sound of the car as he drove by, she rose up and stretched luxuriously.

He let the car roll to a stop in front of the house where he had lived so long. He blew two blasts on the horn, and waited. Nothing! He got out of the car, and walked up the steps into the house. Only after he had entered did he think it a little strange that the door was not even locked.

Inside, things were in good-enough order. He glanced about, apprehensively, but there was nothing at which a man would hesitate to look. He searched around the living-room for some note left behind to tell him where they had gone. There was no note.

Upstairs also everything looked much as usual, but in his parents' bedroom both the beds were unmade. Perhaps it was that which made him begin to feel giddy and sick. He walked out of the room, feeling himself unsteady.

Holding by the rail, he made it downstairs again. "The kitchen!" he thought, and his mind cleared a trifle at the thought of something definite to do.

As he opened the swinging door, the fact of motion within the room struck his senses. Then he saw that it was only the second hand of the electric clock above the sink, steadily moving on past the vertical, beginning its long swoop toward six again. At that moment also he started wildly at a sudden noise, only to realize that the motor of the electric refrigerator, as if disturbed by his coming, had begun to whir. In quick reaction he was deathly ill, and found himself vomiting into the sink.

Recovered, he went out again, and sat in the car. He was no longer ill, but he felt weak and utterly despondent. If he made a detective-like investigation, searching in cupboards and drawers, he could probably discover something. But of what use thus to torture himself? The main part of the story was clear. There were no bodies in the house; of that at least he could be thankful. Neither, he believed, would there be any ghosts—although the faithful clock and refrigerator were rather too ghostlike.

Should he go back into the house, or go somewhere else? At first he thought that he could not enter again. Then he realized that just as he had come here, so his father and mother, if by any chance they still lived, would also return here looking for him. After half an hour, overcoming repugnance, he went back into the house.

Again he wandered through the empty rooms. They spoke with all the pathos of any dwelling-place left without people.

26

Now and then some little thing cried out to him more poignantly—his father's new encyclopedia (purchased with qualms as to the expense), his mother's potted pelargoniums (now needing water), the barometer that his father used to tap each morning when he came down to breakfast. Yes, it was a simple house—what you would expect of a man who had taught history in high school and liked books, and of a woman who had made it into a home for him and served on the Y.W.C.A. board, and of their only child—"He always does so well in his studies!"—for whom they had cherished ambitions and for whose education they had made sacrifices.

After a while he sat down in the living-room. Looking at the familiar chairs and pictures and books, he gradually came to feel less despondent.

As twilight fell, he realized that he had not eaten since morning. He was not hungry, but his weakness might be partly the result of lack of food. He rummaged around a little, and opened a can of soup. He found only the stub of a loaf of bread, and it was mouldy. The refrigerator supplied butter and stale cheese. He located crackers in a cupboard. The gas-pressure at the kitchen stove was very low, but he managed to warm up the soup.

Afterwards he sat on the porch in the dark. In spite of his meal he felt unsteady, and he realized that he was suffering from shock.

San Lupo Drive was high enough on the slope of the hills to be proud of its view. As he sat there looking out, everything seemed just about the same. Apparently the processes behind the production of electricity must be almost completely automatic. In the hydro-electric plants the flow of water was still keeping the generators in motion. Moreover, when things had started to go to pieces, someone must have ordered that the street-lights be left turned on. Now he saw beneath him all the intricate pattern of the lights in the East Bay cities, and beyond that the yellow chains of lights on the Bay Bridge, and still farther through the faint evening mist, the glow of the San Francisco lights and the fainter chains on the Golden Gate Bridge. Even the traffic-lights were still working, changing from green to red. High upon the bridge-towers the flashes silently sent their warnings to airplanes which would no longer ever be flying. (Far to the south, however, somewhere in Oakland, there was one wholly black section. There, some switch must have failed, or some fuse have burned out.) Even the advertising signs, some of them at least, had been left burning. Pathetically, they flashed out their call to buy, though no longer were there any customers left or any salesmen. One great sign in particular, its lower part hidden behind a nearby building still sent out its message *Drink* although he could not see what he was thus commanded to drink.

He watched it, half-fascinated. *Drink*—blackness. *Drink*—blackness. *Drink*. "Well, why not?" he thought, and going in, he came out again with a bottle of his father's brandy.

Yet the brandy had little bite, and brought no satisfaction. "I'm probably not the type," he thought, "to drink myself to death." He found himself really more interested in watching the sign that still flashed there. *Drink*—blackness. *Drink*—blackness. *Drink*. How long would the lights burn? What would make them go out in the end? What else would continue? What was going to happen to all that man had built up through the centuries and now had left behind him?

"I suppose," he thought again, "I ought to be considering suicide. No, too soon. I am alive, and so others probably are alive. We are just like gas molecules in a near-vacuum, circulating around, one unable to make contact with the other."

Again a kind of dullness verging on despair slowly came settling upon him. What if he did live on, eating as a scavenger at all those great supplies of food which were piled up in every storeroom? What if he could live well and even if he could draw together a few other survivors? What would it all amount to? It would be different if one could pick half a dozen friends for fellow-survivors, but this way they would probably be dull and stupid people, or even vicious ones. He looked out and saw still the great sign flashing far off. *Drink*—blackness. *Drink*—blackness. *Drink*. And again he wondered how long it would keep flashing while there were no more vending-machines or salesmen offering whatever it was one was to drink, and from that he thought back to some of the other things he had seen that day, wondering what would happen to the coyote that he had seen loping along the highway, and what would happen to the cattle and horses standing by the watering-trough beneath the slowly revolving spokes of the windmill. How long indeed would the windmill still revolve and pump its water from the depths of the earth?

Then suddenly he gave a quick start, and he realized that he had again a will to live! At least, if he could be no more a participant, he would be a spectator, and a spectator trained to observe what was happening. Even though the curtain had been rung down on man, here was the opening of the greatest of all dramas for a student such as he. During thousands of years man had impressed himself upon the world. Now man was gone, certainly for a while, perhaps forever. Even if some survivors were left, they would be a long time in again obtaining supremacy. What would happen to the world and its creatures without man? *That* he was left to see!

Chapter 2

Yet, after he was in bed, no sleep came to him. As the chilly arms of the summer fog lapped around the house in the darkness, he felt first loneliness, and then fear, and finally panic. He rose from his bed. Wrapping himself in a bathrobe, he sat before the radio, frantically searching the bands. But he heard only, far-off, the rasp and crackle of static, and there was no one.

With a sudden thought he tried the telephone. As he lifted the receiver, he heard the low hum of the clear wire. He dialed desperately a number—any number! On some distant house he heard the telephone ring, ring again. He waited, thinking of the sound echoing through empty rooms. After it had rung ten times, he hung up. He tried a second number, and a third—and then no others.

Working with a new thought, he rigged up a light with a reflector, and standing on the front porch, high above the city, he sent the flashes into the night—*short-short-short, long-long-long, short-short-short*—the old call of the SOS, which had gone out so often from despairing men. But there was no reply from all the expanse of the city. After a while he realized that with all the street lights still burning there was too much illumination; his own petty flashing would hardly be noticeable.

So he went into the house again. The foggy night sent a chill into him. He turned on the thermostat, and in a moment he heard the whir of the oil-burner. With electricity still working and a full tank of fuel-oil there was no trouble. He sat, and after a while turned out the lights in the house, feeling in some strange way that they were too conspicuous. He let the fog and the darkness wrap him round and conceal him. Still he felt the fear of loneliness, and as he sat there, he laid the hammer close at hand, ready for grasping if there should be need.

A horrible cry broke the darkness! He trembled violently,

and then realized that it was only the call of a mating cat, the sort of sound which in any night one might have heard now and then, even on decorous San Lupo Drive. The caterwauling rose to a climax, and then the growl of a charging dog cut across it, and the night was silent again.

For them the world of twenty thousand years was over-thrown. In the kennels, swollen-tongued, they lay dead of thirst—pointers, collies, poodles, toy pekinese, tall hounds. The luckier ones, not confined, wandered loose through city and countryside; drinking at the streams, at the fountains, at the gold-fish ponds; hunting here and there for what they might find for eating—scurrying after a hen, picking up a squirrel in the park. And gradually, the pangs of hunger breaking down the long centuries of civilization, they drew closer to where the unburied corpses lay.

Now no longer would Best-of-Breed go for stance, and shape of head, and markings. Now Champion Golden Lad of Piedmont IV no longer outranked the worst mongrel of the alley. The prize, which was life itself, would go to the one of keenest brain, staunchest limb, and strongest jaw, who could best shape himself to meet the new ways and who in the old competition of the wilderness could win the means of life.

Peaches, the honey-colored spaniel, sat disconsolate, grow-ing weaker with hunger, too stupid to live by craft, too short-legged to live by pursuit of prey. . . . Spot, the children's mongrel pet, had the luck to find a litter of kittens and kill them, not for fun but for food. . . . Ned, the wire-haired terrier, who had always enjoyed being on his own and was by nature a tramp, managed to get along fairly well. . . . Bridget, the red setter, shivered and trembled, and now and then howled faintly with a howl that was scarcely more than a moan; her gentle spirit found no will to live in a world without master or mistress to love.

That morning he worked out a plan. He felt sure that in an urban district of two million people others must be left alive. The solution was obvious; he must find someone, any-one. The problem was how to make contact.

First he set out to walk around the neighborhood, in the hope of discovering someone he knew. But around the well-known houses he saw no sign of people. The lawns were parched; the flowers, wilting.

Returning home, he passed through the little park where he had often played as a boy, climbing the tall rocks. Two of them leaned together at the top to form a kind of little cave, high and narrow. Ish had often played at hiding there. It seemed a natural primitive refuge-place, and he looked into it. There was no one.

He walked on across a broad surface of smooth rock that sloped with the hillside. It was pitted with small round holes marking the places where squaws had once pounded with stone pestles.

"The world of those Indians passed away," he thought. "And now our world that followed theirs has passed too. And am I the only one?"

After reaching the house again, he got into his car, mapping out in his head a route to cover the city so that few areas would be left out of the sound of the horn. He drove along, hooting the horn about every minute and then waiting, listening for some reply. As he drove, he looked about curiously, appraising what had happened.

The streets had an early-morning look. Many cars were parked, and there was little disorder. Fires were burning here and there, as he could see by smoke-columns. An occasional body lay where the man had finally been overcome, and near one of them he saw two dogs. At one street-corner, the body of a man was hanging from the cross-arm of a telephone pole, conspicuously labeled with a placard *Looter*. After he had passed this pole, he came to a good-sized business district, and then he noticed indeed that there must have been a certain amount of disorder. The big window of a liquor-store was broken.

As he came to the end of the business district, he blew his horn again in his regular routine, and half a minute later he started to hear a faint honk from far away. For a moment he thought that his ears might merely be tricking him.

He honked again quickly, and immediately this time he had a reply. His heart sank—"Echo!" he thought. But then he honked again, a long and a short, and as he listened carefully the reply came merely one long.

He turned, and drove in the direction of the sound, which he estimated must be half a mile away. Having driven three blocks, he honked again and waited. More to the right this time! He turned. Twisting through the streets, he came to a blind end, turned around, and sought another way. He honked, and the reply was closer. Straight ahead this time he went on, overshot, and heard the next reply to the right and behind him. He took another turn, and came to a small business district. Cars were parked along the street, but he

31

saw no one. He thought it strange that whoever was signaling back to him did not stand in the street somewhere and wave. He honked, and suddenly the reply was almost at his elbow. He stopped the car, jumped out, and hurried along the sidewalk. In the front seat of a car parked at the curb, he saw a man. Even as he looked, the man collapsed and fell forward on the wheel. The horn, pressed down, emitted a long squawk as the body slipped sideways to the seat. Coming closer, Ish smelled a reek of whiskey. He saw the man with a long, straggly beard, his face bloated and red, obviously in the last stages of passing-out. Ish looked around, and saw that the liquor-store close by was wide open.

In sudden anger, Ish shook the yielding body. The man revived a little, opened his eyes, and emitted a kind of grunt which might have meant, "What is it?" Ish shoved the inert body to a sitting position; as he did so, the man's hand fumbled for the half-empty bottle of whiskey which was propped in the corner of the seat. Ish grabbed it, threw it out, and heard it splinter on the curbing. He was filled only with a deep bitter anger and a sense of horrible irony. Of all the survivors whom he might have found, here was only a poor old drunk, good for nothing more in this world, or any other. Then as the man's eyes opened, and Ish looked into them, he felt suddenly no more anger, but only a great deep pity.

Those eyes had seen too much. There was a fear in them and a horror that could never be told. However gross the bloated body of the drunkard might seem—somewhere, behind it all, lay a sensitive mind, and that mind had seen more than it could endure. Escape and oblivion were all that could remain.

They sat there together on the seat. The eyes of the drunken man glanced here and there, hardly under control. Their tragedy seemed to grow only deeper. The breath came raspingly. On sudden impulse, Ish took the inert wrist and felt for the pulse. It was weak and irregular. The man had been drinking, doubtless, for a week. Whether he could last much longer was questionable.

"This, then, is it!" thought Ish. The survivor might have been a beautiful girl, or a fine intelligent man, but it was only this drunkard, too far gone for any help.

After a while Ish got out of the car. He went into the liquor store for curiosity. A dead cat, it seemed, lay on the counter, but as he looked, it stirred to life and he realized that it had merely been lying, after the habit of cats, in such a position that it looked dead. The cat looked at him with a kind of cold effrontery, as the duchess at the chambermaid. Ish felt uncomfortable, and had to remind himself that this was the way cats had always behaved. The cat seemed contented and looked well fed.

Glancing around the shelves, Ish saw what he had been curious about. The man had not even bothered to pick out the better whiskey. Rot-gut had been good enough for his purposes.

Coming out, Ish saw that the man had now managed to find another bottle somewhere, and was taking a long drink. Ish realized that there was nothing much he could do about it. Still, he wanted to make a last try.

He leaned in at the window of the car. The man, revived perhaps by his last drink, was a trifle more alert. He looked at Ish, seeming able to focus his eyes, and he smiled, rather pathetically.

"Hi-ah!" he said in a thick drawl.

"How are *you?*" said Ish.

"Ah—bar—el—low!" said the man.

Ish was trying to make out what the sounds meant. The man gave his pathetic little child-like smile again, and repeated a trifle more clearly.

"Ah—nay—bar'l—low!"

Ish half caught it.

"Your name's Barello?" he asked. "No, Barlow?"

The man nodded at the second name, smiled again, and before Ish could do anything, he was taking another drink. Ish felt himself close to tears, far from anger. What difference did a man's name make now? And yet Mr. Barlow, in his befuddled mind, was trying to make what had been in civilization the first gesture of good will.

Then quite gently Mr. Barlow slumped down on the seat in stupor again, and the whiskey from the unstoppered bottle gurgled out to the floor of the car.

Ish hesitated. Should he cast in his lot with Mr. Barlow, get him sobered up, and make him reform? From what he knew of alcoholics, he did not think the prospects good. And by staying he might lose the chance to make contact with some more likely person.

"You stay here," he said to the collapsed body, on chance that it might still be able to hear. "I promise to come back."

Having said this, Ish felt he had fulfilled a kind of minimal duty. He had really no hope. The eyes showed that Mr.

Barlow had seen too much; the pulse, that he had gone too far. Ish drove away, making note, however, of the location.

As for the cats, they had known little more than five thousand years of man's domination, and had always accepted it with reservations. Those unlucky enough to be left penned inside houses, soon died of thirst. But those who had been on the outside managed better than the dogs to scramble along one way or another. Their hunting of mice became an industry, not an amusement. They stalked birds now to satisfy the quick pang of hunger. They watched by the mole-tunnel in the uncut lawn, and by the gopher-burrow in the vacant lot. They prowled in the streets and alleys, here and there discovering some garbage-can that the rats had not yet looted. They spread outward from the edge of the city, invading the haunts of the quail and the rabbits. There they met with the real wild-cat, and the end was quick and sudden, as the stronger inhabitant of the woods tore the city cat to pieces.

The sound of the next horn was more lively. *Toot, toot, toot,* it went, *toot-ta-toot, toot, toot, toot!* No drunk man was handling that one. When he came close to the sound of it, he saw a man and woman standing there together. They laughed, and waved at him. He drove up, and got out of the car. The man was a big fellow, dressed flamboyantly in a loud sport-coat. The woman was young enough and good-looking, in a blowsy way. Her mouth was a red blob of lipstick. Her fingers glittered with many rings.

Ish took two steps forward, and then stopped, suddenly. *"Two is company and three is a crowd."* The man's look was definitely hostile. And now Ish noticed that the right hand was in the bulging side-pocket of the sport coat.

"How are you?" said Ish, halting.

"Oh, we're doing fine," said the man. The woman merely giggled, but Ish noticed that there was invitation in her smile, and suddenly, more than ever, he sensed danger. "Yes," the man went on, "yes, we're doing fine. Plenty to eat, plenty to drink, and lots of—" He made an obscene gesture, and grinned at the woman. She giggled again, and again Ish saw invitation and sensed danger.

He wondered what the woman could have been in the old life. Now she looked merely like a well-to-do prostitute. There were enough diamonds on her fingers to stock a jewelry store.

34

"Is anybody else left alive?"

They looked at each other. The woman giggled again; it seemed to be her only answer.

"No," said the man. "Nobody around here, I guess." He paused, and glanced at the woman again. "Not now, anyway."

Ish looked at the hand which the man still kept in the side-pocket of the coat. He saw the woman move her hips provocatively, and her eyes narrowed a little, as if she said that she would take the victor. The eyes of this couple were not suffering like the eyes of the drunk man. They did not seem to have sensitive minds, and yet perhaps they too had suffered more than men and women could stand, and in their own way had gone bad. Suddenly, Ish realized that he was closer to death, perhaps, than he had ever been before.

"Which way are you going?" said the man, and the import of his words was clear.

"Oh, just wandering around," said Ish, and the woman giggled.

Ish turned and walked toward the car, more than half expecting to be shot in the back. He made it, got into the car, and drove away. . . .

He had heard no sounds this time, but as he turned the corner, there she was, standing in the middle of the street, a long-legged teen-age girl with stringy blond hair. She stood, suddenly stopped, as a deer stands surprised in a glade. With a quick movement of a shrewd and hunted thing, she leaned forward, squinting against the sun into the windshield, trying to see who was there. Then she turned and ran swiftly, again like a deer. She dodged through a hole in a board fence and was gone.

He walked down to the hole in the fence, and looked through it, and called, and called again. He had no reply. He half expected there would be at least a mocking laugh from some window, or the flip of a skirt around a corner, and if he had had even as much encouragement as that, he would have continued the pursuit. But there was nothing flirtatious about this one. Perhaps she had had experiences already, and knew that in such times the only safety for a young girl was in quick and final flights. He waited around some minutes, but nothing happened, and so he went on. . . .

Again there had been horn-signals, but they had stopped before Ish could get to them. He drove around in the vicinity for some minutes, and at last saw an old man coming out of a grocery store, pushing a baby-carriage piled high with canned goods and cartons. When Ish came closer, he saw that the old man was perhaps not so very old. If his scraggly white beard had been shaved away, he might have appeared a vigorous sixty. As it was, he was unkempt and dirty, and his clothes looked as if he had been sleeping in them.

Of the few whom he had met that day, Ish found the old man most communicative, and yet he too stood off by himself. He took Ish to his house near by, which he was stocking of all manner of things—some useful, some quite useless. The mere mania of possession had taken command, and the old man was well on the way, without restraints, toward being the typical hermit and miser. In the former life, Ish learned, the old man had actually been married. He had been a clerk in a hardware store. Yet probably he had always been unhappy and lonely, restricted in his contacts with other people. Now, apparently, he was happier than he had been before, because there was no one to interfere with him and he could merely withdraw and store up around himself all these material goods. He had canned food, sometimes in neat boxes, sometimes in mere piles and heaps of cans. But he also had a dozen crates of oranges, more than he could possibly eat before they spoiled. He had beans in cellophane bags, and one of the bags had broken already, spilling the beans across the floor.

In addition to food he had boxes and boxes of electric-light bulbs and radio-tubes, a cello (though he could not play), a high pile of one issue of the same magazine, a dozen alarm clocks, and a host of other miscellaneous materials which he had collected, not with any definite idea of use, but merely for the comfortable feeling of security which came to him from surrounding himself with all kinds of possessions. The old man was pleasant enough, but he was already, Ish reflected, essentially dead. The shock, reacting upon his already withdrawn character, had sent him close to insanity. He would merely go on piling up things around himself, living to himself, withdrawing farther and farther.

Yet, when Ish started to leave, the old man seized his arm in panic.

"Why did it happen?" he asked wildly. "Why am I spared?"

Ish looked in disgust at the suddenly terror-stricken face. The mouth was open; it seemed drooling.

"Yes," he snapped back, angry, and glad to express his anger, "yes—why were *you* spared and so many better men taken?"

The old man glanced involuntarily about him. His fear was now abject, inhuman.

"That's what I was afraid of!" he half-whispered.

Ish reacted into pity.

"Oh, come on!" he said. "There's nothing to be afraid of! Nobody *knows* why you survived. You were never bitten by a rattlesnake, were you?"

"No—"

"Well, no matter. This business of natural immunity, I believe—nobody understands it. But even in the worst pestilences not everybody gets sick."

But the other shook his head. "I must have been a great sinner," he said.

"Well, in that case, you should have been taken."

"*He*—" the old man paused and looked around, "*He* may be reserving me for something special." And he shivered. . . .

Approaching the toll-gates, Ish felt himself automatically begin to wonder whether he had a quarter handy for toll. During a wild second he imagined himself playing an insane scene in which he slowed the car down and held out an imaginary coin to an imaginary hand stretched out to take it. But, though he had to slow the car a little to go through the narrow passageway, he did not stretch out his hand.

He had told himself that he would cross to San Francisco, and see what things were like there. Once on the bridge, however, he realized that the bridge itself had drawn him. It was the largest and boldest work of man in the whole area; like all bridges, it was a symbol of unity and security. The thought of going to San Francisco had been an excuse. He had really wished to renew some kind of communion with the symbol of the bridge itself.

Now it lay empty. Where six lines of cars had speeded east and west, now the white lines on the pavement stretched off unbroken toward their meeting at infinity. A seagull that was perched on the railing flapped lazily as the sound of the car drew close, and slid off on a downward plane.

At a whim, he crossed to the left side and drove unobstructed along the wrong lane. He passed through the tunnel, and the high towers and long curves of the suspension-bridge rose before his eyes in magnificent perspective. As usual, some painting had been in progress; to contrast with the prevailing silver gray, one cable was splotched with orange-red.

Then suddenly he saw a strange sight. One car, a little

green coupé, was parked neatly at the railing, headed toward the East Bay.

Ish approached it, gazing curiously. He saw nobody, or nothing, inside. He passed it; then, yielding to curiosity, he swung his car around in a wide easy loop, and parked beside the coupé.

He opened the door and looked in. No, nothing! The driver, despairing, feeling the sickness upon him—had he parked there, and then leaped over the railing? Or had he, or she, merely suffered a breakdown, and flagged another car, or walked on? Some keys were still dangling from the dash-board; the certificate of registration was fastened to the steering-column—John S. Robertson, of some number on Fifty-fourth Street, Oakland. An undistinguished name and an undistinguished address! Now Mr. Robertson's car had possession of the bridge!

Only after he was again entering the tunnel did Ish think that he might at least have settled the question as to a breakdown by seeing whether he could start the car. But it did not really matter—any more than it mattered that he was heading toward the East Bay again. Having swung around to park beside the coupé, he had merely continued on in the direction toward which he was pointed. He had already realized that there would be no utility in visiting San Francisco. . . .

Soon afterward, as he had promised, Ish came again to the street where in the morning he had talked (if it could be called talking) with the drunk man.

He found the body lying on the sidewalk in front of the liquor store. "After all," Ish reflected, "there is a limit to the amount of alcohol that any human can absorb." Remembering the eyes, he could not be sorry.

No dogs were in the vicinity as yet, but Ish did not like to leave the body merely lying there. After all, he had known and talked to Mr. Barlow. He could not figure out just where or how he could perform a burial. So he found some blankets in a near-by dry-goods store, and wrapped the body carefully in these. Then he lifted Mr. Barlow into the seat of the car, and closed the windows carefully. It would make a tight and lasting mausoleum.

He said no words, for they seemed hardly in place. But he looked through the window at the neat roll of blankets, and thought of Mr. Barlow, who was probably a good guy, but couldn't survive a world going to pieces around him. And

38

then, because in some way it seemed a decent thing to do, Ish took off his hat, and stood uncovered a few seconds. . . .

In that day, as in some ancient time when a great king was overthrown and the remnants of the conquered peoples were jubilant against him—in that day will the fir trees rejoice and the cedars, crying out: "Since thou art laid down, no feller is come up against us?" Will the deer and the foxes and the quail exult: "Art thou also become weak as we, Art thou become like unto us? Is this the man that made the earth to tremble?"

("Thy pomp is brought down to the grave and the noise of thy viols; the worm is spread under thee and the worms cover thee.")

No—none will say such words, and none will be left to think them, and the book of the prophet Isaiah will moulder unread. Only, the spike-buck will graze farther from the thicket without knowing why, and the fox-cubs play beside the dry fountain in the square, and the quail hatch her eggs in the tall grass by the sundial.

Toward the end of the day, swinging in a wide detour to avoid one of those noisome regions where the dead bodies lay thickly, Ish came back to the house on San Lupo Drive.

He had learned much. The Great Disaster—so he had begun to call it to himself—had not been complete.

Therefore he did not need immediately to commit his future to the first person he met. He would do better to pick and choose a little, particularly since everyone he had so far seen was obviously suffering from shock.

A new idea was shaping in his mind and a new phrase with it—Secondary Kill. Of those that the Great Disaster had spared, many would fall victim to some trouble from which civilization had previously protected them. With unlimited liquor they would drink themselves to death. There had been, he guessed, murder; almost certainly there had been suicide. Some, like the old man, who ordinarily would have lived normal enough lives, would be pushed over the line into insanity by shock and the need of readjustment; such ones would probably not survive long. Some would meet with accident; being alone, they would die. Others would die of disease which no one was left to treat. He knew that, biologically speaking, there was a critical point in the numbers of any species—if the numbers were reduced below this point, the species could not recover.

Was mankind going to survive? Well, that was one of those interesting points which gave him the will to live. But certainly the result of his day's research gave him little confidence. In fact, if these survivors were typical, who would wish mankind to survive?

He had started out in the morning with a Robinson-Crusoe feeling that he would welcome any human companionship. He had ended with the certainty that he would rather be alone until he found someone more congenial than the day had offered. The sluttish woman had been the only one who had even seemed to want his company, and there had been treachery and death in her invitation. Even if he found a shotgun and bushwhacked her boy-friend, she could offer only the grossest physical companionship, and at the thought of her he felt revulsion. As for that other girl—the young one—the only way to make her acquaintance would be by means of a lasso or a bear-trap. And like the old man she would probably turn out to be crazy.

No, the Great Disaster had shown no predilection toward sparing the nice people, and the survivors had not been rendered pleasanter as the result of the ordeal through which they had passed.

He prepared some supper, and ate, but without appetite. Afterwards he tried to read, but the words had as little savor as the food. He still thought of Mr. Barlow and the others; in one way or another, each in his own manner, everyone whom he had seen that day was going to pieces. He did not think that he himself was. But was he actually still sane? Was he too, perhaps, suffering from shock? In calm self-consciousness he thought about it. After a while he took pencil and paper, deciding to write down what qualifications he had, why he might be going to live, even with some degree of happiness, while the others were not.

First of all, without hesitation, he scribbled:

1) Have will to live. Want to see what will happen in world without man, and how. Geographer.

Beneath this he wrote other notes.

2) *Always was* solitary. Don't have to talk to other people.

3) Have appendix out.

4) Moderately practical, though not mechanical. Camper.

5) Did not suffer devastating experience of living through it all, seeing family, other people, die. Thus escaped worst of shock.

He paused, looking at his last note. At least he could hope that it was true.

Still he sat staring, and thinking. He could list others of his qualities, such as his being intellectually oriented, and therefore, he supposed, adaptable to new circumstances. He could list that he was a reader and so had still available an important means of relaxation and escape. At the same time he was more than a mere reader in that he knew also the means of research through books, and thus possessed a powerful tool for reconstruction.

His fingers tightened about the pencil for a moment while he considered writing down that he was not superstitious. This might be important. Otherwise he would even now, like the old man, be fighting the fear that the whole disaster had been the work of an angry God, who had now wiped out his people by pestilence as once before by flood, leaving Ish (though as yet unsupplied with wife and children) like another Noah to repopulate the emptiness. But such thoughts opened up the way to madness. Yes, he realized, if a man began to think of himself as divinely appointed, he was close to thinking of himself as God—and at that point lay insanity.

"No," he thought. "Whatever happens, at least I shall never believe that I am a god. No, I shall never be a god!"

Then, his flight of ideas still continuing, he realized that in some ways, very curiously, he felt a new security and even satisfaction at the contemplation of a solitary life. His worries in the old days had been chiefly about people. The prospect of going to a dance had more than once sent him into a sweat; he had never been a good mixer; no one had asked him to join a fraternity. In the old days, such things were a handicap to a man. Now, he realized, they were actually a great advantage. Because he had sat on the edge of so many social gatherings, not quite able to mingle in the conversation, listening, watching objectively, now he could endure not being able to talk, and again could sit and watch, noting what happened. His weakness had become strength. It was as if there had been a blind man in a world suddenly bereft of light. In that world, those with seeing eyes could only blunder about, but the blind man would be at home, and now instead of being the one who was guided by others, he might be the one to whom the others clung for guidance.

Nevertheless the lonely life stretching out before him did not seem so simple and seemed far from secure or pleasant, as he again lay on his bed and through the darkness the cold fingers of the fog reached in from the Bay and folded within them the house on San Lupo Drive. Then again that great fear came upon him, and he cringed in vague dread and listened for noises in the darkness, and thought of his loneliness and of all that might happen to him, too, in the course of that Secondary Kill. A wild desire for flight and escape came upon him. He had a feeling that he must go far away and move fast, and keep ahead of anything that might be pursuing him. Then he rationalized this thought with the feeling that the disease could not have fallen everywhere upon the United States, that somewhere must be left some community, which he should find.

Chapter 3

In the morning his panic had faded, but the deep-seated fear was still with him. He got out of bed carefully, and swallowed apprehensively in terror that he might have a sore throat. He handled himself with all the care of an aged hypochondriac. When he walked downstairs, he balanced himself meticulously, realizing that even a sprained ankle might mean death.

He immediately began preparations for flight, and as always when he began acting upon some definite plan, even though the plan in itself made little sense, he felt a quietness and satisfaction. His own car was old. He therefore began to look around for a better one among the many hundreds that were parked along the streets. Most of these were without keys, but finally in a garage he found a station-wagon which suited his fancy and which contained a key. He pressed the starter, and the engine responded perfectly. He idled it for a minute, raced it, and decided that it was good. He started to engage the gears, and then suddenly paused with a feeling of uneasiness. He did not regret leaving his own car, but still something worried him. In a moment he remembered. He went back to his old car, and took out the hammer. He carried it over to the station-wagon and laid it at his feet. Then he drove out of the garage.

From a grocery he stocked himself, nibbling some crackers and cheese for lunch as he walked about selecting his cans. He realized he might pick up supplies at any town. Still, it would be convenient to have a reserve with him in the car. From other stores he took a sleeping-bag, an ax and a shovel, a rain-coat, cigarettes, enough food to see him through several days, a small bottle of good brandy. Remembering his experiences of the day before, he went into a sporting-goods shop, and selected a variety of weapons—a light shot-gun, a medium-calibre repeating rifle, a small automatic pistol that would go handily into a side pocket, a hunting-knife.

Just when he had finished loading the station-wagon, and was about ready to start, he looked around and first became conscious of a dog. He had seen many dogs in the last two days, and he had tried to shut them out of his mind. They were pathetic, and did not like to think what was happening. Some of them looked starved; some of them looked too well fed. Some seemed uncertain and cringing; others snarled and were all too well assured of themselves. This particular dog was like a small hound, with long drooping ears, of a white-and-liver color—a beagle, probably, although he did not know much about breeds of dogs. It stood at a safe distance of ten feet, looked at him, wagged its tail, and whimpered just audibly.

"Go away!" he said, roughly, for his heart was suddenly bitter within him, and he felt himself building a wall against more attachments which must only end with death. "Go away!" he repeated. Instead, the dog took a step or two closer to him, and put its forequarters down on the ground and laid its head on its forefeet and looked up at him with strangely appealing eyes, which rolled upward. Long drooping ears gave the face an expression of infinite sadness. Obviously, the dog was saying, "You have broken my heart!" Suddenly, without thinking, he smiled and he remembered then, it was perhaps the first time he had smiled, except ironically, since the snake had struck.

He came to himself instantly, and realized that the dog was rubbing against his leg, quick to sense the change of his mood. As he looked down, it scurried away suddenly in fright, or pretended fright, then dashed around in a little circle variegated with two quick dodges, and ended again with its forelegs on the ground and its head between them, giving out an eager little bark which changed into a hound-like howl. Again Ish broke into a smile which this time was really a broad grin, and the dog sensed his mood. It dashed around him again in a swift run, with sudden changes of direction, giving an imitation of what it would do if chasing a rabbit. It ended this little demonstration of varied abilities by running boldly up to Ish's legs again, rubbing against them, and putting its head there as if to be patted, as much as saying, "Wasn't that a good act I put on?" Realizing what was expected of him, Ish dropped his hand on the dog's head, and patted the sleek forehead. The dog gave a little whimper of satisfaction.

The tail wagged so vigorously that the whole body seemed to be wagging from the ears back. The light-colored eyes rolled upwards until the whites showed along the bottom. It was the picture of adoration. The long ears fell on each side, and little wrinkles showed on the forehead. The dog was certainly making a good case of love at first sight. Its actions said, "This is the only man in the world for me!"

Ish relaxed suddenly. Squatting down, he patted the dog unashamedly. "Well," he thought, "I've got myself a dog—whether I want one or not." And then he reconsidered, "I mean, the dog has got me."

He opened the door of the station-wagon; the dog jumped in and lay down, at home on the front seat.

Going into a grocery, Ish found a box of dog-biscuits; he fed the dog one from his hand. The animal took the food without any particular sign of affection or thanks. This was obviously what a man was for. Once you had got yourself a man, there was no need to be particularly grateful to him. Noticing for the first time, Ish saw that it was not a dog, strictly speaking, but a bitch. "Well," he said, "a case of pure seduction, apparently."

He went back to the house, and picked up a few of his personal belongings—some clothes, his field-glasses, a few books. He reflected a moment whether there was anything else needed for a trip which might take him clear across the continent. Then he shrugged his shoulders.

He took out his wallet, and discovered that he had nineteen dollars in fives and ones. He certainly did not need any more money. He even considered throwing the whole wallet away, but finally kept it. He was so used to having it in his hip-pocket that he felt uncomfortable without it. The money would probably do him no harm.

Without any real hope, he composed a note, and left it posted conspicuously on the living-room desk. If they should return while he was away, they would know that they should wait for his return or leave a note of their own for him.

As he stood by the car, he gave another look up and down San Lupo Drive. There was no one in sight, of course. The houses and trees all looked the same as before, but he noticed again that the lawns and gardens already showed the lack of care, particularly of watering. In spite of the fogs, the long drought of the California summer was already settling down.

By now it was mid-afternoon. Nevertheless, he decided to start at once. He was anxious to be off, and he could spend the night at some near-by town.

As with the dogs and cats, so also with the grasses and flowers which man had long nourished. The clover and the blue-grass withered on the lawns, and the dandelions grew tall. In the flowerbed the water-loving asters wilted and drooped, and the weeds flourished. Deep within the camellias, the sap failed; they would bear no buds next spring. The leaves curled on the tips of the wisteria vines and the rose bushes, as they set themselves against the long drought. Foot by foot the wild cucumbers quickly sent their long vines across lawn and flowerbed and terrace. As once, when the armies of the empire were shattered and the strong barbarians poured in upon the soft provincials, so now the fierce weeds pressed in to destroy the pampered nurslings of man.

The staunch motor hummed steadily. He drove, the morning of this second day, with exaggerated caution, thinking of blow-outs and of steering-gear or brakes which might suddenly cease to function, and of cattle wandering on the highway. He tried to keep the speedometer needle at forty.

But that motor had never been designed to keep a car at such a speed, and he constantly found that he had slid up to fifty or sixty without realizing it.

Yet, even to be moving at all kept him from feeling quite so depressed. Mere change of place was a comfort; flight itself, a solace. Deep within, he knew that all this was because he was temporarily escaping from the necessity of decision. As long as he was merely pulling down the curtain of one landscape behind him and raising that of another in front of him, as long as he was merely driving, he did not need to make plans for the future, to decide how he should live, or even whether he should live. The necessity now was only to decide how he should steer around the next approaching curve.

The beagle-bitch lay beside him. Now and then she put her head in his lap, but mostly she slept quietly, and her being so close was also a comfort. In the rear-view mirror he never saw a car behind him, but he looked in it occasionally, out of habit. In it he saw the rifle and shot-gun on the middle seat behind him, and the back seat piled high with his sleeping-bag and the cartons of food. He was like a sailor in his own boat stocked and ready for emergencies, and he also felt the deep desperation of the solitary survivor of a shipwreck, alone in all the vastness.

He followed Highway 99 south through the San Joaquin Valley. Although he drove slowly, he made excellent mileage. He did not have to slow down behind a truck, or to stop for traffic-lights (though most of them were still functioning), or to reduce speed for towns. In fact, in spite of his apprehensions, he had to admit that driving Highway 99 under these conditions was much safer than driving it through thick and madly speeding traffic.

He saw no man. If he had searched through the towns, he might have found someone, but there was no use of it now. A straggler here or there he might pick up at any time. Now he was searching to see whether some greater remnant might be left somewhere.

The broad plain stretched away—vineyards, orchards, fields of melons, fields of cotton. Perhaps a farmer's eye could have seen that already everything showed neglect, and the absence of the hand of man, but to Ish it all still looked about the same.

At Bakersfield he left 99, and turned toward the winding road over Tehachapi Pass. Fields gave way to scattered slopes of oaks, and higher still came open park-like stands of thin-foliaged Coulter pine. Here, too, there was no one. Yet he did not so much feel the absence of people, for this had always been empty country. He came down the side of the pass on the other end, and looked out over the far reaches where the desert began. More sharply than ever he became apprehensive. Although the sun was still well above the horizon, he stopped at the little town of Mojave, and began to make his preparations.

To cross those two hundred miles of desert, men had carried water in their cars even in the Old Times. There were stretches where one might have to walk for a full day to reach even a roadside stand if the car went bad. He could take no chances now, when no one would be coming to help him.

He found a hardware store. The door was massive and strongly locked; so he smashed a window with the hammer and went in. He took three large canteens, and filled them at a faucet from which water was still running, though feebly. He added a gallon jug of red wine from a grocery store.

Still he was not satisfied, and the thought of the desert weighed heavily on him. He drove back along the main street, not just sure what he was seeking, and then his eyes fell on a motorcycle. It was black and white, one of those used by the Highway Patrol. Through all his depression and fear he still felt qualms at stealing a motorcycle belonging to a traffic cop. It was the height of the incredible.

Yet after a minute he got out, fiddled with the motorcycle, found it workable, and rode slowly down the street and back.

After an hour's work in the heavy heat of the late afternoon, using some planks to build a ramp, he managed to wheel the motorcycle up, and to lash it securely on the lowered tail-gate of the station-wagon. Now he was not only like a sailor in his own boat, but he had a tender in which he could take refuge if the boat itself should sink. Even so, he felt more apprehensive than ever, and found himself now and then glancing over his shoulder.

The sun set, and he was tired. He made himself a cold and unsatisfactory meal, and ate it dispiritedly, still feeling the fear. He even considered what he would do if the food gave him indigestion. When he had finished eating, he found a can of dog-food in a grocery store, and fed it to the beagle. She accepted the offering as only her due. Having eaten, she curled up in the front seat. He drove the station-wagon to the best-looking tourist-court in town, found the door of a room unopened, and went in, the beagle following. Only a dribble flowed from the faucets. Apparently the water supplies of this small town were not as automatically adjusted as were those of the city. He washed as well as he could; then went to bed. The dog curled up on the floor.

The fear gripped him hard, and he could not sleep. The dog whimpered in a dream, and he started violently. The fear moved in more tightly. He got out of bed, and tried the door to be sure that he had locked it, although he did not know who or what he should be fearing, or against whom or what he should lock a door. He thought of going to find a drug store and getting some pills to make him sleep, but even that idea frightened him. He thought of trying the brandy, but that too had sinister implications as he remembered Mr. Barlow. At last he slept, but restlessly.

In the morning his head was heavy, and in the crisp heat of the desert forenoon he still flinched at starting across the dry waste. He considered turning back; he considered going south toward Los Angeles, telling himself that it would be a good idea to see what had happened there. But all these ideas, he knew, were excuses, mere flinchings from the carrying-out of his original plan, and he still had enough pride in himself to keep from needlessly turning back or swerving from the course which he had laid out. But he temporized at least to this extent, that he would not start across the desert until nearly sunset. That, he argued, was merely an ordinary precaution. Even in ordinary times many people drove the desert at night just to escape from the heat.

He spent the day restlessly in Mojave—oppressed by the fear, and trying to think of more things which he should do for safety. When the sun was about to touch the western hills, he started, the dog beside him on the seat.

He had scarcely gone a mile before he felt the desert closing in around him. The low sun cast the Joshua trees into strange long shadows. Then the shadows were gone, and soon twilight fell. He turned on his lights, and the high beams illuminated the road before him—empty, always empty. In the rear-view mirror he never saw the far-off twin lights which would mean that some car was overtaking him.

Then it was full darkness, and his anxiety grew deeper and deeper. He thought of all that might go wrong, even though the engine purred steadily along. He drove slowly and still more slowly, thinking of blow-outs, thinking of an overheating engine, or of oil that might fail to flow and leave him marooned, far alone. He even lost confidence in the motorcycle which he carried as insurance. After a long time—he was driving slowly—he passed one of the little desert stations where one might at least expect to get gasoline or a spare tire or something to drink. Now it was dark, and he knew that there was no help. He went on beyond that, the white beams cutting out the road clearly ahead of him; the engine still purred smoothly, but he wondered what he would do if it should stop.

He had gone a long way. At last the dog on the seat beside him began to whimper and stir restlessly. "Shut up!" he said sharply, but still she whimpered and stirred. "Oh, all *right!*" he said, and pulled the car to a stop, not bothering to turn aside off the pavement.

He got out, and then held the door open for the dog. She ran about for a moment, whimpering, and then without stopping to relieve herself, she suddenly lifted her nose, let out a bay tremendous for such a small creature, and struck out at full speed into the desert. "Come! *Come back!*" he shouted, but the dog paid no attention, and her bay went off into the distance.

There was a sudden deep silence as she ceased giving tongue, and in the silence he suddenly started, realizing that another noise, too, had stopped. The idling engine had stalled. In quick panic he leaped back into the car and pressed the starter-button. The engine resumed its steady purring. Yet, he was shaken. Feeling suddenly conspicuous, as if things might see him and he could not see them, he turned out the lights and sat in the darkness. "What a mess!" he said to himself.

Faintly, far off now, he heard again the baying of the beagle. The note rose and fell as she circled somewhere behind the quarry. He considered going on, and abandoning her. After all, he had not wished to take her along in the first place. If now she chose to abandon him in the desert and go off after the first chance rabbit, what debt had he toward her? He slipped the car into gear, and drove ahead. But he stopped after only a few yards. It seemed too mean a desertion. The dog would probably find no water in the desert, and that would be a horrible end. In some way he had already incurred obligations to the beagle, even though she seemed to be using him for her own ends. He shivered in his loneliness and depression.

After a while, a quarter of an hour perhaps, he was suddenly aware that the beagle had returned. He had not heard her; she had merely appeared. She lay down panting, her tongue hanging out. He felt sudden uncontrollable anger against her. He thought wildly of all those vague dangers to which her foolishness seemed to expose him. If he could not leave her to die of thirst in the desert, at least he could put her to a quick end. He got out of the car carrying the shotgun.

Then, as he looked down, he saw the dog lying with its head between its forepaws, panting still from the run. She did not bother to move, but he could vaguely see her large eyes lifted up toward him with the touch of whites along the bottom. Having had her fun chasing the rabbit, she had now come back to her man, the one she had adopted and who had proved extremely useful to supply tasty food out of cans and to transport her to a lovely country which supplied real rabbits for chasing. Suddenly Ish relaxed, and laughed.

With the laughter, something broke inside of him, and it was as if a load had rolled away. "After all," he thought, "what am I afraid of? Nothing more than my death can happen. That has come to most people already. Why should I be afraid of that? It can be nothing worse than that."

He felt infinite relief. He strode half a dozen steps down

the road, springily, giving his body a chance to express what his mind felt.

And surely this was more than the dropping off of any momentary burden. This was a kind of great Declaration of Independence. He had boldly stepped up to Fate, and slapped Fate in the face, and dared Fate to do the worst.

Thereupon he resolved that if he was to live at all he would live without fear. After all, he had escaped a nearly universal disaster.

With a quick decision he hurried to the rear of the car, undid the lashings, and dumped the motorcycle. No longer would he take all these over-cautious precautions. There might not be any Fate which objected to people playing the game too safely. But, even if there were not, such playing was too much trouble. He would take his chances from now on, and at least enjoy life without fear, as long as he lived it. Was he not living, as they said, on borrowed time?

"Well, come on, Princess," he said ironically, "let's get going." And as he said it, he realized that he had at last named the dog. That was a good name; its very triteness seemed to connect him with the old days, and at least she was The Princess, always expecting him to take care of her with the best of service, repaying him only incidentally, in so far as she took him away from thoughts of himself.

Yet, reconsidering, he did not go any farther that night. With his new-found sense of freedom he rather enjoyed merely taking additional chances. He pulled the sleeping-bag out. Unrolling it, he lay on the sand under the slight shelter of a mesquite bush. Princess lay beside him, and went soundly to sleep, tired from her run. Once he awoke in the night, and lay calm at last. He had passed through so much, and now he seemed to know a calm which would never pass. Once Princess whimpered in her sleep, and he saw her legs twitch as if she were still chasing the rabbit. Then she lay quiet; he, too, slept away.

When he awoke, finally, the dawn was lemon yellow above the desert hills. He was cold, and he found Princess close up against his sleeping bag. He crawled out just as the sun was rising.

This is the desert, the wilderness. It began a long time ago. After a while, men came. They camped at the springs and left chips of stone scattered about in the sand there, and wore faint trails through the lines of the mesquite bushes, but you could hardly tell that they had been there. Still later, they laid down railroads, and strung up wires, and made long straight roads. Still, in comparison with the whole desert, you could hardly tell that men had been there, and ten yards aside from the steel rails or the concrete pavement, it was all the same. After a while, the men went away, leaving their works behind them.

There is plenty of time in the desert. A thousand years are as a day. The sand drifts, and in the high winds even the gravel moves, but it is all very slow. Now and then, once in a century, it may be, there comes a cloudburst, and the long-dry streambeds roar with water, rolling boulders. Given ten centuries perhaps, the fissures of the earth will open again and the black lava pour forth.

But as the desert was slow to yield before man, so it will be slow to wipe out his traces. Come back in a thousand years, and you will still see the chips of stone scattered through the sand and the long road stretching off to the gap in the knife-like hills on the horizon. There will be little rust, and even the iron rails may be there. As for the copper wires, they are next to immortal. This is the desert, the wilderness—slow to give, and slow to take away.

For a while the speedometer needle stood at 80, and he drove with the wild joy of freedom, fearless at the thought of a tire blowing out. Later, he slowed down a little, and began to look around with new interest, his trained geographer's mind focusing upon that drama of man's passing. In this country, he saw little difference.

When he came to Needles, the gasoline-gauge stood nearly at empty. Electric power had failed, and the gas pumps would not work. With a little search he found a gasoline depot at the edge of town, and filled his tank from one of the drums. He went on.

Crossing the Colorado River, he entered Arizona, and the road began to rise up among sharp, rocky crags. Here, at last, he saw cattle. Half a dozen steers and two cows with their calves stood in a draw near the road. They raised their heads, idly, when he stopped the car to look them over. These desert cattle, unless when grazing near the road, scarcely saw a man from one month's end to the other. Twice a year, the cowboys came out to round them up. The passing of man would make no difference here, except that actually the herds would breed more rapidly. After a time, perhaps, they might have troubles with over-grazed range, but before then the long-drawn howl of the *lobo* wolves would re-echo

51

again through these ravines, and there would be a new means of control of numbers. In the end, however, he had no doubt that the cattle and the wolves would strike off some unconscious balance and that the cattle, bereft of man, would continue to thrive.

Farther on, near the old mining-town of Oatman, he saw two burros. Whether they had merely been wandering about the vicinity of the town at the time of the catastrophe, or whether they had been some that had gone wild, already, he did not know, but they seemed well contented. He got out of the car, and tried approaching them, but they scampered away, keeping their distance. Returning to the car he loosed the yapping Princess, and she made a wild dash at the two strange animals. The jack laid down his ears, and charged upon her with lips drawn back from teeth and lashing forefeet. Princess turned sharply and scuttled to the car and the protection of her man. The jack, thought Ish, would be more than a match for any wolf, and even a mountain-lion might well regret pressing an attack.

He passed the summit above Oatman, and well down the other side he came for the first time to a partial block in the road. At some time during the last few days a fierce desert thunderstorm must have swept across this edge of the mountains. When the water came tearing down the wash, the culvert had plugged and water had streamed across the road, carrying sand. He got out to investigate. In ordinary times, a road-crew would soon have been along. They would have cleared the sand from the road and opened the culvert again, and everything would have been as before. But now, the culvert remained plugged, and the few inches of sand remained on the road, and when he looked at the lower side of the pavement he saw that the washing water had already cut out half a foot of dirt from under the lower side of the concrete. Now, at the next storm, still more sand would wash across, and still more dirt would be cut away from the underside. In a few years the concrete might begin to crack away from where it was undercut, and the sand and gravel would pile up still higher on the road itself. Now, however, there was no serious question of passability. He drove the car over the sand.

"A road is as strong as its weakest link," he thought, wondering how long it would be possible to travel as he was traveling now. That night he slept again in a bed, helping himself to a place in the best tourist court in Kingman.

The cattle, the horses, the asses—through thousands of centuries they lived their own lives, and went their own ways in forest and steppe and desert. Then man grew strong, and for a while he used the cattle, and the horses, and the asses, for other ends. But after that was finished, they went their own ways again.

Fastened with their stanchions in the long barns, the dairy cattle bawled thirstily for a while and then lay still. Penned in their paddocks, the long-limbed thoroughbreds died slowly.

But on the ranges, the white-faced Herefords looked out for themselves, and even on the farms, the cattle broke through the fences and wandered freely. So too, on the ranges, with the horses and the asses. . . .

The asses seek the desert, as in the ancient days. They sniff the dry east wind, and gallop on the dusty lake beds, and step daintily on the boulder-strewn hills; with their hard mouths they eat the thorny bushes. Their companions are the big-horn sheep.

The horses take the dry open plains. They eat the green grass of spring, and the grass-seed of summer, and the dry grass of autumn, and in the winter, shaggy-coated, they paw the snow, for the dry grass beneath it. With them the herds of the pronghorn pasture.

The cattle seek the greener lands and the forests. In the copses the cows hide the new-born calves until they can follow the mothers. The bison are their companions, and their rivals. The great bulls battle mightily, and in the end, perhaps, the heavier bulls will prevail, and the bison move out over all their old domain. Then the cattle may be pushed deeper into the woodland and there find their haven.

Electric power had failed at Kingman, but the water was still running. The stove in the kitchenette at the tourist-court was supplied from a tank of liquefied gas, and the pressure was at normal. Since there was no electric refrigeration, he could have neither eggs, nor butter, nor milk. But he took his time, and after a raid on a store prepared an excellent breakfast—canned grapefruit, canned sausages, flapjacks, syrup. He made a large pot of coffee, and had it with sugar and canned milk. Princess enjoyed her usual can of horsemeat. After breakfast, to get gasoline, he took the hammer and a cold chisel, and plugged a hole in the tank of a truck. Setting a five-gallon can beneath the spurt of gasoline, he filled it, and then transferred the gasoline to his own tank.

There were dead bodies in the town, but in the dry Arizona

heat they had mummified instead of decaying, and though they were not pretty to look at, they made no assault upon the nostrils.

Beyond Kingman he soon came to where the compact little piñon pines stood evenly spaced across dry rolling country. Except for the highway, man had left little mark anywhere. No telephone line followed the road, and often there were no fences—just the rangeland stretching off on both sides, green because of the summer rains, dotted with the little trees. Actually, he knew that overgrazing had changed the grass and shrubs over all this country, and that with man gone there would now be more changes. Perhaps, with the slaughter-houses no longer at work, the cattle would become more numerous than ever; before their predators could increase sufficiently to control their numbers, they might eat the grass to the roots and start gullies and change the whole face of the country. No, just as likely, he reconsidered. hoof-and-mouth disease would work in across the now open Mexican border, and cattle might almost disappear. Or perhaps he underestimated the rapidity at which wolves and mountain-lions would multiply. All he held fairly certain was that in twenty-five or fifty years some kind of moderately stable situation would result and that the land then would steadily get to look more and more like what it had been before the white men came.

On the first two days he had felt the fear; on the third, he had speeded wildly in reaction. But today, again in reaction he felt a great calm and restfulness. The quiet of everything impressed him. In spite of having spent so much time in the mountains, he had just taken it for granted that mountains were quiet, and had not realized how much of the noise in the world was man-caused. There had been many definitions of Man; he would make another: "The noise-producing animal." Now there was only the nearly imperceptible murmur of his own engine. He had no need to blow the horn. There were no back-firing trucks, no snorting trains, no pounding planes overhead. In the little towns no whistles blew or bells rang or radios blared or people talked. Even if it was the peace of death, still that was a kind of peace.

He drove slowly, though not from fear. When he wished, he stopped to look at something. At every halt he made it a game to discover what he could hear. Often, after he had turned off the engine, he heard nothing at all, even in a town. Sometimes there was the chirp of a bird or the faint humming

54

of an insect; sometimes the wind made a little rustling. Once he heard with a sense of relief the muffled pounding of a far-off thunderstorm.

By that time it was afternoon, and he had come into a higher country of tall pines with a snow-capped peak looming up to the north. At Williams a shiny streamlined train stood in the stationyard, just as the engineer had left it; he saw no one. At Flagstaff, much of the town had been burned; he saw no one.

Just beyond Flagstaff he came around a bend of the road and some distance ahead saw two crows leave something in the road and flap heavily away. He feared a little to come up and see what they had been eating, but it was only a sheep. The body lay tight upon the concrete of the highway, a red smear of blood showing from the torn throat. When he looked around, he saw that there were other bodies of sheep lying close to the road, and on both sides he could see still more. He walked a little way off the road, and counted twenty-six.

Dogs or coyotes? He could not tell, but he could easily reconstruct the scene—the harried sheep driven across the meadow, those on the outside pulled down or separated from those who clung closely toward the center of the flock.

Soon afterwards, out of whim, he turned in at the little road which led toward Walnut Canyon National Monument. He came to the neatly built Superintendent's house which looked down into the deep canyon with its ruined houses of the Cliff Dwellers. There was an hour's daylight left, and he found a grim amusement in walking around the narrow path, looking at what was left of those houses of that old people. He came back, and slept the night in the house at the lip of the canyon. Already there had been a summer thunderstorm, and a little water had run under the door. Since no one had cleaned it up, it had lain in a pool there and damaged the floor. Other rains would come; year by year, their effect would increase until after a while the neat house at the lip of the canyon would fall into ruins, and be not much different from those old houses sheltering along the cliffs. Here the ruin of one civilization would pile up on the ruin of another.

For a while the flocks, too, will remain. Even though the killers kill merely in the rage of the blood-lust, nevertheless millions of sheep are not to be wiped out in a day, or in a month, and thousands of new-born lambs will be dropped. What are fifty or one hundred slain out of millions? Yet not without reason, as symbol of a perishing people, men have said *"sheep without a shepherd."* In the end they will vanish. . . .

They wander helplessly in the blizzards of the winter, and in the summer they stray far from water and are too stupid to find their way back; they are caught in the spring floods, and the bodies wash down by the hundreds; they stampede stupidly over cliffs, and lie in corrupting masses in the depths of the ravines; and always there are more of the killers—the dogs run wild, the wolves and coyotes, the mountain lions, the bears. After a while, the great flocks are broken into a few frightened scurrying fragments; in the end, there will be no more sheep.

Thousands of years ago they accepted the protection of the shepherd and lost their agility and sense of independence. Now, when the shepherd has gone, they too must go.

On the next day he was crossing the wide high plains of the continental divide. This was rich sheep country, and again he saw more bodies where coyotes had harried the flocks. Once, on a far-off hillside, he saw what seemed to be scattered sheep running wildly, but he could not be sure.

Again, however, he saw an even stranger sight; in the rich meadow along a stream, he saw a flock of sheep grazing peacefully. He looked around, half expecting to see the wagon and the sheepherder himself; but instead, he saw only two dogs. The shepherd was gone, but by long habit the dogs were continuing their task, keeping the sheep together, maintaining them in the good pasture along the water of the stream, doubtless fighting off the marauders that came sniffing in the night. He stopped the car and watched, keeping Princess beside him on the seat, so that she would not disturb the situation. The two sheep-dogs grew excited when they noticed the car; they barked excitedly, and rounded up a few stragglers. They kept their distance, a quarter-mile away, and seemed hostile. Just as in the cities the electric power was still pulsating through the wires after man had passed, so here upon the far stretches of the grass lands, the dogs watched the sheep for a little while. But, he thought, it could not be for long.

The road led on across the wide spaces; U.S. 66 read the signs beside the pavement. It had been a great highway, he remembered, in the old days, the road of the Okies to California; there had been a popular song about it; now, it lay empty. No bus roared by with *Los Angeles* imprinted on its front; no truck came from east or west, no jalopy piled high with the household goods of some migrating fruitpicker, no sleek car of tourists going to the Indian dances, not even a Navaho wagon with a bony horse pulling it by the side of the pavement.

He dropped into the valley of the Rio Grande, crossed the bridge, and went up the long street of Albuquerque. This was the largest town he had seen since leaving California; he honked his horn as he went, and waited for a response. He heard nothing, and he did not wait long.

He slept that night at a tourist-court on the eastern edge of Albuquerque, from which he could look back down the long slope toward the town. It was all in darkness; here the power had failed already.

In the morning he went on through the mountains, and came out on the other side into a country of scattered buttes with broad plains between. A frenzy of speed came upon him again, and he drove the car at its limit on the straight roads. The buttes fell away behind; he crossed the state line, and was in Texas, in the flat country of the Panhandle. The day was suddenly blazing hot, and around him lay endless stubble fields from which the wheat had already been cut before the death fell upon the harvesters. That night he slept on the outskirts of Oklahoma City.

In the morning he skirted the city by a by-pass, and went on. He followed 66 toward Chicago, but after a few miles a tree across the road blocked him. He got out to consider the situation. There had obviously been one of those sudden wind-storms which sweep the plains country. A tall poplar standing before a farm house had tipped and gone over, hiding the whole highway in a clutter of leaves and branches. It would be a labor of a half a day to chop any kind of passage through the tangle. Then suddenly he realized that here was a significant scene in that great drama which he had set himself to watch. Highway 66, that famous road! Here it was, blocked by the chance falling of a tree! A man might cut his way through this obstruction, but there were, or would soon be, others. In the thunderstorms, mud would wash across the road and earth slide from the cuts; a bridge would go in the summer freshet; in a few years, to take a car from Chicago to Los Angeles on Highway 66 would be a task for a pioneer in a covered wagon.

He thought of detouring through the fields, but the soil was soft and mucky from recent rains. Consulting his road-map, he saw that he could go south ten miles and strike another paved road, which would bring him back to the highway. He turned the station-wagon around, and started back.

But when he reached the other road, he saw no real reason why he should return to 66. The secondary highway led on directly toward the east, and so far as he could tell, that direction was just as good as another. "Perhaps," he thought, "that fallen tree has changed the whole future course of human history. I might have gone on toward Chicago, and something might have happened there. Now something different will happen."

So he went eastward through Oklahoma, the country empty everywhere. On the rolling hills the scrubby oak-growth looked just as it must have looked before. On the level cultivated stretches, corn and cotton were growing. The corn stood high, head above the weeds; it would bear a fairly good crop. But the cotton was rapidly being choked out.

The full heat of summer was upon him now, and was breaking down more of his remnants of civilization. He still shaved daily, more because he felt comfortable that way than for any sense of his appearance, but he had not had his hair cut, and it hung shaggily about him. He hacked at it with a pair of scissors. He had reverted merely to a pair of blue jeans and an open-necked shirt. He threw the shirt away every morning, and put on a clean one. Somewhere he had forgotten his gray fedora, and from an Oklahoma general store he picked up a cheap straw hat, the kind that any tenant farmer might wear in the summer.

That afternoon he crossed into Arkansas, and though he knew that state-lines were only imaginary, he suddenly became conscious of another change. Here all the dryness of the plains country was left far behind, and the weather was hot and humid. As a result the growth was everywhere pushing in upon the roads and buildings. Runners from vines and climbing roses already dangled across windows and hung swinging from eaves and porch roofs. The smaller houses looked as if they were shrinking back shyly and beginning to hide in the woods. Fences also were being obscured. There was no longer a sharp line between the road and the surrounding country. Grass and weeds were showing green at every little crack in the concrete; blackberry shoots were pushing in from the shoulders, breaking the clean white line. In one place the long runners of some vine reached clear to the white line in the middle of the pavement, and met others advancing from the other side.

Peaches were ripe, and he varied his diet of canned food by raiding an orchard. His entry scared off a few hogs which had been eating the fallen fruit. That night he slept at North Little Rock.

The prize boars will die in their well-kept pens, and the fat brood sows will wander about, squealing for their mash, but on many a farm, the shoats will run wild without restraint of fences. They need nothing from man. In the heat they seek the swamps by the river, and root there, and lie in the mud, grunting happily. When the air grows cool, they wander the oak woods and feed on the acorns. After a few generations, they grow slimmer of leg and thinner of body and longer of tusk. Before the fury of their boars, even the wolf and the bear hurry aside. Like man, they eat flesh or fowl or tuber or nut or fruit. They will live.

An hour on the road next morning, at the edge of a small town, he started, as his eyes fell upon the unaccustomed sight of a well-weeded and tended garden. He stopped, went to investigate, and found for the first time what might, by generous interpretation, be called a social group. They were Negroes—a man, a middle-aged woman, a young boy. By the obvious look of the woman, there would soon be a fourth member.

They were timid. The boy kept in the background, curious but frightened, scratching at his head in a way that suggested lice. The woman stood, stolidly silent except to direct question. The man took off his straw hat and stood fingering its broken rim nervously; beads of sweat, from nervousness or the heat of the morning sun, ran down his shiny black forehead.

Ish could hardly understand the thick dialect, rendered more unintelligible by embarrassment. He made out, however, that they knew of no one else in the neighborhood, and in fact knew very little of anything, not having been beyond walking distance from the spot since the disaster. They were not a family group, but merely a chance association of survivors—three, against the law of chance, having survived in one small town.

Ish soon realized they were suffering not only from the shock of the catastrophe but also from the taboos carried over from before it. They talked with diffidence in the presence of a strange white man, dropping their eyes.

In spite of their obvious reluctance, Ish looked around their place. Although all the houses of the town must have been open to them, they still lived in the crude cabin where the woman had lived before the disaster. Ish did not go in, but through the open door he saw the rickety bed and chairs and the sheet-iron stove, and the oil-cloth-draped table with the flies buzzing about the uncovered food. The outside looked better. They had a luxuriant garden and a good corn-patch, and were actually tending a small field of cotton, although what in the world they expected to do with the cotton was more than Ish could figure out. Apparently they had merely carried on, doing the things that people in their world were supposed to do, and thus gaining a sense of security.

They had chickens in a pen, and some pigs. Their painfully naive embarrassment when Ish saw the pigs was only too plain advertisement that they had appropriated them from some farmer's pen and now felt that the white man would hold them accountable.

Ish asked for some fresh eggs, and for a dozen gave them one of his dollar bills. They seemed to be delighted with the exchange. After a quarter of an hour, having exhausted all the possibilities of the situation, Ish got into the car, much to the relief of the reluctant hosts.

He sat in the front seat for a moment, thinking to himself, "Here," he reflected, "I might be a king in a little way, if I remained. They would not like it, but from long habit they would, I think, accept the situation—they would raise vegetables and chickens and pigs for me, and I could soon have a cow or two. They would do all the work that I needed to have done. I could be a king, at least, in a little way."

But the idea was only fleeting, and as he drove on, he began to think that the Negroes had really solved the situation better than he. He was living as a scavenger upon what was left of civilization; they, at least, were still living creatively, close to the land and in a stable situation, still raising most of what they needed.

Of half a million species of insects only a few dozen were appreciably affected by the demise of man, and the only ones actually threatened with extinction were the three species of the human louse. So ancient, if not honorable, was this association that it had even been used as an argument for the single origin of man, anthropologists noting that all isolated tribes scratched and picked at the same parasites and therefore inferring that the original ape-men must have carried the original insect-ancestors outward with them from their point of dispersal.

Since that first departure, throughout hundreds of millennia, the lice had adjusted their life nicely to their world, which was the body of man. They existed as three tribes, taking as their domains, respectively, the head, the clothing, and the private parts. Thus, in spite of racial differences, they amicably maintained a tripartite balance of power, setting for their host an example which he might well have followed. At the same time, becoming so exactly adapted to man, they lost the capacity of existing upon any other host.

The overthrow of man was therefore their overthrow. Feeling their world growing cold, they crawled off in search of some new warm world to inhabit, found none, and died. Billions perished most miserably.

At the funeral of Homo sapiens *there will be few mourners.* Canis familiaris *as an individual will perhaps send up a few howls, but as a species, remembering all the kicks and curses, he will soon be comforted and run off to join his wild fellows.* Homo sapiens, *however, may take comfort from the thought that at his funeral there will be three wholly sincere mourners.*

He came to the long bridge across the great brown rolling river, and a truck was stalled, blocking the narrow single lane which led across to Memphis.

Feeling like a bad boy, who is doing something forbidden and will be punished for it, he went against all the traffic signs, took the narrow single lane on the lefthand side of the railroad tracks, and headed across toward Tennessee on the road which should lead to Arkansas.

But he met no one, and before long he came to the Tennessee side, and drove out (still in the wrong direction) through the bridge approach. Memphis was as empty as other cities had been, but a south wind was blowing, and it brought a fetid reek from what had been the teeming districts around Beale Street. If this was any indication of what Southern cities would be like, Ish wanted no more of them. He headed fast toward the country again.

Before he had gone far, however, the south wind brought steady rain. Since driving became dull and wearisome, and since he was certainly in no hurry to get anywhere, he holed up in a tourist-court at the edge of a small town, the name of which he did not even bother to ascertain. The gas pressure was still working at the stove in the kitchenette, and he made the fresh eggs his chief dish for dinner. They were a real treat, and yet he ended by being in some way still unsatisfied. "I wonder," he thought, "if I'm getting all the things I

61

should to eat." Perhaps he should raid a drug store for some vitamin tablets.

Later, he let Princess out for a run, and she suddenly vanished into the rain with a long yapping which ended in a bay as she struck on the trail of some animal. He was disgusted, since he knew that he might have to wait up an hour for her pleasure to return. She was back sooner, however, smelling woefully of a skunk. He shut her in the garage, and she complained bitterly with her yapping, at the disgraceful way she was being treated.

Ish went to bed, still with the unsatisfied feeling. "Must be suffering from shock more than I realize consciously," he thought. "Or else the loneliness is getting me, or maybe good old sex is raising its ugly head."

Shock could do strange things, he knew. He remembered hearing the story of a man who had seen his wife killed before his eyes in an accident and who had felt no desire for months.

He thought of the Negroes whom he had seen that day. The woman—middle-aged, far gone in pregnancy, no beauty at any time—could scarcely have thus disturbed him. When he thought of the incident, his memories turned chiefly to the way in which they had found a kind of security by keeping close to the soil. Then Princess bayed from the garage, and he cursed her, and went to sleep.

In the morning he still felt unsatisfied and restless. The storm was not yet over, but at the moment no rain was falling. He decided not to leave, but to take a walk down the road. Before going he looked into the station-wagon, and saw the rifle lying on the middle seat. He had hardly touched it since leaving California; now, without any definite thought, he took it, tucked it under his arm, and walked down the road.

Princess followed him a few yards, then discovered a new trail, and in spite of the last night's experience was off upon it, vanishing over the hill in a series of delighted yelps and bays. "Better luck this time!" he called after her.

Ish himself walked along with no more definite idea than to stretch his legs a little or perhaps find a tree with ripe fruit. He was scarcely thinking of anything when he saw a cow and a calf in a field. There was nothing remarkable in that; he could see a cow and a calf in nearly any field in Tennessee. The remarkable fact was that now the loaded rifle was under his arm, and suddenly he knew what must somewhere have been in his mind.

Carefully resting the rifle on a fence-post he saw the sights come clearly into line with the redness of the calf's shoulder. The range was butcher's distance. He squeezed the trigger, and the rifle spoke and kicked back against him. As the sound died, he heard the calf give a long choking wheeze; it stood with legs braced but shaky, a thin stream of blood bursting from the nostrils. Then it collapsed and fell.

The cow had run a few yards after the shot, and now she stood and turned uncertainly. Ish did not know what she might do in the defense of her calf. Taking good aim again, he put a bullet just behind her shoulder. He fired twice more, for mercy, as she toppled.

He had to walk back to the cabin for the hunting-knife. When he returned, he carried the reloaded rifle. He felt his own reaction as curious. Before this time he had never thought much about weapons, but now it was as if he had declared war upon creation and should look for retaliation upon himself. Yet, when he came to where the cow and the calf were lying, and climbed over the fence, he met no resistance or opposition. The calf, to his dismay, was still breathing. Not liking the job, he cut its throat. He had never been a hunter, and had never butchered an animal; so he made a bad haggling job of it. Getting himself well bloodied in the process, he managed to hack out the liver; when he had got it, he realized that he had no way to carry it, except in his hand. He had to lay the bloody mass back among the entrails of the calf, and go back again to the cabin to get a pan. When he returned to the calf, a crow was already at work upon the eyes.

When he finally had the liver safely at the cabin, he was so covered with blood and dirt that he had lost all desire to eat it. He washed as well as he could at the cabin, and waited around listlessly, since the rain had again begun to fall. Princess returned, and demanded entrance. Since she had, by this time, lost most of the skunk's smell, he admitted her. She was wet and scratched with briers, dirty and foot-sore. She lay on the floor putting herself into shape with her tongue; he himself lay on the bed as if spent by emotion, yet in some way satisfied at last. Outside, the rain fell steadily, and after an hour, for the first time since it all happened, Ish realized that he had a new sensation—he was merely bored.

He looked around at the cabin, and found a six-months-old magazine; he settled down to read a story which dealt with the old boy-meets-girl theme, taking its particular slant from the problems which arose to hinder true love as the result of a housing shortage. It was all as far away, Ish concluded, from his present situation, as if it had been a story about building the Pyramids. In the course of the morning, he read three stories, but he found the advertisements much more fascinating. Not one in ten of them seemed to have any relation to his present situation, because they were not aimed at man, the individual, so much as at man, the member of a group—for instance, you should avoid bad breath, not because it might be a symptom of approaching toothache or digestive discomfort, but because if you had bad breath the girls would not like to dance with you or your boy-friend would not propose.

Yet the magazine had the good effect, at least, of taking him out from himself again. By noon, he was hungry, and when he looked at the liver now lying peacefully in a pan, he found that the memory of the bloody and dying calf had passed out of his mind. He fried a fine succulent piece of it for his lunch, and enjoyed it greatly. A bit of fresh meat, he concluded, was what he had been wanting. He gave a piece to Princess, also.

As he sat quietly after lunch, he had a new feeling of satisfaction and release. To shoot a calf was certainly no feat of sportsmanship, and it was not getting very close toward the production of one's own food. Yet it was a little closer to reality than the opening of a can. He seemed to have moved one step away from a mere scavenging existence, and to be getting a little closer to the state in which the three Negroes were living. To put it that an act of destruction had been an act of creation might seem a paradox, but he felt of it as something of that sort.

A fence was a fact, and a fence was also a symbol. Between the herds and the crops, the fence stood as a fact, but between the rye and the oats, it was only a symbol, for the rye and the oats did not mingle of themselves. Because of fences the land was cut into chunks and blocks. The pasture changed to the plowed land sharply at the fence, and on the other side of the plowed land, at the line of the fence, went the highway, and beyond the highway was the orchard, and then another fence with the lawns and the house beyond it, and again at a fence, the barnyard. Once the fences are broken both in fact and in symbol, then there are no more blocks and chunks of land and sharp changes, but all is hazy and wavy, and fades from one into the other, as it was in the beginning.

After that, he lost track of the time still more. He did not travel far in any day because there was much rain, and the roads were not as smooth and straight as they had been in the West. Moreover he had lost his sense of hurry. He worked northeastward through the hills of Kentucky, then struck the Ohio River bottomland, and went on into Pennsylvania.

He foraged more for himself. He gathered green corn from the weed-grown corn-patches. There were ripe berries and fruit. Now and then in a garden he found a head or two of lettuce which had not been ruined by worms. Frequently, he pulled up carrots, and ate them raw, since he was very fond of raw carrots. He shot a young pig. He used the shotgun to bag two partridges. Again, with Princess shut in the car and protesting loudly, he spent a happy two hours slowly stalking a flock of turkeys which always scurried off just before he was within range. At last, however, he managed to get close enough to knock over a gobbler. Some weeks ago it must have been a tame turkey, but now it had gone wild, and from constant necessity of dodging foxes and wild cats had become almost as wary as if it had lived all its life in the woods.

Between rains the weather was warm, and when he felt like it, he stripped and swam in some likely-looking stream. Since the water from faucets began to seem stale, he drank from springs and wells although by now, he judged, even the larger rivers should be free of sewage and factory refuse.

He became used to the look of the towns, and could generally tell whether they were entirely empty or whether by searching he might somewhere find a survivor or two. The liquor stores were often looted. The other buildings usually undisturbed, although occasionally there had been tampering with the banks—people apparently still putting trust in money. In the streets there would be an occasional pig or dog, less often, a cat.

Even in this once more thickly inhabited part of the country he saw comparatively few bodies, and there was less stench of death than he had feared. Most of the farms and many of the smaller towns apparently had been left deserted when their last inhabitants withdrew to larger centers for medical care or else fled into the hills, hoping to escape infection. On the outskirts of every larger town he saw the piled-up dirt where the bulldozers had worked even in the last days. At the end, necessarily, many bodies must have been left unburied, but these were usually in the areas around hospitals which had been concentration-points. At the warning of his nose he avoided such spots or drove rapidly past them.

The surviving people, he found, were generally singles, occasionally couples. They were anchored firmly in their own places. Sometimes they seemed to wish that he would stay there with them, but they never wished to accompany him. He still did not find any of them with whom he wished to share the future. If necessary, he thought, he could return.

The country in some ways showed more change than the towns, although one would hardly have imagined so to begin with. But in the country the crops were growing up rankly with weeds. In this part, the wheat had not been cut at the time of the disaster, and now it was heavy in the head and the grains in some places had started to fall. The cattle and horses wandered about, and fences were obviously starting to go. Here and there a field of corn would remain undisturbed when the fence was tight, but more often the animals had forced an entrance.

Then, one morning, he crossed the Delaware River into New Jersey, and realized that he could reach New York by early afternoon.

Chapter 4

He came to the Pulaski Skyway about noon. Once before, as a boy of fifteen, he had driven there with his father and mother. Then the streaming traffic had half terrified him; trucks and cars had come roaring in, seeming to converge from all directions, and then suddenly to drop out of sight again as they went off onto the down-ramps. He remembered his father gazing anxiously, this way and that, to watch the traffic-signs, and his mother nervously giving advice. But now, Princess slept on the front seat beside him, and he speeded along the Skyway by himself.

Far ahead now he saw the high towers of the sky-scrapers, pearl-gray against a cloudy sky; there had been a shower, and the day was cool for mid-summer.

When he saw those towers, his feelings were strangely stirred. Now he knew, what he would not have been quite able to explain before, why he had headed for New York, even unconsciously. This, to every American, was the center of the world. According to what happened in New York, so in the long run, he could only think, it must happen elsewhere —"Falls Rome, falls the world."

When he came to the clover-leaf above Jersey City, he stopped in the middle of the Skyway to read the signs. No brakes squealed suddenly behind him; no horns blared; no truck-drivers bawled obscenities at him for blocking the road; no policemen shouted through loud-speakers.

"At least," he thought, "life is quieter."

From far off, he just caught the sound, some bird squawked twice—a seagull probably. The only other sound was the nearly imperceptible murmur of his own idling engine, as drowsy as the hum of bees.

There at the last moment he flinched from trying either of the tunnels. Untended, they might have gradually filled with water, and he had a vague fear of being trapped. He swung north, and at last crossed by the empty George Washington Bridge, and came to Manhattan.

Stretched out between its rivers, the city will remain for a long time. Stone and brick, concrete and asphalt, glass—time deals gently with them. Water leaves black stains, moss shows green, a little grass springs up in the cracks. (That is only the surface.) A window-pane grows loose, vibrates, breaks in a gusty wind. Lightning strikes, loosening the tiles of a cornice. A wall leans, as footings yield in the long rains; after years have passed, it falls, scattering bricks across the street. Frost works, and in the March thaw some flakes of stone scale off. (It is all very slow.) The rain washes quietly through the gutters into the storm-drains, and if the storm-drains clog, the rain runs still through the gutters into the rivers. The snow piles deep in the long canyons, drifting at the street corners; no one disturbs it. In the spring, it too runs off through the gutters. As in the desert, a year is like an hour in the night; a century, like a day.

Indeed the city is much like the desert. From the asphalt and concrete-coated soil the rain runs off both ways into the rivers. Here and there in a crack the subtle grass and the hardy weeds grow up a little, but no tree or vine or tall grass takes root. The very shade trees by the avenues, lacking man's care, die in their shallow pockets. The deer and the rabbits shun the empty streets; after a while even the rats go away. Only the flying creatures find there a refuge—the birds nest on the high ledges, and at morning and evening the bats fly out and in through the few broken windows. It will remain a long time, a very long time.

He turned south on Broadway, thinking to follow it clear to

the Battery. At 170th Street, however, he came to a very official-looking STREET CLOSED sign with an arrow directing him to detour eastward. He could have driven past the sign and ahead, but he felt a caprice to yield docilely to instructions. He drove over to Amsterdam Avenue, and then went south again. His nostrils let him know that the Medical Center must have been one of the last points of concentration, and that the detour sign had been put up to give directions around it.

Amsterdam Avenue was vacant too. Somewhere in these vast accumulations of concrete and brick and mortar and plaster, somewhere in all these cave-like holes that men called rooms, somewhere certainly, some people must be living. The catastrophe had been nearly universal, and in overcrowded Manhattan the disease had probably raged even more severely than elsewhere. Also, he thought, what he had come to call the Secondary Kill might have been more severe in a wholly urbanized population. Nevertheless, he had already learned that a few people had survived elsewhere, and surely among the millions of Manhattan there would be some. But he did not bother to blow his horn; a mere straggler here and there he had found to be of little interest to him now.

He drove on, block after block. Everything was quiet and motionless. The clouds had broken, and the sun stood high overhead, but the sidewalks were as empty as if the sun had been the moon and the hour had been three in the morning. Even then he would have seen a beat-walking policeman or have met a night-hawk cab. He passed an empty playground.

A few cars were parked along the curbs. He remembered that his father had driven him through downtown Manhattan on a Sunday when even Wall Street lay deserted. This was much the same, but worse.

At last, near Lewisohn Stadium, nuzzling around an entryway, two thin-looking dogs supplied the first sign of life. In the next block he saw a few pigeons fluttering about, not many.

He drove on, passed the red-brick buildings of Columbia University, and stopped in front of the high, still unfinished cathedral. It was unfinished now, and so it would remain.

He pushed at the door; it swung open; he entered. Momentarily he had a horrible thought that he might find the nave piled with the bodies of those who at the last hour had gathered there to pray. But there was no one. He walked down a side aisle, and went into the little chapels of the apse, one after another—those where the English and the

68

French and the Italians and all the others of that teeming polyglot city had been invited to kneel and worship. The sunlight streamed in at the stained-glass windows; it was all as beautiful as he remembered from before. He had a wild desire to throw himself on his knees before one of the altars. "There are no atheists in fox holes," he remembered, and the whole world now was nothing but a huge fox hole! But certainly what had happened did not inspire one to think that God was particularly interested in the human race, or in its individuals.

He walked back along the main aisle. Turning, he looked up the nave, and let its grandeur beat in upon him. He felt a little choking in the throat. This, then, was the end of all man's highest striving and aspiration. . . . He went out to the empty street, and got into the car again.

At Cathedral Parkway he swung east, and defying traffic signs entered Central Park and went south along the East Drive, thinking that on a summer day people might go to the Park as they would have done ordinarily. But he saw no one. From his previous visit as a boy he remembered squirrels, but he saw no squirrels either; starving dogs and cats had apparently accounted for them already. On a meadow he saw a bison bull grazing; not far off, a horse. He passed the back of the Metropolitan Museum, and saw Cleopatra's Needle, now doubly orphaned. At Sherman's statue he swung into Fifth Avenue, and a tag-end of verse popped into his mind: "Now all your victories are in vain."

An island within an island, the green oblong of the Park will remain. It has open soil where the rain penetrates. The sun shines upon it. In the first season the grass grows tall; the seeds fall from the trees and bushes, the birds bring in more seeds. Give it two seasons, three seasons, and the eager saplings are sprouting. Give it twenty years, and it is a jungle of second growth with each tree straining upward to gain light above its fellows, and the hardy natives, fast-growing ash and maple, crowding out the soft exotics which man once planted there. You hardly see the bridle path any more; leaf-litter lies thick on the narrow roads. Give it a hundred years, and you walk in full-grown forest, scarcely knowing that man was ever there except where the stone arch still spans the under-pass, making a strange cave. The doe walks in the woods, and the wild-cat leaps upon the rabbit, and the bass jumps in the lake.

In the tall windows of the fashion shops, the mannequins still postured strangely in gay costumes, their jewelry flashing. But Fifth Avenue lay before him empty, as quiet as Main Street of Podunk on a Sunday morning. The windows of one great jewelry store had been smashed. "I hope," thought Ish, "he found the diamonds good eating, poor guy. No, I hope he was somebody who liked pretty stones because they were pretty, like a child picking them up on the beach. Perhaps, with his diamonds and rubies, he really died happier." On the whole, however, there was little disturbance along Fifth Avenue. "The corpse is laid out in good condition," he thought. "Yes, Fifth Avenue makes a beautiful corpse."

A few pigeons fluttered up at Rockefeller Center, disturbed now by the sound of a single motor. At Forty-second Street, yielding to a whim, he stopped the car in the middle of Fifth Avenue and got out, leaving Princess shut up.

He walked east on Forty-second Street, the empty sidewalk ridiculously wide. He entered Grand Central Terminal, and looked in at the vast expanse of waiting-room.

"Waugh!" he called loudly, and felt a childlike pleasure as an echo came reverberating back from the high vault, through the emptiness.

He wandered back to the street, and a revolving door caught his eye. He pushed against it idly, and found himself in the lobby of a large hotel. Flanked by huge chairs and davenports, the lobby led on to the desk.

Standing just inside the door, he had a moment's idea of approaching the desk and entering into an imaginary conversation with the reservation-clerk. He had telegraphed from— well, Kansas City would be a good place. Yes, and his reservation had been confirmed! What were all these excuses now? But the insane notion faded. With a thousand rooms empty and the poor clerk gone—who knew where?—the joke was not very funny.

At the same time also he noticed something different. Over all the chairs and davenports and cigarette-stands and marble floors lay a distinct layer of gray dust.

Perhaps, not being a housekeeper, he had not previously noticed dust, or perhaps this place was particularly dusty. No matter which! From now on, dust would be a part of his life.

Back at the car, he slipped it into gear, crossed Forty-second Street, and continued south. On the steps of the Library he saw a gray cat crouched, paws stretched out in front, as if in caricature of the stone lions above.

70

At the Flatiron Building he turned into Broadway, and followed it clear to Wall Street. There they both got out, and Princess showed interest in some kind of trail which ran along the sidewalk. Wall Street! He enjoyed walking along its empty length. With a little observation he discovered that there was some grass, weeds rather, showing green here and there in the cracks of the gutter. He remembered the family story that an early Dutch settler, one of their ancestors, had owned a good farm in this vicinity. His father, when the bills were high, used to say, "Well, I wish we had held on to that farm on Manhattan Island." Now Ish could take the land back for all that anybody cared. Yet this wilderness of concrete and steel and asphalt was the last place where anybody would really care to live now. He would trade that Wall Street farm for any ten acres in Napa Valley, or even for a small corner of Central Park.

He walked back to his car, and drove south on Broadway still, the little distance to the Battery. There he gazed across the expanse of the lower Bay toward the ocean. This was the end of the road.

There might be communities left in Europe or South America or on some of the islands, but he could not go to find out. Right here, doubtless, his Dutch ancestor had come ashore some three hundred years ago. Now he, Ish, had rounded the full circle.

He noticed the Statue of Liberty. "Liberty!" he thought ironically. "At least, I have that! More than anyone ever thought of, when they put the lady up there with her torch!"

Close to the shore of Governor's Island a large liner was beached. She must have been run aground at high tide, and now at low tide she loomed up far above the water, canted at a crazy angle. Secretly infected before leaving Europe, before long with passengers and crew alike dead and dying, that ship must have made desperately for port—for a port which itself had strangely ceased to send out signals. No tugs came out to meet her. Perhaps a dying boatswain on the bridge lacked even the crew to drop an anchor, and with dimming eyes merely steered her toward the mudbank. There she would rest, and doubtless the waves would wash up mud against her obstructing bulk, and in a century she would be almost indistinguishable—the rust-covered center of a little island with trees growing up around her.

Going on, Ish swung off through the East Side, struck a noisome area again at the great center of Bellevue Hospital, turned west and found the same difficulty around Pennsylvania Station and the adjoining hotels, and finally went north on Eleventh Avenue. He turned into Riverside Drive, and noticed that the sun was getting low over the smokeless smokestacks of the Jersey shore. He was just wondering where he should spend the night when he heard a voice calling out, "Hi, there!"

Princess burst into a frenzy of barking. Stopping the car, he looked back, and saw a man emerging from the entryway of an apartment house. Ish got out to meet him, leaving the barking Princess in the car.

The man advanced with outstretched hand. He was completely conventional-looking, well shaved, wearing a tropical-worsted suit, with even the coat on. He was middle-aged and overweight, with a smiling face. Ish half expected him to break into the conventional shopkeeper's greeting "Well, sir, what can I do for you today?"

"Abrams is the name," he said, "Milt Abrams."

Ish fumbled for his own name—it was so long since he had thought of it. Introductions over, Milt Abrams took him inside. They went into a pleasant apartment on the second floor. A blonde-haired woman, about forty, well dressed, almost smart-looking, was sitting at a cocktail table, and there was a cocktail shaker before her. "Meet—the Mrs." said Milt Abrams, and from the way he hesitated, Ish knew that the Mrs. merely covered up his embarrassment. The catastrophe would scarcely have spared a husband and wife, and there had been no opportunity for any ceremony since. Milt Abrams was obviously conventional enough to let this worry him even under the circumstances.

The Mrs. looked at Ish with a smile, possibly at Milt's discomfort. "Call me Ann," she said. "And have a drink!—Warm martinis, that's all I can offer you! Not a scrap of *ice* in New York City!" In her own way she was as typical a New Yorker as Milt.

"I tell her," said Milt. "I keep on telling her, not to drink that stuff—warm martinis are poison."

"Think of it," said Ann, "spending a whole summer in New York City—and without a *scrap* of ice!" Nevertheless, she seemed to have overcome her dislike of warm martinis sufficiently to have got on the outside of several of them.

"Here, I'll offer you something better," said Milt. Opening a cupboard, he displayed a fine shelf of Amontillado, Napoleon brandy, and selected liqueurs. "And," he added, "they don't call for ice."

Obviously, Milt was a natural connoisseur in liquor. The

72

bottle of Chateau Margaux that he produced for dinner was further proof.

Chateau Margaux over a meal of cold canned corned beef was not perhaps all that could be wished, but the wine was plentiful enough to produce in Ish a slight and happy befuddlement. Ann was definitely befuddled by this time.

The evening passed pleasantly enough. They played cards by candlelight—three-handed bridge. They drank liqueurs. They listened to records on a tinny-toned portable phonograph which had the great advantage of not needing electric power, but of being wound up by hand. They talked—as you might talk on any evening. "That record scratches . . . I haven't won a finesse yet. . . . Let me have another glassful."

It was a kind of make-believe. You pretended there was a world outside the windows; you were playing cards by candlelight because that was a pleasant thing to do; you did not trade reminiscences or talk of what you might think anyone would talk about under such circumstances. And Ish realized that this was proper and right. Normal people, and Milt and Ann seemed to be certainly normal, did not concern themselves much with either the distant past or the distant future. Fortunately, they lived in the present.

Yet, as the cards were dealt and played, by incidental remarks here and there, Ish put together a great deal of the situation. Milt had been part-owner of a small jewelry-store. Ann had been the wife of someone named Harry, and they had been prosperous enough to spend summers on the coast of Maine. The only work for pay that Ann had ever done had been to sell perfume in one of the more exclusive shops, as a kind of lark during the Christmas rush. Now the two of them occupied a fine apartment, vastly better than even Harry had been able to provide. The electricity had failed immediately, because the dynamos which supplied New York had been steam-driven; the water supply remained apparently at normal, and this prevented any sanitary problem.

Actually they were marooned on Riverside Drive. Being ordinary New Yorkers they had never owned a car, and so neither of them could drive. Automobiles were mysteries to them. Since all public transportation had now disappeared, they were left wholly afoot, and neither was of an age or temperament or physique to enjoy walking. Broadway, with its still well-stocked food- and liquor-stores, formed their practical eastern limit; the River lay to the west; they wandered up and down the Drive, perhaps half a mile north and south. That was their world.

Within these narrow limits they did not think that anyone else was living. As to what might be happening in the rest of the city, they had not as much idea as Ish. To them the East Side was as far off as Philadelphia; Brooklyn might as well be Saudi Arabia.

Once in a while, indeed, they had heard cars go by on Riverside Drive, and on rare occasions they had seen one. They had been wary, however, about approaching any of the cars, because from loneliness and a sense of helplessness, a fear had come upon them, and they had a kind of bug-a-boo terror about roving gangsters.

"But everything was getting so quiet that I really wanted to see someone. You weren't driving fast," said Milt almost diffidently, "and I saw you were alone, and didn't look bad, and had an out-of-town license."

Ish started to say that he would give them his pistol, but checked himself. Firearms were as likely to create as to solve difficulties. In all probability Milt had never fired a gun in his life, and he did not look like an apt learner. As for Ann, she gave the impression of being one of those excitable women who would be as dangerous to friend as to foe if she ever started cutting loose with a pistol.

In spite of having no motion pictures and no radio and in spite of lacking even that great and continual show of the passing populace of the city, still Milt and Ann did not seem to be particularly bored. They played cribbage, alternating with two-handed rummy—for high, but of course mythical, stakes. As the result, Ann now owed Milt several millions of dollars. They played endless records—jazz, folk-songs, dance-tunes—on the tinny phonograph. They read uncounted volumes of mystery stories which they got from the circulating libraries on Broadway and left strewn around the apartment. Physically, he guessed, they found each other attractive.

But if they were not bored, neither did they seem to have much pleasure in life. There was a great vacantness somewhere. From shock they were walking in a kind of haze. They were people without hope. New York, their world, had vanished; it would never live again in their time. They had no interest when Ish tried to tell them what had happened in the rest of the United States. "Falls Rome, falls the world."

Next morning Ann was having another warm martini at breakfast, and still complaining that there was not a scrap of ice in New York City. They urged him to stay longer; they urged him even to stay permanently. He could certainly find himself a girl somewhere in New York, they said; she would make a fourth for bridge. They were the pleasantest people he had found since the catastrophe. Yet he had no desire to stay there with them, even if he could locate a girl for a fourth at bridge—and other things. No, he decided, he would strike back for the West again.

But as he drove off and they stood at the entryway of the apartment-house and waved to him, he almost turned back to stay a while longer. He liked them, and he pitied them. He hated to think what would happen when winter struck, and the deep canyons between the buildings were clogged with snow and the north wind whistled down the groove of Broadway. There would be no central heating in New York City that winter, though indeed there would be plenty of ice, and no need to drink warm martinis.

He doubted whether they could survive the winter, even though they piled broken furniture into the fireplace. Some accident would quite likely overtake them, or pneumonia might strike them down. They were like the highly bred spaniels and pekinese who at the end of their leashes had once walked along the city streets. Milt and Ann, too, were city-dwellers, and when the city died, they would hardly survive without it. They would pay the penalty which in the history of the world, he knew, had always been inflicted upon organisms which specialized too highly. Milt and Ann—the owner of a jewelry store, a salesgirl for perfumes—they had specialized until they could no longer adapt themselves to new conditions. They were almost at the other end of the scale from those Negroes in Arkansas who had so easily gone back to the primitive way of living on the land.

The Drive curved, and he knew that they would now be out of his sight, even if he turned around. He felt the warmth and fullness of tears in his eyes—Good-bye, Milt and Ann!

Chapter 5

Headed west—going home, as he still thought of it—he felt often as if he were on a leisurely camping trip. A man and his dog drove in a car, and the days slipped by uneventfully.

He crossed the rich farmlands of eastern Pennsylvania where the ripe unharvested wheat was golden brown and the corn stood shoulder-high. When he came to the empty Turnpike, he stepped hard on the accelerator, and steered deliriously around the neatly banked curves at eighty and ninety miles an hour, careless of danger, intoxicated with the mere joy of speed. He went on into Ohio.

By now gas-pressure had failed almost everywhere, but he picked up a two-burner gasoline stove which functioned perfectly. When the weather was fine, he merely camped in the woods, and built himself a fire. Tinned goods, salvaged from stores, still remained the basis of his diet, but he foraged in the cornfields, and took vegetables and fruit when he could find any.

He would have enjoyed some eggs, but chickens seemed to have vanished completely. He saw no ducks either. Weasels, cats and rats, he imagined, had cleaned out this smaller poultry, grown too stupid under long domestication to live without protection. Once, however, he heard the raucous call of guinea-fowl, and twice he saw geese calmly floating in barnyard ponds. He shot one of them, but found he had had the bad luck to bag an old gander, too tough to be made palatable by any campfire cookery. He often saw turkeys in the woods, and occasionally shot one. If Princess had been a bird-dog, he might have tried for partridges and pheasants, and though she departed hot on the trail of innumerable rabbits, she never brought one back to within range of the shot-gun. In the end he began to wonder whether these always invisible rabbits might not be pure figments of her imagination.

Cattle were common in the pastures, but he found the thought of the butchering too unpleasant, and had no great hunger for meat in the hot weather. He saw occasional small flocks of sheep. When the road went through swampy country, he sometimes almost ran over hogs, which seemed to enjoy stretching out in the shade on the coolness of the deserted concrete pavement. Lean dogs still haunted the towns. He rarely saw cats, but he sometimes heard them at night, and so he judged that they had already returned to nocturnal habits.

Avoiding the larger cities, he drove westward—Indiana, Illinois, Iowa—through the fields of tall corn and all the empty little towns, sun-flooded and empty by day, dark and empty by night. Still he looked for the small things that showed how the wilderness was moving in to take charge— the tiny sprout of a poplar tree standing up in the shaggy grass of a lawn, a telephone wire dangling on the road, the tracks of dried mud where a coon had paused to dip its food in the water of the fountain beneath the statue of the Civil War soldier in front of the court-house.

He came upon people now generally by twos or threes. (The isolated molecules were beginning to find one another.) Usually these people were clinging to some little spot that they had known previous to the disaster. As before, not one of them showed any desire to go away with him, but sometimes they invited him to stay. He found the offer no temptation. These people were physically alive, but more and more he realized that they walked about in a kind of emotional death. He had studied enough anthropology to realize that the same phenomenon had been observed on a smaller scale before. Destroy the culture-pattern in which people lived, and often the shock was too great for the individuals. Take away family and job, friends and church, all customary amusements and routines, hope too—and life became walking death.

The Secondary Kill was still at work. Once he saw a woman whose mind had failed. The clothes indicated an original prosperity, but now she was scarcely able to care for herself and could certainly not last through a winter. Several survivors told him of others who had committed suicide.

As yet, though sometimes he wondered, he himself was conscious of no great strain either of shock or of loneliness. He attributed this to his maintenance of interest in the whole progress of events, and to his own peculiar temperament. He thought many times of his qualifications for the new life, as he had once listed them.

Sometimes, while he drove or sat by his fire, erotic images rose to his mind. He thought of Ann on Riverside Drive, crisp and well-groomed in her blondness. But she was an exception. The usual women were ill-kempt and even dirty, their faces blank with mental apathy, except when they laughed hysterically or giggled. Some of them were obviously approachable, but always he felt desire wither away within him. This, he realized, might be the particular form that shock took with him. But there was no need to force matters; in the end he might change.

All across the blazing plains of Nebraska the wheat had not been harvested. Now it stood, losing its golden color, turning brown. The grains were already dropping from the heads. Next year there would be a volunteer crop, but all around the edges other kinds of grass would also sprout up, grass that could grow more readily when the soil was not disturbed. Soon, he knew these native grasses would form a sod and crowd out the wheat.

Estes Park was restful after the heat of the plains. He

stayed there for a week. The trout had not struck at a hook all summer, and the fishing was excellent.

Next came the high mountains, and then the desert again and the sagebrush. Then he was pressing his foot hard and steering round the curves of U.S. 40 toward the summit of Donner Pass.

On the other side of the Pass he suddenly sensed that the country all ahead was palled in smoke. "What month is it, anyway?" he thought, "August? Early September, more likely. Bad forest-fire season." And he remembered that now there would be no one to battle against the fires which lightning would still start.

By Yuba Gap he suddenly came to the fire. It was burning low on both sides of the road, and he chanced running through it. The highway was wide, and things were not too hot, until on rounding a curve he came squarely upon a snag, fallen and blocking the way completely, blazing along its whole length, fierce with heat. Suddenly he again felt the old fear which he had shaken off, (years ago, it seemed) that morning in the desert—the utter loneliness to face an emergency or recover from any accident.

There was nothing for it but to turn the car around on the highway. He shuttled back and forth twice, killing the engine in his panicky haste. It started again, and he swung on the back trail out of the flames.

Once more in safety, he recovered his calm. He drove back to the junction with California 20, and decided to make another try. There was some fire along this road, too, but generally it had swept past already. He drove carefully, avoiding a few chunks of fallen tree on the road, and managed to get through. He was appalled, however, as he gained the ridge beyond, and saw fire seemingly everywhere. He was lucky to make it.

He had planned to camp that night in the cool of the mountains; instead, to escape being further blocked by fire, he drove on, and unrolled his sleeping-bag in the little park of a foothill town. No lights were burning. He was disappointed, for he had hoped to find lights in California. The forest-fire, however, would undoubtedly have burned out the power-lines, at least locally.

As he lay, trying to sleep, hot and uncomfortable, the dryness of smoke in his nostrils, he had the feeling that now he was trapped. Even though the fires would burn themselves out, the roads across the Sierra would be permanently

78

blocked by many fallen trees and by landslides and washouts upon the denuded slopes.

In the morning, as usual, he felt more cheerful. If he was trapped, California was a comfortably large place to be trapped in, and even though the Sierra would be impassable, the southern road through the desert might remain open for a long time. He was just ready to start, but Princess, with her usual perverseness, suddenly gave tongue, and disappeared on a trail. Irritated, he waited for her, and when she did not return, he changed his plans, and spent most of the day lolling, half naked, in the shade of some trees. In the late afternoon, he started.

At twilight he came to the crest of the hill, and looked out again over the broad expanse of all the Bay cities. With a sudden start of pleasure he saw that most of the street lights were still burning. There had been no electric lights for such a long time that he could really not remember where he had last seen them. All the steam-driven power-plants must have failed almost immediately, and even the smaller hydro-electric systems had not lasted long. He felt a curious local pride mingling with his pleasure; perhaps these were the last electric lights left burning in the whole world.

At the moment he could almost think that it had all been some wild vagary of the imagination, and that he had now returned to a normally functioning city.

The long empty highway ahead of him gave the lie to such thoughts. He looked more carefully. A few sections, he decided, had blacked out through local failure of power since he had been away. The lights on the Golden Gate Bridge were either extinguished, or else he could not see them because of the smoke drift upon the Bay.

He turned into San Lupo Drive. As far as he could see from the street-lights and the headlight glare, everything looked just the same as when he had last left it. "There'll always be a San Lupo Drive!" he thought, and then he realized that at least he was enough like all the other survivors to pick out some particular familiar spot, and though he went away, to return to it again like the homing pigeon.

He opened the front door, snapped the lights on, and looked. Nothing was changed. He had known that it must be so, and yet there had always been hope. He felt no active sorrow, but only dullness.

"The sere and yellow leaf," he thought, saying a line he had heard on the stage, but not knowing what play. *"There would have been a time. . . ."*

Princess made a sudden dash into the kitchen, slipped on the linoleum, skidded, yelped comically, and recovered. Thankful to her again for breaking the tension, he followed her. She was sniffing along the baseboard, but he failed to discover what had excited her.

"Well," he thought, walking back to the living-room, "if I have no feelings left, that is perhaps strange, but at least there is no one now to whom I can pretend. It is probably all part of what I am passing through."

The note which he had left posted on the desk was still there, undisturbed, looking remarkably fresh. He took it, crumpled it, threw it into the fireplace, scratched a match. He hesitated a moment. Then he touched the match to the paper, and watched the flame blaze up. *That* was finished!

In that generation there will be neither father nor mother, nor wife, nor child, nor friend. But it will be as in the ancient tales when the gods reared up a new people from stones or dragons' teeth, and they were all strangers with strange faces, and no man knew his fellow's face.

The next morning he settled down to establish his life. Food, he knew already, was no problem at all. In the nearest business district he began looking into store-windows. Rats and mice were making a mess of everything, and the floors were littered with gnawed cartons and spilled food. Through one window, however, he was startled to see the gaily colored piles of fruit and vegetables as fresh and lovely as ever. He stared incredulously, peering through the dust-coated glass. Then, first with irritation and then with amusement, he realized that the bright colors were merely from the papier-mâché oranges, apples, tomatoes, and avacados which the store in the old days had used for a permanent front-window display.

After a while he saw through the windows a grocery which was unlittered. Apparently it must be rodent-proof. Carefully jimmying a window, he got into the store.

The bread was inedible, and weevils were at work even in some of the carefully sealed boxes of crackers. But the dried fruit and everything inside of tin and glass was as good as ever. As he was picking out some cans of olives, he heard an electric motor start. Curiously, he opened the refrigerator, and found that the butter was still perfectly preserved. Next he investigated the deep-freeze units, and found fresh meat, frozen vegetables, ice-cream, and even materials for a green salad. When he left with his loot, he closed the window carefully behind him, to keep at least that one store free of rats.

After he had returned to the house, he reflected upon his position again, and decided that as yet the mere maintenance of life would be easy, indefinitely. Food, clothing—the shops were full, and he had only to help himself! Water still gushed from the faucets at full pressure. Gas had failed, and if it had been a country of bitterly cold winters, he might have had to consider laying in some kind of fuel supply. But his gasoline stove served excellently for cooking; if the fireplace was not sufficient in the winter, he could round up a battery of such stoves and supply himself with all the heat he needed. In fact, he soon began to feel so pleasantly self-sufficient that he feared he was turning into a hermit like the old man he had once seen.

In those days when there had been death even in the air and civilization tottered toward its end—in those days, the men who controlled the flow of the water looked at one another and said, "Even though we fall sick and die, still, the people must have water." And they thought of plans that they had laid carefully in those times when men feared that bombs would fall. Then they set the valves and opened the channels, so that the water flowed freely all the way from the great dams in the mountains and through the long siphons and into the tunnels and finally to the reservoirs from which it would flow, all at the pull of the earth, through all the faucets. "Now," they said, "when we are gone, the water will flow on—yes, until the pipes rust out, and that will be the time of a generation!" Then they died. But they died as men who have finished their work and lie down quietly, secure in their honor.

So at the end, there was still the blessing of water, and no one thirsted. And even when only a few wanderers walked through the city streets, the water still flowed.

Ish had feared at first that he would suffer from mere boredom, but he soon found himself as busy as he wished to be. The desire for activity which had expressed itself in his eastern trip had now faded out. He slept a great deal. He also found himself sitting for long periods, conscious but in sheer apathy. Such lapses, however, frightened him, and he always tried to force himself into some kind of activity.

Fortunately, though the mechanics of living were not complicated, they took up an appreciable part of his time.

He had to prepare his food, and he soon found that unless he washed the dishes promptly, a stream of ants appeared, to make everything twice as difficult. He was forced, for the same reason, to wrap up the garbage and carry it somewhere away from the house. He had to feed Princess; since she was getting smelly, he even bathed her, over her loud protests.

One day, wanting to shake himself out of his apathy, he went to the Public Library, smashed a lock with his hammer, and after some browsing found himself (a little to his own amusement) walking out with *Robinson Crusoe* and *The Swiss Family Robinson*.

These books, however, did not interest him greatly. Crusoe's religious preoccupations seemed boring and rather silly. As for the Robinsons, he felt (as he had felt when a boy) that the ship remained for the family a kind of infinite grab-bag from which at any time they might take exactly what they wanted.

Although the radio was dead, he still had the family's record-player and collection of records. After a while he located in a music store a better record-player. It was heavy, but he was just able to get it home on the station-wagon tail-gate, and set it up in the living-room. He also took all the records he wanted. Feeling the need of something more too, he helped himself to a fine accordion. With the aid of an instruction-book, he managed to make some very soul-satisfying noises on it, although Princess objected at times with loud howls. He also supplied himself with drawing-materials, but never got round to using them.

His chief interest remained the careful observation of what was happening to the world after the removal of man's controls. He drove around through all parts of the city, and into the near-by country. At other times, carrying his field-glasses, he took long walks through the hills, with Princess trailing now behind him and now dashing off in wild pursuit of that perpetual unseen rabbit.

Once he searched for the old man whom he had found storing up all those supplies of miscellaneous goods. After some trouble he located the house, and found the rat's nest of materials which had been piled in it. But the old man was not in the house, and there was no evidence as to where he had gone or whether he was still alive. Aside from this, Ish made no effort to find people, remembering how unsatisfactory had been the results of his previous attempts.

The look of the streets was changing a little. The drought of summer had not yet been broken, but the winds had blown dust and leaves and trash, and deposited them in little piles here and there. Over most of the city he saw no animals at all, neither dogs nor cats nor rats. In certain areas, however, particularly near the water-front, he saw a good many dogs, although only of a certain kind. They were small and active ones, terriers or terrier-like mongrels. By watching, he saw that they marked the establishment of some new cycle of life. They scavenged in the supplies which they found in the stores, perhaps having learned this from the rats. Where the rats gnawed open a carton of crackers, the dogs came in and ate. But also the dogs apparently lived largely upon the rats. This accounted for their concentration in the areas where rats had been somewhat abundant even before the catastrophe. The dogs had also apparently driven away or killed off the cats, doubtless getting scratched in the process, but also achieving some desperately needed meals.

These dogs amused Ish. They seemed almost to swagger, cocky still, as terriers were supposed to be. Though dirty and thin, they exuded vigor and self-confidence, as if knowing that they had solved the problem of life. Temperamentally they must represent the individuals who had always lived more or less on their own, taking care of themselves as they wished and paying scant attention to man. They showed no interest in Ish, keeping distance, not trying either to make friends or to escape from him. After Princess had tangled in a rough-and-tumble fight with one of the bitches, he took the precaution of keeping her on a leash or in the car whenever he drove through such districts.

In parks and on the edges of the city, wherever there was a good growth of bushes, he occasionally saw a cat. They kept mostly to the branches, apparently fearing the dogs and at the same time ready to prey upon birds.

During his walks in the hills he had never seen any dogs until one day he was surprised to hear a medley of yaps and deeper bays. Gaining a point from which he could look out, he saw a half dozen cattle, on what had once been the golf course, closely pursued and being harried by some eight or ten dogs. Focusing the field-glasses, he saw that the dogs were of different varieties, but none of them of the short-legged ratter type. There was a magnificent Dane, a collie, a spotted Dalmatian and others which had more the mongrel look but were all long of leg and moderately powerful. They were obviously a hunting pack, spontaneously formed and already experienced at their business. They were trying to cut out one of the calves. But the cattle fought back, vigorously, horns toward the pack, or kicking out from behind. They gradually made their way out of the open stretches of grass. When they reached the shelter of some bushes at the edge of the golf course, they seemed to gain the advantage, and the dogs drew off.

Since the show was over, Ish called Princess, and they started to walk back a mile toward where he had left the car. In a few minutes he heard the bay of the pack again. It came closer, and suddenly he knew that they were on his own trail.

Panic struck at him. He started to run. But after a few yards he realized that running would be of no use and only an invitation. He stilled his panic, gathered up a few stones, and selected a fallen branch to serve for a club. He continued to walk toward the car. The baying came closer; then suddenly it stopped, and he knew that the dogs must have sighted him. He hoped that the long-ingrained respect for mankind had survived, but also he suddenly began to wonder what had happened to the old man and the other people whom he had once seen in this region. Now one of the dogs, an ugly black mongrel, came out on the road right in front of him. Fifty yards off, it stopped, sat down, and looked at him. As he drew closer, he raised his arm, and made a gesture of throwing a stone. By age-old reaction the dog jumped up. It loped to the side of the road, and disappeared into the bushes. Ish could hear movement elsewhere in the brush, as if the dogs were circling about. Princess was behaving in her usual irritating and uncertain fashion. Now she cringed, tail between legs, brushing against him. Again she made short provocative dashes with loud barks, this direction and that, as if challenging one and all to combat with her and her man.

Now he could see the car far ahead; he walked steadily, husbanding his stones, looking backward only now and then, depending upon Princess to give warning if a sudden attack should come from behind. He caught a glimpse of the Dane standing in a gap between bushes, a magnificent dog, heavy as a man. With a loud yap Princess made a suicidal dash at the great beast. He sprang toward her, and at the same time the collie dashed out of the bushes on the left. But Princess doubled with the agility of a rabbit, and the two larger dogs collided in their rush, and caromed off each other, snarling. Princess came back again to brush against his legs, her tail drooping. Now the Dalmatian crossed into the road ahead and stood there, red tongue lolling out. Ish continued

84

his steady pace. The Dalmatian was the least fiercesome looking of the dogs, and Ish felt that he might brave that one. A handsome collar still circled the spotted neck, a metal dog-tag dangling from it. Uneasily, Ish saw that it was thin, with ribs showing, and yet did not look in too bad condition. Evidently on rabbits or calves or on whatever the pack might run down or find as carrion, the dogs were managing to get along. He hoped that they had not yet been driven into cannibalism, and that their interest in Princess might be somewhat playful—not to mention their interest in a stray man.

At twenty feet distance, without slacking his steady pace, Ish raised his arm, threatening. The Dalmatian suddenly dropped tail between legs, and slunk off. The car was close now, and Ish relaxed.

He got to the car, opened the door for Princess to jump in, and stilling a last-moment panicky impulse to scramble, he himself stepped in behind her with dignity. As the door clicked shut, he had an immediate feeling of safety. He let his hand close comfortably around the solid handle of the hammer which lay at his feet. He felt sick with the reaction.

Looking out from the car, he saw only the handsome Dalmatian, sitting at the side of the road. Now being safe, Ish felt his attitude quickly changing. Actually the dogs had done him no harm, and indeed had not really even threatened him. During a few minutes he had thought of them as wild creatures thirsting for his blood. Now, they seemed a little pitiful, as if they might merely have been seeking the companionship of a man because of what they remembered long ago—of food laid out in dishes, of crackling logs in the fireplace, of a patting hand and a soothing voice. As he drove away, he wished them no bad luck, but rather hoped that they would manage occasionally to snap up a rabbit or pull down a calf.

The next morning the whole matter had even a more comic aspect when he became aware of Princess's changed condition. Not wanting any puppies, he shut her in the basement.

Yet he could not be sure, and he decided if there was one way rather than another by which he did not care to die, it was to be torn to pieces by the teeth of dogs. After that he made it a rule always to walk in the hills with a pistol strapped at his belt, or else with his rifle or shotgun. . . .

Two days later the problem of dogs had come to seem a petty one compared with the problem of ants. They had already troubled him, but now they seemed to arrive from all directions at once and to cover everything. Even in the old days, he could remember that constant battle—his mother's cry of dismay at finding a line of them in the kitchen, his father's irritation, and the constant debate about whether they should summon the ant-man or try to handle the situation themselves. But now the ants were a hundred times worse than ever before. No longer did ardent householders combat them in the houses, and even wage offensive war against them in their own strongholds. Now after a few months their powers of rapid breeding had brought their numbers to climactic proportions. Probably, also, they had found great supplies of food somewhere.

They streamed everywhere. Ish was sorry not to be a good enough entomologist to ascertain what really was happening and to work out the history of this overpowering increase. But in spite of some investigations, he never even discovered for certain whether the ants were spreading outward from some great center of development or whether they were breeding equally all over the city.

Their scouts ranged everywhere. Suddenly he had to become a furiously meticulous housekeeper, for the slightest scrap of food or even a dead fly brought an immediate stream of ants an inch wide, overwhelming the insignificant prey which had attracted them. He found them wandering upon Princess's coat like fleas, although apparently they did not bite. He found them in his own clothes. Once in the early morning he awoke with a horrible dream because a stream of ants was pouring across his own cheek, bent to some goal which he never discovered.

Actually the house was only alien ground into which they made raids. Their real strength lay outside. Their hills seemed now to be everywhere. He could not overturn a clod without having ants swarm out by thousands from burrows that pierced the earth. They must be annihilating all the other insects, he thought, destroying their means of subsistence even if not killing them. He got bottles of ant-poison and DDT spray from the drug store, and tried to make the house into a hostile island, but the pressure of numbers was so great from the outside that they streamed across his spray. Doubtless all the trespassers inevitably died, but the death of even millions of individuals would not affect such numbers appreciably. He tried to estimate how many ants must be living on this one city lot, but he came out with an unbelievable answer in billions. Had they no natural enemies? Had they broken all limits of control? With the removal of man were they now destined to inherit the earth?

Yet, after all, they were only the little hustling ants which had irritated and plagued California housewives. Making some investigations, he found that actually the range of the plague did not extend appreciably beyond the limits of the city. In some way, like dogs and cats and rats, these ants had come to be domestic animals dependent upon the activities of man. This gave him a certain hope. If he had only been seeking his ease, he would have left the city, but he preferred, even at the cost of some discomfort, to watch what was happening.

Then one morning he realized suddenly that he had not noticed any ants. He looked around carefully, but he could not see any of their scouts. He dropped a bit of food on the floor, then went away about some other business for a few minutes. When he returned to the scene of his experiment, the food lay there without an ant upon it. Curious, realizing that something had happened, he went outside. He turned over a clod of dirt, and no ants swarmed from their holes. He hunted carefully. Here and there he discovered a few stragglers wandering about aimlessly, but they were so few that he could have counted them individually. He hunted still further. He could find no dead bodies of ants. They had simply vanished. Perhaps, if he had had the skill in their ways to dig down and find their nests, he would have discovered that they were lying dead in their billions. But again he could only wish that he knew more of their manner of life and could carry on an investigation.

He never solved the mystery, but he had little doubt as to what had happened. When any creature reached such climactic numbers and attained such high concentration, a nemesis was likely to fall upon it. Possibly the ants had exhausted the supplies of food which had led to this tremendous increase of numbers. More likely, some disease had fallen upon them, and wiped them out. In the next few days he smelled, or thought he smelled, a faint all-pervading putrescence, as if from the decaying bodies of billions of ants. . . .

One evening shortly afterward, he sat reading, and after a while began to feel hungry. He went to the kitchen, and rummaged in the refrigerator for some cheese. Happening to glance at the electric clock, he was surprised to see that the time was only nine-thirty-seven. He had thought it was later. On his way back to the living-room he took a bite of the cheese, and glanced at his wrist-watch. The watch-hands stood at ten-nine, and he knew that he had set the watch by the clock within twenty-four hours.

"The old clock's going to pieces at last," he thought. "Not surprising!" He remembered how the motion of its hands had startled him when he had first returned to the house.

He sat down to read again. A high wind from the north with the heavy smell of smoke in it blew so hard that it rattled the windows occasionally. By now he was used to the smell of smoke, and did not think about it. At many times he could not even get a good view because of the smoke of the burning forests. After a while he blinked his eyes a little, and stared more intently at the page where the letters seemed to have grown strangely indistinct. "This smoke must be making my eyes water," he thought. "I don't seem to see so well." But as he looked closer, it seemed that not only the page before him but the whole room had grown dimmer. With a sudden start he looked at the electric-light bulb in the bridge lamp beside him.

Then quickly, with a jumping heart, he was out of his chair and standing on the front porch looking out over the broad stretches of the city below him. The lights were still burning along the streets. The chains of yellow beads still showed on the great bridge, and at the tops of the towers the red lights were flashing. He looked more carefully. The lights seemed a little dimmer than they should be, but he could be imagining that, or they might be obscured by all the drifting smoke. He went back and sat in his chair again and tried to read, forgetting about it—forgetting what he feared.

But he blinked—and again! Looking at the light beside him, he was puzzled. Then suddenly he remembered the clock!

"Well," he thought, "it had to come!"

His watch now showed ten-fifty-two. He went out to the kitchen, and saw that the clock was at ten-fourteen. He calculated apprehensively. The result was bad. As closely as he could remember, the clock had lost six minutes in about three-quarters of an hour.

The clock was run, he knew, by electrical impulses which were ordinarily timed at sixty to the minute. Now they must be coming less often. An electrical engineer would doubtless have found it an elementary matter to calculate just how much less often. Ish could even have made an attempt at the calculation himself, but he saw no use in it, and he felt suddenly downcast. In any case, once the Power-and-Light system had started to go to pieces, the rate of decline would undoubtedly be progressively faster.

Back in the living-room, he could scarcely doubt now that the light had faded still more. Deep shadows seemed to have moved out from behind the chairs in the corners of the room.

"The lights are going out! The lights of the world!" he thought, and he felt like a child going alone into the dark.

Princess lay dozing on the floor. The fading of the lights could mean nothing to her, but she sensed his nervousness and came up restlessly sniffing, whining a little.

He stood on the porch again. Minute by minute the long chains of street-lights grew less and less luminous, more and more yellow. The high wind, he thought, must be helping, blowing down a power-line here, weakening a switch connection there. The fire too was sweeping across the forested ridges unchecked by men, burning power-lines, perhaps, even power-houses.

After a while the lights seemed to fade no further, but to remain at a constant dimness. He went in again, and pulling another bridge-lamp to the side of his chair, he was able to read comfortably with two lights instead of one. Princess lay down again to doze. By now it was late, but he did not want to go to sleep. He felt as if he were sitting up by the death-bed of his most treasured and oldest friend. He remembered those great words "Let there be light, and there was light!" This seemed the other end of that story.

After a while he went to look at the clock again, and saw that it had stopped with the hands symmetrically upward—at eleven-five.

His watch showed him that by now it was well after midnight. The lights might still continue many hours, or even might burn dimly for days. Yet he did not want to go to bed.

He tried to read again, but finally slipped off to sleep in the easy-chair where he was sitting.

With Power-and-Light it was all so carefully contrived that even in the disaster there was no need for adjustment. The men fell sick, but the generators still sent out along the wires their finely timed pulsations. So, when the brief agony of mankind was ended, the lights still burned.

So it continued through the weeks. If a wire broke and cut out a whole town from the flow of power, the system adjusted before that wire had had time to fall to the ground. If a power-house failed, just as quickly the other power-houses in the system stretching across hundreds of miles took up the slack, and sent out more power to fulfill the need.

Yet in any system, as in a chain or a road, there is always a weakest. link. (That is the fatal flaw of all systems.) The water would continue to flow; the great generators could spin upon their oil-bathed bearings for years. But the flaw lay in the governors which controlled the generators. No one had ever bothered to make them wholly automatic. Once every ten days they were inspected for oil; once a month, perhaps, there was need to add oil to them. After two months without care the oil supplies grew low, and one by one, as the weeks passed, the governors began to go out of action. When one failed, automatically the great water-nozzle changed angle and the water flowed through without touching the wheel. Then the generator ceased revolving, and sent out no more power. As generator after generator was thus cut out of the system, the strain upon the few remaining ones became greater and greater and the decline of the system became cumulative.

When he awoke, he noticed that the lights had faded still more. The filaments in the electric lamps were only an orange-red now. He could look at them without hurting his eyes. Now, although he had not turned off any of the lamps, the room was in half-darkness.

"The lights are going out! The lights are going out!" How often, in how many centuries had those words been said—sometimes in matter-of-fact tones, sometimes in panic—now literally, now as symbol? How much light had meant in all the story of Man! Light of the world! Light of life! Light of knowledge!

A deep shiver shook him, but he stilled his panic. After all, he thought, the great system of Power-and-Light had held up for an amazingly long time, all its automatic processes functioning though the men were gone. He thought clear back to that first day when he had come down out of the mountains not yet even knowing what had happened. Then he had passed the power-house, and felt the reassurance that everything must still be normal because he saw the water pouring out from the tailraces and heard the dim continuous hum of the generators. He felt again a curious touch of local pride in thinking of it. Perhaps no system had lasted so long. These might well be the last electric lights to be left burning in the world, and when they faded, the lights would be out for a long, long time.

No longer sleepy, he sat there, feeling that he should not go to sleep, wishing at least that the end would come quickly and with dignity and not be dragged out too long. Again, he felt the light fading, and he thought, "This is the end!" But still it lingered, the filaments now only a cherry-red.

And then again they faded. As a sled on a hillside, slowly first, then gaining momentum. Just for a moment, he thought (or imagined), they flared more brightly—and then they were gone.

Princess stirred in her sleep, then suddenly barked the half-bark of a dream. Was it a death knell?

He went outside. "Perhaps," he thought, "that was just the failure of some local line." But he was really sure that it had not been. He peered through the darkness, all the thicker for the smoke that was heavy in the air, changing the moon into an orange ball. He could see no light—not along the streets, nor anywhere on the bridge. This, then, was the end. "Let there be *no* light, and *there was no light!*"

"No use being melodramatic!" he thought. Going inside, he stumbled around until he had found the drawer where his mother kept candles. Putting one into a candlestick, he sat again by its feeble but steady and continuing light. Nevertheless he continued to feel a little shaken.

Chapter 6

The fading out of the lights had a strangely severe effect upon Ish. Even in the full daylight, he seemed to feel those shadows creeping in from the edges toward him. The Dark Ages were closing in.

He found himself hoarding matches and flashlights and candles, piling them up in spite of himself, as a psychological protection.

Yet actually, in a little while, he discovered that the absence of electric light was not really as important to him as the absence of electric power, particularly of refrigeration. The ice-box was dead now, and his food spoiled. In the deep-freeze units the fresh meat, and butter, and heads of lettuce soon relapsed into mere smelling masses of corruption.

Now came the change of the season. He was completely lost as to the passage of the weeks and months, but with the geographer's eye he could still tell something about the time of year from the look of things. Now he guessed it must be October, and the first rain came to confirm him; from the way it settled down, it seemed likely to last longer than one expected of the first storm.

He stayed at home, managing to amuse himself fairly well. He played his accordion. He browsed through several books —ones he had always meant to read and now was undoubtedly going to have time to do so. Now and then he looked out at the fine drifting rain and the clouds low over the tops of the houses.

The next day he went out to see what was happening, still thinking of the drama he was prepared to watch. Not so much had occurred, it seemed at first. But after a while he began to notice things. On San Lupo Drive a drain-pipe had plugged with the washing in of all the unswept leaves that lay in the gutter. After the drain-pipe had plugged, the water had swirled across the street to the downhill side and flooded over the curb. The stream of water had worked its way across the tangle of tall grass which had been the Harts' lawn, and seeped under the door. Their floors and rugs must be soaked, and slimy with mud. Below the house the water had broken out, and run through the rose-garden, leaving a small gully behind it, at last disappearing into the drainage of a storm-sewer on the street below. It was just a little matter, and yet it showed what must be happening all over the country.

Men had built roads and drains and walls and thousands of other obstructions to the natural flow of water. These could survive and function only because men were constantly at hand to repair and clean the thousands of little breaks and blockages which showed up at every change of the weather. Ish himself could have cleaned out that clogged drain in two minutes by merely scraping the leaves back from the grating where they had plugged it. But he saw no point to stretching out his hand. There were thousands, millions, of spots where the same thing must be happening. The roads and the drains and the walls had been constructed only for man's convenience, and now that man was gone there was no need of them. The water might just as well follow its natural courses, and cut back through the rose garden. Soaked and muddy, the Harts' rugs would begin to rot where they lay. No matter! To think of that as something bad, was merely to think in terms of what had once been and no longer existed.

As he walked back home, he suddenly came upon a large black billy-goat calmly eating the hedge which Mr. Osmer used to clip so carefully. Ish looked at the billy-goat in amusement and in some curiosity, wondering where he could have come from. (No one kept goats anywhere near such a respectable street as San Lupo.) The goat desisted from eating the hedge, and looked at Ish. Perhaps, thought Ish, the animal was looking also at the man in amusement and some curiosity. Men now had rarity-value. Having looked for a few seconds, as if it might be equal to equal, the goat again returned to the more profitable business of eating the long shoots which had grown out from the hedge. Doubtless they were very succulent.

Princess suddenly returned from some expedition of her own, and flew at the strange animal in a frenzy of barking. The goat put down his horns and made a sudden dash at the dog. Princess, who seldom had much stomach for a fight, turned quickly with her rabbit-like dodge, and raced back to her man. The goat resumed eating.

A few minutes later Ish saw the goat walking calmly along the sidewalk, as if he owned it and all of San Lupo Drive.

"Well, why not?" thought Ish. "Perhaps he does. This is certainly a New Deal."

During this time, when the rain kept him mostly indoors, his thoughts turned a little toward religion, as they had when he walked through the Cathedral. This time he found a large annotated Bible on his father's bookshelves, and tried browsing here and there in it.

The Gospels seemed strangely unsatisfying, probably because they dealt mostly with the problems of a man involved in the social group. "Render unto Caesar . . ." was a strangely unprofitable text when there was no more Caesar, and not even a Collector of Internal Revenue.

"Sell whatever thou hast, and give to the poor. . . . As ye would that men should do unto you . . . Love thy neighbor as thyself"—all these presupposed a functioning society of many people. As the world now was, a Pharisee or Sadducee might perhaps still follow the set rites of formalized religion, but the very humanity of the teachings of Jesus rendered them obsolete.

Turning back to the Old Testament, he began *Ecclesiastes,* and found himself suddenly more at home. The old fellow "The Preacher"—Koheleth, as the notes called him, whoever he might have been—had a curious way of striking the naturalistic note, of sensing the problem of the individual against the universe. Sometimes it was almost as if he had imagined what Ish was now experiencing: "And if the tree fall toward the south, or toward the north, in the place where the tree falleth, there it shall be." Ish thought of that tree in Oklahoma which had fallen to block Highway 66. And again he read, "Two are better than one . . . for if they fall, the one will lift up his fellow, but woe unto him that is alone when he falleth." And Ish thought of the great fear that had been upon him when he was left alone, and he had felt all too vividly that there would be none to help him up, if he fell. He read through, marveling at the clear-eyed naturalistic acceptance of the universe. There was even a line, "Surely the serpent will bite without enchantment."

He came to the end of the last chapter, and his eyes fell to the lines which began on the lower part of the page. "The song of songs, which is Solomon's." He read, "Let him kiss me with the kisses of his mouth: for thy love is better than wine."

Ish stirred uneasily. In all these long months he had rarely had such feelings. Now again he realized that, more than he thought from day to day, the shock of the whole catastrophe had affected him. It was all like some old story of enchantment in which a king sat and watched life pass by, unable to mingle with it. Other men had done differently. Even those who had drunk themselves to death had, in a sense, been partaking of life. But he himself, in observing what happened, had merely been rejecting life.

What made life anyway? Many people had asked that question—even Koheleth, the preacher, was far from the first. And each had come up with a different answer, except those who admitted that no answer could be found.

Here was he, Isherwood Williams, a strange mingling of realities and fantasies and pressures and reactions, and there all outside was the vast empty city with misty rain falling upon the long empty streets, and the twilight now beginning to deepen. Between the two, him and everything outside him, there lay some kind of strange bond; as one changed, so the other changed also.

It was as if there were a vast equation with many terms on each side, and yet only two great unknowns. He was on one side; x, perhaps, you could call him; and on the other side was y—everything which was called the world. And two sides of the equation always were trying to keep more or less in balance and never quite managed it. Perhaps the real balance only came with death. (Perhaps that was what Koheleth in his fine disillusioned mind was thinking when he wrote "The living know that they shall die; but the dead know not anything.") But, this side of death, the two halves of the equation tried always to be in balance. If the x side changed and he Ish felt within him the pressure of some gland or if he suffered shock or if there was even something so simple as that he grew bored, then he did something, and that changed the other side of the equation, if only a little, and then there was again a temporary balance. But if on the other hand, the world outside changed, if there was a catastrophe wiping out the human race, or if merely it should stop raining, then the x side, being Ish, would also have to change, and that would mean more action, and then there would be again a temporary balance. And who could say whether in the long run one side or the other side of the equation began more of the actions?

Then, before he really thought what he was doing, he had risen to his feet, and on second thought he knew that he had done so because again a feeling of desire had stirred within him. The equation had got out of balance, and he had risen restlessly to set it right again, and already he was affecting the world because Princess had leaped up at his rising and was wandering about the room. Yet at the same time he heard the rain beat a little harder against the window. Then he looked up at it to see what was happening. And so the world had also pressed in upon him and caused him to do something. And after that he set out to get himself some supper.

The almost complete removal of man, though in some ways an unprecedented earthly catastrophe, had not in the slightest affected the earth's relation to the sun, or the sizes and locations of the oceans and continents, or any other factor influencing the weather. Therefore, the first autumn storm which swept down from the Aleutians upon the coast of California was ordinary and conventional. Its moisture extinguished the forest-fires; its raindrops washed from the atmosphere the particles of smoke and dust. Behind it a brisk wind swept down cool and crystal-clear and air from the northwest. The temperature dropped sharply.

Ish stirred in his sleep, and gradually came to consciousness. He was cold. "The other side has changed," he thought, and pulled up another blanket. He grew warm. "O prince's daughter!" he thought dreamily, "Thy breasts are like two . . ." And he drifted to sleep.

In the morning the house was chilly. He wore a sweater as he got himself his breakfast. He considered building a fire in the fireplace, but the cooler weather had also made him feel more active, and so he thought that he would not stay indoors much that day.

After breakfast he stood on the front porch to drink in the view. As always after one of these storms, the air was clear. The wind had died down. The red towers of the Golden Gate Bridge, miles away, stood against the blue sky, as if close enough to touch. He turned a little toward the north to look at the peak of Tamalpais, and suddenly started. Between him and the mountain, on this side of the Bay, a thin column of smoke rose straight up through the calm air, a slight wisp, the kind of smoke-column that should come from a small fire, particularly from one burning in a fireplace and ascending through a chimney. It might, he realized, have been rising there a hundred times before when he had looked out, but in the smoky and misty atmosphere he would not have noticed it. Now it was like a signpost.

Of course it might be a fire burning from some natural cause without any human being in its vicinity. He had investigated many smokes like that with no results. But that was not so likely now, because the rain would have smothered such fires.

In any case it could not be more than a couple of miles off, and his first thought was to jump into the station-wagon and investigate. That would cause no more harm than the loss of a few minutes for which he had no particular use anyway. But something stopped him. His attempts to establish human contact had not been rewarding. That old shyness rose up within him, as it had sometimes in the old days when the thought of attending a dance would put him into a sweat. He began to temporize, just as he used to do when he said that he had a great deal of work to do and so buried himself in a book instead of going to the dance.

Did Crusoe really want to be rescued from his desert island where he was lord of all that he surveyed? That was a question that people had asked. But even if Crusoe had been the kind of man who wanted to escape, to renew contacts with other people, that would not mean that he himself, Ish, was such a person. Perhaps he would cherish his island. Basically, perhaps, he feared human entanglements.

Almost in panic, as if fleeing from a temptress, he called Princess, got into the car, and drove off in the opposite direction.

He spent most of the day wandering restlessly through the hills. At times he observed what the rain had done to the roads. By now there was no longer that hard and fast line

96

between road and what was not road. Leaves had dropped from the cold of the autumn and the high winds. Little dead branches had blown off, and fallen on the pavement. Here and there a washing stream of water had left a delta-like deposit of dirt and gravel. Once, very far off, he heard—or thought he heard—the bay of a pack of dogs. But he did not see them, and before the end of the afternoon he was back home again.

When he looked out toward the mountain, he could see no smoke against the sky. He had a certain sense of relief, and yet an even stronger sense of disappointment, now that he had a chance to think it over.

That was the way. When the opportunity was at your hand, you did not dare to seize it. When the opportunity was lost, it became precious. The other side of the equation had changed, and he had adjusted by running away. Of course, he might see the smoke again the next morning, but then again he might not. Perhaps that human being, whoever it was, had merely been passing through that way, and could never be found again.

He felt a quick rebound of excitement, at opportunity re-granted, when he looked out in the early darkness after supper, and suddenly saw a faint but unmistakable light. He hesitated no longer. Now, instead of temporizing, he called Princess, got into the car, and drove in that direction.

It was a slow process. His seeing the light must mean merely that the windows of that house happened to face his porch; probably he could not have seen it at all before the storm had blown down most of the leaves. As soon as he left the house, he could no longer see the light. He drove back and forth along the streets for half an hour, finally relocated it, drove slowly down the right street and past the proper house. The shades had been pulled, but there was light shining through, even illuminating the street a little. It was bright, probably from a gasoline lamp.

He brought the car to a stop on the opposite side of the street, and waited a moment. Apparently, whoever was inside the house had not heard the motor. For a moment still he hesitated, almost ready now to put the car into gear again and slide off undiscovered. Yet, from some deeper drive within him, he leaned forward, and half opened the car door as if to get out. Suddenly Princess leaped by him, and ran toward the house with a fury of barking. She must have scented whoever was there. With a sudden curse, he got out, and started to walk after her. She had tipped his hand, this time, for certain. He hesitated again, suddenly realizing he was unarmed. Yet to advance against the house carrying a gun was not a good opening. Without much thought he reached back into the car, and grabbed his old hammer. Holding it in his hand, he advanced after the dog. In the window of the house he saw a shadow move.

When he had gained the sidewalk, the house-door opened a few inches, and suddenly the beam of a flashlight caught him. He could see nothing beyond it. He stopped, waiting for what the other person would have to say. Princess scuttled back, suddenly silent. Ish had the uncomfortable feeling that whoever was keeping him covered with the flashlight had him covered also with a gun held in the other hand. With the light in his eyes, he was blinded. This had been a crazy thing to do, he thought; an approach under cover of darkness always looked suspicious, and made people nervous. At least he was glad that he had shaved that morning, and that his clothes looked moderately clean.

There was a long pause. He stood waiting for the sharply barked question—the inevitable, if slightly ridiculous, "Who are you?" or else for that curt order, "Put up your hands!" That was why he had a sudden gasp of surprise when a woman's voice came with an affirmation: "That's a beautiful dog!"

There was a momentary silence, the memory of the voice in his ears was gentle and low, with a touch of some soft accent in it. At the sound he felt warm feelings rising up within him.

Now the light fell from his eyes, illuminating a path ahead of him, and Princess bounded up through the beam of light, her tail wagging in joy. The door of the house moved open wide, and against the dim light behind her, he saw a woman on her knees patting the dog. He walked up toward her, still with the hammer dangling ridiculously but comfortably from his hand.

Then Princess, in a sudden flurry of excitement, burst away and went tearing into the house. The woman leaped up with an exclamation, half-screamed, half-laughed, and also dashed in. "My God, she must have a cat!" thought Ish, and rushed after her.

But when he arrived in the living-room, Princess was merely dashing around the table and smelling at the chairs, and the woman was standing erect beside a gasoline lamp sheltering it against being overthrown by the excited dog.

She was above middle height, brunette, not very young—
no mere girl, certainly, but a fully developed woman.

She glanced at the antics of the scampering dog and
laughed, and the sound of laughter was like something remembered from Paradise long ago. She turned to him, and
he saw the flash of white teeth in the dark face. Then suddenly a barrier burst within him, and he laughed joyously.

After a moment she spoke again, neither questioning nor
demanding. "It's good to see someone." This time Ish replied, but he could think of nothing better than an apology
for the ridiculous hammer which still dangled from his hand.
"Pardon me for bringing this thing in," he said, and he set it
down on the floor upon its head with the handle sticking
stiffly into the air.

"Don't worry," she said, "I understand. I went through it
too—having to have something around to make you feel
comfortable. Like a pocket-piece or a rabbit-foot, you remember. We're still about the same as we used to be, all of
us."

After the sudden release of the laughter, he was trembling.
All his body seemed growing weak. He felt, almost physically,
more barriers breaking—those necessary barriers of defense,
built up through the months of loneliness and desperation. He
must touch another human being, and he put forward his
hand in the old conventional gesture of the handshake. She
took it, and doubtless as she noticed his trembling, she drew
him toward a chair and almost pushed him into it. As he sat
down, she patted his shoulder lightly.

She spoke again, once more neither questioning nor commanding: "I'll get you something to eat."

He did not protest, though he had just eaten heartily. But
he knew that behind her quiet affirmation lay something more
than any call of the body for food. There was need now for
the symbolic eating together, that first common bond of human beings—the sitting at the same table, the sharing of the
bread and salt.

Now they were sitting opposite each other. They ate a little, more in symbol than in reality. There was fresh bread. "I
made it myself," she said, "but it's getting hard to find flour
now that's got no weevils in it." There was no butter, but
honey and jam for the bread, and a bottle of red wine.

And now, like a child, he began to talk. This was nothing
like that time when he had sat with Milt and Ann on Riverside Drive. Then the barriers had still been up. Now, for the
first time, he talked of all those days. He showed even the

little scar of the fangs on his hand and the larger scars where he had slashed himself to apply the suction-pump. He told of his fear and of his flight and of the Great Loneliness that he had never quite dared face or imagine. And as he talked, she often said, "Yes, I know. Yes, I remember that, too. Tell me more."

As for her, she had seen the catastrophe itself. She had faced more than he had, and yet he could see that she had come through better than he. She talked little, seeming to have no need, but she drew him on.

As he talked with her, he knew now at last that this, at least as far as he was concerned, was no mere casual meeting —or passing moment. In this lay all the future. Since the disaster he had seen men and women here and there, and no one before had ever held him. Perhaps time had healed him. More likely, she herself was different.

Yet she was a woman. As the minutes slipped by, he sensed that basic reality more and more, with an intensity that made him tremble. As between man and man the breaking of bread was the reality; the shared table, all the symbol needed. But as between man and woman there must be still more, in reality and in symbol, a further sharing.

They realized suddenly that neither knew the other's name although each had been calling the dog Princess.

"Isherwood," he said. "That was my mother's maiden name and so she stuck it on me. Bad, wasn't it? Everybody called me 'Ish'."

"I'm Em!" she said. "Emma, that is, of course. Ish and Em! We won't get very far writing poetry about that combination!" And she laughed. And they laughed together.

Laughter—that was another sharing! And yet it was not the final one. There were ways these things were done. He had known men who could do them, had seen them at work. But he, Ish, was not the right kind. All those qualities which had permitted him to be by himself and survive through the bad days, alone—all those qualities now came up to work against him. And he sensed too, very deeply, that they would be wrong. The old methods had worked in the days when there were girls in every cocktail-bar, looking for adventure. But now such methods were not right, he knew, and knew deeply—at this time, when the vast city stretched away empty in all directions outside of the windows and all the ways of the world had vanished and this woman had lived through all the catastrophe and the fear and the loneliness and now had

100

come out on the other side, still with courage in her eyes, and affirmation, and laughter.

For a wild moment he had an idea that they might say some kind of marriage vows. Quakers could marry themselves. Why couldn't others? They could stand up together, and face toward the east where the morning sun would rise. And then he sensed that the mere babbling of words was in itself much more dishonest even than a straightforward feeling for the knee under the table. He realized that he had been silent for what might have been a full minute. She was looking across at him with level calm eyes, and he knew that she read his thoughts.

In his embarrassment he rose suddenly to his feet, upsetting the chair as he got up. Then the table between them had ceased to be a symbol joining them together and now held them apart. He stepped from behind it, and across toward her as she rose up too. And then there was the softness of her body against his.

O Song of Songs! Thine eyes, my love, are gentle, and the fullness of thy lips is soft and firm. Thy neck is ivory, and the smoothness of thy shoulders like warm ivory. The softness of thy breasts against me is like fine wool. Thy thighs are firm and strong like the cedars. O Song of Songs!

She had gone now, into the inner room. He sat, still with breath and heart quick, tense and waiting. He had only one fear now. In a world where there were no doctors and even no other women, how could anyone risk the chance? But she had gone. He realized that she, too, in her great affirmation, would consider this also and care for it.

O Song of Songs. My love, thy bed is fragrant as boughs of the pine tree, and thy body is warm. Thou art Ashtoreth. Thou art Aphrodite, that keepest the gate of Love. Now my strength is upon me. Now the rivers are pent up. Now is my hour. Oh, receive me in thine infinitude.

Chapter 7

He lay quietly awake after she slept beside him, and his thoughts rushed by him so fast that he could not stop them long enough to get to sleep. That was what she had said before, earlier in the evening—no matter what happened to the world, it did not change the person, and he remained what he had been. Yes, that was the way! Though so much had happened, and even though he might be deeply moved by that great experience, yet still he was the observer—the man who sat by the side, watching what happened, never quite losing himself in the experience. The strangeness! In the old world it might well never have happened. Out of destruction had come, for him, love.

He slept. When he woke, it was daylight, and she was gone. He looked around the room fearfully. Yes, it was really a shabby little room, and he suddenly h d a fear that pe haps all this seemingly great experience of love was, after all, only something which in the old days wou'd have been no more than a pick-up of a restless waitress and a grimy room in a cheap hotel. And she—she was no goddess, no hamadryad glimpsed whitely in the dusk! Except at the moment of desire, she would never be Ashtoreth or Aphrodite. He trembled a little to think of how she might look in the morning light. She was older than he; perhaps he was merely mixing her in some vague kind of mother-image. "Oh, don't worry," he thought, putting it into words, "there never has been perfection yet, and it certainly isn't going to start now for me." Then he remembered how she had first spoken, not in question or command, but merely in affirmation. Yes, that was the way it ought to be. Take what was good in a situation, not worrying about what might not be there.

He got up and dressed. As he dressed, he sniffed the aroma of coffee. Coffee! That was a kind of modern symbol, too.

She had the table set in the breakfast-nook when he came out, as any commuter's wife might have done. He looked at her almost bashfully. He saw again, more clearly by morning light, the wide-set black eyes in the dark face, the full ripe lips, the swelling curve of the breasts beneath a light-green smock.

He did not offer to kiss her, and she did not seem to expect it. But they smiled back and forth, one at the other. "Where's Princess?" he said.

"I put her out for her run."

"Good—And it's going to be a good day, too, I think."

"Yes, looks like it. Sorry there are no eggs."

"No matter. What is it? Bacon, I see."

"Yes."

They were little words, meaning nothing, yet there was a great joy to say them. A greater joy, perhaps, saying the little things than saying something much greater. A whole content-

102

ment came over him. This was no affair of the rented room. His luck was in! He looked across into her level eyes, and felt new security and courage rise up within him! This would endure!

They moved back, later that day, to the house on San Lupo Drive, chiefly because he seemed to have more possessions—books, especially—than she did. It was less trouble to move to the books than to move the books to them.

The days went more swiftly and more comfortably after that. There were many ways of sharing. "What was it?" he thought. " 'A friend doubles joys and cuts griefs in half'?"

She never talked about herself. Once or twice he tried to draw her out with questions, thinking that she might need to tell things. But she did not respond easily, and he decided that she had already made her adjustment in her own way. She had drawn the veil across the view toward the past; now she looked forward only.

Yet she made no apparent attempt at secrecy. He learned from casual remarks that she had been married (happily, he was sure), and had had two small children. She had gone to high school but not to college; her grammar lapsed occasionally. Her soft accent, which he had noticed when she first spoke, had perhaps the touch of Kentucky or Tennessee in it. But she never mentioned having lived anywhere except in California.

Her social status must have been, Ish judged, somewhat lower than his. But there was nothing more ridiculous to contemplate, now, than all that business of social classes.

"Amazing, how little everything like that matters now!" And the days slid by easily.

One morning, finding that they needed some supplies, he went down to start the car. He put his thumb on the starter button. There was a sudden click, nothing more.

He pressed it again, and it clicked. That was all.

He heard no sudden comforting whir as the motor took over, no reassuring little bangs as the cold cylinders began to fire. Panic fell upon him again. He pressed the button once more, and still once more, and every time came only the little click. "Battery gone!" he thought.

He got out, raised the hood of the car, and stared hopelessly at the orderly but complex array of wires and gadgets. It was too much for him. He had a sudden hopeless feeling within him; he went back to the house.

"The car won't start," he said. "Battery gone, or something!" He knew that his face must be even more woebegone than his voice. That was why he could hardly believe it, when she laughed. "There's no place we have to go so badly as all that," she said. "To look at you, you'd think that things had gone to pieces!"

Then he laughed too. It made all the difference in the world whether you had that other to cut the grief in half, and the trouble suddenly seemed tiny. A car was convenient when you wanted to go to the stores and load up with some more supplies. But they could live just as well without a car. She was right—they had really no place that they needed so badly to go!

He had imagined a desperate day, trying to find a new car or to fix up the old one. As it was, they made it a sport, even though it did take them most of the morning before they located another one. Most of the cars had no keys in them, and while he might have shorted a wire somewhere, they agreed that it would be an inconvenience to have to drive a car without a key. And when they found one with a key in it, the battery, unused now for several months, would not work. At last they found one that had a key in it, and was parked on a hill. The battery was too weak to turn the engine over, but it would burn the lights faintly, and Ish judged that it would send out enough of a current to fire the spark-plugs.

They got the car rolling downhill, and then after a minute the cylinders began to bang and putter and backfire. Ish and Em laughed together happily at the adventure of it. At last the gasoline worked up through the feed-pipes, and the engine warmed, and began to run smoothly. Now they laughed in triumph, and went speeding at sixty miles an hour down the empty boulevard, and Em leaned over and kissed him. And suddenly, queer as it seemed, Ish realized that he had never felt so happy in his life.

This car was not such a good one as the station-wagon. Because of this, they used it merely to make some explorations through the warehouse district, checking up in the classified telephone book to locate dealers in batteries. At last they forced the entrance to the proper room and found dozens of batteries with the acid not yet in them. There were also supplies of acid, and although neither of them was mechanically minded, they made the experiment of pouring the acid into a battery of the right size. They took it back, and put it into the station-wagon. It worked perfectly, the first time.

As at last the motor of the station-wagon hummed tunefully, responding to the pressure of his foot on the throttle,

Ish thought that on that day he had met, and faced, two problems. First, he had seen that he could do a great deal toward keeping a car running for a long time. But of even greater importance, he had faced the possibility that there would come a time when there would no longer be any cars, and yet still he could live happily and without fear.

The next day, indeed, the new battery in the station-wagon was dead again. Either it was defective or he had made some mistake in installing it. This time, however, he was in no panic. In fact he did not even bother to do anything about it for a couple of days. Then they repeated the process. Either by luck or by greater care, they had better success, and the battery continued to work.

Sleek with lacquer, shining with chromium, their motors machined to the thousandth of the inch, their commutators accurate as watches, they had been the pride and the symbol of civilization.

Now, they were locked ingloriously in garages, or stood in the lots, or were parked at the curb. The dead leaves dropped, the blowing dust settled. The rains fell, and spotted the dust, and made the leaves stick more tightly, and then more dust and more leaves fell. The windshields were so thickly coated that you could scarcely see through them now.

More deeply, they changed little. The rust ate here and there, but on the grease-smeared surfaces it could not work rapidly. Unused, the coils and the timers, the carburetors and the spark plugs, all remained as good as ever.

In the batteries the slow processes of chemistry worked day and night, breaking down, neutralizing. A few months, and the unused batteries were dead. But as long as the battery and acid were kept separate, neither deteriorated, and it would always be a small matter to add the acid and start out again with a new battery; the batteries were not the weakest link.

More likely it was the tires. In the rubber the processes of decay worked slowly. The tires would last a year, five years. But nevertheless, the weakness worked in them. The air leaked from the tires, and after the car had stood on the flat tires for a while, they were no longer of any use. Even in the warehouses, decay worked in the rubber. The stored tires would have ten years, and still some life. Twenty years they would last, perhaps even more. Quite likely the roads, themselves, would be broken and men forget how to drive cars

105

and lose the desire for driving them before the cars them-selves were rendered undrivable.

Her head rested in the crook of his arm, and he looked down upon the black liquid eyes. They lay on the davenport in the living room. Her face looked darker than ever now in the twilight.

There was one question, he knew, that they had not yet faced, and now she brought it forward.

"That would be fine!" she said.

"I don't know."

"Yes, it would."

"I don't like it."

"You mean you don't like it about me?"

"Yes. It's dangerous. There'd be no one else but me, and I wouldn't be any use."

"But you can read—all the books."

"Books!" he laughed a little as he spoke. *"The Practical Midwife? The Pathology of Parturition?* I don't think I'd like to face it, even if you would."

"But, yet, you really could find some books and read them. That would be a lot of use. And I wouldn't really need so much help." She paused a moment: "I've been through it twice before, you know. It wasn't bad."

"Maybe not. But it might be different this time without hospitals and doctors and all that. And just why, why do you think so much about it?"

"Biology, don't they call it, or something like that? I guess it's natural."

"Do you think life must go on, we have a duty to the future, all that?"

She paused a minute. He could tell that she was thinking, and thinking was not the best thing that she did; she reacted at deeper levels than those of mere thought.

"Oh, *I* don't know," she said. "I don't know whether life needs to go on. Why should it? Just as likely I'm selfish. I want a baby for myself. I mean, oh, I don't talk this sort of thing well. I'd like to be kissed, though." He did it.

"I wish I could talk," she said. "I wish I could tell what it is I think about it."

Then she stretched her arm out, and took a match from the box on the table. She smoked, more than he did, and he expected her to take a cigarette also. But she did not. It was a big kitchen-match, the kind she liked. She turned it be-

106

tween thumb and finger, saying nothing. Then she scratched it against the box.

The matchhead spurted into a flare. Then the fierceness faded out, and the wood of the match-shank burned quietly in yellow flame. Suddenly she blew it out.

Vaguely he knew that she, who did not find words easily, had tried—perhaps half unconsciously—to act out something that she could not say. Slowly he thought that he understood. The match lived, not when it lay in the box, but merely when it burned—and it could not burn forever. So too with men and women. Not by denying life was life lived.

He thought then of his old fear during the first days and of the time when he had overthrown it, when he had unlashed the motorcycle from the tailgate of the station-wagon in the desert and tossed it to one side. He remembered the wild feeling of exaltation which had come when he had offered defiance to death and all the powers of darkness.

He felt her body stir gently in his arms. Yes, he thought humbly, that strong courage was his only at great moments —with her it was part of daily life.

"All right," he said, "I suppose you're right. I'll read the books."

"You know," she said, "I might need a little more help than that!"

Her body was close and warm against him. Still he held back, feeling all the loneliness and the emptiness and the terror. Who was *he* to set mankind again on the long and uncertain road to the future? But it was only for a moment. Then her courage and the confidence of her courage flowed out from her to him. "Yes," he thought, "she will be the mother of nations! Without courage there is nothing!"

And then suddenly he was conscious again of her body, and his strength came upon him.

To thee be the glory, because the love of life was brighter before thy face than the fear of death was dark. Thou art Demeter and Hertha and Isis; Cybele of the Lions, and the Mountain-Mother. From thy daughters shall spring tribes; and from thy grandsons, nations! Thy name is The Mother, and they shall call thee blessed.

There will be laughter and song again. Maidens will walk in the meadows; young men, leap by the brooks. Their children's children shall be again as the pine trees of the mountainside. They shall call thee blessed, because in a dark time thy look was toward the light.

107

While they were still uncertain, Em looked out one morning and said, "See, some rats!"

He looked. Sure enough, two rats were nosing their way along the base of the hedge, foraging about or merely investigating. Em pointed out the rats to Princess through the window, and then opened the door. But being a dog who gave tongue to tell the hunter where the chase was leading, she leaped out baying, and the rats vanished before she was anywhere near them.

That afternoon they saw more rats at several times, one place and another, near the house, in the street, or running in the gardens.

Next morning the wave had engulfed them. Rats were everywhere.

These were merely ordinary-looking rats, no larger or smaller than rats were expected to be, not particularly fat or particularly lean—just rats. Ish thought of the way the ants had been some time ago, and felt a cold shiver run through him.

The only thing to do was to make an investigation, and thus render the rats less horrible, because when you knew something about the situation, you saw the interest that lay in it.

In the station-wagon they drove about here and there, often crushing some rat which decided to dash across the street, just ahead of their tires. At first they shuddered a little at the soft squash, and looked at each other, but before long it had become so common that they thought nothing about it. The area which the rats were occupying was roughly the city, although they spread outward from the built-up area, covering somewhat larger an area than the ants had done.

What had happened, in general, was clear enough. Ish remembered some kind of statistics which declared that the number of rats in a city was generally about equal to the number of people.

"Well," he explained to Em, "you start then with, say, a million rats, half of them being does or bitches or whatever you call lady rats. Some of the stores and warehouses are rat-proof, but still there has been for all this time what you can call an unlimited supply of food."

"Then how many rats should there be now?"

"I can't do that problem in my head. I'll try later."

That evening at home he sat down to it as a mathematical problem. With the aid of his father's encyclopedia he determined that rats had approximately one litter a month, with an average of about ten young. That is, one month of uninterrupted breeding might have produced about a population of ten million rats in this given area. These young females, in turn, would begin to breed before they reached the age of two months. There must be some casualties, of course, and he had no way of determining just how many of the rats would live to maturity. But, certainly the increase must be prodigious under the circumstances. His mathematics broke down.

But even if the rats should only be increasing at the rate of doubling their numbers every month, an estimate which seemed ridiculously conservative, there should by this time be already somewhere in the neighborhood of fifty million. If they were increasing threefold each month, an estimate which still seemed conservative, there would now be in the area approximately one billion rats.

As he considered the problem, he saw no reason at all why the rats, with unlimited food, might not possibly quadruple their numbers every month. In the Old Times man had been the only important natural enemy of the city rats, and even man had had to maintain constant war against them to keep their numbers under control. With man gone, their only enemies would have been the small number of dogs whose instinct led them to catch rats, and somewhat larger number of cats. But here a secondary result must have influenced the situation in favor of the rats. As he had noticed, the rat-catching dogs seemed to hold the ground alone without the help of any cats. Probably the dogs had killed the cats as much as they had the rats, and so had eliminated the chief control. And in the end, the dogs themselves had probably been overwhelmed in the mere increase of numbers. Now he no longer saw any dogs. It seemed unlikely that they had actually been killed by the rats, although the rats may very well have cleaned out many litters of puppies. Probably, the dogs had merely retreated before the swarms of rats, and were still hanging around on the outskirts, now having been driven from the city into the suburbs.

Whether there were a billion rats or only fifty million made very little difference. There certainly were too many rats, and Ish and Em felt themselves in a state of siege. They watched all the doors carefully. Nevertheless, one rat appeared in the kitchen from some unknown quarter, and they had a mad scurry as Ish pursued it with a broom. Cornered, it leaped viciously at the broom-handle, and left teeth marks in the hard wood before he was able to crush it against the floor.

After a few days, moreover, they began to see a kind of

109

difference, both in the appearance and in the behavior of the rats. Apparently, the supplies of food, vast though they were, had at last begun to yield before the attack of an ever-pyramiding number of rats. The rats now appeared thinner, and they ran around even more feverishly in search of food. They began to burrow in the ground. They dug up the tulip bulbs, first of all, seeming particularly fond of them. Then they attacked the less palatable bulbs and roots. They ran along the branches of the trees, apparently eating any insects they could find or any remains of seeds or fruit. They even, at last, began to gnaw the bark of young trees, like rabbits.

Ish parked the car as close to the house as he could now, and made a dash for it, wearing high boots. But actually the rats never made any attempt at an attack. Ish kept Princess in the house mostly, although the rats had offered her no violence either.

Still driving about to investigate, Ish became more and more accustomed to the soft squash beneath his tires. He began to feel as if he were plastering the streets with a continuous line of crushed rats. In the angle of two walls, as he drove slowly by, a small white object caught his attention. Stopping the car and looking carefully, he saw that it was the skull of some small dog. The long teeth, still shining white, indicated that it had probably been a terrier. Apparently, the rats had cornered the dog in the angle of the walls; or else, the dog, fighting for its life, had retreated there. Whether the rats had dared attack a strong and healthy dog, Ish could not know. Perhaps it had suffered an accident or had been chewed up in a fight with another dog. Perhaps it was old or sick. But apparently, for once, the swarm of rats had been too much even for the ratter. Ish saw only a few of the larger bones; the rest had apparently either been gnawed to pieces or dragged away. In the vicinity, he saw also the skulls of several rats, indicating that the terrier had gone down fighting. He tried to imagine the scene. The swarming gray bodies clambering all over the struggling dog, the dog unable to attack those which hung to its back. Others must have slashed at the hamstrings like wolves attacking an old bison-bull. Though the dog might kill a dozen or fifty, in the end the mad, hunger-frenzied rodents must have gnawed through the skin and tendons until the dog collapsed. Ish drove away from the spot feeling definitely sober, and deciding that they must keep an even more careful watch on Princess.

He remembered, hopefully, that the ants had vanished almost overnight, and he kept expecting that something like that also might happen to the rats. But there was no indication of it.

"Are the rats going to take over the world?" Em asked. "Now that men are gone, are the rats going to be next?"

"Of course I don't know for sure," said Ish, "but I hardly think so. They've got a head-start because they know how to use the food-supplies in the city and because they breed fast. But once they get away from the city they'll have to forage on their own, and the foxes and snakes and owls are going to build up too because man is gone and because they'll have lots of rats to feed on."

"I never thought of that!" she said. "You mean rats are kind of domestic animals because people supply them food and kill off their enemies."

"More like parasites on man, I suppose really." And then, just to be saying something to keep her interest, he ran on: "And speaking of parasites, of course rats have them too. Just like the ants! When anything gets too numerous it's likely to get hit by some plague—I mean—" (Something had suddenly exploded in his mind at the word.) He coughed to cover up his hesitation, and then went on, without making a point of it. "Yes, some plague is likely to hit them."

Em, to his relief, did not seem to have noticed.

"All we can do then," she said, "I guess, is to sit around and cheer for the rat's parasites."

Ish did not tell her what had disturbed him. It was the realization that not just *plague* in the general sense, but bubonic plague was a common epidemic among rats. It was spread, he knew, by fleas, and those infected fleas readily hopped from dead rats to living people. The thought of being among the few people left in an area inhabited by millions of rats being killed off by bubonic plague was a horrible situation to contemplate.

He began to deluge the house with DDT and spray it upon his clothing and Em's. Naturally then she became suspicious, and he had to tell her.

She was not disturbed. Her natural courage rose superior to even the thought of plague, and perhaps there was a vein of fatalism in her too. The simplest and safest thing would have been to hurry out of the city, and get to some place—the desert, perhaps—where few rats could live.

But each of them had already decided independently that life was not to be lived on the basis of fear. Her courage

111

indeed was stronger than his, and the horror of the rats pressed in more closely upon him. Occasionally he even felt panic and was ready to force her into the car for flight. But always in such times her courage seemed to flow out from her and sustain him.

As the days passed, he watched individual rats carefully to see if they seemed sickly. On the contrary, they seemed more active than ever.

Then Em called to him one morning from the window. "Look, they're fighting!" He went to look, quickly, but without too much interest. Probably, he thought, it was merely whatever kind of sex-play rats indulged in. But it was not.

He saw a large rat definitely attacking a smaller one. The small one fought back, and dodged desperately, and seemed just about to make its escape through a hole which might be too small for the larger one. Then suddenly a third and still larger rat appeared, and sprang also upon the small one. The little pool of blood spread out from the torn throat, and then the largest rat dragged the body away, the one who had made the original attack scurrying close after.

In high boots, well gloved, carrying a stout stick in his hand, Ish made an expedition to the nearest business-center and foraged for some more food. Curiously, to him, he found very few rats in the stores, and when he investigated, he found that everything which a rat could get and eat had been completely wiped out. The stores were a great disgusting litter of torn papers, and chewed cartons and rat-droppings. They had even chewed the labels on the cans and bottles, so that sometimes it was difficult even to tell what was contained in them. Certainly, as yet, starvation and not disease was closing in upon the hordes. He took the news back to Em.

Next morning they let Princess out for her daily run. (They had been allowing her out only once a day as a matter of precaution.) After a few minutes they heard her wild howling, and she came tearing back to the door with rats skirmishing all around her, and two or three actually clinging to her back. Opening the door they let her in, and necessarily admitted three or four rats along with her. Princess retired under the davenport in a flurry of howling. Deserted by the cause of the disaster, Ish and Em spent a lively quarter hour routing out the rats and killing them. They hunted the house most carefully, aided by a now partially recovered Princess, to find whether any rat was still lurking in a closet or behind the books of the bookcase. But they decided that they had killed them all. They kept Princess shut up, after that, out of necessary precaution, and they also muzzled her for fear of hydrophobia.

By now they were quite sure that the rats were preying one upon another. Sometimes they saw a large rat pursuing a smaller rat, and sometimes it seemed as if several banded together in a pack to attack a single one. They seemed less numerous now, but that might be because they were keeping out of sight under the new conditions.

To Ish the whole affair, in spite of a certain horror that he still held of it, came to be a most interesting study in ecology, almost a laboratory problem. The rats had first lived upon the stores of food which men had laid up for them, and these had gradually been transformed into a great reservoir of rat-flesh. Then, when the cereals and dried fruit and packaged beans were depleted, there was left—for certain individual rats at least—this other supply of food. Under such circumstances, it seemed a question whether any single rat would die of starvation, even though the rats as a species might be dying of starvation.

"The old and sickly and weak and immature will go first," he said, "and then those that are not quite so old or sickly or weak or immature—and so on."

"And eventually," said Em, who sometimes showed disconcerting logic, "there'll just be two great strong rats left to fight it out—like (what was it?) the Kilkenny cats?"

Ish explained that before such a fate ensued the rats would have become so scarce that they would again have begun to forage upon other sources of food.

When he thought more deeply, he saw that the rats were not actually destroying the species for their own individual preservation; they were really saving the species. If the rats had been sentimental and had decided that they would all starve together without indulging in cannibalism, then indeed there might have been some danger. But rats were realists, and so their racial future seemed secure from this emergency.

Day by day, the numbers of rats became fewer, and then one morning they seemed to be gone entirely. Ish knew that there still must be many rats in the city, but what had happened was merely what would happen in the decline of any species. Under natural circumstances, the rats kept out of sight, liking narrow passageways and holes and brush-filled gullies. Only when their numbers became so great that they could not all find such refuges did they spill over and inhabit the open places where they could be seen.

Doubtless, at the end, disease may have helped, but he was never sure of this. One great advantage of the disappearance through cannibalism was that there were no bodies of rats left around. They had gone on to preserve the species into the next generation. Also, he knew, although he did not investigate, that the rats must have done a great deal toward removing the bodies of the human beings who had died in the original disaster.

As he collected his thoughts upon the subject, he was surprised that there had been no plague of mice. The ants had come first, and then had come the rats. Between the two there should have been a rapid increase of mice, because the mice should have had almost as good an opportunity as the rats and because their breeding rate was even faster. He never learned the answer, but merely had to suppose that some control of which he knew nothing had acted to prevent the rapid increase of mice.

Both Ish and Em took a little while to recover from the horror with which the rats had filled them. But after a while they decided that Princess had not contracted hydrophobia. They loosed her, and life became more normal, and they forgot about the constant crawling of the gray bodies.

The fables were wrong. Not the Lion, but Man, was the King of Beasts. Throughout his reign the rule was heavy, often harsh.

But though the cry rise up, "The King is dead!" it shall not go on: "Long live the King!"

As in the old days when some conqueror died, leaving no tall son, and the captains strove together for the scepter and none proved strong enough and the realm fell apart, so it shall be again, for neither the ant nor the rat nor the dog nor the ape is wise enough above his fellows. For a little while there will be jostlings, quick rises and sudden falls; then, a quiet and a peace such as the earth has not known in twenty thousand years.

Again her head lay in the crook of his arm, and he looked down into the dark eyes. She spoke. "Well, you'd better get busy at that book-work now. I guess it's happened."

And then suddenly before he could say anything, he felt her tremble and she was crying. He had not thought this of her—this fear! He felt the sudden weakness of his own terror. What if she collapsed?

"Oh, darling," he cried out. "Maybe we can still do some-

114

thing! There are ways. You mustn't try to go through with it!"

"Oh, it's not that! *It's not that!*" she cried out, still trembling. "I lied. Not what I said, what I didn't say! But it's all the same. You're just a nice boy. You looked at my hands, and said they were nice. You never even noticed the blue in the half-moons."

He felt the shock, and he knew that she felt the shock in him. Now everything came together in his mind—brunette complexion, dark liquid eyes, full lips, white teeth, rich voice, accepting temperament.

Then she spoke again, scarcely in more than a whisper, "It didn't matter at first, of course. No man cares then about that. But my mother's people never had much luck in the world. Maybe when things are starting out again, it shouldn't be with them. But mostly, I guess, I think it wasn't right with you."

Then suddenly he heard nothing more, for the whole vast farce of everything broke in upon him, and he laughed, and all he could do was to laugh and laugh more, and then he found that she, too, had relaxed and was laughing with him and holding him all the closer.

"Oh, darling," he said, "everything is smashed and New York lies empty from Spuyten Duyvil to the Battery, and there's no government in Washington. The senators and the judges and the governors are all dead and rotten, and the Jew-baiters and the Negro-baiters along with them. We're just two poor people, picking at the leavings of civilization for our lives, not knowing whether it's to be the ants or the rats or something else will get us. Maybe a thousand years from now people can afford the luxury of wondering and worrying about that kind of thing again. But I doubt it. And now there are just the two of us here, or maybe three, now."

He kissed her while she still was weeping quietly. And he knew that for once he had seen more clearly and more deeply, and been stronger than she.

Chapter 8

On the day after she had told him, he drove to the University campus, and parked in front of the Library. He had never entered it since the Great Disaster, although he had often gone to the city library for books. The great building stood undisturbed. Its surrounding bushes and trees had not,

115

in the few months, grown appreciably taller. The drain pipes all seemed to be functioning perfectly, and no stain of water showed on the white granite walls. There was only a general impression of dirt and litter and disuse.

He did not want to force an entrance by breaking a window, thus giving access to animals and also to the rain. In the end, however, he could find no other way. He tapped gently with his hammer, and managed to break only a part of a pane, reaching through, he unlocked the window and raised it. After all, he told himself, he could bring some boards and patch the window again, so that it would still be ratproof and weatherproof.

He had been in the Library hundreds of times before, as a matter of course, during his years at the University. But now under the changed conditions, he felt a strange new sense of awe. Here rested in storage the wisdom by which civilization had been built, and could be rebuilt. Now that he knew himself soon to be a father, he had suddenly a new attitude, a feeling for the future. The child should not grow up to be a parasite, scavenging forever. And it would not need to. Everything was here. All the knowledge!

He had come to hunt up some books on obstetrics, but after looking into the main reading-room and then wandering through two levels of the stacks, he became so excited that he left the building in a frenzy of imagination. He did not need to worry about the obstetrics today. There was plenty of time still for that.

He drove home in a kind of trance. Books! Most of the knowledge was in books, and yet he soon saw that they were not all. First of all, there must be people who could read, who knew how to use the books. He must also save other things. Seeds, for instance. He must see to it that the more important domestic plants did not vanish from the earth.

Suddenly he felt that all civilization depended not only upon men but also upon these other things which had marched with him like kinsmen and friends and companions. If Saint Francis had hailed the sun as brother, might not we also say, "Oh, Brother Wheat! Oh, Sister Barley!" He smiled to himself. Yes, one could go on: "Oh, Grandfather Wheel! Oh, Cousin Compass! Oh, Friend Binomial Theorem!" All the discoveries of science and philosophy also might be imagined as standing shoulder to shoulder with man, even though the putting of the matter into words made it all sound a little ridiculous.

He hurried, still hot with boyish enthusiasm, to tell it all to

116

Em. He found her trying, not at all successfully, to teach Princess to retrieve. Em was not as enthusiastic as he had expected. "Civilization!" she said. "Oh, you mean airplanes going higher and higher, and faster and faster. That kind of thing!"

"Oh, yes. But art, too, you know. Music, literature, culture."

"Yes, mystery-stories and those funny Negro jazz bands that always made my ears hurt."

He was crestfallen, even though he knew she was having a little fun with him.

"Another thing, though, about civilization," she said. "There's this matter of time. We don't really know what month it is. We'll want to be sure when his birthday comes, so that we can celebrate it, something less than two years from now."

Perhaps, he felt in his mind, *that* was the difference! That was the difference between woman and man. She felt only in terms of the immediate, and was more interested in being able to spot her child's birthday than in all the future of civilization. Again, he felt superior to her.

"One thing I didn't do, though," he said, "was to read any of those obstetrics books today. I'm sorry—but there's no hurry, is there?"

"Oh, no. Maybe not even any use of it at all. Don't you remember that even in the Old Times babies were always being born in taxis and hospital lobbies? Once they're started, nobody can stop them."

Later, when he had thought things over, he could not but admit that she had made a suggestion of something important. The more he thought about it, the more fundamental he considered her idea of keeping track of time. After all, time was history, and history was tradition, and tradition was civilization. If you lost the continuity of time, you lost something that might never be recovered. Probably it had already been lost unless some of the other survivors had been more careful about the matter than he had been. Take the seven-day week, for instance. Even though you were not religious, you had to admit that the seven-day week with its one day of rest was a fine old tradition of mankind. It had been going on for at least five thousand years, clear from Babylonian times, and no one knew how much further. Would he ever be able to figure out again just which day was Sunday?

As for getting the proper day of the year, that should not be too difficult. He knew enough about the fundamentals of

117

astronomy to do that, and if he got the time of the solstice correct, he could figure back on last year's calendar and perhaps re-establish the day of the week.

This was the time of the year to get busy on the problem. Although he did not know exactly, he could tell from the progress of the weather and from his general knowledge of how much time had elapsed since the catastrophe, that it must have come now pretty well toward the middle of December. If the solstice was to be in a week or so, he could easily tell by watching where the sun set.

Next day he found a surveyor's transit, and although he did not know much about the use of it, he set it up on the porch, facing the west. He blackened its lenses with soot, so that he could observe the sun without hurting his eyes. His very first observation showed that the sun was going down behind the hills of San Francisco, to the south of the Golden Gate. From memory he knew that this was very near to its most southern point of setting. He left the transit in position, and recorded the angle of the sunset.

The next evening it set still a little farther south. And then, as systems do, his system went to pieces. A heavy storm blew in from the ocean, and during a whole week he could not observe where the sun set. Next time he saw it, it had already started north.

"Well, anyway," he said, "we must be pretty close to it. If we add one day to the time when we last saw the sun, we ought to be very near to the solstice, and then if we add ten days to that, we would get to New Years."

"Isn't that rather silly?" she said.

"Why?"

"Well, I mean, that is, shouldn't the year really start when the sun turns north again? Don't you guess really that was what people tried to do once, and things got mixed up some way or other, and got about ten days out of kilter?"

"Yes, I imagine it was that way."

"Well, why don't we just start our New Year then with—what you call it?—the solstice? It seems simpler."

"Yes, but you can't just go fooling with the calendar. That's been established for a long time. You can't just shift it."

"Well, didn't someone named Julian do it, and weren't there riots and things? But still, they did change it."

"They did change it! Yes, you're right—and I suppose we can change it now if we want to. It certainly gives a person a sense of power!"

Then in playfulness of imagination they decided that living where they did, they had a system all worked out before them, so that they would not even bother to have months and things like that unless they wanted to, because from the hill they could see the sun setting around its whole arc. They could merely date things by the time the sun set in the middle of the Gate, or the time it had reached the first big hump to the north, or the time it had begun to reach the various points along the long slope of the mountain. What was the use of merely having months?

"Say!" she said, suddenly, "it must be pretty nearly Christmas, too. I hadn't thought of that. You think I can get down before the stores close to pick you a tie?"

He looked back at her with a little smile. "I suppose we ought to feel pretty lugubrious this Christmas, and yet, some way, I can't."

"Next year," she said, "this ought to be even more fun. We'll have to get him his first tree."

"Yes, and he can have a rattle, too, can't he? What I'm looking forward to, though, is when he can get an electric train, and I can run it. No, poor guy, I guess there'll never be an electric train for him. Maybe, though, when we have grandchildren, in twenty-five years, maybe, we'll be able to get the electricity working again."

"Twenty-five years! I'll be a pretty old woman by that time. It's strange, thinking forwards now, as well as backwards. For a while, I only thought backwards. But that thinking ahead brings up something else to my mind, also—the years! We'll have to keep track of the years. Don't people on desert islands cut notches in trees or something like that? You see, he'll want to know what year it is; so he can vote or get a passport, or report to his draft board, maybe. Only perhaps, you aren't going to restore things like that for us in this new civilization. What is this year, anyway, now?"

Again he thought that was like a woman, to put even such an all-important thing as the very date in terms of her unborn child. But yet, as so often, her instinct was right—a great pity if the historical record should be broken at some point! Doubtless in the long run, archeologists could restore the continuity by means of varves or dendrochronology, but it would save a lot of work if someone merely kept the tradition.

"You're right," he said. "And it's simple, too, of course. We know what year it is now, and when we decide we've come to New Years, we'll just chisel a new date on some good rock, and then every year chisel the next one. The chiseling will

119

be quite a job, and so we'll always remember whether we are up-to-date or not."

"Isn't that rather silly, too?" she said. "I mean, starting out with a date in four figures. As far as I'm concerned," she paused for a moment and looked around with that quiet air which sometimes was so impressive, "as far as I'm concerned, this past year might as well be the Year One."

That evening there was no rain. The clouds still hung low, but the air was clear beneath them. You could have seen the lights of San Francisco, if there had been any lights.

He stood on the porch, and looked out toward the dark west, breathing the cool damp air in deeply. His mood was still close to exaltation.

"Now we have finished with the past," he thought. "These last few months, the tag-end of the year—we shall let the past have them. This is the Moment Zero, and we stand between two eras. Now the new life begins. Now we commence the Year One. The Year One!"

Now there lay before him no longer the mere drama of a world without men and of its constant adaptation. No longer would personal readjustment be his own dominating problem. Now there stretched away in the years ahead, the unfolding drama of a new society, reconstructing itself, moving on. And now he would not be the lonely spectator, at least, not merely that. He could read. He was equipped with the background of much knowledge already. He would extend that into technics, into psychology, into political science, if that were needed.

There must be others that he could find also to join with them—good people who would help in the new world. He would start looking for people again. He would look craftily, trying to keep away from all those who had suffered too much from the shock, whose minds or bodies were not what one wanted to build up the new society.

Somewhere within him there lingered still that one deep fear that she might die in childbirth, that the whole hope of the future might thus fade. And yet, he could really not fear it very deeply. Her courage burned too brightly. She was life. He could not associate her with death. She was the light for the future, she and those that would spring from her. "O mother of nations! And her children shall call her blessed!"

He himself would have had only the courage to live on, feeling death creep in closer year by year as once the darkness had crept in from the corners of the room when the lights were failing. Her stronger spirit had struck back against death, and already life built up anew within her. From her depths courage flowed out to him.

It was curious, doubtless even illogical, that the thought of the coming child should make so much difference. But he granted the difference. He had known despair, but now he knew hope. He looked forward with confidence to the time when the sun would again be setting at the southern end of its long arc and the two of them—or the three—would go to carve into some rock the numeral commemorating the end of the Year One. It was not finished. The thing would go on.

A phrase leaped into his mind.

"Oh, world without end!" he thought. As he stood there, looking out into the dark west over the empty city, breathing deeply of the cool damp air, the words sang in his mind, "Oh, world without end! World without end!"

> *Here ends Part I. The inter-chapter called* Quick Years *follows, after a time-interval of one year.*

Quick Years

Not far from the house on San Lupo Drive there was that area which had once been a small public park. Tall rocks rose picturesquely, and at one place the tops of two of them leaned together, forming a high narrow cave. Near by, a smooth rock-surface, as large as the floor of a small room, sloped with the hillside, but was not too steep to sit on comfortably. In those older times which had been before even those that were now called the Old Times, some tribe of simple people had lived thereabouts, and on the smooth rock-surface you still saw the little holes where those people had pounded with stones to make their acorn-mash.

One day, after the round of the seasons had passed and the sun for the second time sank well to the south of the Golden Gate, Ish and Em climbed the hillside toward the rocks. The afternoon was calm and sunny, warm for mid-winter. Em carried the baby, wrapped in a soft blanket. (She was pregnant again, although not yet heavy on her feet.) Ish carried his hammer and a cold-chisel. Princess started with them, but as always went baying off on the trail of one of her rabbits.

When they came to the rock, Em sat down on it in the sun and nursed the baby, and Ish worked with hammer and chisel, cutting into the smooth surface the single numeral. The rock was hard, but with the heavy hammer and the sharp chisel, he soon finished an upright line. But it was fun to adorn the work a little, and some ceremony seemed fitting to mark the end of their first full circuit of the sun from south back to south. So Ish cut a clean serif at the base of the line, and a little hook at the top, so that the finished figure resembled the neat 1 which he remembered in the times of printing.

When he was done, he sat close beside Em in the sun. The baby had finished feeding, and was happy. They played with him.

"Well," said Ish, "that was the Year One!"

"Yes," said Em, "but I think I shall always remember it as the Year of the Baby. Names are easier to remember than numbers."

Thus from the very beginning it came about that they called each year not so often by its number as by a name based on something that had happened during that time.

In the spring of the second year, Ish planted his first garden. He had never like gardening, and that probably explained why, in spite of good resolutions and two half-hearted attempts, he had not grown anything during the first year. Nevertheless, as he turned over the dark moist soil with the spade, he felt a deep satisfaction at being in touch again with primeval things.

That was about all the satisfaction he got from the garden. To begin with, the seed (he had had a hard time to find any at all because of the ravages of the rats) was several years old, and much of it failed to sprout. Snails and slugs soon moved in, but by scattering a box of Snale-Killa he eliminated them, and felt triumphant. Then, just as the lettuce was making a good growth, a buck jumped the fence and wrought havoc. Ish put another layer on the top of the fence. Next, some rabbits burrowed beneath—more destruction, and more work! One evening he heard crashing noises and rushed out just in time to scare off a predatory cow on the point of smashing a way through the fence. More work!

By this time he was waking up at night with thoughts of ravening deer, rabbits, and cattle prowling around his fence and ogling his lettuces with eyes that gleamed like tigers' eyes.

Then, in June, the insects arrived. He sprayed poison until he was afraid he would not dare eat the lettuce even if any lived to be harvested.

The crows were the last to find the garden, but when they arrived in July their numbers made up for their late arrival. He stood guard, and shot some of them. But they seemed to post sentries and swoop down as soon as his back was turned, and he could not watch during all the daylight hours. His scarecrows and dangling mirrors kept them off for a day, but after that they lost their fear.

In the end he actually erected a shelter of fly-screen over the few rows of garden which seemed worth saving, and he harvested a little lettuce, along with some scrawny tomatoes and onions. But he conscientiously let some of the plants go to seed, and saved the fresh seed for the future.

He was as thoroughly discouraged as any amateur gardener had ever been. It was one thing apparently to grow vegetables when thousands of others were doing the same, and quite another when yours was the only plot and so from miles around every vegetable-hungry animal and bird and mollusk and insect came galloping or flying or oozing or hopping, and apparently sending out by signals to its fellows the universal shout, "Let's eat!"

Toward the end of summer the second baby was born. They called her Mary, just as they had decided finally to call the first one John, so that the old names would not vanish from the earth.

When the new baby was only a few weeks old, there was another memorable event.

This was the way of it. . . . In those first years though Ish and Em stayed contentedly close at home, they now and then had visits from wanderers who had seen the smoke on San Lupo Drive and headed for it, sometimes in cars, more often on foot. These people, with one exception, seemed to be suffering from shock. They were bees who had lost the hive, sheep without a flock. By now, Ish concluded, the ones who had made a good adjustment must already have settled down. (Besides, no matter whether the wanderer was a man or a woman, the old problem of three's-a-crowd reared up.) So Ish and Em were glad when one of these restless and unhappy people decided to continue wandering.

The exception was Ezra. Ish always remembered how Ezra came strolling along the street that hot September day, his face florid, his half-bald head even redder, his jaw narrow and pinched, his bad teeth showing suddenly when he saw Ish and stopped and smiled.

"Hi-ya, boy!" he had said, and though the words were American, still behind them somewhere was the ghost of a North-of-England accent.

He stayed until after the first rains. He was always pleasant, even when his teeth were growling. He had that inexpressibly great gift of making people feel comfortable. The babies always smiled for Ezra.

Ish and Em would have urged him to stay permanently, but they feared the triangle-situation, even when the outsider was as easygoing and perceptive as Ezra. So one day when he seemed restless they sent him off, telling him jokingly to find himself a pretty girl and then come back and join them. They were sad after he had gone.

At the time of his leaving the sun was again far to the south. So, when they went to the flat rock and cut the numeral 2, Ezra was still in their minds, though he was gone and they did not expect to see him again. He would have been, they thought, a good helper, a good person to have around. To his memory they called it the Year of Ezra.

The Year 3 was the Year of the Fires. Just after midsummer the smoke suddenly drifted over everything, and it stayed, lighter or heavier, through three months. The babies sometimes woke up coughing and choking, their eyes watering.

Ish could realize what was happening. The western forests were no longer primeval woodlands of big trees through which a fire could sweep and do little damage. On the contrary, because of logging and man-caused fires, the forests consisted mostly of thick and highly inflammable second-growth, made all the worse by slash-piles and brush-fields. Man had produced this kind of forest, and it was dependent upon him, surviving only because of his vigorous efforts at fire-suppression. Now the hoses lay neatly coiled and the bulldozers reddened with rust, and in this summer, a very dry one, over all northern California, and doubtless in Oregon and Washington too, the lightning-set fires were raging uncombatted through the tangled second-growth and blazing up in the tinder-dry slash-piles. One horrible week they even saw the fires burning brightly in the night, all along the north side of the Bay, sweeping the slopes of the mountain from bottom to top, and dying out only when there was nothing left to burn. The broad arms of the Bay fortunately kept the fire on the north side, and there were no lightning storms on the south side to start new fires. When it was all over, Ish believed that there must be very few forests left unburned in California, and centuries would be required to grow them again.

In this year also Ish really settled down to reading—another sign that he was finally adjusting to the situation. He got his books from the City Library, and kept the million volumes of the University as a great reserve to be tapped when the time was ripe. Although he often thought that he should use his reading to make himself skillful in such fields as medicine and agriculture and mechanics, he found that what he actually wanted to read was the story of mankind. He plunged through innumerable volumes of anthropology and history, and went on into philosophy, particularly the philosophy of history. He read novels and poems and plays, which also were the story of mankind.

Sometimes in the evening, when he was reading and Em was knitting, and the babies were asleep upstairs and Princess was lying lazily in front of the fire—sometimes then Ish would look up and think that his father and mother had passed many evenings in just the same way. But then he

125

would see the gasoline lamp and turn his eyes up to the dead electric-light bulbs in the ceiling-fixture.

The Year 4 was the Year of the Coming. . . . One day in early spring, about noon, Princess leaped up barking wildly and dashed for the street, and then they heard a car-horn tooting. Ezra had been gone for more than a year, and they had stopped thinking about him. But there he was—in a jalopy-looking car, overflowing with people and household goods. Ish couldn't help thinking of an Okie outfit arriving in California in the Old Times.

Besides Ezra, there crawled out of the car a woman of about thirty-five, a younger woman, a frightened-looking half-grown girl, and a little boy. Ezra introduced the older woman as Molly, and the younger as Jean, and after each name he added calmly and without embarrassment, "My wife."

Ish suffered only mild shock at the fact of bigamy. He had been through a great many experiences already, and he reacted quickly to realize that plurality of wives had been an accepted part of many great civilizations in the past and might well be again in the future. It was certainly a practical situation when there were two women available and only one man, especially when the man was like Ezra, able to live comfortably with people under all sorts of conditions.

The little boy was Ralph, Molly's son. He had been born only a few weeks before the Great Disaster, and had presumably either inherited immunity or absorbed it through his mother's milk. This was the only case, so far as they knew, of two members of the same family surviving.

The half-grown girl they called Evie, but nobody really knew her right name. Ezra had found her living in squalor and solitude, opening cans to find what she needed, grubbing for worms and snails. She must have been five or six years old at the time of the Great Disaster. Whether she had always been half-witted, or whether the shock of death and solitude had rendered her so, no one knew. She cowered and whimpered, and even Ezra could win a smile from her only now and then. She knew a few words, and after they had been kind to her for a long time, she gradually came to talk more, but she never grew normal.

Later in the same year Ish and Ezra went off together for a few days in Ish's old station-wagon. The trip was not a pleasant one; they had tire-trouble and engine-trouble, and the roads were rough. Nevertheless they accomplished what they had set out to do.

They located George and Maurine, whom Ezra had found

on one of his wanderings. George was a big shambling fellow, gray around the temples, good-natured, uncertain in speech but deft in his trade, which was carpentry. ("Too bad!" thought Ish. "A mechanic or a farmer would have been better for us!") Maurine was his female counterpart, except that she was some ten years younger, around forty probably. She loved housekeeping as George loved carpentry. As for their mental processes, you might call George dull, but you would have to call Maurine stupid.

Privately Ish and Ezra discussed George and Maurine, and decided that they were good solid people, comfortable to have around, more a source of strength than of weakness. (It was a little, Ish thought wryly, like deciding whether you would give someone a bid to your fraternity, and when there were so few to choose from, you couldn't be too choosy.) In the end George and Maurine came along back in the station-wagon.

Ish and Maurine found that they had one experience in common. As a little girl in South Dakota, she had been bitten by a rattlesnake.

Toward the end of this year Em bore her second son, whom they named Roger. So by that time the people living on San Lupo Drive numbered seven adults, and four children, and Evie besides. About then they began, at first as a joke, to talk of themselves as The Tribe.

The Year 5 supplied no very startling occurrence. Both Molly and Jean had babies, and Ezra was as pleased as a two-time father should be. In the end they called it the Year of the Bulls. This was because there was a plague of cattle that year, just as from the first months they all remembered the plagues of the ants and the rats. Cattle had gradually got to be more and more numerous. Very rarely did anyone see a horse; never, a sheep. But it was good country for cattle, and they reached a climax in this year, and became a nuisance. To be sure, you easily got all the steak you wanted, though it was tough. But you had continual trouble running into a cross bull when you were merely wanting to walk here or there. You could always shoot a bull, but shooting one near the houses either meant that you had to go to all the trouble of burying the carcass, or of dragging it away, or else you suffered from the smell. They all had to become adept at stepping quickly out of the way when a bull charged, and they came to make something of a sport of this, and to call it "bull-dodging."

The Year 6 was an eventful one. During its course all four of the women bore children—even Maurine, who had seemed too old. There was, however—now that Em had led the way —a strong drive toward the having of many children. Each of the adults had for a time lived alone, had experienced what they now called the Great Loneliness, and the strange dread that went with it. Even now their little group was only a tiny candle against the pressure of surrounding darkness. Each new-born baby seemed to give the uncertain flame a stronger hold and to push the darkness of annihilation back a little. At the end of this year the number of children, which was ten, exceeded the number of adults— and then of course there was Evie, who was hardly to be counted in either group.

But it was an eventful year for other reasons too. It was a year of drought and of little grass, and the too numerous cattle grew thin and wandered everywhere, searching food. Driven madly by hunger, they crashed the strong fence around the little vegetable plot one night. The aroused men emptied rifles into the milling cattle at short range, but before they could be driven off, the garden was utterly ruined—ironically, by being trampled out, for in the confusion of the milling herd no animal had been able to eat.

To crown all this, came the grasshoppers. They descended suddenly, and ate up everything that the cattle could not reach. They ate the leaves from the trees and the flesh from the ripening peaches, so that the bare seeds hung from the ends of the leafless branches. Then the grasshoppers died, and their stench was everywhere.

After a while the cattle also lay dead by hundreds in the dry stream beds and muddy waterholes, and their stench too filled the air. By now the land was stripped bare, as if it would never recover.

A horror fell upon the people. Ish tried to explain to them that it was all a part of the jostling for readjustment after the loss of human controls. There was bound to be, for instance, a plague of grasshoppers during the first year when conditions favored them, now that their breeding-grounds were not disturbed by cultivation. But with the stench in the air and the whole earth looking dead, he could not be very convincing. George and Maurine took to prayer. Jean made fun of them openly, saying that what had happened in the last few years didn't give her confidence in this god-business. Molly went into depressions, and wept loudly at times. In spite of his rationalistic explanations even Ish was

128

despondent for the future. Of the adults only Ezra and Em showed the capacity for taking things as they came.

The older children seemed to be little affected. They gulped their canned milk greedily, even when the stench was thickest. John (they already were calling him Jack) held his father's hand with confidence, and looked with mild six-year-old interest at a cow which had tottered along the street and lay dying in the sun. He obviously accepted it as just part of his world.

But the nursing babies, except Em's, absorbed a sense of disaster through their mothers' milk. They wailed fretfully. Thus disturbing their mothers all the more, they set up a vicious circle.

October was a month of horror.

Then came the miracle! Two weeks after the first rain they looked out, and the hills were a faint green with sprouting grass. Everyone was suddenly happy, and Molly and Maurine wept with pleasure. Even Ish was relieved, for in the last weeks the despair of the others had shaken his confidence in the basic recuperative powers of the earth itself, and he had begun to doubt whether any seed remained.

When, at the time of the winter solstice, the people all gathered once more at the smooth expanse of rock to cut the numeral into the surface and to name the year, they were uncertain what they should call it. It might be, for good omen, the Year of the Four Babies. But it might be the Year of the Dead Cattle, or the Year of the Grasshoppers. In the end the evilness of the year prevailed in their thoughts. So they called it simply the Bad Year.

The Year 7 was a strange one also. The mountain-lions suddenly seemed to be everywhere. You hardly dared to walk between houses without carrying a rifle, and having a dog at heel to give warning, and the dog kept usually very close at heel also. The lions never quite dared attack a man, but they picked up four dogs, and you were never quite sure whether one of them might not just suddenly leap from a tree. The children had to be kept indoors. What had happened was again obvious enough to Ish. During the years when there had been so many cattle, the lions must have bred rapidly, and now that the cattle had perished in the drought, the lions were left without food and ravenously were closing in.

In the end there was bad luck, because Ish missed his shot and instead of killing a lion merely raked it across the shoulders, and it charged and mauled him before Ezra could get another shot home. After that he walked with a little limp, and became very tired when he had to sit long in the same position, as in driving a car. (But by now the roads had gone to pieces badly and the cars were unreliable and there were few places to go anyway, so that there was very little car-driving.) Naturally, they called it the Year of the Lions.

The Year 8 was comparatively uneventful. They called it the Year We Went to Church. (The name amused Ish, for its wording implied that that experiment was over and done with.)

This had happened in this way. . . . Being merely seven ordinary Americans, they were of varied religious affiliations or of none at all, and even among the church-members no one had felt any creative religious drive. Ish had gone to Sunday-School as a child, but when Maurine asked him what church he belonged to, he had to say that he was a skeptic. Maurine did not know the word, and jumping to the wrong conclusion she always referred to Ish thereafter as being a member of the Skeptic Church.

Maurine herself was a Catholic, and so was Molly. They could still cross themselves and say a *Hail Mary*, but otherwise they were in a bad situation, having no confessor and no way of celebrating mass. As Ish reflected, the Catholic Church had considered almost all possibilities, but apparently never the one of getting reorganized after the Apostolic Succession was broken and only two women remained.

Of the others, George had been a Methodist, and a deacon. But he was too inarticulate to turn preacher, and not enough of a leader to organize a congregation. Ezra was tolerant of everyone's beliefs, but never let himself be pinned down as to his own, and so probably lacked any convictions. Jean had been a member of some loud-praying modern sect called Christ's Own. But she had seen the congregation pray in vain at the time of the Great Disaster, and now she had turned definitely anti-religious. Em, who never liked to turn toward the past, was reticent. As far as Ish could tell, she never prayed. Now and then, apparently without thinking of religious implications, she sang hymns or spirituals in her full throaty contralto.

George and Maurine, sinking the Methodist-Catholic differences, were the ones who suggested church services— "for the sake of the children." They appealed to Ish, who was something of a leader, especially in things intellectual.

130

Maurine, broad-mindedly, even told him that she would not object to the use of "the Skeptic form of services."

Ish felt the temptation. He could easily piece together some harmless bits of religion, give comfort and confidence to people who might often need it badly, and supply a core of solidity and union to the community. George, Maurine and Molly would welcome it; Jean should be easy to convert again; Ezra would not stand in the way. But Ish himself hated building upon a foundation of insincerity, and he knew that Em would see through the sham.

In the end they held a service each Sunday—George had kept track of Sunday, or at least thought so. They sang hymns, and read from the Bible, and stood uncovered for silent prayer, each for himself.

But Ish never prayed during the period of silence, and he did not think that Em or Ezra did either. Moreover, Jean maintained her hostility stoutly, and never attended. Ish felt that if he had had more fervor, or more hypocrisy, he could have argued Jean over. As it was, however, the church services were cultivating disunion rather than unity of feeling, and sham more than true religion.

One day, on the spur of the moment, Ish put an end to them. He did it rather neatly, he thought, ending his speech with the idea that they were not really giving up the services but merely extending the period of silent prayer indefinitely—"letting each one of us carry on in his heart as he wishes."

Molly wept a little at what seemed to her such a lovely thought, and so the experiment with the church at least was ended in harmony.

At the beginning of the Year 9 there were seven adults, and Evie, and thirteen children, ranging in age from newborn babies up to Molly's Ralph, who was nine, and Ish's and Em's Jack, who was eight.

Everybody had a pleasant sense of confidence and security in the growth of the community, or of The Tribe, as they now said more often. The birth of each baby was a time of real rejoicing, as the shadows seemed to draw back a little and the circle of light to enlarge.

Soon after the beginning of that year, a decent-looking oldish man came up to George's house one morning. He was one of those wanderers who still occasionally, though less and less often, passed through.

They received him hospitably, but like the others he showed little reaction to what they did for him. He stayed only over one night, and then went off again, without even saying good-bye, in the aimless way of those shocked ones.

He had scarcely gone, it seemed, before people began feeling irritable. All the babies started crying. Then soon there were sore throats and running noses and aching heads and swollen eyes, and The Tribe was suddenly in all the throes of an epidemic.

This was all the more remarkable because throughout the preceding years the general health had been so unbelievably good. Ezra and some of the others had suffered with bad teeth; George, who was the oldest, had complained of various aching joints which he described under the old-fashioned term "rheumatism"; occasionally a scratch became infected. But even the common cold seemed to have vanished entirely, and there were only two diseases that remained active. One of these struck each of the children sooner or later; it was a great deal like measles in its symptoms, and doubtless it *was* measles, and that was what they called it, lacking any doctor to make them sure. The other began with a violent sore throat, but yielded so quickly to sulfa pills that no one really knew its full course. As long as there were sulfa pills in any drug store and they kept potent in spite of age, Ish saw no need to find out experimentally just how this sore throat would develop, if left untreated.

Why so few diseases remained—this seemed miraculous to people like George and Maurine, and they were inclined to be superstitious about the matter. They felt that God in some great anger had nearly wiped out the human race in one vast plague, and thus being satisfied, had seen fit to remove the minor plagues as a kind of compensation—just as, after Noah's flood, he had set the rainbow in the sky as a sign that there would never again be another such flood.

To Ish, however, the explanation was plain. Since so large a proportion of the people had died, the chain of most infections had been broken, and many individual diseases had, you might say, "died" when their particular kinds of bacteria became extinct. Of course there would still be the diseases which might spring from the mere deterioration of the human body, such as heart-failure and cancer, and George's "rheumatism," and there might also be animal-borne infections, like tularemia and tick-fever. Also there could be, here and there, individual survivors who carried some disease in chronic form, but could still pass it on to others, just as some one of themselves had probably been responsible for the survival of "measles."

132

The old man, everyone remembered too late, had blown his nose occasionally. Doubtless he had an infected sinus, and so had infected them all with what used to be called "the common cold," although lately it had been so *un*common as to seem extinct.

In any case there was something almost comic in the way so many disgustingly healthy people were suddenly transformed into sneezers and coughers and hawkers and noseblowers.

Fortunately, the cold ran its course without complications, and in a few weeks everyone was well again. Throughout the rest of that year Ish lived in fear of another outbreak. There was a good chance, he knew, that the infection might be quiescent in one of them, and then break loose again when the short-time immunity of the others had worn off. But the long dry summer (it was particularly sunny that year) doubtless helped everyone to throw off the last vestiges of the infection. That was great luck! Ish had been highly susceptible in the Old Times. He had sometimes said, not altogether as a joke, that the loss of the common cold compensated for the accompanying loss of civilization.

That autumn, however, the good luck ran out. No one ever knew exactly what happened, but three of the children fell ill with violent diarrhoea, and died. Most likely they had been wandering about at play in one of the near-by uninhabited houses, and had found some poison—ant-poison, perhaps. Tasting it curiously they had found it sweet, and shared it. Even when dead, civilization seemed to lay traps.

One of the children had been Ish's own son. He had always worried, not about himself, but about Em, in such a case. Yet, though she mourned for the child, he saw that he had underestimated her strength. Her hold on life was so strong that, paradoxically, she could accept death also as a part of life. Both Molly and Jean, the other bereaved mothers, grieved hysterically, and were much more stricken.

That year two children were born, but nevertheless the total number of The Tribe for the first time was smaller at the end than at the beginning of a year. They called it the Year of the Deaths.

The Year 10 had no remarkable events, and no one was convinced as to what it should be called. But when they sat on the flat rock and Ish poised his hammer and began to cut with the chisel, for the first time some of the children spoke up, and they said it should be called the Year of the Fishing.

133

This was because during this year they had discovered that the bay was swarming with beautiful striped bass, and they had had a great deal of fun going fishing and catching them. Besides supplying a very fine variety to the diet, the fishing had also been a real source of amusement to everybody. But in general, Ish was surprised how little actual necessity they had to seek amusement. In the kind of life that they lived there always seemed to be a good deal to do just to get food and to support oneself in comfort and there was in it a great deal of satisfaction which did not call for anything as definite as amusement.

In the Year 11, Molly and Jean bore children, but Molly's died at birth. This was a great disappointment, because it was the first one that they had lost at childbirth, and in the course of the years the women had become very skillful at helping one another. They thought that perhaps this death was caused from Molly's being old now.

When it came to naming the year, however, there was a dispute between old and young. The older ones thought it should be called the Year when Princess Died. . . . She had been ailing, an old dog, for some time. No one knew just how ancient she was, because she might have been anywhere from one year to three or four when she first picked up Ish. She had remained the same—always the princess, expecting the best of treatment, always unreliable, always ready to disappear on the trail of an imaginary rabbit just when you wanted her. But for all you might say against her, she had shown a very real character, and the older people could remember the time when she seemed very important along San Lupo Drive, almost another person.

By now there were dozens of dogs around. Nearly all of them must be children or grandchildren or great-grandchildren of Princess, who on various occasions had disappeared for a day or two and apparently met an old friend among the wild dogs or picked up a new one. As the result of a lot of in-breeding and out-breeding and cross-breeding, these present dogs were very little like beagles, but varied tremendously in size and color and temperament.

But to the children Princess had been an old and not very interesting dog of uncertain temper. They said that this should be the Year of the Wood-Carving, and after a momentary hesitation Ish supported them, even though Princess had meant more to him than to anyone else. She had taken him out of himself in those first bad days and let him free himself of fear, and her wild barking dash had taken him into the house where he found Em. when otherwise he might have hesitated and driven on. But also, he thought, Princess was over and done with, and only a link with the past, to be remembered by people who were growing older and older. Soon the younger children would not remember her at all. After a while she would be wholly forgotten. (Then the icy thought came to him: "So too I may grow old, and older, and be merely a link to the past, and be an unregarded old duffer, and then die and be soon forgotten—yet that is as it should be!")

Then, as the others argued, he thought of the wood-carving. It had swept over them as a kind of fad or craze, like bubble-blowing or mah-jongg in the Old Times. Suddenly all the children were raiding lumber yards for good boards of soft sugar-pine, and were trying to carve running designs of figures of cattle or dogs or people. They worked awkwardly at first, but soon some of them grew skillful. Though, like all fads, it had fallen off, still the children worked at it on rainy days.

Ish had studied enough anthropology to know that any healthy people should have creative outlets, and he was worried that The Tribe had not developed artistically but was still living under the shadow of the past, listening to old records on the wind-up phonographs and looking at old picture books. Accordingly he had been pleased at the fad for wood-carving.

At a pause in the argument he spoke up, supporting the children. So it came to be known as the Year of the Wood-Carving, and in Ish's mind the Year 11 had a symbolic value, as a breaking with the past and a turning to the future. Yet the naming was a small matter, and he was not sure that he should attach any significance to it.

In the Year 12, Jean lost a child in childbirth, but Em made up for it by bearing the first pair of twins, whom they called Joseph and Josephine, or more commonly, Joey and Josey. So this was the Year of the Twins.

The Year 13 saw the birth of two children who both lived. It was a quiet and comfortable year, with nothing to mark it especially. So, for lack of anything better, they merely called it the Good Year.

The Year 14 was much like it, so they called that the Second Good Year.

The Year 15 was also excellent, and they considered calling it the Third Good Year, but there was a difference. Ish and the older people again felt that first loneliness and the drawing in of the darkness. Not to grow more numerous was essentially to grow fewer, and this was the first year since the very beginning when there had been no children born. All the women—Em, Molly, Jean and Maurine—were now getting old, and the younger girls were not yet quite old enough to marry, except for Evie, the half-witted one, who should never be allowed to have children. So they did not like to call this the Third Good Year, because it was not wholly good. Instead, the children remembered that this year could be thought remarkable because Ish had got out his old accordion and to its wheezing they had sung songs together— old songs like *Home on the Range* or *She'll Be Comin' Round the Mountain*, and so they called this, at the children's prompting, the Year That We Sang. (No one except Ish seemed to think that anything was wrong with the grammar.)

The Year 16, however, was remarkable because the first marriage actually took place. Those married were Mary, who was Ish's and Em's oldest daughter, and Ralph, who had been born to Molly just before the Great Disaster. They were younger than would have been thought suitable or even decent for marriage in the Old Days, but in this also standards had changed. Ish and Em, when they discussed the matter privately, were not even sure that Mary was especially fond of Ralph, or Ralph of Mary. But everyone had always assumed that the two of them would get married because there was nobody else available whom either of them could take, just as it once was with princes and princesses. So perhaps, as Ish concluded, romantic love had merely been another necessary casualty of the Great Disaster.

Maurine and Molly and Jean were all for "a real wedding," as they said. They hunted up a Lohengrin record for the wind-up phonograph, and were making a wedding costume in white with a veil, and everything to go with it. But, to Ish, all this seemed a horrible parody of things that had once been; Em, in her quiet way, supported him. Since Mary was their daughter, they controlled the wedding. In the end, they had no ceremony at all, except that Ralph and Mary stood before Ezra, and he told them that now they were being married and that they would assume a new responsibility to

136

the community and that they must try to fulfill it well. Mary bore a child before the year was out, and so for that reason, it was called the Year of the Grandchild.

The Year 17 they called, mostly at the children's prompting, the Year the House Busted. The reason was that one of the nearby houses had suddenly collapsed and crashed down with a great noise just in time for some of the children to see it as they came running out at the first crack. On investigation, the matter proved simple enough, because termites had had a chance now to work in the house for seventeen years undisturbed, and had eaten through the underpinning. But the incident had made a great impression upon the children, and so it gave the name to the year, although it was not really a matter of importance.

In the Year 18, Jean bore still another child. This was the last of all that were born to the older generation, but by this time there were two marriages of the second generation, and two more grandchildren were born.

This was called the Year of the Schoolteaching. . . . Ever since the first children had been old enough, Ish had tried, in a more or less desultory way, to give them some kind of teaching so that they could at least read and write and do a little arithmetic, and know something of geography. But it had always been difficult to get the children together, and there seemed to be so many things that they wanted to do, either in play or in earnest, and the schoolteaching had never accomplished very much, although most of the older children could read after a fashion. At least they had once been able to read, but Ish doubted whether some of them—such as Mary, who was now a mother with two babies—could at the present moment do more than spell out words of one syllable. (Though she was his own beloved oldest daughter, he admitted to himself that Mary was not intellectual—no need to say she was stupid.)

In this Year 18, however, Ish really tried to get together all of the children who were of proper age, so that they would not grow up completely ignorant. It worked for a while, and then again it lapsed, and it was hard to say whether he had accomplished anything or not, and he felt a sense of frustration.

The Year 19 was named the Year of the Elk, again because of a little incident which impressed the children. One morning some of them saw Evie, now grown to be a woman, looking

137

out and pointing and crying excitedly in her strange voice, which did not quite form words. When they looked, they saw that she was pointing at a new kind of animal. This turned out to be an elk, which was the first one that they had seen in all these years. Apparently, the herds had now increased enough so that they had worked down from the north and were coming back into this region, where they had lived before the arrival of white men.

There was no question about the Year 20. It was the Year of the Earthquake. The old San Leandro Fault stirred again, and early one morning there was a sharp jolt and the sound of falling chimneys. The houses in which they all lived stood the shock, because George always kept them in excellent repair. But the houses that had been weakened by termites or undermined by washing water or damaged by rot came crashing down. After that there was hardly a street which was not littered here and there with brick or with other debris, and because of damage from the earthquake deterioration began to accelerate.

The Year 21 Ish had thought they might call the Year of the Coming of Age. They now numbered thirty-six—seven of the older ones, Evie, twenty-one of the second generation, and seven of the third.

In the end, however, this year was named, like many others, from a small incident. . . . Joey was one of the twins, who were the youngest of the children born to Ish and Em. He was a bright boy, though small for his age and not so good at play as some of those who were even younger than he. He got a certain favoring from both his father and mother, because he was, with his twin, the youngest. On the whole, however, in such a large group of children, nobody had paid him any great attention, and now he was nine years old. But just at the end of this year, they suddenly discovered to their great amazement that Joey could read—not only could read in the slow, halting way of the other children, but could read quickly and accurately and with pleasure. Ish felt a sudden warming of his heart toward the youngest son. This was the one in whom the light of intellect really was still burning.

The other children also were much impressed, and so at the ceremony they cried out that this should be called the Year When Joey Read.

End of the inter-chapter called Quick Years.

138

2

The Year 22

There must be in their social bond something
singularly captivating, and far superior to anything to be boasted of among us; for thousands
of Europeans are Indians, and we have no examples of even one of those Aborigines having
from choice become Europeans!

—J. Hector St. John
de Crèvecoeur,
*Letters from an
American Farmer*

Chapter 1

After the ceremony at the rock was over and the numerals 2 and 1 stood out sharply and freshly cut on the smooth surface, the people started back toward the houses. Most of the children scuttled ahead, calling back and forth, eager with ideas about the bonfire which traditionally ended the New Year celebration.

Ish walked beside Em, but they talked little. As always at the date-carving Ish felt himself thinking deeper thoughts than usual and wondering what would happen in the course of the year. He heard the children shouting out:

"Go to the old house that fell down; you can pull off lots of dry wood there. . . . I think I can find a can of gasoline . . . . I know where there is toilet paper; it burns fine."

The older people, as was the custom, gathered at Ish's and Em's house, and sat around for a little conversation. Since it was a time for festivity, Ish opened some port, and they all drank toasts, even George, who ordinarily did not drink. They agreed again, as they had at the rock, that the Year 21 had been a good year and that the prospects for the coming one were good also.

Yet in the midst of the general self-congratulation, Ish himself felt a renewed sense of dissatisfaction.

"Why," he thought, feeling the words flow through his mind, as if he were arguing aloud, "why should *I* be the one who in times like this always has to start thinking ahead? Why am *I* the one that has to think, or try to think, five years or ten years, or twenty years into the future? I may not even be *alive* then! The people who come after me—they will have to solve their own problems."

Yet he knew, as he thought again, that this last was not altogether true either. The people who live in any generation do much, he realized, either to create or to solve the problems for the people who come in the generations later.

In any case, he could not help wondering what would happen to The Tribe in the years that were ahead. It worried him. After the Great Disaster, he had thought that the people, if any survived at all, would soon be able to get some things running again and proceed gradually toward re-establishing more and more of civilization. He had even dreamed of a time when electric lights might go on again.

But nothing like that had happened, and the community was still dependent upon the leavings of the past.

Now he looked around, as he had often looked before, at the ones who were with him. They were, so to speak, the bricks out of which a new civilization must be fashioned. There was Ezra, for instance. Ish felt himself growing warm with the mere pleasure of friendship as he looked at that thin ruddy face and pleasant smile, even though the smile showed the bad teeth. Ezra had genius perhaps, but it was the genius of living on easy and friendly terms with people, and not the creative drive that leads toward new civilizations. No, not Ezra.

And there beside Ezra was George, good old George—heavy and shambling, powerful still, though his hair had turned wholly gray. George was a good man, too, in his fashion. He was a first-class carpenter, and had learned to do plumbing and painting and the other odd jobs around the house. He was a very useful man, and had preserved many basic skills. Yet Ish always knew that George was essentially stupid; he had probably never read a book in his life. No, not George.

Next to George, was Evie, the half-witted one. Molly kept her well groomed, and Evie, blonde and slender, was good-looking, if you could forget the vacantness of her face. She sat there glancing right and left at whoever was talking. She even gave an illusion of alertness, but Ish knew that she was understanding little, perhaps nothing, of what was being said. She was no foundation-stone for the future. Certainly, not Evie.

Then came Molly, Ezra's older wife. Molly was not a stupid person, but she had had little education and could certainly not be called intellectual. Besides, like the other women, she had expended her energy at bearing and rearing children, and now five of hers were still alive. That was enough contribution to ask of anyone. No, not Molly.

Beyond Molly, the next person was Em. When Ish looked at Em, so many feelings boiled up within him that he knew any judgment he might try to make of her would be of no value. She, alone, had made the first decision to have a child. She had kept her courage and confidence during the Terrible Year. She it was to whom they all turned in time of trouble. Some strong power lodged within her, to affirm and never to deny. Without her they might all have been as nothing. Yet, her power lay deep in the springs of action; in a particular situation, though she might inspire courage and

141

confidence in others, she herself seldom supplied an idea. Ish knew that he would always turn to her and that she was greater than he, but he also knew that she would not be of help in planning toward the future. No—though it seemed disloyalty to say so—not even Em!

Beyond Em, lolling on the floor, were Ralph and Jack and Roger, the three who were still called boys, even though they themselves were married and had children. Ralph was Molly's son who was married to Ish's daughter, Mary; Jack and Roger were Ish's own sons. But as he looked at them now, Ish felt very far from them, even though his connection by family was as close as could well be. Though he was only some twenty years older, still he seemed separated from them by centuries. They had not known the Old Times, and so they could not look forward much and think how things might again be in the future. No, probably not the boys either.

Ish's eyes had moved around the circle, and he was looking now at Jean, Ezra's younger wife. She had borne ten children, and seven of them were still alive. She had a mind of her own, as her refusal to join in the church-services had shown. Still, she was not a person of new ideas. No, not Jean.

As for Maurine, George's wife, she had not even bothered to come to the gathering, but had gone directly from the rock to her own house, where she would already be engaged at sweeping or dusting or some other of her perpetual and beloved tasks of housewifery. Of all persons, certainly not Maurine.

Three other adults also were not present. They were Mary, Martha, and young Jeanie, who were married to the three boys. Mary had always seemed to Ish the most stolid of all his children, and now with her own children coming so fast, she grew a little more bovine, yearly. Martha and Jeanie also were mothers, and motherhood was absorbing them. No, none of these.

Present and absent, twelve adults! He still had difficulty in realizing that there was no vast reservoir of humanity from which to draw.

Half a dozen children were interspersed among the adults or circled around restlessly on the outside of the circle. Instead of going to help with the bonfire, these few had kept with the adults—half-bored, and yet apparently thinking that such a large gathering of their elders was important and should be watched. Ish let his attention shift to them, speculatively. Sometimes they listened to what the older people were

142

saying, and sometimes they merely poked each other or scuffled. Yet, in them, careless as they seemed, rested the hope. The older people could probably slide along on the present arrangements as long as they lived, but the children might have to adapt. Could any of them supply the spark?

And now, as he began to focus on the children, Ish saw that one of them was not scuffling with any other, but was sitting there, steadily listening to what the older ones were saying, his big eyes glancing back and forth with a bright glow of intelligence and interest. This was Joey.

No sooner had Ish's eyes focused for a moment upon Joey, than Joey's alertly wandering glance noticed the attention his father was giving him. He squirmed with delight, and his face broke into the all-embracing grin of a nine-year-old. Upon the impulse of the moment, Ish winked slyly at his youngest son. Joey's grin could scarcely have become any broader than it was, but in some way it seemed to spread. Ish caught the flutter of an eyelid in return. Then, not to embarrass Joey, Ish turned his glance elsewhere.

There was a slow argument going on among George and Ezra and the boys. Ish had heard it all before, and was not enough interested to participate or even to listen to all of it.

"One of them things don't weigh more'n four hundred pounds anyway, I think," George was saying.

"Yes, maybe," Jack replied. "But just the same, that's a lot to lug up here."

"Aw, that's not so much!" said Ralph, who was heavy-set and powerful, and liked to show off his strength.

And so, thought Ish, the argument would go on, as he had heard it often before, about whether it was possible to get a gas-refrigerator somewhere, and set it up, and supply it with still charged tanks of pressurized gas, and so have ice again. Yet, in the end, nothing would be done, not because the project was impossible or even inordinately difficult, but merely because everybody was fairly well contented with things as they were, and in a region of notably cool summers there was no great drive which led anyone to want to have ice. Yet, in a vague way, the old argument disturbed him.

He let his gaze shift back to Joey. Joey was small, even for his age. Ish enjoyed watching the little boy's face, the quick way in which his eyes shifted from one speaker to another, never missing a point. In fact, Ish could see that Joey often picked up the point of a sentence, even before the speaker arrived at the end of it, especially with a slow speaker, like old George. This must be, Ish reflected, a tremendous day for Joey. A year had actually been named after him, the Year When Joey Read. No other child had ever had any such honor as that. Perhaps it was even such a distinction as to be bad for him. Yet, the idea had come spontaneously from the other children, a tribute to sheer intellect.

The languid argument was still going on. George was talking now:

"No, there shouldn't be no great trick to connecting up the pipes."

"But, George," this voice was Ezra's with its quicker tempo and faint tone of Yorkshire still noticeable after all these years, "has gas-pressure kept up in those tanks of compressed gas? I should think, p'raps, after all this time. . . ."

Ezra's voice trailed off that moment at a sudden rumpus between two of the children. Weston, Ezra's own twelve-year-old son, was engaged in a punching contest with Betty, his half-sister.

"Stop it, Weston," Ezra snapped out. "Stop it, I say, or I'll warm your pants for you!"

The threat did not carry conviction, and as far as Ish could remember, he had never seen the easygoing Ezra punish a child. Nevertheless, at the paternal order the scuffle subsided with no more than the conventional protest from Weston, "Aw, Betty started it!"

"Yes, but what do you want ice for anyway, George?" This was Ralph speaking. It was a natural and never-failing phase of the argument. The boys, who had never known what it was to have ice, had no urge to make them go to the work of obtaining it.

Ish was thinking to himself that George had been asked that question a great many times in the course of this argument before. He really should have had his answer ready, but George was not a quick thinker and was not a man to be hurried. He shifted his tongue in his mouth, shaping words before he actually set out to reply, and in the pause Ish again watched Joey. The little boy's glance moved quickly from the hesitant George to Ezra and to Jack, as if to see how those others were taking the pause; then Joey's eyes sought his father's again. All at once there was a quick comradeship and sense of understanding in the glance. Joey seemed to be saying that either his father or he would find an answer quickly and not hesitate as George was doing.

Then something exploded inside Ish's brain. He did not

144

hear the words that at last began to unroll slowly from George's mouth.

"Joey!" Ish was thinking—and the name seemed to reverberate all through his consciousness. "Joey! He is the one!"

"Thou knowest not," Koheleth wrote in his wisdom, "how the bones do grow in the womb of her that is with child." And though the centuries have passed since Koheleth looked upon all things and found them fickle as wind, yet still we know little of what goes to the making of a man—least surely of all, why usually there issue forth only those who see what is, and why rarely, now and then, there comes forth among them the chosen one, Child of the Blessing, who sees not what is, but sees what is not, and seeing thus what is not, imagines also what may be. Yet without this rare one all men are as beasts.

First in the dark depths and the flooding, those unlike halves must meet that carry within them each the perfect half of genius. But that is not all! Also the child must be born to the world in fitting time and place, fulfilling its need. But even that is not all. Also the child must live, in a world where death walks daily.

When each year children are born in millions, now and then the infinitesimal chance will happen, and there will be greatness and vision. But how will it be, if the people are broken and scattered, and the children only a few?

Then, almost without knowing what had happened, Ish found himself on his feet. He was talking. In fact, he was making a speech. "Look here," he was saying, "we've got to do something about all this. We've waited long enough!"

As he stood there, he was only in his own living-room, and he was talking only to the few people who were there. He knew that they were only a few, and yet it seemed to him not so much as if he were talking just to these few in this little room, but rather that he was in some great amphitheater and talking to a whole nation or to all the people of the world.

"This has got to stop!" he said. "We mustn't go on living forever just in this happy way, scavenging among all the supplies that the Old Times left here for us, not creating or doing anything for ourselves. These things will all give out some day —if not in our years, in our children's, or grandchildren's. What will happen then? What will they do when they won't know how to produce more things? Food, they can get, I

145

suppose—there will still be cattle and rabbits. But what about all the more complicated things we enjoy? What, even, about building fires after the matches have all been used, or spoiled?"

He paused, and looked around again. They all seemed pleased, and seemed to be agreeing with him. Joey's face was transcendent with excitement.

"That refrigerator you were talking about just now, all of you!" Ish went on. "That's an example. We talk about it, but we never do anything. We're like that story—that old king in the old story—the one who sat enchanted and everything moved around him, but he could never make any move to break the spell. I used to think we were just suffering from the shock of the Great Disaster. Perhaps that was it, in those first days. When people have their whole world go to pieces around them, they can't expect to make a fresh start immediately. But that was twenty-one years ago, and many of us have even been born since that time.

"There are lots of things we should do. We should get some more domestic animals, not just dogs. We ought to be growing more of our own food now, not just raiding the old grocery stores still. We ought to be teaching the children to read and write more. (No one has ever supported me strongly enough in that.) We can't go on scavenging like this forever, we must go forward."

He paused, searching for words by which to point out to them the old truism that unless we go forward we inevitably go back, but suddenly they all applauded loudly, as if he had finished. He thought that he had really swayed them by a sudden flood of eloquence, but then he realized, as he looked around, that the applause was largely in good-natured irony.

"That's the fine old speech again, Dad," Roger remarked. Ish glared at him angrily for a moment; having really been the leader of The Tribe for twenty-one years, he did not like to have himself put down thus as merely an old codger with some funny ideas. But then Ezra laughed good-naturedly, and everybody joined in the laughter, and the tension fell off.

"Well, what are we going to do about it then?" Ish asked. "I may have made the same old speech before, but even if I have, it's true, nevertheless."

He paused expectantly. Then Jack, who was Ish's oldest son, unlimbered himself from where he was lolling on the floor, and got to his feet. Jack was taller and much more powerful than his father now; he was, himself, a father.

"I'm sorry, Dad," he said, "but I've got to go."

146

"What's the matter? What is it?" Ish snapped back to him, a little irritated.

"Well, nothing so very much, but there's something I have to do this afternoon."

"Won't it wait?"

Jack was already moving toward the door.

"I suppose it might wait," he said, as he put his hand on the door knob. "But I think I'd better be going anyway."

There was silence for a moment, except for the sounds of the door opening, and shutting, as Jack went out. Ish felt himself suddenly angry, and he knew that his face was flushed.

"Go on talking, Ish," Ish heard the voice, and knew through his anger that it was Ezra's. "We would like to hear just what you think we ought to do; you have the ideas." Yes, it was Ezra's voice, and Ezra as usual was saying something quickly to cover up the difficulty and make people feel better. He was even flattering Ish.

Nevertheless, at the voice, Ish relaxed. Why should he be angry with Jack for acting independently? He should, rather, be happy. Jack was a grown man now, no longer a little boy and merely a son. The flush faded from Ish's face, but still he felt a profound sense of trouble within him, and he was led on to talk more. If the incident could do nothing else, at least it could supply him with a text.

"This business with Jack right here now, that's something I want to talk about, too. We've drifted along all these years not doing anything about producing our own food and getting civilization back into some kind of running-order, as regards all the material things. That's one matter, and an important one, but it isn't the only one. Civilization wasn't just only gadgets and how to make them and run them. It was all sorts of social organization too—all sorts of rules, and laws, and ways of life, among people and groups of people. The family—that's all we have left of all that organization! That's natural, I suppose. But the family can't be enough when there get to be more people. When a little child does something we don't like, the father and mother correct it, and bring it into line. But when one of the children grows up, that's all over. We haven't any laws—we aren't a democracy, or a monarchy, or a dictatorship, or anything. If someone—Jack, for instance—wants to walk out on what seems to be a kind of important meeting, nobody can stop him. Even if we take a vote here and decide to do

147

something, even then, there's no means of enforcement—oh, a little public opinion, perhaps, but that's all."

He had trailed off to a lame ending, rather than coming to a conclusion. He had been speaking more from the emotional drive that Jack's move had aroused in him. He was not a trained orator, and had certainly no practice.

Yet, as he looked around, he saw that the speech had apparently made a very good impression. Ezra was the one who spoke first.

"Yes, you bet!" he said. "Don't you remember all of those wonderful times we used to have back in those days. Golly, what wouldn't I give just now to be over there with George's big radio and turn it right on and hear Charlie McCarthy again! Don't you remember the way that little guy would talk, making fun of the other guy, whatever his name was, you know, and here that other one was just the same as him all the time."

Ezra took out the big Victorian penny that had served him for a pocket-piece during all these years. He tossed it back and forth from one hand to the other in sheer stimulation at the thought of hearing Charlie McCarthy again.

"Yes, you remember too," he went on. "Why, you used to be able to go right down to the picture-house and pay your money and go right in! And you would hear all that music going with the film, and see—oh, maybe—Bob Hope or Dotty Lamour. Yes, those were the days all right! Do you suppose that p'raps if we all got together and worked hard we could find some of those films and rig them up to show them to all the kids? I can just hear them laughing. Maybe we could get a Charlie Chaplin film somewhere!"

Ezra took out a cigarette and a match, and as he scratched the match it broke into a bright flame. Matches never seemed to deteriorate if they were in a fairly dry place. Yet nobody now knew how to make matches, and at every sudden spurt of flame there was one match the fewer. Ish had a strange feeling about Ezra, who was thinking of civilization chiefly as the return of motion-pictures, and at the same time was scratching a match.

George was the one who spoke next:

"If there was any way of making people help me, just one or two of the boys, I could get that gas refrigerator fixed up and working in two, three days, maybe."

George stopped speaking, and Ish supposed that he had finished, for George was never much of a talker. Surprisingly, he went on:

148

"About those there laws, though, that you was talking about. I don't know. I was kind of glad that we live in a place where we don't have no laws. These days, you can do just about the way you want. You can go out and park your car anywhere you want to. Right by a fire-hydrant, maybe, and nobody's going to give you a ticket, that is, you could park it right by the fire-hydrant if you had a car that would run."

This was as far in the way of a joke as Ish had ever heard George go, and George responded to his own humor by chuckling quietly. The others all joined in. The standard of humor in The Tribe, Ish realized, had never been very high.

Ish was about to say something more, but Ezra spoke again.

"Come on, now, I propose a toast," he said. *"To law and order!"* The older people laughed a little at hearing the old phrase again, but to the younger ones it meant nothing.

They drank the toast, and then everything slipped back quite naturally into merely a social occasion again.

After all, Ish reflected, it *was* a social occasion, just as well perhaps, not to let business interfere too much. Perhaps the seed he had planted with this rendition of his impassioned little speech would have some effect in the future. Yet, he felt doubts. You used to have the jokes about never fixing the roof until it rained. People were undoubtedly the same now, or worse. They might well wait until something happened that forced them to act; that something would almost certainly be unpleasant—most likely, serious.

Yet he drank the toast with the others, and with half his mind he listened to the talk. With the other half, nevertheless, he still kept to his own thoughts. This had been a good day; yes, on this day he had carved 21 into the smooth surface of the rock, and the Year 22 had begun; on this day, also, partly because the year had been named as it was, he had become more conscious of the possibilities in his youngest son.

He glanced to where Joey was sitting, and caught in return a quick bright glance, full of the small boy's admiration for his father. Yes, perhaps, there was one at least who could understand fully.

In all that immense and complex system of dams and tunnels, aqueducts and reservoirs, by which water was brought from the mountains to the cities, one particular section of

149

steel pipe in the main aqueduct supplied the fatal flaw. Even at the time of its manufacture certain imperfections had been apparent. It had happened, however, to go past the inspector just at the close of a day, when his senses were dulled and his judgment impaired.

No great harm resulted. The section of pipe was set into place by the workmen, and functioned without difficulty. Shortly before the Great Disaster, a foreman had noticed that this section had developed a slight leak. By the welding of a patch upon it, however, it would be made as good as new, or even stronger than the average.

Then through the years no man passed that way again. A little trickle of water from the faulty section of pipe grew very gradually larger. Even in the dry summers a small patch of green showed by the dripping pipe; birds and small animals came there to drink. And still rust ate from the outside, and from the inside the corrosive action of the water itself slowly bored outward to meet the rust pits, piercing pinprick after pinprick in the tough skin of steel.

Five years, ten years—now a dozen jets of fine spray played from the surface of the pipe. Now the puddle was a drinking-place for cattle.

In five more years a little stream ran off from beneath, the only summer stream in all that dry foothill region. By now the pipe was beginning to be honey-combed with rust, its actual structure grown weak.

Beneath the pipe the ground had long been soft and muddy, and the tramping of animals had aided the erosion of a little gully. Finally, the erosion was sufficient to start a mud flow in the soft wet soil on which the concrete pier rested, the one which supported the pipe with its heavy load of water. As the pier settled, the weight of the water was thrown upon the weakened pipe. A long rent opened in its rust-riddled steel, and a broad stream of water poured out and gushed down into the gully. This torrent soon undermined the footing still more, and it shifted again. Once more the pipe tore, and the stream of water issuing from it became like a small river.

Just as Ish had crawled into bed that evening the sharp crack of a rifle shot brought him sitting full upright, tense. Another resounded, and then a fusillade began popping in the night.

He felt the bed shaking gently, as Em laughed quietly beside him. He relaxed.

150

"Same old trick!" he said.

"Fooled you badly this time!"

"I've been thinking too much about all the future today, I suppose Yes, I suppose my nerves are stirred up a little too much today."

The fusillade was still popping in a good imitation of guerrilla warfare, but he lay down and tried to relax. He knew now what had happened. After everyone had left the bonfire, one of the boys had sneaked back and thrown a few boxes of cartridges into the hot ashes. As soon as the boxes were burned through and things became hot enough, the cartridges had let loose. Like most practical jokes it involved a certain element of risk, but at this time of year the grass was green, and there was no danger of starting a fire. Also, most of the people had been warned in advance or knew what was likely to happen and so would be sure to keep a long way from the hot ashes. Indeed, Ish reconsidered, he himself might have been the particular object of this joke, and everyone else might have known about it.

All right! If so, he was successfully baited. He felt a sense of irritation, but for more serious reasons, he thought, than because he had been fooled.

"Well," he said to Em, "there they go again—more boxes of cartridges popping off uselessly, and no one left in the world who knows how to make cartridges! And here we are in a country overrun with mountain-lions and wild bulls, and cartridges the only way we have of keeping them under control, and for food we don't know how to kill cattle or rabbits or quail except by shooting them."

Em seemed to have nothing to say, and in the pause his mind ranged petulantly over the events of the bonfire itself. That fire had been built up largely out of sawed timber brought from a lumber-yard, interspersed with cartons of toilet-paper, which burned beautifully because of the holes through the middle. In addition, boxes of matches had been scattered through the fire because they went up with fine flares, and there had also been cans of alcohol and cleaning-fluid to give further zest. Doubtless, if you had had to buy all those materials with money, the bonfire would have cost ten thousand dollars in the Old Times; now, those materials might be considered even more valuable, because they had come to be completely irreplaceable.

"Don't worry, dearest," he heard her say now. "It's time to go to sleep."

He settled down beside her, his head close against her

151

breast, seeming as always to draw strength and confidence from her.

"I'm not worrying much, I suppose," he said. "Maybe I really enjoy all this, feeling a little lugubrious about the future, as if we were living dangerously."

He lay still for a moment more, and she said nothing, and then he went on with his thinking aloud.

"Do you remember I've been saying this a long time now, that we have to live more creatively, not just as scavengers? It's bad for us, I think, even psychologically. Why, I was saying this way back even at the time when Jack was going to be born."

"Yes, I remember. You've said it a great many times, and yet, some way or other, it still seems easier just to keep on opening cans as long as there are plenty of cans in the grocery stores and warehouses."

"But the end will come some time. Then, what will people do?"

"Well, I suppose, whatever people there are then—they will just have to solve that problem for themselves. . . . And, dear, I've *always* wished you wouldn't worry so much about it. Things would be different if you had a lot of people who were like you, that thought about things a long way off. But all you have are usual people like Ezra and George and me. And we don't think that way. Darwin—wasn't that his name? —said that we all came from apes or monkeys or something, and I suppose apes and monkeys and things like that never thought much about the future. If we'd come from bees or ants, we might have planned out things ahead, or even if we had been trained like squirrels to store up nuts for the winter."

"Yes, maybe. But in the Old Times people thought about the future. Look at the way they built up civilization."

"And they had Dotty—what was *her* name?—and Charlie McCarthy, just like Ezra says." Then suddenly she went off on another tangent. "And about all this scavenging business that worries you so much! Is it so very different from what people used to do? If you want some copper now, you go down to one of the hardware stores, and find a little copper wire, and take that and hammer it up. In the Old Times, they just went and dug some copper out of a hill somewhere. It maybe was copper ore and not just copper, but still they were scavenging in a way, for it was there all the time. And as far as the food goes, they grew it by using up what was stored in the ground, and changing that into wheat. We

152

just take most of our stuff out of what is stored up somewhere else. I don't know that there's too much difference!"

The argument stopped him for a moment. Then he rallied.
"No, that's not just right either," he said. "At least, they
were *more* creative than we are. They were a going concern.
They produced what they used as they went along."

"I'm not too sure about that," she said. "It seems to me I
can remember reading even in cheap things like the Sunday
supplements that we were always just at the point of running out of copper or oil, or were exhausting the soil so we
wouldn't have anything to live on in the future."

Then from long experience, he knew that she was wanting
to go to sleep. He gave her the last word, and said nothing
more. But he himself lay awake, his thoughts still running
fast. He remembered clear back to times just after the Great
Disaster when he had thought of ways in which civilization
might again start to go. Then he remembered how he had
thought of change itself—how sometime it comes from the
inside of a man, reacting outward against the environment,
and how sometimes the environment presses in against the
man, forcing him to change. Only the unusual man perhaps
was strong enough to press outward against the world.

And from thinking of the unusual man, he went naturally
to thinking of little Joey, the bright one with the quick eyes,
the only one who seemed to follow all the things that Ish
had been saying. He tried to guess what Joey would be like
when he grew older, and he thought how some day he might
be able to talk to Joey. He imagined the words.

"You and I, Joey," he would say, "we are alike, we understand! Ezra and George and the others, they are good
people. They are good solid average people, and the world
couldn't get along without having lots of them, but they
have no spark. We have to give the spark!"

Then from thinking of Joey, who was at the top, his mind
ran rapidly through the others, ending with Evie, who was
at the bottom. Should they have ever kept Evie all these
years? He wondered. There had been a word—euthanasia,
wasn't it?—for that kind of thing. "Mercy-killing," they
called it sometimes. Yet who was qualified in a group like
this to take the responsibility of removing someone like Evie,
even though she was probably no source of happiness to herself nor to anyone else? To do anything like that, he realized,
they would have to have a power much stronger than the
mere authority of an American father over his children,
much stronger than that of the group of friends exercising a

mild public opinion. Something would happen some time, not necessarily about Evie of course. But something *would* happen some time, and then they would have to organize and take stronger action.

His imagination stirred him so powerfully that he made a quick movement of his body, as if already he were taking countermeasures against whatever it was that might have happened.

Either Em had not been asleep, or else his sudden movement waked her.

"What is it, dearest?" she said. "You jumped like some little dog that dreams it's chasing a lion!"

"Something's going to happen some time!" he said, speaking as if she already knew the course of his thoughts.

"Yes, I know," she said—and apparently she *did* know his thoughts. "And we're going to have to do something. 'Organize' I think is the word. We're going to have to do something about what has happened."

"You knew what I was thinking?"

"Well, you've said the same thing before, you know. You've said it very often. Especially around New Years you say it. George talks about the refrigerator, and you talk about something going to happen. Some way or other, nothing has happened yet."

"Yes, but some time it will. It's bound to! Some year I'll be right."

"All right, dearest. Go on worrying. You're probably the kind that don't feel comfortable unless you've got something to worry about—and that particular worry, I guess, won't do you much harm."

She said nothing more, but she reached over and took him into her arms, and held him close. From the touch of her body, as always, he took comfort, and so he slept.

From the broken pipe of the aqueduct the water had now been gushing out like a small river during a period of several weeks. No more water flowed on into the reservoirs. At the same time, from thousands of leaks which had developed through the course of the years, from the many faucets left running at the time of the Great Disaster, from the major breaks occurring at the time of the earthquake—from all of them, the stored water ran out from the reservoirs, and their levels fell steadily.

154

Chapter 2

As Ish had expected, they did nothing. Weeks passed. There was no heaving and grunting of men as they carried the refrigerator up the hill, no click and crunch of spades preparing a garden plot. Ish worried occasionally, but in general life drifted along, and even he could not be much concerned. With his old student's habit of observing even when he did not participate, he often wondered just what might be happening.

Was it really, as he sometimes imagined, that all the individuals were still suffering under a kind of shock as the result of the sudden destruction of their old society? His studies in anthropology supplied him with examples—the head-hunters and the plains Indians, who had lost the will to readjust and even the will to live, after their traditional way of life had rudely been made impossible. If they could no longer go head-hunting or ride out to steal horses and take scalps, they had no desire for anything else either. Or, with a mild climate and food-supplies easy to obtain, was there now simply no stimulus to change? He could recollect possible examples of this kind also—some of the South Sea islanders, or those tropical peoples who lived chiefly on bananas. Or was it something else?

Fortunately, he had enough background of philosophy and history to keep his perspective. He was actually, he realized, struggling to solve a problem which had baffled philosophers from the time when they had first become conscious of problems at all. He was facing the basic question of the dynamics of society. What made a society change? He, as a student, was more fortunate than Koheleth or Plato or Malthus or Toynbee. He saw a society reduced in size until it had attained the simplicity of a laboratory experiment.

Yet, whenever he had arrived at this stage of argument, another thought cut across and disturbed the simplicity. He began to feel himself less scientific but more human, to think more nearly as Em thought. This society along San Lupo Drive was not really a philosopher's neat microcosm, a small dip out of the general ocean of humanity. No—it was a group of individuals. It was Ezra and Em and the boys—yes, and Joey! Change the individuals, and the whole situation changed. Change even one individual! In the place of Em, if we had had—well, say, Dotty Lamour? Or, instead

155

of George, one of those high-powered minds that he remembered from his University years—Professor Sauer, perhaps! Again the situation would change.

Or would it? Possibly not, for in the test the physical environment might be stronger, and might force the aberrant individuals into its mould.

But in one detail Ish thought that Em was wrong. She did not need to fear that he was worrying too much about the situation and would end up with ulcers or a neurosis. Instead, his observation of what was happening kept him interested in life. At first, just after the Great Disaster, he had devoted himself to observing the changes in the world as the result of the disappearance of man. After twenty-one years, however, the world had fairly well adjusted itself, and further changes were too slow to call for day-to-day or even month-to-month observation. Now, however, the problem of society—its adjustment and reconstitution—had moved to the fore, and become his chief interest.

Then at this point in the recurrent course of his thinking he always had to correct himself again. He could not, and should not, be merely the observer and student. Plato and the others—each of them could merely watch and comment, even cynically, if he so felt. Through his writings he might influence future generations, but he himself was in no appreciable way responsible for the growth and development of the society in which he lived. Only now and then had the scholar also become the ruler—Marcus Aurelius, Thomas More, Woodrow Wilson. To be sure, Ish realized that he himself was not a ruler exactly, but he was the man of ideas, the thinker, in a community of only a few individuals. Necessarily the others turned to him in their rare times of trouble, and if any real emergency should arise, he would almost certainly have to assume leadership.

The thought had already in the course of the years sent him to the City Library after books about scholars who had also become rulers. Their fates were not comforting. Marcus Aurelius had worn himself out, body and soul, in bloody and fruitless campaigns on the Danube frontier. Thomas More had gone to the scaffold, and afterwards, ironically, he had been canonized as a martyr of the Church. The biographers often called Wilson a martyr also, although no Church of Peace had made him St. Woodrow. No, the scholar in power had not prospered notably. Yet he, Ish, in a community which even yet numbered only thirty-six people, was so placed that he probably could wield more influence in the shaping of its future than an emperor or a chancellor or a president in the Old Times.

Heavy rains in the week after New Years had slowed the falling of the water level in the reservoir. Then, a little earlier than usual, came the mid-winter dry spell.

Like the blood of some leviathan oozing from a hundred thousand pin-pricks, the life-giving water flowed away through open faucets and leaking joints and broken pipes.

And now, where the still-standing gauge showed that the depth had recently been twenty feet, only a thin skim of water covered the bottom of the reservoir.

When Ish woke up that morning, he realized that it was a fine sunny day, and that he had slept well and was rested. Em was gone from the bed, and he heard the familiar little sounds from downstairs which meant that breakfast would soon be ready. He lay still for a few minutes, thoroughly enjoying himself, coming back more slowly than usual to full consciousness. He felt it a very fortunate circumstance to be able to lie in bed a little while longer if you wished, not merely on Sunday morning, but on any morning. There was no sharp looking at clocks, in the life that they lived now, and no need for him or for anyone else, to catch the 7:53 train. He was living a life of greater freedom than anyone could possibly have lived in the Old Times. Perhaps, with his special temperament he was even living more happily now than he could have lived then.

When he felt ready, he got up and shaved. There was no hot water, but he did not care about that particularly. As a matter of fact, nobody would have minded if he had not shaved at all, but he liked the sense of cleanliness and stimulation that the shave gave him.

He dressed—a new sport shirt and a pair of blue jeans. He stuck his feet into some comfortable slippers, went slopping down stairs, and steered toward the kitchen.

As he came to the door, he heard Em say, rather more sharply than she was used to speak, "Josey child, why don't you turn that faucet farther, so you can really get some water?"

"But, Mommie, it *is* turned on, as hard as I can turn it."

Ish, coming into the kitchen, saw that Josey was holding the tea-kettle in the sink under the faucet, and that only a trickle of water was running.

"Morning!" he said. "I guess I'll have to get George to

157

come over and fix up that plumbing a little bit. Josey, why don't you run out into the garden, and get some water from one of the outside faucets?"

Josey trotted off agreeably, and when she was gone, Ish took the opportunity to kiss Em, and to tell her what he was planning for the day. Josey was gone for a little while, and then came back with the kettle full.

"The water out there ran faster for a little while, and then it just died out to a trickle, too," she said, setting the kettle on the gasoline-stove.

"That's a nuisance!" said Em. "We'll need more water for washing the dishes."

Ish recognized the tone of voice. This was one of the times when a crisis was laid directly at the feet of the men-folk to do something about.

Breakfast was served on the dining-room table, and the table looked just about the way it might have looked in the Old Times. Ish sat at one end, and Em at the other. They had only four children at home now. Robert, who was six-teen, and almost fully grown up, according to the standards of The Tribe, sat on one side. Beside him was Walt, who was twelve, and very big and active for his age. And on the other side, close to the kitchen door, sat Joey and Josey, part of whose work was to help with breakfast, by aiding with the cooking and setting of the table, and running in and out to wait on table and helping to wash the dishes afterwards.

As he sat down, Ish could not help thinking how little this particular scene differed from what it might have been in the Old Times. To be sure, he would never have expected then to be the father of so many children. But, granting the numbers, the family group was just what it might have been at any time in almost any society—father, mother, and chil-dren, tightly grouped to form the basic social unit, so basic in fact that it might be considered biological rather than social. After all, he thought, the family was the toughest of all human institutions. It had preceded civilization, and so it naturally survived afterwards.

There was grapefruit-juice, out of cans, of course. Ish had long since begun to doubt seriously whether after all this time there was anything valuable in the way of vitamins left in canned juices. Even the taste had gone flat. But they con-tinued drinking it, because it felt good on the stomach, even though there might not be any vitamins, and at worst it probably was doing them no harm. There were no eggs, be-

158

cause there had been no hens since the Great Disaster. There was no bacon, either, because canned or glassed bacon was hard to find now and there were no pigs in this vicinity, as far as they had ever discovered. But they had beef-ribs, braised and well browned, which were a fairly good substitute for bacon, even to Ish's taste. The children, of course, liked nothing better. In fact, they made the principal part of their breakfast on the beef-ribs because they had grown up being largely meat-eaters and expecting or wanting little else. Ish and Em, on the contrary, had always been used to having toast or cereal, and now that the rats and weevils had ruined all flour and packaged cereals, they had hominy, from cans, cooked up so as to be something like a breakfast-food. They ate it with canned milk and to sweeten it there was white corn-syrup, because lately they had been unable to find any sugar that rats and weather had spared. The grownups also had coffee. Ish used milk and corn-syrup in his; Em had always preferred hers black and unsweetened anyway. The vacuum-packed coffee, like the grapefruit juice, had lost much of its flavor.

They had settled gradually upon this menu as their standard one for breakfast. Except perhaps for lack of vitamins, it seemed to offer a fairly well balanced meal, and to supply vitamins they had fresh fruit whenever they could find any, though now that blight and insects and rabbits had ruined the orchards, there was little fruit to be had, except for wild strawberries and blackberries, a few wormy apples, and some sour plums from trees gone wild. On the whole, however, Ish found it a satisfying breakfast.

After he had finished, Ish slumped into an easy chair in the living room, picked a cigarette from the humidifier, and lighted it. But the cigarette was not very satisfactory. They were no longer able to find vacuum-packed ones, and the ordinary ones had dried out almost completely in the packages now, no matter how well sealed. You had to keep them in the humidifier a while to get them decently smokable, and then the trouble was that you were likely to get them even too damp. That was what was wrong with this one. And then also, he could not quite enjoy the cigarette because his conscience was bothering him. From the kitchen he could hear uncertain sounds from Em and the twins, and he gathered that they were still having trouble getting water.

"Might as well go over," he thought, "and see George, and get him to clean out that pipe or whatever it is." He got up and went out.

On the way to George's, however, he stopped at Jean's house to pick up Ezra—not that Ezra could fix anything, or that he needed Ezra for any negotiation with George, but just because he always liked to see Ezra. He knocked, and Jean came to the door.

"Ez is not here now," she said. "He's over at Molly's this week." Ish had the funny feeling that he often had when facing the actual practice of bigamy. He did not exactly see how Jean and Molly kept on such good terms, and even helped each other out in all the little emergencies of house-keeping. It was merely another triumph of Ezra's at getting along with human beings and making them get along with each other.

Ish turned to go, and then he recollected, and looked back.

"Oh, Jean," he said. "Say, is your water running all right this morning?"

"Why, no," said Jean. "No, it isn't. There's just a little trickle coming out."

She closed the door, and Ish went down the porch steps and headed for Molly's house. He felt a sudden little chill of apprehension.

He picked up Ezra at Molly's, and discovered that she at least had had no difficulty with water. That, however, might be the result of her house being several feet lower than Jean's so that the water might not yet have run out of the pipes.

They went over to George's house, which stood neat and trim inside its freshly painted white picket-fence. Maurine showed them into the living-room, and told them to sit down while she went to get George, who was puttering around somewhere as usual. Ish sat down in one of the big velour-covered overstuffed chairs. Then, as always, he looked around the living-room with a sense of amazement, mingled with an almost perverted pleasure. The living-room in George and Maurine's house looked exactly the way the living-room of any prosperous carpenter would have looked back in the years before the Great Disaster. There were bridge-lamps with pink shades, and tassels hanging from them. There was a very expensive electric clock, and a magnificent console radio-phonograph, which had four different bands of reception. There was also a television set. On both tables were scarfs carefully crumpled up to give an elegant look to things, and on one table were neat piles of several popular magazines.

The bridge-lamps did not work, because there was no electricity, and the hands of the electric clock always stood at 12:17. The magazines were at least twenty-one years old. There were no programs on the air for the radio to pick up, even if there had been any electric current by which the radio and the phonograph could run.

Yet all these things were the symbols of prosperity. George had been a carpenter in the Old Times. Maurine had then been married to a man who must have been about the social and financial equal of George. Such people always wanted to have fine bridge-lamps and electric clocks and radios and all the rest, and now that it was possible to have all these things, they had merely gone out and got them and put them into the house. Their not working was secondary. In the evening Maurine merely brought in a kerosene lamp, and stood it on the table and they got their light from it instead of from the bridge-lamps, and they had a wind-up phonograph for actual use. It was ridiculous, and also a little pitiful. Yet, when Ish considered the matter, he always remembered Em's first reaction to it.

"Well," she had said, "don't you remember in the Old Times people would have a piano, maybe a grand piano, in the living-room, even though nobody could play it? And they had a set of those books—what did they call them?—the Harvard Classics, though they never read them. And maybe they had a fireplace that never even had a chimney attached to it. All those things were just to show off that you could afford them. They were proof that you had arrived. So I don't see much difference now if George and Maurine want to have their bridge-lamps, even if they can't get any light from them."

They heard George coming in from the back, and then his bulky form filled the doorway. He held a pipe-wrench in one hand, and was wearing his usual costume of carpenter's overalls, rather dirty and well stained with paint smears. He could have used new overalls every day, but apparently he felt more comfortable in ones that were well broken in.

"Hi, George," said Ezra, who usually managed to say the first word.

"G'morning, George," said Ish.

George seemed to chew his tongue for a moment, as if really considering what the situation demanded. Then he said:

"Morning, Ish. . . . Morning, Ezra."

"Say, George," said Ish. "No water over at Jean's or at our place this morning. How about here?"

There was a pause.

"None here, neither," said George.

"Well," said Ish, "what do you make of it?"

George hesitated, working his mouth and lips, as if he were chewing the end of an imaginary cigar. Ish felt a sense of irritation at George's lumpishness. Yet he reflected, controlling himself, that George was a solid person and a very good one to have around.

"Well," he repeated, "what do you make of it, George?"

George made a motion as if to put the imaginary cigar into one corner of his mouth, and then he replied. "Well, if she's off over there too, I guess there's no use looking any more for some block in my pipes around here, way I was. I guess she's broke or clogged up somewheres on the main pipe that comes to all these houses."

Ish caught a sidelong glance from Ezra, and a ghost of a smile on his face as much as to say that after all any of them might have figured that out and that George's pronouncement was not exactly the word of a mental giant.

"I guess you must be right, George," Ish said. "But what are we going to do about it?"

George shifted the imaginary cigar again, and then spoke: "Well, I dunno."

Like Em, George obviously considered this to be out of his province. Give him a dripping faucet or a plugged toilet, and he would be happy taking care of it for you. But he was no mechanic, and certainly no engineer. So, as it always happened, Ish had to take the lead.

"Where did all this water come from anyway?" he asked on the impulse.

The others both were silent. It was curious. Here they had been for twenty-one years merely using water that continued to flow, and yet they had never given any real consideration to where the water came from. It had been a gift from the past, as free as air, like the cans of beans and bottles of catsup that could be had just by walking into a store and taking them from the shelves. Ish indeed had vaguely thought about the matter sometimes, and wondered how long the water would continue to run, and even considered vaguely what they should do to develop another supply. But he had never got round to doing anything. Water which had already run for many years might well continue to run for many years more, and so there was no pressure for action. In all those years there had never been one single day, until this one, when there had been any immediate reason why he should say to himself: "Today I must do something about the water-supply."

So now Ish glanced from George to Ezra, and had no response to his question. George merely stood, shifting weight from one foot to the other. Ezra had a little twinkle in his eyes, to indicate that this was not his department. Ezra knew people. When he had clerked in that liquor-store he must have been good at jollying his customers along and making tie-in sales. But when it came to handling ideas and things, Ish was better than Ezra. Ish saw that he would have to answer his own question.

"This water must come from the old city water-system, somewhere," he said. "Must *have* come, I mean. The old pipes are still there. I think the best thing for us to do would be to go up to the reservoir and see whether there is any water in that."

"O.K.," said Ezra, agreeable as ever. "Maybe, though, we should see what the boys think about it."

"No," said Ish. "They won't know anything about it. If it was a question of hunting or fishing, we could ask the boys. But the boys wouldn't know anything about this."

They went out and began calling the dogs, and getting ready to harness up the teams to the wagons. The reservoir was not more than a mile away, but ever since he had been mauled by the mountain-lion, Ish was not good at long walks, and George was beginning to suffer from the stiffness of old age in his legs. Getting the dogs together and making everything ready always took some time. At moments like these, Ish regretted that horse-taming had come to be a lost art. There were no wild horses left in the immediate vicinity, but he was sure that they could find plenty of them farther east in the open plains country of the San Joaquin Valley. But the trouble really was that all three men had been city-people who were used to driving automobiles; not one of them really knew anything about horse-keeping or horse-managing, and so they had never made the effort to keep horses. Actually, the dogs were in many ways more convenient because they demanded little care, and fed on the less choice cuts of the many cattle which could be killed easily in the surrounding country. But to have horses, you would have had to see that they were kept on good pasture, and protected from wolves and lions. So on the whole, now that automobiles were difficult to keep running, the dog-teams were probably the simplest answer to their modest requirements for transportation, and George

163

was very happy to make the little wagons and keep them in repair. It had taken Ish years to get over the feeling, when he was driving in one of the wagons behind four dogs, that he was acting in some kind of ridiculous pageant, and made a ludicrous spectacle. But, of course, no one else felt the same, and he had gradually come to accept the situation. After all, people had thought it natural to have dogs pull sleds. Why not wagons?

They left the dog-teams at the foot of the final slope, and climbed up along the old path, breaking their way through thick blackberry bushes. They stood at the edge of the reservoir, and looked across its empty expanse. There was a little skim of water in two or three low spots, but the outlet-pipe stood up into the air. They took a long look, and it was Ezra who spoke at last:

"That's that!"

They discussed the possibilities a little, but without much interest or conviction. They were already half way through the rainy season, so that there was little possibility that rain-fall would put water into the reservoir again. They went down the path, picked up the dog-teams, and started home.

As they neared the houses, the dogs began to bark, and the house-dogs barked back at them. Everyone had time to assemble at Ish's house to hear the news. When they had heard it, the older people looked so glum that the children caught the infection, and one little fellow, who was probably too young to understand anything actually, began to cry. In the babble of conversation it soon became evident that no one was much worried about actual thirst, but that the women were greatly concerned that the toilets would no longer work. They did not mind this one day, but it was the thought that they would never work again! It seemed that all life had taken a step backward.

Only Maurine accepted the situation philosophically. "I growed up my first eighteen years on the old farm in South Dakota," she said. "I run out to the outhouse, all kinds of weather, and I never seen a flusher except maybe when we was in town on Saturdays. That was one of the things I liked best when pappy piled us into the old Chevy and we went to California. But I always felt it wouldn't last, and I'd end up, a-runnin' out in all weathers, way I began. Flushers was nice. But it's all over now, and I say, 'Thank the good Lord the weather ain't so cold here as in South Dakota.'"

The older men were more concerned with the problem of

drinking-water. At first, like the confirmed city-dwellers that they had been, they thought in terms of finding where supplies of bottled water had been left in the stores and warehouses. But soon they saw that even in the approaching dry season, there could be no real lack of water. In spite of the long rainless summer, the area was not a desert, and the little streams in the gullies, though no one had ever paid much attention to them, must actually be supplying the water for all the cattle and the other animals which wandered in the region.

Just at this point, a distinction between the older generation and the younger began to show itself. Ish, in spite of having been a geographer, could not have told off-hand where there was a single spring or dependable stream in the neighborhood, although he could still locate positions by names of streets and intersections. The youngsters, on the other hand, could quickly tell him where there was a stream of running water at this season of the year, or where there would be pools of water, or where there were springs. They could not locate these places by reference to streets, but they could tell in general where they were, and could go to them without hesitation. Ish suddenly found himself being instructed by his own son Walt, who assured him that at this season of year there would be running water in a little gully which Ish had scarcely ever noticed because it flowed through under San Lupo Drive by means of a storm drain.

Before long, the original consternation changed to a kind of warm excitement. Some of the youngsters were sent off with the dog-teams and some five-gallon cans to bring back water from the nearest spring. The older ones began to dig holes vigorously, and to set up outhouses.

The enthusiasm lasted for several hours, and resulted in a noticeable amount of work. Steady pick-and-shovel labor, however, was something to which no one was accustomed, and by noon there was widespread complaint about blisters and weariness. When they separated for lunch, Ish suddenly became aware that no one was coming back for work. It was amazing how many important matters seemed to be planned for that afternoon—such as going fishing, and wiping out an ugly-acting bull who might prove dangerous, and shooting a mess of quail for dinner. Besides, by now the enthusiastic youngsters had brought in a supply of water which was plentiful for all immediate needs of drinking and cooking. The difference between having a small water-supply and no

165

water at all was tremendous, psychologically. A five-gallon can sitting in the kitchen-sink took away all sense of strain.

After lunch Ish again relaxed with a cigarette. He was not going to go out and dig by himself. As the story-books told things, this would have been setting a noble example Practically, it would m ke him look rid culous.

Little Joey came, and stood nervously for a moment on his left foot with his right leg bent at the knee, and then reversed.

"What's the matter, Joey?" said Ish.

"Don't we want to go out and work some more?"

"No, Joey. Not th s .fternoon."

Joey continued balancing, letting his gaze wander around the room and then come b ck to his father.

"Go along, Joey," said Ish gently. "Everything's fine! We'll have the lesson at the regular time."

Joey went off, but Ish was touched, even if a little humiliated, by the wordless sympathy which his youngest son was offering. Joey scarcely could understand the larger issues, but his quick mind had sensed that his father w s unh ppy, even though there had been no argument between him and the others. Yes, Joey was the one!

Since that idea had first come to Ish on New Years Day, he had been pressing the lessons, and Joey had been absorbing them eagerly. There was even danger that he might turn out to be a learned pedant. He showed little abi ty t leadership among the other children, and sometimes Ish had begun to doubt.

This small incident just now, for instance! It might show intelligence and thought for the future, and it might show a tendency to escape from contacts with those of his own age, who were better at games than he, and to seek security in the presence of his father, by whom he felt himself appreciated. Ish hoped that the other children did not feel how strongly Joey had become his favorite. It was not right for a father to play favorites, but this situation had arisen suddenly and involuntarily, that New Years Day.

"Oh," he thought, "don't worry about it!" And suddenly he felt as if he were explaining it all to Em. "There on New Years Day, I was suddenly sure that Joey was the Chosen One. Now of course it's all blurred. Maybe this is only the feeling a father gets for a small son. Later we may squ bble, just the way I do with Walt now. Yet, I hope! The other boys were never like this—bright, I mean, lightning-quick at lessons. I don't know. I wish I knew. I'll keep on trying."

Then, as he lit another cigarette, he was suddenly angry. He himself had not been so very bright! He had missed the opportunity. During the years he had been saying, "Something is going to happen!" It had not happened, and they had smiled at him for a gloomy and not-to-be-regarded prophet. Now this morning it *had* happened! It had been a shock! He could remember the scared faces when he and Ezra and George had first come back with the news. Then was the time to have made his I-told-you-so speech. He should have rubbed it in. He should have painted the future with disaster. That might have got something done.

As it was—perhaps he himself had been a little scared at the moment—everyone had made as light as possible of the matter, searched for the easiest makeshifts, and thus dulled the edge of what might have been made to seem a disaster. The tribe had really taken the matter in its stride. Or—the identity of the word popped an old comparison into his mind—it had rolled off, "like water off a duck's back!" Four or five hours later, and everybody had apparently settled again into the old happy-go-lucky life!

"Apparently," yes! But after all, some sense of shock and uncertainty must still be lingering. Some had gone fishing and some had gone quail-shooting, and already he had heard two reports of a shot-gun. But all of these must certainly feel a slight sense of irresponsibility, even of guilt, at having left the more important work. They would come in tired at evening, and then the reaction might go the other way. He would get everybody together for a meeting then. If the iron would not still be red-hot, it might at least have re-warmed a little.

Then he himself incongruously crunched out his second after-lunch cigarette, and settled back to rest, comfortable and unharassed by worry, in the big chair.

"This is comfortable," he thought, "This is . . ."

In those days they will look toward the sea, and cry out suddenly, "A ship, a ship! . . . Yes, a ship certainly! . . . Do you not see the plume of the drifting smoke? . . . Yes, it is making for our harbor!" Then they will be merry with one another and say gaily: "Why were we despondent? . . . It stood to reason that civilization could not be destroyed everywhere! . . . Of course, I always said. . . . In Australia, or South Africa, one of those isolated places—or one of the islands." But there will be no ship, and only a wisp of cloud on the horizon.

Or one will wake from his nap in the afternoon, and look upward quickly. "Surely! . . . I knew it must come! . . . That was the motor of a plane. . . . I could not be mistaken." But it will be only the locust in the bush, and there will be no plane.

Or one will rig batteries to a radio-set, and sit with earphones, fingering the dials. "Yes?" he will say sharply. "Be quiet there, all of you! . . . Surely, surely! . . . Just at 920! . . . Someone talking. I heard distinctly, sounded Spanish. . . . . There again! . . . Now it's faded!" But there will be no words on the air, only the tricks of the far-off thunderstorms.

"Yes, this is comfortable," thought Ish, resting in the big chair. . . . And then suddenly he started! From the street came the noise of two loud reports, and he knew at once that they could be nothing but the backfiring of a large truck! Then, so quickly that he did not seem to take time at all, he was standing on the sidewalk in front of the house, and there was the truck in the middle of the street. It was a fine large truck painted bright red with blue trim, and in large white letters on its sides he saw: U. S. GOVT. A man got out of the truck, and though he had been driving it, he was now (quite understandably) wearing a cut-away coat and a high silk hat. The man said nothing, but Ish of course knew that this was the Governor of California. Ish felt himself filled suddenly with an inexpressible happiness. For again there was security and constituted authority and the strength of the many, instead of only the few in the midst of surrounding darkness, and now he, Ish, was no longer a weak and neglected child wandering alone in the vast unfriendly world. . . .

In that bewilderment of happiness too great to be borne, he awoke. The insides of his hands were moist, and his heart pounded. As he looked around the familiar room, the happiness faded out like a dying light, and in its place succeeded a woe, equally unutterable.

After another moment the woe too faded out as his conscious controls took over. That intense happiness of the dream, so overwhelming that it had awakened him—he knew now that it had sprung again from that often-repeated dream —"wish fulfillment," they used to say. How many times throughout these twenty-one years had he dreamed it in some form or other! Not during the first year or two indeed —his sense of loneliness and insecurity had seemed to grow cumulatively with the years, piling up faster than the birth of new children could counteract it.

Yes, today the symbolism had been very plain. It varied, though usually it was plain enough. He felt a little surprised that it so often took the form of the return of the United States Government. In the Old Times he had never considered himself a flag-waving patriot, and he had not thought often about such things as the benefits of citizenship. But no more, indeed, did a person think of the air he breathed, until it was taken away. A sense of the vastness and solidity of the United States of America must have affected the sub-conscious feelings of its citizens, he reflected, much more than most of them had imagined.

By now he had brought his mind back to his actual world. He stirred in the chair. By the position of the sun he judged that he had slept an hour. Again he heard the distant report of the shotgun from the quail-hunters. He smiled wanly, associating it with the back-firing truck. Anyway—now he would set about getting the others together for the meeting which he had planned for that evening.

Water supplies remained scanty throughout the day, but at least no one suffered from thirst. That evening the older ones, including Robert and Richard who were only sixteen, gathered at Ish's house at his invitation. Ish found no one very much disturbed. It would be a good idea (this seemed to be the general opinion) to try digging a well near one of the houses, rather than to move to some houses nearer a natural water supply. Yes, they probably would have to watch sanitation carefully under the new arrangements and see that the children were instructed in such matters.

There was no presiding officer. Occasionally someone deferred to Ish to settle a point, but this deference, he realized, might be because he held a faintly recognized natural leadership of intellect or even for no better reason than that he was the host. There was no secretary taking a record of what happened. But then, there were no motions made and no votes taken. As always, it was more a social than a parliamentary gathering. Ish listened to the conversation back and forth.

"Come to think of it, though—how's anybody know we'd get water in that well?"

"Can't be a well till you *do* get water."

"Well, that hole-in-the-ground then?"

"You got something there!"

"Maybe this would do better. . . . Run a pipe over to some crick or spring, and hitch it onto our old pipes."

"How about it, George? That sound O.K.?"

". . . .Why, sure . . . I guess so . . . Yeah . . . I guess I could connect up some pipes."

"Trouble would be, though, when everybody wants water at once."

"Have to build a dam—earth-dam would be all right—so's to have a little bitty head behind your water."

"Guess we could do that?"

". . . . Sure . . . Be some work, though."

As the conversation wandered on almost complacently, Ish found himself gradually becoming more disturbed. To him it seemed as if this day had seen a retrograde and perhaps irretrievable step. Suddenly he found himself on his feet, and he was really making a speech to the ten people who were there before him.

"This shouldn't have happened," he said. "We shouldn't have let this creep up on us. Any time in the last six months we should have been able to see that the water in the reservoir was failing, but we never even went to look at it. And here we are, caught suddenly, and shoved back so that we'll perhaps never be able to catch up with things again. We've made too many mistakes. We ought to be teaching the children to read and write. (No one has ever supported me strongly enough in that.) We ought to send an expedition to find out what's happening other places. It's not safe not to know what may be happening just over the hill. We should have more domestic animals—some hens, anyway. We ought to be growing food . . ."

Then, when he was really in full career, someone started clapping, and he stopped for applause, feeling pleased. But everyone was laughing good-naturedly, and again he realized that the applause was ironic.

Through the noise of the hand-clapping he heard one of the boys saying:

"Good old dad! He's said it again!"

And another replied:

"Time for George and the refrigerator!"

Ish joined in the laughter. He was not angry this time, but he was crestfallen at having unconsciously repeated himself and even more at having again failed to make his point. Then Ezra was speaking—good old Ezra who was always quick to cover up anyone's embarrassment!

"Yes, that's the old speech, but maybe there's a new point

170

there. How about that business of sending out an expedition?"

To Ish's surprise a vigorous discussion arose, and in its course he was struck again by the unpredictable quality of people, particularly in a group. He had thrown out the new idea without any special forethought; it had sprung spontaneously from the events of the day—the surprise which had come upon them because they had not taken the pains to explore around the reservoir. He would have considered it the least important of his suggestions, but this was the one that caught the group-imagination. Suddenly everyone was in favor of it, and Ish joined the crowd in vigorous support. It was better, he felt, to do something—anything to break the lethargy.

Soon he felt himself becoming more enthusiastic. His original idea of an "expedition" had merely been that they should explore the country for a hundred miles or so roundabout, but he found that the others had understood him to envisage something much more. Soon, his imagination kindling, he went along with them. In a few minutes everyone was talking of a transcontinental expedition.

"Lewis-and-Clark in reverse!" thought Ish to himself, but he said nothing, knowing that few of those present would know anything about Lewis and Clark.

The talk ran on vigorously:

"Too long for walking!"

"Or dog-teams either!"

"Horses would do better, if we had some!"

"There're sure to be some over in the big valley."

"Take a long time to catch and break them."

As he listened, still another thought crossed Ish's mind. His old dream, the one which had come again that afternoon! How did they really know that the Government of the United States had actually failed? Even if it had, it might have been reconstituted. It would be small and weak, of course, and might not yet have been able to re-establish touch with the West Coast. By their own effort they might make the contact.

Another curious feature was that nearly everyone wanted to go! It was the best evidence you could want as to the way in which people generally—males, at least—were born with itchy feet, always ready to go somewhere else and see new things. The question became one of elimination. Ish was ruled out, scarcely being able to put up a good protest, because of his disability where the mountain-lion had clawed

171

him, far back in the Year of the Lions. George was too old. Ezra, in spite of his vigorous arguments, was disqualified as being the worst shot of them all and generally the least fitted to take care of himself in the open. As for the "boys," everyone except themselves agreed that they should not leave their wives and young families. In the end the decision was for Robert and Richard, youngsters, but well able to take care of themselves. Their mothers, Em and Molly, looked doubtful, but the enthusiasm of the meeting overrode their objections. Robert and Richard were delighted.

The more ticklish questions were really as to the route and the means of transportation. In the last few years no one had used an automobile, and several once-fine cars stood forlorn and ruinous along San Lupo Drive on hopelessly flat tires; the children used them for playhouses. The trouble of keeping automobiles going was more work than pleasure, and the roads in all directions had become so clogged with fallen trees and the bricks of chimneys brought down by the earthquake that there would have been little practical advantage to trying to travel about the city by car, even if you had a workable one. On top of all that, the younger men had never known the fun of driving a car under good conditions, and so had no interest. Finally, where would you go if you had a car? You had no friends to visit in the other part of town, and no movies to go to. To bring cans and bottles home from the grocery stores, the dog-teams did well enough, and they also served for fishing-expeditions to the bay-shore.

Still, the older ones agreed, it might be possible to get an automobile running again, and to drive it for a considerable distance, even on rotten tires, if you kept the speed down below, say, twenty-five miles an hour. And that was really traveling, compared with a dog-team! Fast enough too to take you to New York in a month easily—provided the roads were passable!

That was the other difficult point—the route! Ish was suddenly at home, bringing into play his old knowledge of geography. Everything to the east, across the Sierra Nevada, would be completely blocked by fallen trees and landslides, and the roads to the north would probably be the same. The best chance would certainly be through the more open country toward the south, actually the route by which Ish had gone to New York once long before. The desert roads might still be almost as good as ever. The Colorado

172

River bridges might still be standing or might have fallen. The only way to find out would be to go and see.

His excitement rising, the old road-maps standing out more clearly in his mind, Ish planned the route eastward. Beyond the Colorado the mountains should not be too difficult, and there were no big rivers for a long way—until you came to the Rio Grande at Albuquerque. Beyond there, if you could just get through the Sandia Mountains, you had open plateau country, and farther east there would be more and more choice of roads. (You could still find gasoline in drums; that would be no great problem.) Once on the plains, you should be able to get to the Missouri or the Mississippi, and even across those largest rivers; the high steel bridges should still be in good condition, to judge by the Bay Bridge.

"What an adventure!" he burst out. "I'd give anything to be able to go! You must look everywhere for people—not just one or two, but communities. You must see how other groups are going at solving their problems and getting started again."

Beyond the Mississippi (he resumed planning the route) it would be hard to say. That was natural forest country, and the roads might be badly blocked. On the other hand, fires might have kept the growth down, at least across the old prairie country in Illinois. All they could do would be to go and find out, if they even got that far, and to make decisions then.

By now the candles were getting well burned down. The clock pointed to ten o'clock, although that was only an approximation. (Ish checked time once in a while by watching the shadow at noon, and the big clock in his living-room was considered standard for the community.) But it certainly was a late hour for people who had no electric lights, and so had gradually got around to making more and more use of sunlight.

Suddenly the others were all on their feet and taking leave. When they had gone, Ish and Em sent Robert to bed, and then started to straighten up the living-room.

Ish felt a nostalgic touch. Things had changed so much, and yet sometimes seemed to have changed not at all! This might have been away back in the Old Times, and he instead of Robert might have been the youngster just sent upstairs. He instead of Robert might be the one peeping down through the stairway (as Robert probably was), seeing his father and mother moving about, emptying cigarette trays, shoving cushions back into place, and generally putting the room to rights so that it would not look too devastating when they came down in the morning. It furnished a kind of comfortable little domestic interim which rounded off the evening and let your nerves settle down from the buzz of conversation.

When they had finished, they sat on the davenport for a last cigarette. Ish's mind could not help snapping back to the evening's discussion. Even though things had not turned out as he had at first planned, still he felt that he had carried a main point.

"Communications," he said. "Communications—maybe that's the big thing! Take it anywhere in history. When a nation or a community got isolated all by itself, it went conservative and then retrograded. It got to acting just the way George and Maurine are over there, gathering in all the things out of the past, and freezing just at that point. That sort of thing, maybe, happened to Egypt and China. But then when there's contact with some other civilization, everything loosens up again, and gets going. That's the way it will be with us."

She did not say anything, but he knew from the very fact of her silence, that she did not altogether agree.

"What is it, darling?" he asked.

"Well, you see, I was thinking maybe it wasn't so good for the Indians when they got into communication with the white people, was it? Or how about all my people on the coast of Africa when they got into contact with the slavers?"

"Yes, but maybe that's just my point. How would we like it if some slavers came over the hill some fine morning, and we had never known they were anywhere around before? Wouldn't it have been better if the Indians could have sent some scouts over to Europe, and been ready for white men who came with horses and guns?"

He was pleased that he had countered so cleverly. After all, her argument had merely been for letting things slide and for living in ignorance. That kind of philosophy could never win in the long run.

But all she said was: "Yes, perhaps, perhaps."

"Do you remember?" he went on. "I was saying this a long time ago. We've got to live more creatively, not just as scavengers. Why, I was saying this way back even at the time our first baby was going to be born!"

"Yes, I remember. You've said it a *great* many times! And still some way or other, it seems to be easier just to go on opening cans."

174

"But the end will come some time, and it shouldn't come suddenly the way this stopping of the water has today."

Chapter 3

When he awoke that next morning, Em was gone from the bed. He lay still, relaxed, calmly happy. Then his mind seemed to turn over suddenly and take hold—and there it was, starting to make plans, thinking.

After a minute, a slight sense of irritation came over him. "You think too much!" he said to himself.

Why did not *his* mind, like other people's minds, allow him to rest and be happy without any planning ahead into the future, whether of the next twenty-four hours or of the next twenty-four years? Why could he not lie quiet for as long as sixty seconds? No, something took over with a rush and a whir, and even though his body lay still, his mind turned over and started, and there it was running on, like an idling engine. *Engine?* Well, naturally, today he would think of engines!

But the quiet happiness between sleep and waking had definitely left him, and pure contentment was gone. With a resentful push of his arm he threw back the blankets.

This morning was bright and sunny. Though the air was cool, he went out to the little balcony, and stood there, looking off toward the west. During all these years the trees had everywhere grown taller, but he could still see the mountain-top and much of the Bay with its two great bridges.

The bridges! Yes, the bridges! To him they still were the most poignant reminders of the great past. The children, indeed, as he had often observed, scarcely thought of bridges as anything different from hills or trees; they were just something that was there. But to him, Ish, the bridges stood testifying daily to the power and the glory that had been civilization. So, he thought, some tribesman—Burgund or Saxon—might once have looked at a strong-built, not yet decayed, Roman gateway or triumphal arch.

But, no, that analogy did not hold. The tribesman was sure and content in his own ancient folkways; he was first of the new, confident master of his own world. He, Ish, was more like the last of the old, a surviving Roman—senator or philosopher—spared by barbarian swords and left to brood over an empty and ruinous city, anxious and uncertain, knowing that never again would he meet his friends at the baths or know the deep security that came to a man when he saw a cohort of the Twelfth march down the street. But no, he was not just like the Roman either.

"History repeats itself," he thought, "but always with variations."

Yes—he had had a chance to think a great deal about history! Its repetitions were not those of a stolid child going over and over the multiplication table. History was an artist, maintaining the idea but changing the details, like a composer keeping the same theme but dulling it to a minor or lifting by an octave, now crooning it with violins, now blaring it on trumpets.

As he stood on the little balcony in his pajamas, he felt a light breeze cool on his face. He sniffed it in more deeply, and again it brought to him the realization that even the smell of things had changed. In the Old Times you were not conscious of any characteristic smell to a city, and yet there must have been a complex mingling of smoke and gasoline-fumes and cooking and garbage and even of people. But now there was only a fresh tang to the air, such as he had once associated with country fields and mountain meadows.

But the bridges! His glance came back to them, as if to a light in the darkness. The Golden Gate Bridge he had not visited in many years. Such a journey would mean a very long walk, or even a long pull for a dog-team; it would mean camping out overnight. But he still knew well what the Bay Bridge was like, and even from where he stood he could see it clearly.

He remembered what it had once been—six crowded lanes of swiftly moving cars, the trucks and buses and electric trains rumbling on the lower level. There was, he knew, only one car on the Bridge now—that little empty coupe parked neatly at the curb near this end of the West Bay span. The yellowed certificate of registration had been, when he had last noticed, still fastened to the steering-column—John S. Robertson (or, he could not surely remember, it might have been James T.) of some number on one of the numbered streets in Oakland. Now the tires were flat, and the once-bright green paint had weathered to moss-gray.

On the surface, to the eye, they had changed. The towers that hid their tops in the summer clouds, the mile-long dipping cables, the interlocked massive beams of steel—no longer they cast back the morning sun with a bright sheen of silver-gray. Over them now rested softly the neutral pall of

176

rust, red-brown color of desolation. Only, at the tops of the towers, and along the cables at good spots for perching, the quiet monotone was capped and spotted with the dead-white smears of the droppings of birds.

Yes, through the years the sea-birds had perched there— the gulls and pelicans and cormorants. And on the piers the rats scurried, and fought, and bred and nested, and lived as only rats can—squeaking and fighting, and breeding and nesting, and at low tide feeding on mussels and crabs.

The broad roadway, unused, showed few signs of change —only roughnesses and a few cracks here and there. Where blown dust had settled into cracks and corners, a little grass was growing, and a few hardy weeds, not many.

Within its deeper structure also, the bridge was still intact and unchanged. The superficial rust had done no more than wipe out a small fraction of the safety-factor. At the eastern approach, where salt water during time of storms splashed against the long-unpainted steel supports, corrosion had eaten somewhat deeper. An engineer, if there had been one, would have shaken his head, and ordered the replacement of some members before allowing traffic to resume.

But that was all. In the enduring structure of the bridge, long-dead civilization still defied the attacks of all the powers of air and sea.

Ish roused himself from his trance-like contemplation, and went in to shave. The clean touch of the steel was at once soothing and stimulating. Cheerfully now, happy with the expectation of purposive action, he found himself thinking of the things to be done that day. He would have to see that they started in again with work on the outhouses and the well. He would make more plans about the expedition into the far interior. (President Jefferson giving instructions to Lewis and Clark!) He would have to see what could be done about making a car work once more. Perhaps, he thought happily, this would be the day on which they would take the road again, not only in a car literally, but also figuratively—the road toward the rebirth of civilization.

He finished shaving, but the moment seemed golden. So he lathered again, and started over his face once more. . . . This community now, these thirty-some people who held the seed of the future—they were fair enough individuals, not brilliant by a long way, but sound. The original adults had been better in spite of their shortcomings than you would have expected to get if you had merely reached down into the great bin of humanity in the old United States and taken the first that came by chance. He ran over them ag 'n rapidly in his mind, and ended upon himself. How did he stack up among the others?

Yes, he could remember years ago, in this same house, he had even sat down and listed his qualifications for the new life. Such things, for instance, as having had his appendix out. Well, having no appendix was still an advantage, although actually, no one had been bothered with that kind of trouble. But he had listed other things which now, he realized, had ceased to be advantageous. He had listed, for instance, his quality of being able to get along without other people. That was no longer a virtue. Perhaps, it was even a vice. But he himself had changed also in those years. If he listed his qualities now, they would not be exactly the same ones. He had read widely, and learned much. Even of more importance, he had lived with Em, and had become the father of a family. He had matured, as a man should. He had a stronger will, he realized, than George or Ezra. If the test came, they would yield to him. He, alone, could think into the future.

He disassembled the razor, and threw the blade into the medicine closet, where there were already a lot of blades lying around. He never bothered to use a blade more than once, because there were so many thousands of them available that there seemed no need of economy. And yet this problem of what to do with the old razor blades was still curiously present. He remembered jokes about that, from long ago. Funny how a little thing remained the same after so many big things had changed irrevocably!

After breakfast Ish went over to talk with Ezra. They sat on the steps of the porch. Before long, more people came along, and a little group formed, as always happened when anybody seemed to be having an interesting conversation. There was talk back and forth, and a good deal of easygoing fun-making, with a little horse-play among the younger people. Everybody seemed to agree, in general, that they ought to get to work again, but nobody was in a special hurry to begin. The delay chafed Ish, especially when George in his slow way began again to bring up the old question of the gas-refrigerator.

At last, however, Ezra and the three younger men with an accompanying rag-tag of little boys and girls moved off to begin work. As soon as they had really started, a kind of enthusiasm fell upon them. Everyone, even Ezra, suddenly began to run, trying to see who would be the first one there to start digging. Ish could see Evie running with the rest—although she could not know what was happening—her blond hair streaming wildly behind her. Who got there first, he could not tell, but in a moment dirt started to fly in all directions. He did not know whether to be amused or perturbed. Everyone seemed to be turning serious work into a kind of play, as if unable to distinguish between work and play. That might sound fine, but you could not accomplish much, he thought, without settling down to labor. As it was, the playful enthusiasm would wear out in half an hour, and the dirt would move more slowly; then, children first, older ones soon afterward, everyone would probably drift off to something else.

When once they stalked the deer, or crouched shivering in the mud for the flight of ducks to alight, or risked their lives on the crags after goats, or closed in with shouts upon a wild boar at bay—that was not work, though often the breath came hard and the limbs were heavy. When the women bore and nursed children, or wandered in the woods for berries and mushrooms, or tended the fire at the entrance to the rock-shelter—that was not work either.

So also, when they sang and danced and made love, that was not play. By the singing and dancing the spirits of forest and water might be placated—a serious matter, though still one might enjoy the song and the dance. And as for the making of love, by that—and by the favor of the gods—the tribe was maintained.

So in the first years work and play mingled always, and there were not even the words for one against the other.

But centuries flowed by and then more of them, and many things changed. Man invented civilization, and was inordinately proud of it. But in no way did civilization change life more than by sharpening the line between work and play, and at last that division came to be more important than the old one between sleeping and waking. Sleep came to be thought a kind of relaxation, and "sleeping on the job" a heinous sin. The turning out of the light and the ringing of the alarm-clock were not so much the symbols of man's dual life as were the punching of the time-clock and the blowing of the whistle. Men marched on picket-lines and threw bricks and exploded dynamite to shift an hour from one classification to the other, and other men fought equally hard to prevent them. And always work became more la-

borious and odious, and play grew more artificial and febrile.

Only Ish and George were left standing there by Ezra's porch-steps. Ish knew that George was getting ready to say something. Funny, Ish thought, you wouldn't think anyone could pause *until* he had said something; George paused *before* he said anything.

"Well," said George, and then he paused again. "Well. . . . I guess I better go get some planks . . . so I can wall in the sides . . . after she gets deeper."

"Fine!" said Ish. George at least, Ish knew, would get the work done. He had carried the habit of work over so strongly from the Old Times that he perhaps could never really play.

George went off after his planks, and Ish went to find Dick and Bob, who had been collecting and harnessing the dog-teams.

He found the two boys in front of his own house. Three dog-teams were ready. A rifle-barrel was sticking out from one wagon.

Ish considered for a moment. Was there anything else he should take along? He felt a lack.

"Oh, say, Bob," he said, "run in, please, and get my hammer."

"Aah, why do you want that?"

"Oh, well, nothing in particular, I guess. It might come in handy for breaking a lock."

"You can always use a brick," said Bob, but he went.

Ish used the momentary delay to pick up the rifle and check that the magazine was full. This was pure routine, but Ish himself was the one who insisted on it. There was only a very small chance of meeting a rambunctious bull or a she-bear with cubs, but you took the rifle along for insurance. Ish, at times when he woke up in the night, still remembered very vividly the occasion when the dogs had trailed him.

Bob came back, and at once handed the hammer to his father. As Ish gripped the handle, he felt a strange little sense of security. The familiar weight of the dangling four-pound head brought him comfort. It was the same old hammer that he had picked up long ago, just before the rattle-snake bit him. The handle had been weathered and cracked then, and it still was. He had often thought of choosing a new handle in some hardware store and fitting it to the head. As a matter of fact he could just as well have picked out a whole new tool. Actually, however, he had very little use for the hammer. By tradition he took it along every New Years Day when he cut the numerals into the rock, but that was about its only practical value, and even for that purpose a lighter one might have been better.

So now he stuck the hammer into the wagon by his feet, and felt comfortable.

"All ready?" he called to Dick and Bob, and just then something caught his eye.

A small boy was standing, half-hidden in the bushes, looking out at the wagons. Ish recognized the slight figure.

"Oh, Joey!" he called on impulse. "Want to go along?"

Joey stepped out from the bushes, but hung back.

"I have to help digging the well," he said.

"Oh, never mind, they'll get the well dug without you—or" [he added to himself] "they more likely won't get it dug either with or without you."

Joey took no more urging. Obviously this was what he had really been hoping. He ran to Ish's wagon, and climbed in snugly at his father's feet where he could just find room. He held the hammer in his lap.

Then the dogs were off with a furious rush and an outburst of barking, as they always liked to start out. The two other teams followed, with the excited boys yelling and their dogs barking too. The dogs around the houses barked back. It made a fair imitation of a riot. As always, hunched in the little wagon behind six dogs, Ish felt ridiculous, as if he were acting in some silly pageant.

Once the dogs had started, they stopped wasting breath at barking, and settled to a slower pace. Ish collected his thoughts, and went over his plans.

He made his first stop at what had once been a service station. The door was open. Inside the little office, though it was walled in glass, the sunlight filtered through in subdued yellow. Twenty-one years of fly-specks and blown dust had coated the windows thickly.

He saw the old telephone directory hanging from its hook beside the long-dead telephone. As he took the book and opened it, bits of brittle yellowed paper broke off from the pages and went fluttering to the floor. He found the address of what had once been the local agency for jeeps. Yes, with the roads in the condition they were, a jeep would be the thing.

Half an hour later, when they came to the proper street-corner, Ish looked through the dirty display-window, and his heart jumped with boyish excitement at seeing a jeep actually standing there.

The boys tied up the teams, and the dogs, well-trained, lay down in orderly fashion without snarling the traces.

Dick tried the door; it was locked.

"Here," said Ish, "take the hammer, and smash the lock."

"Oh, here's a brick!" said Dick, and then went running off down the street toward the remains of a chimney that had fallen in the earthquake. Bob went with him.

Ish had a feeling of irritation. What was wrong with those boys? At best a brick was not as good as the hammer for smashing a door in. He ought to know; he had smashed a lot of them.

He stepped three strides across the sidewalk, and swinging with the hammer on the rhythm of his last stride, he sent the door crashing inwards. That would show them! After all, there had been sense in bringing the hammer!

The jeep that was standing there in the display-room had four flat tires, and showed a thick layer of dust, but under the dust the red paint was shiny. The speedometer showed a total of nine miles. Ish shook his head.

"No," he said, "this one's too new. I mean, she *was* too new! One that was better broken in will be easier for us."

In the garage behind the display-room, there were several others. All their tires were flat, extremely flat. One had its hood up and various of its parts were scattered around. It must have been in for a repair-job. Ish passed that one by.

There seemed little to choose between the others. The speedometer of one of them stood at six thousand, and Ish decided to try that one.

The boys looked at him expectantly, and Ish felt that he was putting himself to the test.

"Now remember," he said defensively, "I don't know whether I can get this thing going or not. I don't know whether anyone could—after twenty years and more! I'm not even a mechanic, you know! I was just one of those ordinary fellows who had driven a car quite a lot and could change a tire, or tighten a fan-belt, maybe. Don't expect too much. . . . Well, first, we might try to see if we can move her."

Ish made sure that the brake was off and the gears in neutral.

"All right," he said. "The tires are flat, and the grease is stiff in the wheel-bearings, and for all I know maybe the bearings themselves have gone flat from standing twenty years the same way. But come on and get behind her, and

182

we'll shove. This floor is level anyway. . . . All right, now. All together—shove!"

The car lurched suddenly forward!

The boys were yelping with pleasure and excitement, and their noise set the dogs to barking. You would have thought it was all over, whereas all that had been proved was that the wheels still would turn.

Next Ish put the gear into high, and they shoved again. This was a different story. The car did not budge.

The question was now whether the engine and gears were merely stiff from disuse or whether they were actually rusted tight somewhere.

Looking under the hood, Ish saw that the engine was well smeared with grease, as engines usually were. There was little sign of external rust, but that might show nothing about what had happened inside.

The boys looked at him expectantly, and he thought of expedients. He could try the other car. He could have the boys bring the dog-teams in and hitch them to the car. Then he had another idea.

The jeep which had been in the process of being repaired was only some ten feet behind the one they had chosen to try. If they could shove that one forward out of gear, they might send it against the rear of the other with enough momentum to make something give. Also they might smash something, but that was no matter!

They brought this jeep within two feet of the other, and rested. Then, altogether, they shoved again.

There was a satisfactory bang of metal on metal. Going to look, they found that the first jeep had moved three inches. After that, they could move it with hard pushing, even when it was in gear. Ish began to feel triumphant.

"You see," he said, "once you get something moving it's easier to keep moving!" (Then he wondered whether that principle applied to groups of people, as well as to engines.)

The battery of course was dead, but Ish had faced that problem before. First, however, he gave the boys instructions to drain all oil out of the car and replace it with oil from sealed cans, using the lightest oil available.

Leaving them at work, he went off with a dog-team. In half an hour he was back with a battery. He connected it, and turned the key in the ignition switch, watching the needle on the ammeter. Nothing happened. Perhaps the wiring was gone somewhere.

But he tapped the ammeter, and the long unused needle

suddenly disengaged and went jiggling over to *Discharge.* There was life!

He felt around for the starter-button.

"Well, boys," he said, "here's a real test. . . . Yes, I guess this is the acid test, seeing that that's what we have in the battery!" But the boys grinned blankly, never having heard the expression, and Ish found himself a little disturbed that he had been able to make a pun at such a climax.

He pressed the starter-button. There was a long grunt. Then slowly the engine turned!

After the first turn it moved more easily, and then more easily still. So far, so good!

The gasoline-tank was empty, like most of them these days. Probably their caps were not air-tight, or else the gasoline seeped through the carburetor—Ish did not know.

They found gasoline in a drum, and poured five gallons into the tank. Ish put in fresh spark-plugs. He primed the carburetor, feeling a little proud that he knew enough to do so. He got into the seat, set the choke, snapped the ignition on again, and tramped on the starter-button.

The engine grunted, turned over, turned faster, and then suddenly roared into life.

The boys were shouting. Ish sat triumphantly, nursing the throttle with his foot. He felt a sense of pride in the old achievements of civilization—in all the honest design and honest work of engineers and machinists which had gone into fashioning this engine, fit to work after twenty-some years of idleness.

The engine, however, died suddenly when the gas in the carburetor was exhausted. They primed and ran it again, and still again, and finally the ancient pump brought up gas from the tank, and the engine ran continuously. The problem now—and perhaps the worst of all—was tires.

In the same display-room there was one of the usual tire-racks well raised above the floor. But the tires had been standing upright for so long that they had sagged a little under their own weight, and the rubber, where it had rested against the rack, was badly indented. Such tires, even though they might last for a few miles, held obviously little possibility for a long run. By searching carefully, they finally found some tires which had been resting on their sides, and these seemed to be in better condition, although the rubber was hard and full of little cracks, and gave an impression of being dead.

They found a jack, and raised the first wheel from the

184

ground. Even to get the wheel off was a struggle, for the nuts had begun to rust to the threads.

Bob and Dick were unaccustomed to the use of tools, and little Joey kept getting in the way with his eagerness, and was more hindrance than help. Even in the Old Times Ish had never demounted a tire except once or twice in an emergency, and he had forgotten the tricks, if he had ever known them.

They spent a long time sweating the first tire off the rim. Bob barked a knuckle, and Dick tore a finger-nail half off. Getting the "new" tire onto the rim was even more of a struggle, both because of their clumsiness and because of the tire's own aged stiffness. At last, tired and thoroughly irritated with one another and with the whole job, they finished getting this one tire onto the rim.

Just as they were pausing, triumphant but tired, Ish heard Joey calling to him from across the garage.

"What is it, Joey?" he answered, a little petulantly.

"Come here, Daddy."

"Oh, Joey, I'm tired," he said, but he went, and the two other boys trailed with him.

Joey was pointing at the spare wheel of one of the jeeps.

"Look, Daddy," he said, "why couldn't you use that one?"

All Ish could do was to burst out laughing.

"Well, boys," he said to Dick and Bob, "that's the time we made fools of ourselves!"

The tire on the spare wheel had been suspended in the air all these years, and it was already on a wheel. They had not needed to shift any tires. All they had needed to do was to take this and the other spares, pump them up, and put them on their own jeep. They had done a lot of work for no purpose because they had just barged along and not used their heads.

Then Ish, suddenly recognizing his own stupidity, strangely gained a new pleasure. Joey was the one who had seen!

But by now it was time for lunch.

They had brought along only their spoons and always essential can-openers. Now they went off to the nearest grocery-store.

Like all the others it was a scene of devastation and litter and ruin. A mess! It was depressing to Ish, even horrible, in spite of the many times he had seen its like. The boys, however, thought nothing of it, never having seen a grocery store in any other state. Rats and mice had chewed into all the cartons, and the floor was deep with the remnants of cardboard and paper, mixed with rodent droppings. Even the toilet paper had been chewed, probably for nesting.

But the rodents could do nothing with glass or tin, and so the bottles and cans were undisturbed. They even looked startlingly neat, at first glance, in contrast with the mess elsewhere. When you looked closer, they were not really neat. Droppings were scattered even on these shelves, and many labels had been chewed, probably because of the paste beneath the paper. Also the colors had faded, so that the once bright red tomatoes on the labels were a sickly yellow, and the rosy-cheeked peaches had almost disappeared.

The labels, however, were still readable. At least, Ish and Joey could read them, and the others, though they got stuck on many hard words like *apricots* and *asparagus,* could at least tell what was inside by looking at the pictures. They selected what they wanted.

The boys were quite ready to sit down in the litter and eat. Ish, however, wanted to get outside. So they went and sat on the curb in the sun.

They did not bother with a fire, but ate a cold lunch out of the cans, each to his choice, from a selection of baked beans, sardines, salmon, liver loaf, corned beef, olives, peanuts, and asparagus. Such a meal, Ish knew, ran high in proteins and fats and low in carbohydrates, but there were few carbohydrates that had been canned or bottled, and the few that you could find, like hominy and macaroni, called for heating. For drink, they had tomato juice. They ate a desert of canned nectarines and pineapple.

When they had finished, they wiped off the spoons and can-openers and put them back into their pockets. The half-empty cans they merely left lying. There was so much litter in the street already that something more did not matter.

The boys, Ish was glad to notice, were in a hurry to get back to work at the car. They had apparently begun to feel a little of the intoxication that was likely to come from a mastery over power. He himself was a little tired, and a new idea was shaping in his mind.

"Say, boys," he said, "Bob and Dick, I mean. Do you think you can go back and shift those wheels by yourselves?"

"Sure," said Dick, but he looked puzzled.

"What I mean is—well, Joey is too little to be much use, and I'm tired. It's only four blocks to the City Library from here. Joey can go with me. Want to, Joey?"

Joey was already on his feet with the excitement of the idea. The other boys were happy to get back to the tires.

As they walked toward the Library, Joey ran ahead in his eagerness. It was ridiculous, thought Ish, that he had never taken Joey there before. But all this matter of Joey's reading and intellectual interests had developed very rapidly.

Because of his policy of saving the great University Library as a reserve, Ish had been using this library for his own purposes for many years, and had long since forced the lock on the main entrance. Now he had pushed the heavy door open, and entered proudly with his youngest son.

They stood in the main reading-room, and then wandered through the stacks. Joey said nothing, but Ish could see his eyes drink the titles in as he passed. They came out from the stacks again, and stood in the main lobby by the entrance, looking back. Then Ish had to break the silence.

"Well, what do you think of it?"

"Is it all the books in the world?"

"Oh, no! Just a few of them."

"Can I read them?"

"Yes, you can read any you want to. Always bring them back, and put them in place again, so they won't get lost and scattered."

"What's in the books?"

"Oh, something of pretty near everything. If you read them all, you would know a lot."

"I'll read them all!"

Ish felt a sudden warning shadow fall on the happiness of his mind.

"Oh, no, Joey! You couldn't possibly read them all, and you wouldn't want to. There are dull ones and stupid ones and silly ones, and even bad ones. But I'll help you pick out the good ones. Now, though, we'd better go."

He was actually glad to get Joey away. The stimulation of seeing so many books so suddenly seemed almost more than was good for the frail little boy. Ish was glad that he had not taken him to the University Library. In due time now he could take him there.

As they walked toward the garage, Joey did not run ahead. This time he kept close to his father; he was thinking. Finally he spoke:

"Daddy, what is the name of those things that are on the ceilings of our rooms—like shiny white balls? You said once they used to make light."

"Oh, those are called 'electric lights.' "

"If I read the books, could I make them make light again?"

Ish felt a sudden intoxication of pleasure, and immediately after it a sense of fear. This must not go too fast!

"Well, Joey, I don't know," he said, trying to speak with unconcern. "Maybe you could, maybe not. Things like that take time, and a lot of people working together. You've got to go slow."

Then they walked without speaking. Ish was proud and triumphant that Joey had absorbed so much of his own feeling, and yet he was fearful. Joey was moving even *too* fast. The intellect should not run ahead of the rest of the personality. Joey needed physical strength and emotional solidity. Still, he was going far!

Ish came out of his thoughts to the sound of retching, and saw that Joey was vomiting upon a pile of rubble.

"That lunch!" thought Ish guiltily. "I let him eat too much mixture. He's done this before." Then he realized that the excitement had probably been more a factor than the lunch.

When Joey felt better, and they finally got back to the garage, they found that the boys had finished the work of shifting tires and pumping them up. Ish felt his old curiosity about the car and the expedition rising up again.

He got into the car, and once more started the engine. He nursed it lovingly, and then raced it a little to let it grow warm. Well, the engine was running and the tires were holding, at least temporarily. But there were a lot of questions about clutch and transmission and steering-gear and brakes, besides all those mysterious but vital things which lurked somewhere in the make-up of automobiles and of which he scarcely even knew the names. They had filled the radiator, but the water-circulation might well be clogged somewhere, and even that was enough to render a car of no value. But here we are again worrying about the future!

"All right!" he said. "Let's go!"

The engine was muttering contentedly. He threw the clutch out, and worked the stiff transmission into low gear. He let the clutch in, and the car lurched forward heavily, as if its bearings were almost too stiff to be started again, as if their fine steel balls like the rubber tires, had flattened from long standing in one position. Yet the car moved, and he felt it respond to the stiff steering gear. He pressed upon the brake, and the car came to a stop, having moved only six feet. Yet it had moved, and (of equal importance) it had stopped.

He had a sudden feeling of more than pleasure, reaching to the height of exaltation. It was not all a dream! If, in one day's work a man and three boys could get a jeep to running again, what could not a whole community accomplish in the course of a few years?

The boys unloosed the dogs from one of the wagons to run home by themselves. They hitched the wagon behind one of the others. Then Dick drove one team, and Bob the other. Ish, with Joey beside him, started out bravely.

Fallen buildings had left heaps of debris in the street. The blowing winds had drifted leaves and dust upon the bricks, and the winter rains had washed the whole into semblances of natural banks and hillocks. Grass was growing thickly; on one little mound there was even a fair stand of bushes. Ish steered stiffly hither and thither, finding a way along the debris-clogged streets. He was nearing home when he bumped sharply over a brick and heard a bang as the left rear tire went out. He ended the day driving home on one flat tire, bumping badly, but taking it slowly and making the last grade successfully, a little ahead of the dog-teams. In spite of this final mishap, he felt that he had done well.

He let the jeep roll to a stop in front of the house, and leaned back in triumphant relief. At least he had got it home. Then he pressed the horn-button, and after all these years of silence it responded wonderfully—TOOT-A-TOOT-TOOT!

He expected children, and older people too, to come hurrying from all directions at the unaccustomed sound, but there was no one. Only a sudden barking of dogs sprang up from everywhere. Then the team-dogs joined in the chorus, as they now came up the hill, and the boys joined him. Ish felt a sudden emptiness of fear inside him. Once before, long ago, he had come into a strangely empty town, and blown the horn of his car, and now it was easy enough to think that something might have happened when your whole universe consisted of only some thirty more or less defenseless people. But that was only for a moment.

Then he saw Mary, her baby on her arm, come unconcernedly out of the house down the street, and wave to him. "They've all gone bull-dodging!" she called.

The boys were suddenly excited to join the sport. They loosed the dogs from the carts, and were off, not even asking permission of Ish. Even Joey, now wholly recovered from his illness, rushed off with the others. Ish felt suddenly left alone and neglected, his triumph at restoring transportation gone suddenly sour in his mouth. Only Mary came to look at the jeep. She stared with big enough eyes, but was as untalkative as the baby, who also stared.

Ish got out of the jeep, and stretched. His long legs were

189

cramped from its close quarters, and his bad loin ached from even this small amount of bumping.

"Well," he said with a little pride in his voice, "what do you think of it, Mary?" Mary was his own daughter, but she was not much like either of her parents, and her stolidity often bothered him.

"Good!" she said with a Choctaw-like imperturbability.

Ish felt that there was not much to follow up along that line.

"Where's the bull-dodging?" he asked.

"Down by the big oak tree."

Just then they heard the loud sound of yelling, and Ish knew that someone had made a good maneuver at dodging.

"Well, I guess I might as well go down and see the *national sport,*" he said, though he knew the irony would be wasted.

"Yes," said Mary, and began to stroll back with her baby toward her own house.

Ish went off on the path down the hill, across lots, through what had once been someone's back yard. "National sport!" he was still thinking to himself bitterly, although he realized that the bitterness might be partly because his own triumphant entry had been spoiled. He heard another shout from ahead which indicated that again someone put himself within a few inches of the bull's horns.

Bull-dodging was dangerous, too, although actually no one had ever been killed or even badly hurt. Ish rather disapproved of the whole business, but he did not feel that he was in a position to set himself firmly against it. The boys needed some way to get rid of their energy, and perhaps they even needed something dangerous. By and large, life was perhaps too quiet and too safe these days. Possibly—the image of Mary came to his mind again—too safe and unadventurous life tended to produce stolid people. These days children never had to be warned against crossing the street because of automobiles, and there were dozens of other daily hazards of the old civilization such as the common cold, not to mention atomic bombs, which nobody ever needed to consider. You had the ordinary run of sprains, cuts, and bruises, what you expected among people living largely in the open, and handling tools like hatchets and knives. Once, too, Molly had burned her hands badly, and there had been a near-drowning when a three-year-old had slipped from the pier at fishing.

Now he came into the edge of the little open space on the

side of the hill, fairly level, close to the flat rock where the numerals of the years were incised. It had once been a park. The bull was being played in the center of the grassy spot. It was not a lawn such as you expected in a park. The grass was a foot tall at this time of year, and would have been taller if it had not been eaten down by cattle and elk.

Harry, Molly's fifteen-year-old, was playing the bull, and Ish's own Walt was backing him up—what they called "playing halfback"—a bit of jargon surviving from the Old Times. Although Ish did not consider himself an expert, his first glance was enough to let him know that this particular bull was not very dangerous. He must have been of almost pure Hereford blood, and still had the red coat with the white face and front markings. Nevertheless he showed the cumulative effects of ancestors who for twenty-one years had lived as range cattle, knowing no man-supplied shelter or food and surviving as best they could. The legs were longer; the barrel of the body, slimmer; the horns, bigger. At the moment, there was a pause in the game as the already tiring bull stood uncertain, and Harry was taunting him to charge.

At the edge of the glade among the trees on the uphill side, the spectators were sitting—almost everybody from the community in fact, including Jeanie with her baby. Among the trees they would have no trouble getting out of the road of the bull, if by any chance he should suddenly decide to leave the open ground. There were several dogs to be loosed in an emergency, and Jack sat with a rifle across his knees.

The bull suddenly came to life, and charged ponderously uphill with enough power to have wiped out twenty boys. But Harry dodged neatly, and the bull came to a halting stop, uncertain and confused.

A little girl (she was Jean's Betty) sprang suddenly from the group, and cried out that she wanted to take over. She was a wild, dashing little figure, her skirts tucked up high around her thighs, her long sun-tanned legs flashing back and forth in the sunshine. Harry yielded place to his half-sister. The bull was tired now, and fit for a girl to take over. Betty, aided by Walt, managed to provoke a few charges which were of no difficulty to dodge. And then, suddenly, a little boy cried out loudly, "I'm going in!"

It was Joey. Ish frowned, but he knew that he would not have to exert himself to forbid it. Joey was only nine, and it was strictly against the rules for anyone so young to try bull-dodging, even as halfback. The older boys enforced this discipline quickly enough. They were kindly, but firm.

"Aah, Joey," said Bob from his age of sixteen, "you're not big enough yet. You've got to wait a couple of years, anyway."

"Yeah?" said Joey. "I'm as good as Walt is, anyway."

The way he said it, suggested to Ish that Joey might have been doing a little practice on his own, sneaking off to find some easy-looking bull and playing it for a while, perhaps with the aid Josey, his devoted twin sister. Ish felt a quick coldness pass through him at the thought of any danger to Joey—to Joey, particularly.

After a few more half-hearted protests, however, Joey had to subside.

By this time the bull, fat from the good grazing, was thoroughly tired and winded. He stood, only pawing the grass a little, while the wildly cavorting Betty swarmed around him, and even turned a handspring. But the sport was obviously over, and the spectators began to drift off. The older boys called to Betty and Walter. Suddenly the bull, much to his relief doubtless, was merely left standing alone in the center of the grassy spot.

Back at the houses, Ish went to look at the well, to see how much work had been done during the day. He found that it had been sunk only a foot or so. Shovels and picks were left scattered about. All too obviously, the easygoing nature of the community and the special attraction of bull-dodging had prevented much labor being performed. Ish looked at the shallow hole a little grimly.

Yet during the day enough water had been carted in from a spring to provide plenty for all practical purposes. At dinner the veal roast was extremely good, and the only thing lacking to make a really excellent meal for Ish was that his Napa Gamay had soured a little in the bottle, after standing for better than a quarter-century, if the vintage-date on the label could be trusted.

Chapter 4

He planned that the boys should leave on the fourth day. That was another difference between the Old Times and these now. Then it was all so complicated that anything important had to be worked out a long time ahead; now you just decided on something, and did it. Besides, the season of the year was favorable, and he feared that delay would only permit the enthusiasm for the expedition to seep away.

Throughout the intervening days he kept the boys busy. He practiced them at driving. He took them to the garage again, and picked up some spare parts, such as a fuel-pump and a coil. To the best of his ability he showed them how to change parts, and they practiced a little.

"Or," he said, "you might find it easier, if you have trouble, to stop in at some garage and get another one running, just as we did here. That might be easier than to try patching this one."

But most of all Ish enjoyed the planning of the route. In the service stations he found road maps, yellow and faded. He studied them eagerly, bringing into play his old knowledge of the land, trying to imagine how flood and windstorm and tree-growth would have affected the roads at different points.

"Head south first, for Los Angeles," he concluded finally. "That was a big center of population in the Old Times. There are probably some people left, maybe a community."

On the map he let his glance run southward toward Los Angeles, following the old familiar red lines of the routes.

"Try 99 first," he said. "You can probably get through. If it's blocked in the mountains turn back toward Bakersfield and work across to 466, and try it over Tehachapi Pass. . . ."

He paused, and in the pause he suddenly felt his throat tight, and his eyes brimming. Nostalgia filled him. The names, it *must* have been, that did it! Burbank, Hollywood, Pasadena—once they had been living towns. He had known them. Now coyotes hunted jack-rabbits through their drought-stricken parks and back-lots. Yet all the names still stood out black and plain on the maps.

He swallowed and winked, for he saw the two boys looking at him.

"O.K.," he said briskly. "From Los Angeles, or from Barstow, if you can't make Los Angeles, take 66 east. That was the way I went. Across the desert, things should be easy. But watch your water. If the Colorado River bridge is there, well and good. If not, swing north and try the road across Boulder Dam. The dam will be there still, certainly."

On the maps he showed them how to figure out alternate routes, if they found themselves blocked anywhere. But with the jeep he thought that they could usually get through with no more than the occasional cutting back of a fallen tree, or an hour's work with pick and shovel to make a track across a landslide. After all, even in twenty-one years, the great highways would not be entirely blocked.

"You may have some trouble in Arizona," he went on. "After you get to the mountains, but then. . . ."

"What's Arry—? What is it?—Arry-*zone*-a?"

Bob was asking, and it was a fair enough question. But Ish found himself stumped to answer it. What Arizona once had been—even that was a hard one. Had it been a certain amount of territory, or had it been essentially a corporate entity, an abstraction. Even so, how could he explain in a few words what a "state" had been? Much less, how could he explain what Arizona now was?

"Oh," he said finally, "Arizona—that was just a name for that part over there beyond the river." Then he had an inspiration, "See, on the map it's this part inside the yellow line."

"Yes," said Bob, "I suppose they had a fence around it?"

"Well, I doubt whether they had."

"That's right. They wouldn't have needed a fence where the river was."

(Let it pass, thought Ish. He thinks Arizona is like an old fenced-in backyard, only bigger.)

After that, however, he stopped referring to states, and mentioned cities. The boys knew what a city was, that is, it was a lot of littered streets and weather-beaten buildings. Of course, since they themselves lived in a city, they could easily imagine another city and another community like their own.

He routed them through Denver, Omaha, and Chicago, wanting to see what would have happened in the great cities. By that time it would be spring. Beyond that, he told them to try for Washington and New York, by the route that seemed the most passable.

"The Pennsylvania Turnpike may still be the best way to get across the mountains. It will be hard to block a four-lane highway like that, and even the tunnels should still be open."

For the return route he left them to their own choice; by that time they would know more about conditions than he did. He suggested, however, that they swing far to the south, since on account of the cold winters there would probably have been a drift of population toward the Gulf Coast.

They drove the jeep every day, and thus, by the process of elimination through blow-outs, they got tires which seemed likely to stand up under some wear.

On the fourth day they left, the back of the jeep jammed

with an extra battery, tires, and other equipment; the boys themselves, half-wild with the excitement of the prospect; their mothers, close to tears at the thought of so long a separation; Ish himself, nervous with the desire to go along.

The boundaries, like the fences, drew lines that were hard and uncompromising. They too were man-made, abstractions dominating reality. Where you crossed by the highway, on a line, the road-surface changed. It was smooth in Delaware, but when you went into Maryland, you felt a change in vibration, and all at once the tires hummed differently. "State line," the sign read. "Entering Nebraska. Speed limit 60 M. P. H." So even right and wrong altered with the sharp snap of a discontinuity, and you stepped harder on the throttle.

At the national boundary the flags showed different colors, though the same breeze blew them. You stopped for customs and immigration, and were suddenly a stranger, unfamiliar. "Look," you said, "that policeman has a different uniform!" You got new money, and even for picture post-cards the stamps had to have another face on them. "Better drive extra carefully," you said. "Wouldn't be good to get arrested over here." That was a funny business! You stepped across a line you couldn't see, and then you were one of those queer people—a foreigner!

But boundaries fade even faster than fences. Imaginary lines need no rust to efface them. Then there will be no quick shifts, and adjustments, and perhaps it will be easier on the mind. They will say as in the beginning: "About where the oaks start to get thin, and the pines take over." They will say: "Over across there—can't tell exactly—in the foothills where it gets drier and you start seeing sage-brush."

After the boys had left, there seemed to be a settling down into another one of those calm and happy periods which had led them to name one certain time the Good Year. Day after day things drifted, week after week. The rains held on late—hard showers, quickly clearing afterwards, with fine blue weather, so that the far-off towers of the Golden Gate Bridge stood out clean-etched and still majestic against the western sky.

In the mornings, Ish usually managed to herd enough of them together to get some work done on the well. Their first shaft hit bed rock before water, for on the slope of the hill the soil was thin. But they managed to take the second shaft

195

down until they struck a good flow. They walled the well in with planking, and covered it, and rigged a hand-pump. By this time, they had all become accustomed to using the outhouses, and the thought of the labor involved to make the toilets work again by means of pipes and tanks and hand-pumping seemed more than was worthwhile. And so they put it off.

The fishing was good now. Everyone wanted to go fishing, and other matters seemed to take second place.

In the evenings, they often gathered together, and sang songs to the accompaniment of Ish's accordion. He sometimes suggested that they should try singing parts. When they did, old George carried a good resonant bass, and the others caught on to the idea, but no one seemed very much interested in this sophistication.

No, Ish decided again as he had decided long before, they were not a very musical group. Years before, he had tried bringing home records of symphonies and playing them on the wind-up phonograph. Such rendition of course was not very good; even so, you could follow the themes. But he never got the children interested. At some melodic passage they might leave off their own playing or wood-carving and look up, listening with pleasure for a moment. As soon, however, as the development became a little complicated, the children went back to their own play. Well, what could you expect of merely a few average people and their descendents? (No, a little better than average, he insisted—but possibly not in musical appreciation.) In the Old Times one American in a hundred might have had a deep or real appreciation of Beethoven, and those few were probably just among those more sophisticated and intense people who, like the more highly bred dogs, had apparently been less able to survive the shock of the Great Disaster.

As an experiment, he also tried jazz records. At the loud blare of the saxophones, the children again left off their own enterprises, but again the interest had been momentary. *Le jazz hot!* It too, with all its involuted rhythms, had been a sophistication; it appealed, not to a simple and primitive mind, but to one that was highly developed and specialized, at least along that particular line. You might as well expect the children to appreciate Picasso or Joyce.

In fact—and this was something that encouraged him—the younger generation showed little interest in listening to the phonograph at all; they preferred to do their own singing.

196

He took this as a good sign: that they would rather participate than listen, rather be actors than audience.

They failed, however, to take the next step and compose tunes and words of their own. Ish himself occasionally tried making up a verse with topical references, but either he had no knack for it or else his efforts met with unconscious resistance as being a violation of tradition.

So they sang in unison against the background of the standardized chords and bumping bass of the accordion. The simpler tunes, he observed, they liked the best. The words seemed to make little difference. They sang "Carry me back to old Virginny" although they had no idea what "Virginny" was or who was asking to be carried back. They sang "Halleluiah, I'm a bum!" without caring what a bum was. They sang plaintively of Barbara Allen although none of them had even known of unrequited love.

Often, in those weeks, Ish thought of the two boys in the jeep. Perhaps the children would call for "Home on the Range," and as his left hand shifted to the G-buttons, he would have a sudden thought, and a pang with it. Just now Bob and Dick might be somewhere far out in the old range country.

Playing mechanically, he would wonder. Were the deer and the antelope playing there now? Or was it cattle? Or had the buffalo come back?

More often, however, thoughts of the boys came to him in the dark hours of the night when some dream, caused by his very anxiety, brought him out of sleep in sudden terror to lie nervously considering possibilities.

How could he ever have let them try it? He thought of all the dangers of flood and storm. And the car! You could never trust young fellows with a car, and even though there was no danger from traffic, they might run off the road. There would be many bad places. The boys would take chances.

There would be mountain-lions and bears and bad-tempered bulls. Bulls were worst of all, because they never seemed to have lost a certain contempt for men, sprung perhaps from age-old familiarity.

No—more likely, the car would break down. Then they would be marooned, hundreds or even thousands of miles away!

But what raised the worst shivers in Ish at such moments in the night was the thought of *men!* What people might the boys encounter? What strange communities—warped and perverted by curious circumstances, unrestrained by any flywheel of tradition! There might be communities with universal and death-dealing hostility to the stranger. Outlandish religious rites might have developed—human sacrifice, cannibalism! Perhaps, like Odysseus himself, the two youngsters would encounter lotus-eaters and sirens and unspeakable Laestrygonians.

This community of their own, here on the hillside, might be stodgy and dull and uncreative, but it had at least preserved the human decencies. That was no guarantee that other communities had done the same.

But in the morning light, all these bug-a-boos of the darkness lost their reality. Then he thought of the two boys as enjoying themselves, stimulated by new scenes, perhaps by new people. Even if the car should break down and they were unable to start another one, still they could walk back over the same road they had driven. There would be no lack of food. Twenty miles a day, at least a hundred a week—even if they had to walk a thousand miles, they should be home before fall. Actually, if they kept a car running, they should be home a great deal sooner. When he thought of it, he could scarcely contain himself for excitement at the thought of all the news they would bring.

So the weeks passed, and the rains were over. The grass on the hills lost its fresh greenness, and then seeded and turned brown. In the mornings the low summer clouds hung so close that the towers of the bridges sometimes reached up into them.

Chapter 5

As time passed, Ish stopped thinking, and dreaming, so much about the two boys. Their being gone so long seemed to show that they had traveled far. It was barely time to expect their return from a transcontinental journey, and certainly not time to begin worrying over their failure to return. Other thoughts, and worries, occupied his mind.

He had reorganized the school, and was back at what he felt to be his essential work of teaching the young ones to read and write and work a little arithmetic, and thus to maintain for The Tribe some hold on the basic skills of civilization. But the young ones, ungratefully, fidgeted on their chairs, and looked restlessly toward the windows, and he knew that they wanted to be outside, running on the hillside, playing at bull-dodging, fishing. He tried various lures, attempting the techniques which in the old days he remembered had been called "progressive education."

Wood-carving! Curiously to Ish, wood-carving had become the chief means of artistic expression. Obviously this was a heritage from old George. Perhaps, stupid as he was, George had unconsciously managed to pass along to the children his love of wood-working. Ish himself had no interest in it, and no knack.

No matter what it had come from! Could he, Ish, as a teacher, make use of this hobby to stimulate an intellectual interest?

So he began to teach them geometry, and to show them how with compass and ruler they could lay out designs on the surface of the wood.

The bait took, and soon with great enthusiasm everyone talked of circles and triangles and hexagons, and had laid out a geometrical design, and was eagerly carving. Ish himself became interested. He felt the fascination of the work as the mellow sugar-pine block—aged for almost a quarter century—began to peel off from his knife-edge.

But even before the first geometrical designs were executed, the children were losing interest. To draw your knife along the edge of a steel square and thus get a straight line—that was easy and uninteresting. To follow the outline of a circle—that was difficult enough, but was mechanical and dull. And the designs when finished, even Ish had to admit, looked like bad imitations of old-time machine-work.

The children reverted to free-running handwork, often improvising as they went. It was more fun to do, and in the end it looked better also.

Best of them all at carving was Walt, although he could never read, except in a halting stammer. But when it came to doing a frieze of cattle on the smooth surface of a plank, Walt carved with sure touch. He did not have to measure things out ahead, or to use the tricks of geometry. If his row of three cows did not quite fill up the space, he merely carved a calf at the end of the line to take up what was left. And yet, when he had finished, it all looked as if he had planned it from the beginning. He could work in low relief, or in three-quarters, or even sometimes in the full round. The children admired his work, and him, tremendously.

So, Ish realized, he had failed in what had seemed his shrewdly planned attempt at using a hobby to stimulate an intellectual interest, and again he was left with little Joey. Joey had no talent at wood-carving, but of them all, only he

199

had kindled at those eternal truths of line and angle which had survived even the Great Disaster. Once Ish found him cutting different-shaped triangles from pieces of paper and then recutting the ends from each triangle and placing them together to form a straight line.

"Does it always work?" Ish asked.

"Yes, always. You said it always would."

"Why do you do it then?"

Joey could not explain why he did it, but Ish shared enough of the workings of his son's mind to be sure that Joey must be really paying a kind of homage to universal and unchangable truth. He was as much as saying to the powers of chance and change: "Here, make this one come out different, if you can!" And when those dark powers could not prevail, it was again a triumph for intellect.

So Ish was left with little Joey—spiritually, and sometimes also physically. For, when the other children ran out of school whooping loudly, Joey often made a point of not going, but of sitting with some biggish-looking book, and even seeming a little superior in his attitude.

Physically, the other boys were stalwart young giants, and Joey lagged at all sports and outdoor adventures. His head seemed big for his body, though that might be, Ish realized, because you thought of it as containing an undue amount of knowledge. His eyes also were big for his head, and exceptionally quick and alert. Alone among the children, he suffered from sick spells, with an upset stomach. Ish wondered whether these attacks were truly physical or sprang from some emotional disturbance, but since there was no chance of sending Joey to either a doctor or a psychiatrist, the actuality would never be known. In any case, Joey remained underweight, and often came home exhausted after playing with the other boys.

"It's not good!" said Ish to Em.

"No," said Em, "but still, you like him interested in books and geometry. That's merely the other side of his not being as strong as the others."

"Yes, I suppose so. He has to find his satisfaction somewhere. But still I wish he would get to be stronger."

"You wouldn't really have him different, would you?"

And, as she went away about some other matter, Ish thought that again she had been right.

"No," he thought, "we have plenty of galumphing young huskies. Still I wish he were stronger. Yet, even if he is something of a weakling, and even a freak and a pedant,

200

we must have one person like that, to carry on intellectually."

And so, of all his children, his heart went out to Joey. He saw in Joey the hope of the future, and he talked often with him, and taught him many things.

Thus the school dragged along through those weeks while they waited for Dick and Bob to return. Even Ish could hardly use a more optimistic word than "dragged." Altogether there were eleven children whom he taught, or tried to teach, that summer.

He held school in the living-room, and the eleven children came there from all the houses. The session lasted only from nine to twelve, with a long recess. Ish realized that he must ride them with a light rein.

He taught them arithmetic, now that he had failed in his attempt to sugar-coat the pill of geometry. He tried to make practical applications of arithmetic, and found it surprisingly difficult. "If A builds 30 feet of fence . . ." the old book read. But nobody built any fences now, and he found himself having to start by explaining why people once had built them —a much more complicated matter to explain than you would think, until you tried it. He thought of emulating the progressive school again by setting up a shop where the pupils could buy and sell and keep accounts. But this was not practical, for there were no more store-keepers now. He would have had to start with a whole exposition of ancient economics.

Then he tried valiantly to present to them some of the wonders of pure number. For himself, indeed, he was successful, and the more he tried to tell it to the children the more he himself felt the basic quality of mathematics to all that had been civilization. At the same time, he felt more and more, even though he could not express it, all the wonder that lay in the relations of one number to another. "Why is it," he would think, "that two and two eternally make four— and not, sometimes, five? *That* has not changed! Even though wild bulls bellow and fight in Union Square!" Thus too, he played games with triangular numbers, showing the way they built up one on top of the other. But except for Joey the children showed no sense of wonder, and Ish saw their sidelong looks toward the windows when he tried to impress them with it all.

He attempted geography also. This, his own subject, he should at least be well qualified to teach. The boys enjoyed drawing maps of the near-by country. But neither boys nor girls were interested in the geography of the world as a whole. Who could blame them? Perhaps when Dick and Bob came back in the jeep, there might be more interest. But just now the children's horizon was limited to the few miles round about. What to them was the shape of Europe with all of its peninsulas? What to them, the islands of the sea?

He made a somewhat better case for history, although what he taught was more anthropology than history. He told them of all the growth of man, that struggling creature, who had gradually learned this, learned that, learned to develop himself here, and restrain himself there, and through infinite error and trouble and foolishness and cruelty, at last had achieved so spectacularly before the end came upon him. They were mildly interested.

Yet most of his time he spent at teaching them to read and write, because reading he felt was the key to everything else and writing was its counterpart. But only Joey took naturally to reading, and romped ahead. He knew the meanings of words, and grasped even the meaning of books.

Civ-vil-eye-za-shun! That is what Uncle Ish talks about. There are lots of quail by the stream today. Two-and-six? I know that! Why should I say it to him? Two-and-nine? That is hard. It is more than my fingers. It is the same as "a lot." Uncle George is more fun than Uncle Ish. He can show you how to carve. My daddy is more fun still. He says funny things. But Uncle Ish keeps the hammer. It is there now on the mantel. Joey makes up stories about the hammer, I think. You can't be sure. I would like to pinch Betty now, but Uncle Ish would not like it. Uncle Ish knows most of anybody. Sometimes I am afraid. If I could tell him what seven and nine is, maybe we would have civ-vil-eye-za-shun, and I could see the pictures that act like people. Daddy used to see them. It would be fun. Eight-and-eight. Joey knows right off. Joey is no good at finding quail nests. Soon we can go now.

In spite of recurrent discouragement, Ish still kept trying, and he always fastened quickly on any opportunity that the children themselves seemed to offer him.

One afternoon the older boys had gone on a longer expedition than usual, and the next morning they brought with them to school some native walnuts. They had not seen such nuts before, and were curious. Ish quickly decided to crack some of the nuts, and thus perhaps give a little lesson in biology. It would be taking advantage of the children's own

202

curiosity, and would be following up something that they themselves had initiated.

He sent Walt outside for two stones to use in cracking the hard shells. Walt returned with two half bricks—bricks and stones not being distinguished in his vocabulary.

Ish ignored that detail, but he found that trying to break the hard shells with a brick was more likely to result in a smashed finger than a smashed nut. He cast around for something better to use, and his eyes fell upon his hammer. It was standing, as usual, on the mantelpiece.

"Go get the hammer for me, Chris!" he said, pointing, to the little boy who was nearest it.

Usually Chris was only too glad to spring up from his seat, and do something active. But now a strange thing occurred. Chris glanced this way and that, at Walt and at Weston, who were next to him. He looked embarrassed, or alarmed.

"Go get the hammer, Chris!" Ish repeated, thinking that possibly Chris had been day-dreaming, and had merely heard his name without noting the words that went before.

"I—I don't want to!" said Chris, hesitantly. Chris was eight years old, and not given to being a cry-baby, and yet Ish could see that Chris was, for some reason, close to tears. He dropped the matter with Chris. "Bring me the hammer, one of you others," he said. Weston looked at Walt, and Barbara and Betty, the sisters, looked at each other too. Those four were the oldest. All four of them looked back and forth, and did not make a move to rise. Naturally, the little ones did nothing. But Ish could see all the children glancing furtively at each other.

Although Ish was wholly puzzled, he saw no reason to make an issue of the matter, and he was just about to get the hammer himself when something else strange began to happen.

Joey rose. He walked over toward the mantelpiece. All the childrens' eyes followed him. The room, Ish realized, was deathly quiet. Joey stood at the mantelpiece. He reached out his hand, and took the hammer. There was a strange little cry from one of the smaller girls. In the hush that followed, Joey walked back from the mantelpiece, and gave the hammer to Ish. Joey went back to where he had been sitting.

The room was still, and the children were looking at Joey. Joey sat down, and Ish broke the silence by pounding on a nut with the hammer. At that noise the tension, whatever it was, seemed to break.

Only after it had come to noon and he had dismissed school did Ish have time to think the matter over and come, with a start, to the conclusion that it had been a case of pure superstition. The hammer—all the children associated it vaguely with something strange and mystical in the far past! It was used on state occasions; it stood on the mantelpiece by itself. Generally speaking, no one touched it except Ish. Even Bob, Ish now remembered, had handled it with reluctance on that occasion when they had started out with the dog-teams. The children had come to think it an implement of power, dangerous for any of them to touch. He could see how such an idea might have begun half seriously as a game and in a few years have come to be taken seriously. And as for Joey, again he realized that Joey was the one who stood out from the crowd. Perhaps Joey had not rationally figured out that Ish's hammer was only like any other hammer. Perhaps, he had merely let his superstition work at a higher level, and assumed that he had something in common with his father, such as was shown by his reading, so that he, as the High Priest's child, the Son of the Blessing, might touch the relics which would blast the others. Possibly even, he might be capable of it, Joey had helped build up the superstition in the others in order to build up his own importance. It could not be much work, Ish decided, to overcome this superstition.

Yet that same afternoon he began to have doubts. On the sidewalk in front of the house some children were playing. As they played, they were jumping from one block of the sidewalk to another and crying out that old rhyme:

> Step on a crack,
> Break your mother's back!

Ish had heard children singing it often in the Old Times. It meant nothing then, just a little childish rhyme. Children, as they got older, had always learned that such things were merely childish. But now, he thought, what would there be to teach the children that such things were mere superstition? Here was a society with almost no stored-up tradition, and apparently a society that was not going to develop its traditions greatly by reading.

He sat in his easy-chair in the living-room, and heard the children, outside, playing and shouting their rhyme. As the

204

smoke of his cigarette curled up, he remembered more and more disturbing evidences of superstition. Ezra carried his pocket piece, the old Victorian penny, and doubtless the children looked on that much as they looked on the hammer. Molly was a confirmed rapper on wood; Ish was disturbed when, now that he considered, he remembered the children also rapping on wood. Would they ever learn that that was just the thing that someone did to make himself feel more comfortable, although it had no real meaning?

Yes, he reluctantly concluded, this matter of the children's beliefs was extremely serious. In the Old Times the beliefs held by the children of any family or small group of families might be momentous enough, but still those children on growing up would come into contact with other beliefs and make adjustments. Besides, there had been a great, even overwhelming, mass of tradition—the tradition of Christianity, or of Western civilization, or of Indo-European folkways, or of Anglo-American culture. Call it what you wished, it was still so tremendous that you might say it was omnipotent, for good or bad absorbing the individual.

But now their little community had lost much of the tradition. Part of it had been lost because no seven survivors (Evie did not count) could preserve and transmit all of it. Part had been lost because for so long a time there had been no big children to pass on the tradition to the small ones. The oldest of the younger generation had been taught games by their parents, not by older comrades. The community should therefore be plastic to an unprecedented degree. This was an opportunity, but also a responsibility—and a danger.

It would be a danger—and he shuddered at the thought— if any evil force, such as a demagogue, should begin to work.

To be sure, he recollected wryly, he had not found the children particularly plastic as regards learning to read! Yet that might be only that a stronger force—the whole environment—was already working against his efforts.

But take now again this matter of superstition. Perhaps this had all grown up because, as it happened, there was no one in The Tribe who was creatively religious. Perhaps there was some kind of vacuum in the childish mind, and it had to be filled up with supernatural beliefs. Perhaps all this represented some kind of subconscious straining toward an explanation of the basis of life itself.

Years ago they had organized those church services, and then discontinued them as meaningless. That discontinuance might have been a mistake.

Now, more certainly even than before, he knew that he had the opportunity to be the founder of a religion for a whole people. What he told the children in school, they would probably believe. He could insure their memory of it by mere insistence and iteration. He could tell them that the Lord God created the world in six days, and found it good. They would believe. He could tell them a local Indian legend that the world was the work of Old Man Coyote. They would believe.

Yet what could he really tell them in honesty? He might tell them any one of half a dozen theories of cosmogony which he remembered from his old studies. Probably they would believe these too, although their complications did not make for quite as good a story as one of those others.

Actually, no matter what he said, it might easily be twisted and made into some kind of religion. Again, as years before, he revolted from the idea, for he treasured the honesty of his own skepticism.

"It's better," he thought in words, remembering some bit of reading, "to have no opinion of God at all than to have one that is unworthy of Him."

He lighted another cigarette, and settled back into the chair again . . . Yet this matter of the vacuum! It worried him. Unless it could be positively filled, his own descendants at the third or fourth generation might be practicing primitive rites of incantation, trembling in terror of witchcraft, and experimenting with riualistic cannibalism. They might believe in voodoo, in shamanism, in taboo . . . !

He started, almost guiltily. Yes, already there were beliefs in The Tribe which approached the intensity of taboo, and he himself was inadvertently their chief author.

There was the matter of Evie, for instance. He and Em and Ezra had talked it over long ago. They wanted no half-witted children of Evie's—to be a care and drag. So they had made her, at least for the boys, a kind of untouchable. Evie, with her blond hair and startled blue eyes, was perhaps the best-looking girl of them all. But Ish was sure that none of the boys had even seriously considered her. Probably they had no specific idea that anything would happen to them if they did, but such action was merely outside their scope of imagination. The prohibition was stronger than law. Such a one you could only call taboo.

Again, there was all the allied matter of fidelity. Always fearing the disruption of quarrels arising from jealousy, the older men had not so much taught marital fidelity as assumed it. Young people had been married at the earliest possible moment. Ezra's bigamy, having always been present, was not questioned. Although Ish did not doubt the utility of this practice for their particular situation, still its acceptance as a matter of faith rather than of reason seemed to come close to taboo. The first violation—and there would surely be one—might bring a tremendous shock.

A third possible example of taboo, though a minor matter perhaps, was the turning of the University Library into a sacrosanct building. Once, when the oldest boys were youngsters, Ish had gone with them on a long walk which had taken them to the campus. While he was napping, two of them had worked loose a board which, long before, he had nailed across the broken window; they had gone into the stacks, and started throwing books onto the floor. Horror-stricken with a sense of the violation of that great treasure house, Ish had followed them. He had been ashamed of himself later, but at the moment he had been outraged beyond reason and had beaten the boys. The very unreasoning quality of his rage and horror must have impressed them much more than the beating. They had certainly passed this impression on to the younger children. The Library had been safe, and Ish had been pleased. But this might also be called an example of taboo, and now he wondered.

There was a fourth one too, of course—but this brought him back to where he had started. He got out of the chair and went to the mantelpiece.

The hammer was there, as he himself had replaced it. He had not asked any child to take it back, not even Joey. He had preferred not to raise the issue again.

There it stood, balanced on its four-pound head of dull, rust-pitted steel. The hammer had been with him a long time. He had found it just before the rattlesnake had struck him, and so it might be called his oldest friend. It had been with him longer than Em or Ezra.

He looked at it curiously, considering it carefully and self-consciously. The handle was actually in bad shape. It had weathered from lying so long in the open, and even before the hammer had been left to lie, the handle had apparently been banged accidentally against a rock and cracked a little. What was the wood? He really did not know. Ash or hickory, he supposed. Hickory, most likely.

The simplest thing, he concluded impetuously, would be to get rid of the hammer. He could throw it into the Bay.

No, he reconsidered, that would be merely treating the

symptom, not the disease. With the hammer removed, the children's tendency to superstition would still remain, and would merely fix upon something else, and perhaps take some more sinister form.

He thought of destroying the hammer, as a symbolical lesson to the children that it had no strength in itself But he remembered that he did not actually have the power to destroy it. The handle he could burn easily, but the steel head was next to indestructible by any means at his disposal. Even if he found a carboy of acid and dissolved the steel in it, to go to so much trouble would make the children think that the hammer must really have possessed some deep-seated power.

So he looked at the hammer with new interest, as something which was coming to have a life and power of its own. Yes, it had the qualities which went toward the making of a good symbol—permanence, entity, strength. Its phallic suggestion was obvious. Curiously, as he thought now, he had never named it, though men were likely to give names to weapons, which also were symbols of power—Madelon and Brown Bess and Killdeer and Excalibur. Hammers had been signs of godhead before this; Thor had carried a hammer, probably other gods too. Among kings there had been that old Frankish one who drove back the Saracens—Martel, they had called him, Charles of the Hammer! *Ish of the Hammer!*

Thus, for one reason or another, when the children reassembled in school the next morning, Ish said nothing about superstition. It would be better, he told himself, to bide his time a little, to observe more closely for a day or two, or a week. Most of all, he wished to learn more about Joey.

As the result of this observation, over a period of some weeks, Ish came to the conclusion, somewhat reluctantly, that Joey had many of the qualities of a first-class brat. He had passed his tenth birthday during the summer. His precocity was sometimes painful; he was, in the old phrase, "too big for his britches." In age, he was half way between Walt and Weston, who were twelve, and Chris, who was eight. But Joey's precocity put him naturally into the company of the two older boys, and he and the younger one had nothing in common. This must be hard on Joey, Ish concluded, because he was always overreaching to attain the physical power of boys two years older and naturally stronger as well. Josey, his own twin, he neglected also, for he was at a stage when boys had no interest in girls, and Josey, besides, was not nearly so bright as he.

There was thus, Ish saw, always a kind of strain about what Joey was doing or trying to do. Again and again Ish thought of that little incident in which the other children had been afraid to pick up the hammer, but had acquiesced in Joey's doing something that they themselves did not dare to do. Obviously, in their minds, there was some kind of power inherent in Joey. Ish thought far back to the times of his studies, and he remembered the wide-spread belief that certain members of a tribe had a special power within them. *Mana*, the anthropologists had called it. Perhaps the children believed that Joey had *mana;* possibly Joey himself believed it.

Yet, though Ish recognized Joey's limitations and disabilities and bad qualities, still he kept his thoughts centered more on Joey than on any of the others. Joey held the hope for the future. Only by the power of intelligence, Ish believed firmly, had mankind ever risen to civilization, and only by further exercise of that same power, would mankind ever rise again. And Joey possessed intelligence. Possibly also he possessed that other power. *Mana* might be a fallacy of simple minds, but even the most civilized peoples had realized that certain individuals carried within them some strange power that went for leadership. Had anyone ever explained why certain men became leaders, and others, though they seemed better qualified, did not?

How much of all this did Joey realize? Many times Ish asked himself the question, but he could not as yet answer it. Yet more and more, as the summer progressed, he felt that in Joey lay the hope of the future.

All mysticism aside! All idea of *mana* discounted! Still, only Joey could keep the light burning through this dark time. Only he could store up and transmit the great tradition of mankind!

But mere acquisition of knowledge was not all in which Joey excelled. Even though he was only ten, he was beginning to branch out for himself, to experiment, to discover things on his own. Indeed, that was the way he had really taught himself to read in the beginning. To be sure, all this development was still at a childish level.

There was that matter of the jig-saw puzzles, for instance. The children had developed a sudden craze for the puzzles, and had set about rifling some of the stores. Ish had watched them at their play, and at first Joey had not been as good as the others. He seemed to lack some basic spatial sense. Sometimes he tried to join pieces which obviously did not fit, and the others indignantly told him so. Joey had been irked at his inferiority, and for a while had withdrawn from the game.

Then Joey had suddenly got a new idea of how to go about it. He collected himself a number of pieces bearing the same shade of yellow, and thus was able to put them together more rapidly and make better progress than the other children.

When he proudly displayed what he had done, the others were impressed. But even after he had explained his system, they did not want to adopt it.

"What's the use anyway!" Weston had argued. "We might be able to do it faster your way, but it wouldn't be any more fun, and nobody cares how soon we get this finished."

Betty had agreed. "Yes, it's no fun just going through all the work, picking up the yellow pieces and the blue pieces and the red pieces, and putting them in different places!"

Joey, Ish noticed, could not put up a good argument for his method, and yet Ish could understand his motives. In the first place, granted there was no need to finish the puzzle in a hurry, still to work efficiently was just as natural and as pleasant for Joey as not to crawl when he could walk. Besides, he had the competitive spirit, the old-time drive, so characteristic of Americans, for getting to the front. Lacking a native gift for distinguishing shapes, really as much a physical endowment as having strong muscles, he had seen the way to take the lead by intellectual means. He had "used his head," as they once had liked to say.

Though the "discovery" was at all remarkable only because made by so young a child, still Ish was pleased to note that it was the discovery of one phase of classification, that basic tool of man's progress. Logic rested upon classification; language, too—by its nouns and verbs grouping things and actions into neat workable compartments. Only by his discovery of classification had man been able to impose some workable degree of order upon the infinite apparent disorder of the natural world.

Ish saw Joey's experimental mind also at work with language. To him language was not merely a practical matter, an unconscious implement used to express wants and feelings. Language to him was also a wonderful plaything. He had, for instance, a sense of puns and of rhymes, although none of the other children showed much interest in such things. He liked riddles.

One day Ish heard him asking a riddle of the other children. "I made this one up myself," Joey was saying proudly. "Why are a man, a bull, a fish, and a snake all alike?"

The other children were not much interested.

"Because they all eat things," Betty suggested languidly.

"That's too simple," said Joey. "Everything eats things. Birds eat things too."

They made one or two other suggestions, and then there came up a suggestion to run off and do something else. Joey saw that he was in immediate danger of losing his audience; to prevent complete anticlimax, he had to come out with his own answer.

"Why, they're all alike because not one of them can fly!"

At the moment Ish was not impressed with the riddle, but as he thought about it afterwards, he felt that it was a highly developed and curious kind of ten-year-old mind which could evolve the idea of negative likeness. And into Ish's mind popped suddenly an old definition: "Genius is the capacity for seeing what is not there." Of course, like every other definition of genius, that one could be shot to pieces also, because it obviously included the madman, as well as the genius. Yet there might be something in it, too; the great thinkers of the world must necessarily have made their reputations by sensing what was not there and looking for it and discovering it, but the first requisite for making the discovery, unless it depended upon mere luck, was the realization that something unseen was there to be discovered, something lacking in the picture.

This was Joey's summer for experiment apparently, and one day he came home reeling strangely and with a strong smell of liquor on his breath. The story came out that he, along with Walt and Weston, had visited one of the liquor stores in the nearest business district. This was a problem that Ish had often considered. He had once even gone into one of the stores and started opening and emptying the bottles. After an hour's work, however, he had found that he had made too little progress; the project was obviously impossible, and the children must take their chances with an unlimited liquor supply. And yet, when he thought about it, the situation for his children was not so different from that which he himself had experienced. In those days his father had always had a shelf holding a bottle or two of whiskey and brandy and sherry, and there would have been nothing to stop Ish from carrying on a clandestine experiment of his own. He had not, and so also his own children and grandchildren apparently were not greatly attracted by the unlimited stores available to them. In fact, drunkenness had never been a problem in the community at all. Perhaps the simpler life they were leading took away the need for such stimulation, or perhaps the mere fact that alcohol, like air, was free to everyone, removed the lure of difficulty which had previously surrounded it.

As for Joey, Ish was pleased to see that the little fellow had still been sufficiently clever to drink only a small amount —not enough to make him really sick or even to make him pass out. He had obviously again been showing off before the older boys, and had again succeeded in impressing them; they had come home in worse shape than he.

Nevertheless Joey was definitely tipsy, and made no objection to being put immediately to bed. Ish took the opportunity to sit at the bedside, and to deliver a lecture on the dangers of too much and too reckless experimentation, particularly if it was designed chiefly to show off before others. He looked down at the small face in the bed, with its big eyes. There was intelligence in the eyes, and he knew that in spite of being tipsy, Joey was comprehending. There was also sympathy in the eyes, as if they were again saying to Ish, "We understand together. We both know things. We are not like these others."

In a sudden flood of affection for his youngest son, Ish reached down and took one of the little hands in his own. He saw an answering look of affection come into the big eyes, and suddenly Ish knew that behind all the boyish bumptiousness, Joey was really a timid, sensitive child, just as he himself had once been. In fact, Joey's brashness was only the expression of timidity gone too far the other way.

"Joey, boy," he said impulsively, "why do you keep straining so hard? Weston and Walt—they're two years older than you are. Why don't you go easier? In ten years— twenty years—you'll be away ahead of anything they can do."

He saw the boy smile slightly, happily. But Ish knew that the happiness was merely that a new-found sympathy with his father, not at an impression that the words might have made. Any child, even a precocious one like Joey, lived in the present; to talk of ten years away was merely, for a child, to talk of centuries.

Ish looked at the little face again, and he saw the eyes roll slightly outward with drunkenness and sleepiness, and there was incongruity in the two. Yet Ish felt this love for his son welling up more strongly than ever within him. "This one, this one," he thought, "is the Child of the Blessing! This one will carry on!"

He saw the eyes lose focus, and the eyelids drop shut, and so he spoke no more, but he sat there by the bed, holding the hand in his own. Then, perhaps because sleep is so like death, a horrible fear swept in upon him. "Hostages to fortune!" he thought. When a man loved greatly, he laid himself open. He himself had had good luck. He had loved greatly with Em, and now, again perhaps, with Joey. With Em he had had the luck—but then one could never even think of Em in terms of death. She was the stronger. With Joey it was different. Holding the hand, he could feel the faint throb of the pulse in the wrist, and it seemed very close to the surface. A mere scratch would be enough. What were the chances for a little boy, not strong of body, driven on always by too powerful a mind?

Yet, this might be the one who could shape the whole future. He had only to grow in stature and in mind, to gain wisdom with the years, and to live.

Between the plan and the fulfillment lies always the hazard. Heart-beat flutters, knife flashes, horse stumbles, cancer grows, more subtle foes invade. . . .

Then they sit around the fire at the cave-mouth, and say, "What shall we do? Now that he is no longer here to lead us!" Or, while the great bell tolls, they gather in the courtyard, and say, "It should not have happened so. Who is there now to give us counsel?" Or they meet at the street corner, and say sadly, "Why did it have to be this way? Now there is no one to take his place."

Through all of history it runs as a plaint. "If the young king had not fallen ill. . . . If the prince had lived. . . . If the general had not so recklessly exposed himself. . . . If the president had not overworked. . . ."

Between the plan and the fulfillment stands always the frail barrier of a human life.

Once more the fogs thinned out, and then came the first hot days. "I have seen it again," Ish thought to himself. "The great pageant of the year! Now is the time of dryness and death. Now the god lies dying! Soon the rains will come, and then the hills will be green. At last one morning I shall look out westward, here from the porch, and I shall see the sun setting far to the south. Then we shall all go

213

together, and I shall carve the number into the rock. What shall we call this year, I wonder!"

By now also it was time to be expecting Dick and Bob to return from their expedition in the jeep. Ish still worried and felt guilty sometimes at having allowed the boys to go, but now they had been gone so long that he was somewhat accustomed to the idea and did not feel the strain so much as he had earlier. And at the same time he had another worry and sense of guilt that tended to counteract this one.

The children! Their superstition and their ideas about religion! He had said to himself that all this would be easy to counteract; he had said that he would do something that next day. Yet all summer he had been flinching.

Was it actually that he did not want to do anything? Did he really want the children to think of Joey as the possessor of some special power? Deep within himself, did he want the children to think of him, Ish, as a god? Not every day or every year could a man have reason to play with the intoxicating idea that he was becoming a god. Oh, well— say, at least a demi-god, a being of some degree of special power!

Ever since the incident of the hammer, he had been studying curiously the children's attitude toward him. It was changeable and uncertain. Sometimes, he sensed that feeling of awe which he had seen on that day of the incident with the hammer. He, like Joey, but even more so, had *mana* within him. He could perform strange feats. He knew the meanings of the puzzling words. He knew the curious ways of numbers. He knew, by some strange power, what the world was like, away beyond the horizon, out through the Golden Gate, that there were islands far in the ocean beyond the little rock-tips of the Farallones, that they sometimes saw standing up above the horizon on clear days.

The children, he came to realize, were not only children, but they were also unsophisticated and inexperienced as children in the Old Times had rarely been. None of them had ever seen more than a few dozen people. Though their lives, he believed, had been happy, they had been happy with the simplicity of a few satisfying experiences, repeated again and again. They had not suffered the continual shock of change which had so affected children in the old days, both for good and for bad, making them nervous on the one hand, and yet alert on the other.

Children so unsophisticated might easily come to feel a certain dread of him, to regard him as a being with powers

214

different from their own, not altogether earthly. At times he sensed this feeling and even saw definite evidences of it.

Yet at other times, indeed generally, he was merely their own father or grandfather, or Uncle Ish, a person they had known all their lives, with whom they had romped on the floor when they were little. They had no more respect for such a person than children ever had. In fact the bigger ones already showed the adolescent feeling that the older man was blundering and quite obtuse. Perhaps they stood in some awe, but still they played tricks on him.

Once, not a week after the incident of the hammer, they had set a tack for him in his chair, though that was one of the oldest of all tricks to play on a teacher. And again, after they had left the room with much suppressed giggling, Ish discovered that someone had worked that other old trick of pinning a strip of cloth to his rear, so that it hung down like a white tail behind.

Ish accepted such tricks in good spirit, and did not attempt to find out which one of the children had done them or to inflict any punishment. In some ways the tricks pleased him, for they showed him that children considered him one of themselves. But the tricks also chagrined him a little. His ego was not above being pleased with the belief that he was a folk-hero or demi-god. Was this a way to treat a demi-god, by putting tacks on his chair or pinning a tail on him, behind? Yet, as he thought farther, he realized that the two attitudes were not incompatible or altogether unprecedented.

That is a strange thing—to be a god! They bring the fat ox with the gilded horns, and at your altar they strike him down with the pole-ax. You are proud of the sacrifice. But then they take head and horns and tail and hide, and in the hide they wrap the entrails. All this noisomeness they burn before your altar, and then go to feast themselves on the fat haunches! You see the deceit, and you are angry with a god's anger. You gather the thunderbolts, and your black clouds assemble. But, no, you think then, "They are my people!" This year they are fat and proud and insolent— but who would wish his people to be mean and meeching? Next year, if there is pestilence, they will really burn the ox— nay, many oxen! So you pass it off, with only a little thunder, scarcely noticed in the pleasant confusion of the feasting. "I am not stupid," you say to The Son, "but there are times when a god should seem stupid!" Then you wonder if you should have shared with him any secret of godship, but rather

*have looked for a convenient mountain to pile upon him.
He is altogether too handy with a sickle these days. . . .*

*Even you terrible ones who call for human sacrifice, you
too must wink! Ah, it is magnificently horrible! The shrieks
of his wife and the moans of the victim and the flailing
axes of the killers! There he lies, covered with blood, his
tongue hanging out, a picture of loathsome death! Yet soon,
in the confusion of the dance, he rises suddenly and dances
with the others and the red mulberry juice mingles with his
sweat and disappears. Then you, the terrible one, must be a
wise god and remember only the horror of the seeming
death, though every child in the village knows you are
tricked. . . .*

*"No, there is no need to grovel and rub the face in the
dirt. Merely bow the head, as you enter, ever so slightly."*

Yet in the end, though he half feared the test, Ish could
not resist an experiment. Perhaps the incident of the hammer
had really meant nothing. He was curious.

He picked the time carefully—late one morning, when it
was only a few minutes before dismissal. He was preparing
himself a retreat, if things got too embarrassing. There was
no difficulty, since he was the teacher, in bringing a discussion
around to the point where he could put the question casually
enough.

"How was it, do you think, that all these things . . ." he
gestured widely with his hands, "how was it that the world
happened to be made?"

The answer came quickly. Weston was the spokesman, although apparently any of the children could have answered:

"Why, the *Americans* made everything."

Ish caught his breath. Yet, immediately, he saw how the
idea had arisen. After all, if a child asked who made the
houses or the streets or the canned food, any of the older
ones would have said naturally that the Americans did. He
followed up with another question.

"And the Americans—what about them?"

"Oh, the Americans were the old people."

This time Ish found it a little harder to adjust quickly. In
"the old people" he sensed not merely a reference to time,
but also something close to superstition. "The old people"
—that had once meant fairies, people of the Other-world.
That might be its meaning now again. Here was something
he should work to counteract.

"I was . . ." He began simply. Then he paused and corrected himself, seeing no reason to use the past tense.

"I am an American."

When he spoke, though they were the simplest of words, he had a curious feeling of pride come over him, as if flags were flying and bands playing. It had been a great thing, in those Old Times, to be an American. You had been deeply conscious of being one of a great nation. It was no mere matter of pride, but also there went with it a profound sense of confidence and security in life, and a comradeship of millions. Yet now he had hesitated to speak in the present tense.

In the silence of his pause he saw the children looking at him, and then suddenly he sensed that his explanation had missed fire. He had merely been trying to explain that there was nothing supernatural in those old people who had been the Americans. He had tried merely to say, "Look at me, I'm Ish, father of some of you, granddad of one. I've rolled on the floor with you. You've mussed my hair. Yes, I'm only Ish. And now when I say, 'I'm an American', I mean that there is nothing supernatural about Americans. They were only people too."

This was what he had thought they would understand, but it had gone the other way round. When he had said, "I am an American," they had nodded inwardly, interpreting, "Yes, naturally, you are an American. You have many strange knowledges which we simple ones do not have. You teach us reading and writing. You tell tales about the world being round. You talk about numbers. You carry the hammer. Yes, it is plain that people like you made all the world, and you are merely one who lingers over from the Old Times. You *are* one of the Old People. Yes, naturally *you* are an American!"

As he looked about, almost wildly at this new thought, the silence was deep, and he saw Joey smiling at him. It was a knowing smile, as if Joey were saying, "We two have something in common. I am like one of the Old People who has been left over. I can read; I understand those things. Without being hurt, I carry the hammer."

Ish was glad that he had had the foresight to ask his question just before noon. There was nothing he could muster now, either for question or reply.

"School dismissed," he said. *"School dismissed!"*

Chapter 6

One late afternoon Ish was talking with Joey, or actually they were continuing Joey's education by means of play-school. Ish had collected some money, and was teaching Joey a little about history and the old economics. Joey liked the bright jingly nickels with the figure of the strange humped animal. As a young child would have done even in the Old Times, he preferred the nickels to the uninteresting bills with their picture of a bearded man who looked something like Uncle George. Ish was trying to find ways to explain.

Just as he thought he had put the point across, he heard a strange and yet old and familiar sound. He lifted his head and waited tensely, mouth open to listen. It came again, much closer—the *toot-a-toot-toot* of a horn!

"Hey, Em!" he yelled. "They're *back!*" He jumped up, letting the bills scatter from his hand to the floor.

He and Em and the children all came rushing out, and there was a universal running and yapping of dogs, just as the jeep came down the road. It was dirty and travel-worn and banged-about, but it had got through. Ish had still a moment of tension. Then the boys jumped out, yelling loudly, obviously alive and well. A sudden sense of profound relief let him know how much he had really been worrying about them.

The boys stood there, surrounded by a little mob of yelling children. Ish held back, almost diffident. Then his eyes caught another movement. There must be someone else in the jeep. Yes, now the person was starting to get out. Ish had a sharp sensation of alarm, of resentment, at the intruder.

First, as the head was thrust out from the low door, Ish saw a bald crown and a brown beard, which would have been handsome if it had not been stained with tobacco and dirty-looking, and scraggly around the edges where it had been haggled with scissors. The man stepped out, and slowly straightened up.

Ish, almost in panic, appraised him. A big fellow—tall and large-framed and heavy! He was powerful, and yet there had been little vigor in his movement as he straightened up. Yes, powerful, but with some inner trouble, and too heavy! The pudgy fat of the thick-featured face had squeezed in upon the eyes, narrowing them.

"Pig-eyes!" thought Ish, still in resentment.

The children were milling around, and the man stood in their midst, just as he had stepped down from the car. He looked up, and saw Ish, and their glances met. The man's little fat-encroached eyes were bright blue. He smiled at Ish.

Ish smiled back, though he raised the corners of his mouth only by conscious effort. "Should have smiled first," he was thinking. "He put me at my ease. I should have done it with him. He's powerful, even though his fat looks soft and unhealthy."

Ish broke up the situation by striding forward to grasp Bob's hand. But even as he did so, the newcomer was still in his mind—"About my age," he was thinking.

Now Bob was making the introduction.

"This is our friend Charlie!" he said simply, and he slapped Charlie on the back.

"Glad to see you!" Ish managed to say, but even the old meaningless words did not slide out naturally. He looked straight at the narrow blue eyes, and in the tenseness of his look there was perhaps a conscious defiance. No, those others were not pig-eyes. Boar's eyes! Strength and ferocity behind the baby-blue. As they shook hands, Ish felt his own grasp the weaker. The other could have squeezed and hurt him if he had wished.

Now Bob had taken Charlie away, to introduce him to the others. Ish felt his resentment growing, not decreasing. "Careful!" he thought.

But he had imagined the return as a reunion with no discordant elements. And here was Charlie!

Handsome, no doubt—in a way! A good companion—so the actions of the boys seemed to testify! But—yes—Charlie was dirty. That thought gave a background of rationality to the unreasoning dislike. Charlie was dirty, and from inner reaction Ish felt himself going on to think that Charlie must be in some way dirty inside, through and through, as well as outside.

Dirt—the ever-present dirt of the earth—that was something which bothered Ish no more than it bothered anyone else these days. But the impression of dirt that Ish gained from Charlie was something different. Perhaps, he analyzed quickly, it was the clothes. Charlie was wearing what had in late years become a rarity, a business suit. He was even wearing the vest, because the afternoon was cold with low-drifting clouds. But the suit seemed greasy, and you would have said that it was egg-spotted, if there had been possibility of a man's having had eggs to eat recently.

They all went trooping up to the house suddenly, Ish with them, not leading. The living-room was jammed. The two boys, and Charlie, held the center. The children looked marveling at the boys, as explorers returned from a far expedition, and they eyed Charlie with as much wonder, because they were unused to seeing any stranger. It was one of the biggest occasions that anyone could well imagine. Ish thought to himself it was a time to open champagne, if he had any ice. Then he wondered why the idea seemed ironic.

"Did you make it?" everyone was asking at once. "How far did you get? What about that big city—what's its name?"

Yet in the midst of all the excitement, Ish felt himself sliding sidelong looks at the greasy beard and spotted vest, and gradually resenting Charlie more than ever.

"Watch your step," he thought to himself. "You're just being the provincial, resenting the intrusion of anyone else who may have different manners and ideas. You keep saying that the community needs the stimulation of new thoughts, and yet when someone else comes in, you start resenting him, and rationalizing to yourself, because you say, 'He's dirty on the outside, and so must have something dirty about him on the inside.' Relax—this is a great day!" Nevertheless, all thought of its being a great day went sour inside him.

"No," Bob was saying, "we never got to New York. We got to that other big city—Chicago. But past there the roads kept getting worse and worse—trees grown up, trees fallen around everywhere, lots of washouts, bridges gone. So we had to shift one way or the other, looking for . . ."

Someone cut in with another question before Bob could even finish his answer. There were half a dozen questions, each one canceling out the one before. In the hubbub, Ish caught Ezra's eye. In that glance he seemed momentarily to sense danger, and he knew that Ezra too was watching Charlie.

Ish felt himself both reassured and justified. Ezra knew people, Ezra liked people. If Ezra was so quickly perturbed at Charlie, there must be something about which to be wary. Ish trusted Ezra in such a case much better than he trusted himself.

"Come on," he thought again. "You don't really know at all what Ezra's thinking. Maybe he's disturbed because he senses what you're thinking. And what's that? Maybe I'm only thrown off because I'm like any small tribesman, and fear the horrible stranger with his new ideas and his new gods to fight against mine."

He brought himself back to what was being said. ". . . wear funny clothes," he heard Dick's voice saying, "Long white gowns, sort of, I don't know what you call them, and they have long white sleeves in them. The men and the women both wear them. They threw stones at us. They yelled, 'Unclean! unclean!' They kept crying, 'We are the people of God!' They made us keep away."

Then Em spoke. The rich roll of her voice, deep but feminine, seemed to cut in beneath the high-pitched almost yelping noises of the excited little crowd. Any of the others would have had to pound on the table and shout for attention. For her, the room grew quickly quiet, even though she did not raise her voice and the words were commonplace:

"It's late," she was saying. "Time for dinner. The boys are hungry. . . ."

Half-witted Evie gave one last little senseless giggle, and then she too was quiet.

Em was saying that everyone should go home now, and come back later. Ish watched Charlie, and saw that Ezra was still watching him too. Charlie's eyes looked at Em, perhaps a moment too long. His glance shifted to Evie's blond hair, and took on, it might have been, an appraising look. Then everyone was getting up, starting to go.

Dick took Charlie off to dinner at Ezra's.

After dinner had been got on the table and they were seated, there were a great many questions to ask. Ish let Em do most of the talking with Bob. She had all the mother's worries to settle. Had they been sick? Found plenty to eat? Slept warm?

Discussion of the trip itself was being reserved until the others returned after dinner, and Ish felt also that he should not pump Bob about Charlie. Yet he could not resist the temptation entirely, and Bob showed no reticence.

"Oh," he said, "Charlie? Sure, we just picked him up about ten days ago, down near Los Angeles. There are quite a few people, I guess, living around Los Angeles. There are some all together, like us, and a few just scattered. Charlie was by himself."

"Did you ask him to come along, or did he just come with you?"

Ish watched, carefully. He saw that Bob was surprised by the question, but apparently not disturbed.

"Oh, I don't just remember. I don't know that I asked him. Maybe Dick did."

Ish dived into his thoughts again. Perhaps Charlie had reasons for wanting to get from Los Angeles to some other place. No, that was merely slandering a man out of prejudice without trial, and then he heard Bob going on.

"He tells lots of funny stories, Charlie does. He's a very good guy." Funny stories, yes, and one could imagine what kind. They were frank enough in all their language, these days; the concept of obscenity, you might say, had disappeared, largely because there was only one word for things in their vocabulary, at least among the younger ones. Obscenity seemed to have died a natural death, possibly as a counterpart to the death of romantic love. But Charlie—*he* might still be able to tell a dirty story. Although Ish had never been a prude about stories, still he felt his original resentment shifting to a kind of righteous indignation, in spite of his continually telling himself that he really knew nothing about Charlie, except the boys' opinions that he was a very fine person. Ish felt himself wishing that the water had never gone off, and shocked them into doing something about the future, and thus bringing an outsider in among them.

After dinner, they all built up a big bonfire on the hillside, and gathered about it. There was much singing and skylarking of the youngsters. It was a time of celebration.

There was much excitement, but the boys gradually got their story told. . . . They had encountered only a few minor washouts and landslides on the highway to Los Angeles, nothing that the jeep could not negotiate in four-wheel drive. The group of religious fanatics, wearing white nightgowns and calling themselves the People of God, lived in Los Angeles. They had focused upon religion, Ish assumed, under the influence of some strong leader who had happened to survive, just as in The Tribe for lack of such a leader, they had developed almost no interest in such things.

Out of Los Angeles, the boys had taken 66 eastward, just as Ish remembered so vividly he had done in the days following the Great Disaster, when he had not been much older than the boys were now. The highway across the desert was easy and open, except for an occasional stretch where sand had blown across. They had gone along with no more trouble than blowouts here and there. The Colorado River bridge they had found shaky, but still passable.

The next community was apparently at one of the old

222

Indian pueblos near Albuquerque. From what he could make out from the boys' description, Ish concluded that most of the few dozen people at this little community were not very dark in complexion, but that the dominant spirit must be Indian, because their pattern of life was based on growing corn and beans as the Pueblo Indians had done for many hundreds of years. Only some of the older people talked English. This community also had drawn inward upon itself, and looked with suspicion upon the strangers. The people there had horses. They did not drive automobiles, and they rarely went into any town.

From there, the boys had swung north to Denver, and then out eastward across the plains.

"We followed a road," said Bob. "It's like 66, only just part of it." He paused, hesitant. Ish thought for a minute, and then realized that the boy was trying to describe Highway 6. Some of the markers would still be standing along it, and Bob had sensed that they were the same shape as the numerals on 66, although there was only one of them. Ish was embarrassed that his own son was not sure of the numerals.

Highway 6 had led them on through the corner of Colorado, and across the plains of Nebraska.

"Lots of cattle everywhere!" Here Dick was taking up the story. "Cattle everywhere, you always see cattle."

"Did you ever see the big brown ones with humps on their shoulders?" asked Ish.

"Yes, once we saw a few of them," said Dick.

"How about the grass? Does any of it grow straight and stiff looking, with a head on the end, and little grains forming. When you went through they should have been still soft and milky, perhaps. When you came back, you might have seen it somewhere standing all golden, with the grain hard. We called it 'wheat'."

"No. We saw nothing like that."

"And how about corn? You know what that is. They were growing it there by the Rio Grande."

"No, there is no corn growing wild anywhere."

Onward still they had gone, finding the roads now blocked more often, since they had come to the wetter country with ranker and faster growth and heavier rains, combined with hard frosts in winter. The highways were splitting up into great chunks and blocks as the frost worked under them, wherever the surface was cracked, grass and weeds, and even bushes and young trees were springing up to block the way. Yet they had crossed what was once Iowa.

"We came to the big river," said Bob. "It is the biggest of all, but the bridge was good."

They had come to Chicago, but it was a mere desert of empty streets. It would be an inhospitable place, thought Ish, when the winter winds swept in from Lake Michigan. He was not surprised that people, with the whole continent to choose from, had drifted away from the once great city by the lake, leaving it ghost-like behind.

Leaving Chicago, the boys had lost themselves in the maze of roads in the outskirts, and had ended up (the day was cloudy, and they lost direction) by going south instead of east.

"After that," said Bob, "we got one of these things out of a store. It points direction—" And he looked at Ish for the word.

"Yes, a compass," said Ish.

"We hadn't needed one before, but now we used it and got going east again, until we came to the river we couldn't cross."

Ish figured out quickly that it might have been the Wabash. Floods of twenty-two years, or—more likely—just one great flood, had swept away the bridges. After exploring southward and finding no passage, the boys had had to go northward to Highway 6 again, which more or less followed a height of land.

The progress eastward had become more and more laborious. Floods, windstorms, and frost had transformed the once open and smooth highways into rough lines of concrete chunks strewn with gravel from washouts, overgrown with vegetation, and crisscrossed with fallen tree-trunks. Sometimes the jeep could push through the bushes or detour the tree-trunks. But often the boys had had to make a passageway with ax or shovel, and the constant work wore them down. Also the loneliness began to oppress them.

"There was a cold day with a north wind," Dick confessed, "and we were afraid. We remembered what you used to tell us about snow, and we thought we might never get home."

Somewhere, probably near Toledo, they had turned back. At turning back, a kind of panic came upon them. At the same time heavy rains began to fall, and the roads were often flooded. They had the fear that some of the bridges over the larger rivers might be carried away, leaving them cut off from their own people. They had not tried to go south, as Ish had wished, but had back-tracked along their own trail, gradually being reassured by their ability to get back to places that they had seen already. On their return home, therefore, they had learned little that they had not learned on the way east.

Ish did not blame them at all. In fact, he thought that they had acted with great determination and intelligence. He blamed himself, if anyone—for sending the boys toward Chicago and New York, the great cities of the Old Times. He might have done better to have chosen some southern route toward Houston and New Orleans, instead of a route into the inhospitable country of northern winters. And yet, east of Houston at least, floods would have been more severe and growth of vegetation much more rapid than farther north. Because of climate, Arkansas and Louisiana would have reverted to impassable wilderness much sooner than Iowa and Illinois.

The children were dancing and shouting around the bonfire. Was there a kind of wild primitiveness in the scene, or was that merely his imagining? Perhaps any children would have done the same. Evie, who of course was mentally a child, was dancing with them. Her blond hair streamed spectacularly behind her.

Ish sat, looking on, and thinking. Well, the chief result of the expedition was not the discovery that the country was returning to the wilderness. Anybody would have known *that!* The important thing was the making of contact with two other communities. That is, if you could call it contact, when the other communities were fighting off all advances from strangers. Was that from mere blind prejudice, or was it from some deep instinct of self-preservation?

Yet, at least, to know that there were people in Los Angeles and near Albuquerque—going communities—took away a little of that basic feeling of loneliness.

Two little groups of people, discovered on a single trip, going and coming by the same road! At that rate, there should be several dozen in the area of the whole United States. He remembered the Negroes whom he had seen in Arkansas, long ago. In that rich country of easy winters, there was no reason in the world why those three should not have survived and become a nucleus to which others, either black or white, could attach themselves. Yet that community in its ways of life and thought would be vastly different from the one in New Mexico and from either of the two in California. This divergence opened vast questions for the distant future.

But this was no time to be carrying philosophical speculation far into the future. The dancing and shouting of the children around the fire had become even more bacchanalian. In the excitement the older boys, even some of the married ones, were joining the revel. They were playing crack-the-whip, all the more exciting because the one who was thrown off the end of the whip had to dodge the fire. Suddenly Ish felt himself stiffen. *Charlie* was playing! In the line, linked between Dick and Evie, he was swinging the whip. The children were obviously delighted to have a grown-up, especially this stranger, playing with them.

Ish tried to argue down his resentment. Why not? Why shouldn't one of the older ones play that way? Me—I'm just as bad as those people in Los Angeles and Albuquerque, not wanting to accept the stranger! Yet I don't think I'd have minded, if Charlie had been a different kind of person.

But, try as he could, Ish felt himself unable to stifle some deep-seated sense of dislike. He began to revise his estimate of the importance of the boys' trip. However important the discovery of the other communities could be for the distant future, the immediate problem was Charlie.

By now it was getting late, and mothers were gathering their children. But after the celebration was over, most of the older ones went home with Ish and Em, to hear still more from the two boys and from Charlie.

"Sit here," said Ezra to Charlie, pointing to the big chair in front of the fireplace. It was a place of honor, and comfort too, and Ish thought how characteristic that was of Ezra, to sense the human relationship so quickly. He himself, though he was host, had not thought of it, and so had not been able to make Charlie feel really welcome. And then he wondered, in quick reaction, whether he really wanted to make Charlie feel at home.

It was a chilly evening, and Ezra called for a fire. The boys brought some wood, and before long the sticks were blazing cheerily. The room grew comfortably warm.

They talked, Ezra leading the conversation, as usual. Charlie asked if he might have a drink. Jack brought him a bottle of brandy and a glass. He drank steadily, but with the habitual drinker's slow absorption. He gave no sign of either excitement or drunkenness.

"I'm still chilly," said Ezra.

"You're not getting sick, are you?" said Em.

Ish himself felt a little chill of uneasiness. Sickness was so uncommon with them that any occurrence of it was a matter of note.

"Don't know," said Ezra. "If this was the Old Times, I'd think I was getting a cold. Of course, it can't be that now."

They piled more wood on the fire, and the room grew so uncomfortable to Ish that he took off his sweater and sat in his shirt sleeves. Then Charlie took off his coat also, and unbuttoned his vest, but did not take it off.

George comfortably settled down into his end of the davenport, and went to sleep. His absence did not make much difference in the conversation. Charlie continued his work on the bottle of brandy, but still it made no difference in him except that from the heat of the fire and from the brandy, his forehead was greasy with perspiration.

Ish could tell now that Ezra was swinging the conversation around, this way and that, to get more information about Charlie's background. But finesse seemed not to be required, for Charlie talked frankly enough whenever the subject came close to him.

"So, after she croaked—" he said. "That was after we'd lived together for quite a few years, ten or twelve, I guess. Well, after my woman died, I didn't want to stay there no more, not around that place. So, when your boys came along, and I liked them, I picked up and came."

As Charlie talked, Ish began to feel himself swinging in the other direction again. The boys liked Charlie immensely, and they had been with him for some time already. There was strength in Charlie, and charm also. Perhaps he would be a good man to add to the community. He noticed now that whole beads of sweat were standing out on Charlie's forehead.

"Charlie," he said, "you'd better take that vest off and be comfortable." Charlie started, but did not say anything.

"I'm sorry," Ezra said. "I don't know what's wrong with me. Maybe I'd better go home, get to bed." But he made no move to go.

"Surely you can't be getting a cold, Ez," said Em. "There's never been a cold!"

They persuaded Charlie to move, himself and his brandy bottle, to a place farther from the fire, but he kept his vest on.

Charlie sat there, and the two house-dogs came nuzzling around him. Obviously, even the dogs were interested in the stranger; he must mean a lot of new smells. But they sensed that the stranger had been received. Although at first they were merely neutral, soon they relaxed comfortably under

Charlie's pulling of their ears and scratching of their backs. Their tails wagged.

Ish, always realizing that people were likely to baffle him, felt himself swing back and forth. Now he sensed both power and charm in Charlie, and felt almost warm toward him. And then the very sense of power and charm caused him to react, perhaps with fear for his own position as a dominant force in the community, and he felt Charlie only as a thing of evil.

At last George woke from his nap, stretched his big body and rose, saying that it was time for him to get home to bed. The others made ready to go with him. Ish knew that Ezra would want to say a word to him personally before going, and so he drew Ezra aside into the kitchen.

"You feeling bad?"

"Me? No," said Ezra. "Never felt better in my life."

Ezra smiled, and Ish began to see light. "You weren't chilly?" he asked.

"Never felt less chilly in my life," said Ezra. "Just wanted to see if we could make Charlie take his vest off. I didn't think we could. He don't like to be away from it. Makes me pretty sure about what I think I see anyway. He's got a vest-pocket he's deepened himself, enlarged it. He's got in it one of those little things they used to make for ladies to carry around in their purses—just a small piece of hardware!"

Ish had a sudden sense of relief. Anything as simple and concrete as a pistol—that could be handled! His relief faded as Ezra went on:

"I wish I was sure about him. Sometimes I think there's something ugly and dirty and mean—clear to the middle of him. Sometimes I think he'll be my best friend. Always, though, I know he's one that knows what he wants and generally gets it."

When they went back to the living-room, George was just leaving.

"This is the best thing that's happened to us for a long time," he was saying to Charlie. "We've needed another strong man. We hope you stay with us."

There was a general confirmatory chorus from the others, as all of them, Charlie and Ezra included, went out the door.

Ish was left standing with his thoughts. He had tried to join in the chorus, but his tongue had been suddenly stiff and his mouth dry. All he could think now was: "Something dirty and ugly and mean—clear to the middle of him."

Chapter 7

After they had gone, Ish thought of something that he had not done during all these years. In fact, after he had decided to do it, he was not sure whether he still could. Yet, when he went into the kitchen, he found that there was a bolt on the back door. He could remember his mother having had it put there because she never trusted the ordinary locks. He shot that bolt. Then he went to the front door, and found that there was still a workable night-latch.

In all these years, there had been no need to secure a door. No one in the community was to be feared; no stranger, if there had been one, would have had a chance of getting through the cordon of dogs. But now there was someone, perhaps not to be trusted, and he had made friends with the dogs. Had that patting of the dogs had calculation behind it?

When Ish had gone to bed and shared his apprehensions with Em, he found her not very responsive. Sometimes, he realized, she was too all-accepting for him.

"What's so remarkable about him carrying a gun?" she said. "You carry one yourself, lots of the time, don't you?"

"Not concealed! And I'm not afraid to take my vest off, and be away from my weapon."

"Yes, but maybe you should give him a break for being nervous and uncomfortable, too. You don't like his looks; maybe he don't like yours. He's among strangers—surrounded!"

Ish felt a surge of resentment, almost anger, against Charlie, the intruder.

"Yes," he said, "but we are on the ground here; this is our place; he comes breaking in; he must adapt himself to us; not we to him."

"You're right, darling, I guess. But anyway, let's don't talk about it any more now. I'm going to sleep."

If there was any one thing that Ish had always envied in Em, it was her capacity to go to sleep merely by saying so. As for him, the harder he thought about going to sleep, the longer he was likely to take, and he could never slow down his mind as he wanted to. Now again he felt it settle to work. For suddenly he had had a new idea, and a disturbing one. The trouble was, he decided, that he had to think of himself as pitted against Charlie in a personal struggle. If The Tribe had been really drawn together already into some firm organization, if there were some symbolic unity by which they presented an unbroken front, then the mere advent of any stranger, strong though he might be as an individual, would be of little moment. Now it might be too late. The stranger had come already, and he must be met as man to man.

And Charlie would be no mean opponent. Already he had won the loyalty and friendship of Dick and Bob, and doubtless of others of the younger ones. George was obviously impressed. Ezra seemed doubtful. What was this strange charm, backed by strength?

Ish could not sense why anyone felt a liking for Charlie, but the fact was that they did. And the fact might be also that he himself was too narrowly prejudiced against the man, out of a spirit of rivalry, to feel Charlie's real strength. But of one thing he began to feel certain. There would be some contest between the two of them. Just what form this contest would take, he could not yet know. But since they lacked the solidarity of anything that could be called a state, the contest would be an individual one.

Or at worst, it would be a struggle of factions with two opposing leaders. On whom could he, Ish, depend? He was not really a leader. He had been a leader so far, doubtless, by default—because George had been too stupid and Ezra too easygoing to offer any competition. Oh, intellectual leadership, yes! But in any basic struggle for power, the intellectual man went under. He thought of the deceptively pretty eyes of baby-blue; yet they had a coldness such as dark eyes could never show.

"Who will follow my banner?" he questioned dramatically. Even Em seemed to be failing him. She had made light of things, almost defended Charlie. All at once Ish felt himself the scared little boy of the Old Times. Of all these people Joey alone was the one who could thoroughly understand, the only one on whom he could always count. And Joey was a little boy, physically frail even for his years. What help could he be against the rush of Charlie's power? No, not pig-eyes, he thought again. They are a boar's eyes!

Finally, however, he said to himself, "This is the mere madness of midnight; these are only the wild fantasies that come to a man in the darkness when he cannot sleep." And he managed, at last, to dismiss the thoughts from his mind, and to sleep.

In the morning things indeed looked better—not altogether rosy, perhaps, but at least not too dark. He ate breakfast in a good enough mood. He was happy to see Bob at the breakfast table again, and by questioning got from him some more details of the trip.

Then, just as he was beginning to feel comfortable, the whole thing broke loose on him when Bob spoke.

"I guess," he said, "I'll go over and see Charlie now."

Ish felt a sudden desire to snap out a bit of fatherly advice, "I wouldn't see so much of that fellow, if I were you." But he saw Em's eyes saying no, and he himself knew that such advice would only make Charlie seem forbidden and more attractive. He still kept wondering what fascination Charlie exercised upon the two boys.

Bob went, and after the morning chores were finished, the other children drifted off too.

"What is the fascination?" said Ish to Em.

"Oh, don't worry," she said. "It's just the attraction of a stranger, something new. Isn't that natural?"

"There is trouble ahead!"

"Perhaps," said Em, and Ish suddenly realized that that was the first time she had admitted the possibility, and then she changed the direction of his thoughts with a second remark, "But be careful that you're not the one who starts the trouble."

"What do you mean?" he snapped, angrily, although he did not often get angry at Em. "You mean that this is just a fight for domination?"

"I think that you'd better go over and see what's happening now," she said, disregarding his last question.

The advice seemed good in any case, for perhaps he too was curious. He started to follow it, and just as he was opening the front door, he had a feeling of uncertainty. He closed the door behind him, and stood on the front porch wondering. His hands felt strangely empty; he needed something. He felt defenseless, and he considered going back into the house to strap a pistol on. In the vicinity of the houses they never needed to carry firearms any more, because the dogs gave plentiful warning; but he could make an excuse that he was going somewhere farther off. Still, he hesitated, realizing that to carry a pistol would look like aggression—besides, it would be a confession of his own weakness and insecurity. Yet he could not deny his feeling of uncertainty.

He went back into the house, and immediately saw the hammer on the mantelpiece. "So that's it!" he thought irritably. "You're as bad as the children. You're letting the children's ideas work into you!" Nevertheless he picked up the hammer and took it along. Its weight and solidity gave him comfort. The handle's firm hardness filled up the emptiness of his right hand.

Over from where the bonfire had been, he heard a sound of people laughing, and he walked that way. He was alone, and then suddenly he felt again the Great Loneliness.

It came upon him with paralyzing force. Once more he was the ant lost from the hill, the bee from the destroyed hive, the motherless child! He paused and stood still, feeling the cold sweat start. No, the United States of America was only a name far in the past! He must act by himself, or with what support he himself could rally. There was no policeman or sheriff, or district attorney or judge, anywhere, to whom he could look.

He was gripping the hammer-handle so hard that his knuckles hurt. "I can't go back!" he thought. Then he mustered all his courage, and slid one foot forward in front of the other.

Once he was moving again, once action had succeeded thought, he felt better. He saw them now, ahead, as he had expected, at the ashes of the bonfire. Almost all the younger ones were there, and Ezra with them. They stood and sat and lounged around Charlie, and he was telling them things, laughing and joking as he went along. All this was just about what Ish had expected, and only when he had looked more closely did a sudden feeling of coldness seem to begin at his stomach and then flow out until it came clear to the ends of his fingers and toes. His right hand had gripped harder, vise-like, on the hammer-handle.

Close to the center of the group, right beside Charlie, Evie was sitting, the half-witted one, and there was a look on her face that Ish had never seen there before.

Ish was about ten paces from Charlie when he noticed. He halted. Some of the children had seen him, but they were interested in the story, and no one had paid him any attention. He stood there, as if not yet officially present.

He paused. It seemed a long time. But he could feel his heart throbbing, and it did not pound more than a few times.

He felt the coldness ooze away. Now he was ready for action. He was almost happy. The problem had suddenly taken form, and even the worst problem in definite form was better than a fog lurking in corners. You could not combat a mere suggestion of evil.

Still, through the long period of a few more heart-beats, he stood there. The problem had revealed itself and taken shape suddenly. That too was part of their present way of life. In the Old Days a crisis simmered and stewed, and you read the newspapers for weeks and months before the strike broke or the bombs fell. When you were dealing with only a few people, a crisis came quickly.

He looked. Evie was at the center of the group, and usually you could count upon her being somewhere on the outskirts. Usually she paid only furtive attention to what was happening; now she kept her face directed at Charlie's, seeming to drink his words in, although she certainly did not understand much of what he was saying. There was something more there than the desire to understand his words. They were sitting close together.

Was it for this, Ish thought with bitterness, that they had cared for Evie. Ezra had found her—dirty, groveling, and unkempt, living in filth with merely enough intelligence to open cans to feed herself on whatever they contained, without cooking or preparation. It would have been better, he had often thought, if they had merely put a can of sweet ant-poison within her reach somewhere. As it was, they had cared for her through so many years, and she had certainly been no pleasure to them and probably no pleasure to herself. Their caring for her had been, he thought sometimes, merely a curious lingering of an old standard of humanitarianism.

Now he looked again at the group before him, and in Evie he noticed something that had never been so apparent to him before. That was the trouble of too long familiarity; just as a picture on the wall became something you did not notice at all, so a person whom you knew for many years tended to lose individual characteristics. Evie, he realized now, was a fully developed woman, startlingly blond, in a special way, beautiful. You had to forget, of course, the strangeness of her eyes, and a vacancy in her face. And that was something which he, Ish, could never really do. But to a man like Charlie, such matters were not important. Yes, as Ezra had said, Charlie knew what he wanted, and what he wanted he wanted quickly. Indeed, was there any reason why he should delay?

Ish gripped hard on the hammer-handle. He took comfort

from it, but he had become very conscious that it was not a pistol.

A sudden burst of laughter came at something which Charlie was saying. Looking at Evie again, Ish saw that she too was laughing in a high, uncontrolled giggle; as she laughed, Charlie reached across and pinched her in the ribs. She screamed girlishly, high and shrill. Then as Ish drew near, his presence all at once seemed to become official, and everyone turned to look at him. Instantly, Ish realized that they had been waiting for him, that the new situation had disturbed them all, and that they were looking for some suggestion of what to do. He walked forward steadily toward Charlie, still gripping hard with his right hand, but taking care not to clench his left fist, in spite of his rising anger.

As Ish drew near, Charlie—nonchalantly almost—reached out with his right arm, and put it around Evie and drew her close to him. She seemed surprised, but yielded comfortably. Charlie looked at Ish, and Ish knew that this was the crisis of open defiance.

Ish mutely accepted the challenge; he felt calmer now. This was no time to let anger disturb one's thoughts. Now that there was action, he could think more clearly.

"All of you go somewhere for a while!" he said loudly. There was no need for finesse or excuses; they all knew something was going to happen.

"I want to talk to Charlie here alone for a few minutes. Ezra, you take Evie over to Molly's. She needs her hair combed."

There was no argument; everybody left so readily that they must really have been a little frightened. By having Ezra go, Ish was losing his best ally, but to have had him stay would have been a confession of weakness before all of the others, including Charlie.

Then the two of them were left there alone—Ish standing, as he had been when he spoke; Charlie, still sitting. Charlie made no gesture of rising; so Ish too sat down. He would not stand when the other sat so lazily. Charlie was still wearing his vest, although he had no coat on and had unbuttoned the vest so that it hung loosely from him. There were six feet between them as they sat on the ground and looked at each other.

Ish saw no reason to beat about the bush.

"All I want to say is that you must quit this with Evie."

Charlie was equally direct.

"Who says so?"

Ish considered for words. He might say "we" but that was vague. If he could have said "We. the people" that would have been better, but he knew that Charlie would think it ridiculous. He did not want to pause longer, and so he spoke.

"*I* say so."

Charlie said nothing in return; he sat there. He picked up a few little pebbles from the ground and idly twitched them with his left hand, throwing them here and there. He could not have stated, any more clearly, his disrespect.

At last Charlie spoke. "There's lots of old wise-cracks you can say when any guy says to you 'I say so'. You know what they are; so let's skip them. I'm reasonable, though. Why don't you tell me just why you want me to lay off Evie? She your girl, maybe?"

Ish spoke quickly.

"This is it," he said. "It's simple enough. We're a pretty good bunch of people here, not mental giants, any of us I guess, but still nobody too downright stupid. We don't want a lot of little half-witted brats running in on us, the sort of children Evie would have."

Only when he had stopped speaking, did he realize that by speaking at all in reply to Charlie's question, he had made a mistake. Like any intellectual, he had been happy to stop commanding and begin arguing, and so he had admitted that his command was non-effective. Now, in spite of himself, he felt in second place, with Charlie the leader.

"Hell!" said Charlie. "What makes you think she's been around here all this time and not had plenty of chances to have kids with all those boys around, if she was going to have any?"

"The boys never touched Evie," said Ish. "She was something they grew up with; she was taboo. And besides, all the boys were married off as early as they could be."

He was still arguing, and was perhaps at the bad end of the argument.

"So *you* say again!" Charlie's words had the confident ring of the voice of a man feeling himself in control. "What you really ought to be glad for is that I picked on that one around here, the only one old enough who ain't married already. What if I'd liked one of the others, and she, me? Then you might have a pretty mess on your hands. You better be glad I was so agreeable."

Ish thought wildly for something to say. What more *could* be said? You could not threaten with the police or say that

235

the district attorney might be interested. He had flung the challenge and been met head on.

No, there was nothing more to say. Ish got up, turned on his heel, and walked off. He had a sudden quick memory in his mind of once long before, when he had met a man just after the Great Disaster, and had turned, and walked away with the feeling that he might be shot in the back. Yet, after that first memory, he was not afraid, and it was the more humiliating that he was not. He realized that Charlie would think there was no need of shooting. He, Ish, had come off second-best.

He was in the depths of bitterness as he walked back toward his own house. He had forgotten how deep humiliation would be. The hammer was mere weight now, not a symbol of power. For years things had gone easily, and he had been a leader. But after all he was not so different from the strange youth that he now could hardly remember. The youth who had existed in the old days before the Great Disaster; the one who was afraid to go to dances, the one who was never quite at ease with other people, and had never been a leader. He had changed much; he had outgrown much; but he could not outgrow it all.

Then as he came, deep in bitterness, through the door of the old house, Em was there waiting for him. He laid down the hammer. He took her into his arms, or perhaps she took him into hers, he was not sure. But after that he felt suddenly a new confidence. Sometimes she did not agree with him. They had argued just the night before about Charlie, but in the end he knew that he would renew his confidence from her.

They sat on the davenport, and he poured out the story. He did not wait to hear what she thought, but he felt her sympathy flow out and enfold him. He felt the raw edge of his humiliation healing over.

She spoke at last:

"You shouldn't have done it! You should have had the boys to back you. He might have shot you right there. You're strong at thinking and knowing things, not in meeting a man like that."

Then it was she who began to take the next action.

"Go get Ezra and George and the boys," she said. "No, I'll send one of the children. No one can move in on us like this, and say what he and we are going to do!"

Yes, Ish realized, he had been wrong. There had been no need to feel again the Great Loneliness. Small and weak

236

though it might be, there was still the strength of The Tribe to rally warmly about him.

George was the first to come, and after him, Ezra. Ish caught the movement as Ezra's quick eyes shifted from George to Em and back again. "He has something," Ish thought, "he wants to say to me alone." But Ezra made no attempt to gain the opportunity. Instead he ended by looking at Em in a half-embarrassed manner.

"Molly's had to lock Evie up in one of the upstairs rooms," he said. Ish could tell what a hard matter it was for Ezra, a highly polite and civilized person, to have to speak in public thus about the burst of passion that had suddenly come upon a half-witted girl at a man's caresses.

"What's to keep her from jumping out the window anyway?" said Ish.

"Nothing, I guess," said Ezra.

"I could fix up some bars," said George, eagerly. "We could put something across the window, all right."

They all laughed a little in spite of the seriousness. George was always so happy to do a little more carpentry somewhere on the houses. But it was obviously impossible to keep Evie locked up for the rest of her life.

Just then Jack and Roger, Ish's own sons, came in; after them, Ralph, who was the last of that trio.

At the boys' coming, there was a little relaxing, and people began to sit down and make themselves comfortable. In a moment, Ish knew they would all expect him to begin to say something and he felt again that this was all happening too rapidly. What he was actually facing was almost like the organization of a new state. And yet, they could not sit down quietly and start out by writing a constitution with a good old-fashioned preamble. No, a particular and troublesome situation faced them, and they must act in the face of it.

He put the question sharply: "What are we going to do about Evie and this Charlie?"

There was a babble of talk, and almost immediately Ish had the chilly feeling that of all the men, only Ezra was solidly with him. The boys, even George, seemed to think that Charlie might bring a new force from the outside to enliven and enrich the life of The Tribe. If he liked Evie, so much the better. They had enough loyalty to Ish to insist that Charlie must apologize for what had happened this morning. But it was evident also, Ish felt, that they all considered him to have acted precipitously—he should have talked with the rest of them before confronting Charlie.

Ish brought up the argument that they could not afford to let Evie start a line of half-witted children. But his words made less impression than he had thought they would. Evie had always been a part of the boys' life, and the thought that there would be others around of the same kind made little impression upon them. They could not think far enough ahead to conceive that the descendants of Evie would necessarily mingle with the rest of the group and bring the whole level down.

Then curiously enough, George's slow mind brought forth an even sounder argument. "How do we know," he said, "that she really is half-witted anyway? Maybe it was just all that trouble she had when she was a little girl when everybody died and left her all alone to take care of herself. That would put anybody crazy. Maybe she's just as bright as any of us really, and so her children will be all right."

Though Ish could not imagine Evie's ever having normal children, still there might be something in the argument, and he saw that it impressed the others, except Ezra. In fact, there was almost a feeling that Charlie was a benefactor to the community, and was going to bring Evie into it again as a normal part. And just then Ish noticed that Ezra was really wanting to say something.

Ezra stood up. That was unusual of him, too, being so formal. And it was also unusual that he seemed to be embarrassed. His florid face was even redder than usual, and he glanced back and forth, particularly at Em, it seemed, in an uncertain manner.

"I've got to say something more," he said. "I talked with that fellow, Charlie, last night after we went home, quite a while. He'd been drinking a lot, you know—talked pretty freely." He paused, and Ish noticed again his half-embarrassed glance toward Em. "He boasted, kind of, you know." And now Ezra glanced toward the boys, as if realizing that they, poor half-savages, would not know really what a civilized man was discussing. "He told me quite a bit about himself, which was what I was after."

Again he paused, and Ish could not remember Ezra ever having been like this before.

"Come on, Ezra," he said. "Tell us. This is just us."

Suddenly the bonds of Ezra's reticence broke. *"This guy, Charlie!"* he burst out. "He's rotten inside as a ten-

238

day fish. Diseases, Cupid's diseases, I mean. Hell, he's got all of them there are!"

Ish saw the news visibly shake George's big body as if it had been a jolting blow on the chest. He saw the flush spread over Em's creamy-colored face. To the boys the news was nothing. They did not know what Ezra was talking about.

Ezra would not even try to explain to the boys until Em had left the room, and then he had difficulties because the whole conception of disease was very hazy to the boys.

As Ezra tried his explanation, Ish sat feeling his thoughts run by him fast. This was something for which neither the old life nor the new life held precedent. He knew vaguely that lepers had been restrained by law, and he remembered stories of leper colonies. A typhoid-fever carrier might, he thought, be legally kept from working in a restaurant. But what use was it to remember such precedents anyway? Now there was no law of the land.

"Let the boys go," he said suddenly to Ezra. "This is for us to talk over and decide on." The boys, he realized suddenly, were disqualified in two ways—they did not know the dangers of disease to a community, and they did not know the force which any society was privileged to exert in its own defense.

The boys filed out, in spite of their years and inches and paternity, seeming mere children again. "Keep quiet about this," Ezra told them.

The three older men turned to each other again after the younger ones had gone.

"Let's get Em back in," said Ezra. Em joined them, and then there were four.

They stood for a minute in silence as if under the actual threat of danger. There was a feeling of death in the air, not of clean death in the open, but of a mean and defiling death.

"Well, what about it?" said Ish, knowing that he must take the lead again.

Once the silence was broken, they discussed the situation fully. They were agreed, first of all, that The Tribe had the right to protect itself and must do so. They would look for no more law or precedent than the primary one of self-defense, which could be applied to a community, as well as to a person.

Granted the right, however, and the necessity, what could be the means? Mere warning, "Do this or else!" they all agreed, would probably be useless and would certainly offer no sure protection. Once the thing was done, the punishment which they could mete out to Charlie would be mere social vengeance, and no avail against the spread of the diseases. They had no means of actually imprisoning Charlie, and the weight of all that responsibility, if they should improvise a jail of bars and locks would be too much for a small community to enforce indefinitely. The obvious thing was banishment. They could merely take him away from the community and tell him to go on. He could manage to live well enough. If he returned, the penalty would be death.

Death—they stirred uneasily even at the mention of it! Now it had been a long time since there had been either war or execution. That their society might have to inflict such a final penalty, the very thought was strangely disturbing to all their minds.

"But what about it?" Em seemed to voice all their fears. "What if he sneaks back somewhere? After all, there are only a few of us older people, and he makes friends easily with the younger ones. What if he makes friends with some of the boys and they protect him? And he could make friends with some of the girls, too, not necessarily Evie."

"We might take him a long way down the road," said Ezra. "We could take him in the jeep and drop him off fifty miles, maybe a hundred miles, away." And then after a pause, he corrected his own judgment. "Yes, but still, he could get back easy in a month or so—and then . . . well, I was just thinking, what would keep him from hanging round with a rifle and bushwhacking one of us. Oh, maybe the boys could run him down with the dogs afterwards, but one of us would be good and dead anyway! I don't want to spend the rest of my life being afraid to get within rifle-range of every clump of bushes."

"You can't punish a man for something he ain't done yet," said George stolidly.

"*Why not!*" said Em sharply. They all turned quickly toward her, but she was silent.

"Why . . . you can't . . . of course, you can't," George was laboriously stating the case. "He's got to do something, and then there's . . . a joo-rie. It says so . . . the *law*."

"*What law?*"

There was a pause, and then the talk shifted away, as if no one quite had the courage to follow Em.

Ish, feeling that he must be fair, brought up another matter.

"Of course we don't know he really has any diseases at

all. We've no doctor to find out. Maybe he had something a long time ago. Maybe he's just boasting. Some men would!"

"That's just it!" said Ezra. "Not having a doctor, we don't know. Yes, he might be just boasting. Do we want to take a chance? If this thing ever gets started. . . . Besides, I think the guy is sick. He moves slow, like something was wearing on him."

"They say sulfa pills work," said Ish, trying still to be fair, to suppress that deep feeling of triumph.

Then, as he looked at George, he was almost appalled at the horror and revulsion that he saw—George, the middle-class citizen, full of superstitions against the "social diseases"; George, the deacon, remembering that text about "the sins of the fathers."

But Em was speaking:

"I asked 'What law?' " she said. "There are the laws in the old law-books still, I guess. They don't mean much to us, now that things are different. That old law, like George said—it waited till somebody did something, and then it punished. But the thing was done. Can we take that responsibility now? There are all the children."

Suddenly there seemed nothing more to say. They all sat silent, each considering possibilities.

"No," Ish found himself thinking, "she does not have a philosophy. She mentions the children and makes it a special case. Yet there is perhaps something deeper even than a philosophy in her. She is the mother; she thinks close to all the basic things of life."

Probably it was not so much a long time that passed as what seemed a long time. Then Ezra spoke.

"While we sit here, even—things happen fast these days! We'd better do something." And then he added, more as if thinking aloud, "I saw, in those days—yes, I saw lots of good ones die. Yes, a lot of good ones have died. I almost got used to death . . . no, never quite."

"Should we take a vote?" asked Ish.

"What on?" said George.

Again there was a pause.

"We can run him out," said Ezra, "or . . . the other. We can't imprison him, and what else is there?"

Then Em faced the issue squarely.

"We can vote Banishment, or we can vote Death."

There was plenty of paper in the living-room desk. The children enjoyed drawing pictures on it. After a little hunting around, Em located four pencils. Ish tore a sheet of paper into four small ballots, kept one himself, and gave one to each of the others. With four people to vote, there might, of course, be a tie.

Ish took his own slip of paper, and wrote a big B on it, and then paused.

This we do, not hastily; this we do, not in passion; this we do, without hatred.

This is not the battle, when a man strikes fiercely and fear drives him on. This is not the hot quarrel when two strive for place or the love of a woman.

Knot the rope; whet the ax; pour the poison; pile the faggots.

This is the one who killed his fellow unprovoked; this is the one who stole the child away; this is the one who spat upon the image of our God; this is the one who leagued himself with the Devil to be a witch; this is the one who corrupted our youth; this is the one who told the enemy of our secret places.

We are afraid, but we do not talk of fear. We have many deep thoughts and doubts, but we do not speak them. We say, "Justice"; we say, "The Law"; we say, "We, the people"; we say, "The State."

Still Ish sat with his pencil poised above the B on his slip of paper. He knew, far within the deeper reaches of his thought, that Charlie's banishment would, in all likelihood, not solve the situation. Charlie would be back; he was a strong and dangerous man, and could exert much influence upon the younger people. "What's the matter?" Ish was thinking. "Am I still just worrying about the leadership? Am I worrying that Charlie will replace me." He could not be sure. Yet, at the same time, he knew that The Tribe faced here something real and dangerous and even dreadful, in the long run threatening its very existence. In that final realization he knew that he could write only the one word there, out of love and responsibility for his children and grandchildren. He scratched out the B and wrote the other word. Its five letters stared back vacantly at him, and then for a moment he had a sudden revulsion of feeling. Was this ever right? By writing that word, was he not bringing back into the world all the beginnings of war and tyranny, of the oppression of the individual by the mass, in themselves diseases worse than any which Charlie could carry. And why did it all have to move so fast?

He started to scratch the word out, but stopped again. No,

he was torn two ways, but he could not quite scratch it. If Charlie should kill someone, that might make it easier to inflict the final penalty, and yet that was only the old conventional way of thinking. The eye for the eye, and the tooth for the tooth! To execute the murderer never brought back the murdered, and was only vengeance. To be effective, punishment should not be retribution so much as a prevention.

How long had he paused? He suddenly came to the realization that he was sitting there silent, staring at the paper, while the other three were waiting for him. After all, his was only one vote; the others could out-vote him, and so he could have his conscience to himself and still Charlie would only be banished.

"Give me your slips," he said.

They passed them in, and he laid them face up before him on the desk. Four times he looked, and he read: "Death . . . death . . . death . . . death."

Chapter 8

They shoveled the dirt back into the grave beneath the oak tree. They dragged branches and carried heavy stones to cover it, so that what lay beneath would be safe from burrowing coyotes. After that, they all walked back, the long mile.

They kept close together, as if needing one another's support. Ish walked among them, swinging his hammer in his right hand. He had had no use for the hammer, but still he had taken it along. Now the downward pull of its weight seemed to keep him firmly on the ground. He had held it in his hand, like a badge of office, when they had gone to find Charlie and, flanked by the boys' leveled rifles, Ish had said the words and heard Charlie begin to curse obscenely.

Now it would never be the same again. Ish did not like to think of what had happened, and when he did think of it, he felt a little sick, physically. Perhaps, if it had not been for George's solidity, they could never have gone through with it finally. George, with his practical skill, had knotted the rope and set up the ladder.

No, he would never like to think of it in the future, either. He was sure of that also. This was an end, and this was also a beginning. It was the end of those twenty-one years when they had lived, now he thought, in a kind of idyllic state, as it might have been in some old Garden of Eden. They had known their troubles; they had even known death But it had been simple, as he looked back toward it. This was an end; yet, it was also a beginning, and a long road lay ahead. In the past, there had been only a little group of people, scarcely more than an overgrown family. In the future, there would be the State.

Yet there was an irony. The State—it should be a kind of nourishing mother, protecting the individuals in their weakness, permitting a fuller life. And now the first act of the State, its originating function, had been to bring death. Well, who could say? Likely enough, in the dim past reaches of time, the State had always sprung from the need to crystallize power in some troublous time, and primitive power must often have expressed itself in death.

"It was necessary. . . . It was necessary," he kept saying to himself. Yes, he could justify the act on the highest of all grounds—the safety and happiness of The Tribe. By the one sharp act, evil and ugly though it seemed, he and the others had prevented—so at least they would hope—all that chain of ugliness and evil which ran on, once started, through the years. Now—so at least they would hope—there would be no endless succession of blind babies, and of trembling, witless old men, and of marriages defiled even in their consummation.

Yet he did not like to think about it. He could justify it rationally. Even though the facts were not wholly proved, the chance had been too great to take.

But he would never be sure how much other motives, secondary and personal, had swayed him. Guiltily he remembered how his heart had leaped when Ezra's words had given support to his own dislike and fear, and to his apprehension that his leadership was challenged. Well, he would never know. Now, in any case, it was finished. No, he would only say, "It is done." Too often, he remembered his history, executions had finished nothing, and dead men had risen from their graves, and their souls had marched on. But Charlie had not seemed to have much of a soul.

He walked with the others. They were all silent, except that the three boys were beginning to recover their spirits and chaff back and forth at one another. There was no reason why they should be less concerned than the older men. The boys had not voted originally, but they had concurred. "Yes," Ish thought, "if anyone is guilty, we are all guilty together, and in time to come no one can raise a word against any other one."

Along the littered and grass-grown streets, between the rows of half-ruined houses, there was never a longer mile than that one back from the new grave beneath the oak-tree to the houses on San Lupo Drive.

When he went into his own house, Ish went to the mantel-piece, and set the hammer there, head down, handle sticking stiffly upward. Yes, it *was* an old friend, but his thought of the twenty-two years altered a little when he remembered the day when he had first used the hammer. Those years—per-haps they had been lived, as he had thought a little while ago, in a kind of Garden of Eden! Yet, also, they had been the years of anarchy, when there was no strong force to protect the individual against whatever might rise up against him. He remembered that day vividly still—the one when he had first come driving down from the mountains and had stood in the street of the little town of Hutsonville, pausing for a moment, hesitant, looking up and down the street, realizing that he was about to do something illegal and irrevocable and ter-rible. Then, he still remembered the feeling, he had drawn back deliberately with the hammer and smashed the flimsy door of the little poolroom and gone inside to read the news-paper. Oh, yes—when you had had the United States of America around and about you, as all-present as the air you breathed, then you had thought little of it except to complain about income-tax and regulations, and you felt yourself the strong individual. But when it had vanished! How was it the old line had gone?—"His hand shall be against every man's and every man's hand against him." So it had been. Even though he had George and Ezra, they had all acted only from day to day; no battle-tested symbol of unity had bound them. Though things had worked comfortably and pleasantly in all these years, that might only have been good luck.

Now from across the street he heard the sound of a saw, and he realized that George was back at work with his be-loved wood. George would not spend much time thinking about what had happened. Neither would Ezra, or the boys. Of them all, only he, Ish, thought much. And now, since he could not help it, he thought back again. Again he wondered, as so often before, what really were springs of action. Did it come from the man inside? Or from the world, the outside? Take all this that had just happened. The water had failed, and then they had sent the boys on their expedition as the result of losing the water, and from the expedition had come Charlie, and from Charlie, who was part of the outside, had come all that had happened afterwards. Yet he could not

245

say, either, that this was all an inevitable succession of happenings from the initial failure of the water. His own mind had worked creatively, throwing out the suggestion for the expedition, seeing imaginatively what might be done. And then again he thought of Joey, that other one who saw what was not there, who looked to the future.

Em came in. She had not been at the oak-tree; that was not woman's work. But she too had written the word upon the ballot. Yet Em, he realized, would not consider too much or worry. She was a person too unified in nature.

She spoke: "Don't think about it now. Don't worry about it."

He took her hand in his, and pressed it against his cheek. For a moment it was cool, and then he felt it warm to the flush of his own skin. Many years it was now since he had first seen her standing in the light of the doorway, and heard her speak, not a challenge or a question, but in quiet affirmation. Twenty-one, twenty-*two*, years—and now he knew that no matter what happened there would be no question in the final relationship between the two of them. They would have no more children; yet that relationship still was warm. She was ten years older than he. Some might say that she was the mother more than the wife for him. Let it be! As things were, so let them stand.

"I'll never keep from it!" he said at last. "From worrying, I mean. I suppose I really get pleasure from it. But I have to try to look ahead, peering into the mist. I guess I had picked out the right profession for myself in the Old Times; I'd have made a good research professor. But it's something of a bad joke, I think, that I was left as one of the survivors. What was needed was only men like George and Ezra; they drift without thinking much, or acting, either. Or else the new times needed men who could act, be leaders, without too much thinking. Men, maybe—well, maybe Charlie was really that kind. Me, I only try. I'm not one like Moses, or Solon —or, or—Lycurgus. Those were the ones who made the laws and founded nations. What has happened—yes, what is going to happen to us all—it would all be different if I were different."

She pressed her cheek against his for a moment.

"Anyway," she said, "*I* don't want you different."

Well, that was what a wife should say! It was trite, but it was comforting.

"Besides," she went on, "how do you know? Even if you were Moses, or—one of those others with the funny names

246

—still you couldn't control what the world does, all of it, pressing in around us."

One of the children called, and Em went away. Ish rose, and went to the desk, and from one of the drawers he drew out the little cardboard box which the boys had brought back with them from the tiny community near the Rio Grande. Ish knew what was in it, but because of all that had been happening with such incredible speed he had not yet had the time, or the peace of mind, to examine it.

He opened the little box, and put his fingers down among the cool and smooth kernels. He squeezed some of them in his palm, took a handful out, and looked at them. They were red and black, small, pointed at the ends—not the large flat kernels, yellow or white, that he had expected to see. Yet this was what he *should* have expected. The large kernels were from a highly developed, perhaps even artificially hybridized, variety of corn. The little black and red ones were more primitive, what the Pueblo Indians had always raised.

He took the box back to his chair. Again he put his hand into it; he picked up more of the black and red kernels, and let them run into the box again through his fingers. He played with them, and as he played, merciful forgetfulness moved in upon him, and there was a new peace in his heart. This also had come from the expedition eastwards. In the corn was life, and the future.

Looking up, he saw Joey—ever the curious one—gazing at him from across the room with interest. He felt himself warm toward Joey, and called to him to come and see. Joey was interested, as always. Ish explained to him about the corn. During the passage of the years their own community had delayed so long in trying to raise corn that in the end he had not been able to find any still living seed. Now there was another chance.

Then, even though it seemed a terrible thing to do, Ish took the little box, and went out into the kitchen with Joey. They lighted a burner in the gasoline stove, and took a frying-pan. Carefully, allowing themselves only two dozen kernels, they poured some corn into the frying-pan, and parched the kernels over the flame.

Even though they thus wasted some of the seeds, Ish felt too much moved emotionally to resist the temptation, and he justified himself by thinking that the actual demonstration to Joey, immediately, was necessary.

The corn did not parch well, and was barely edible. Neither of them cared for it much. Actually Ish could only remember having eaten parched corn as a sophisticated cocktail-relish, but he explained to Joey that parched corn had been a regular food on the American frontier and that his ancestors must often have depended largely upon it.

The big eyes, bright in the thin little face, showed that Joey appreciated the story.

"I wish," thought Ish, "that he might grow stronger, and be something firmer to count on. Well, I have wasted two dozen of them, but perhaps in Joey's mind I have planted a more important seed."

Wheat and corn—they too, like dog and horse, marched and shared with man, friends and helpers on the long way. . . .

Far in some dry corner of the Old World the little spiked grass sprouted more thickly around the edges of the campsites where the disturbing and enrichment of the soil gave it ground to its liking. So first, perhaps, it adopted man, but soon man adopted it. The more it repaid his care, the more he coddled it. With his fostering it grew taller and stronger, yielding more seed; but also it came to demand the tilled soil and the seed-bed free of the competition of the wilder grasses.

The first year after there were no more plowed fields, the volunteer wheat sprang up on thousands of acres, but soon there was less of it and then still less. Like wolves upon the sheep, the fierce native grasses returned. They formed tough sod; year after year, they grew from the same roots, thriving the better for lack of cultivation.

After a while there was no more wheat, except that far off in the dry lands of Asia and Africa, here and there, the little spiked grass still was growing, as it had grown before an incident called Agriculture. . . .

So also with the maize. From the tropics of America, it too journeyed far with man. Like the sheep it traded its freedom for a fat and pampered life. It could no longer even shed its own seeds, held tight within the tough husk. Even sooner than the wheat, the maize vanished. Only, on the Mexican Highlands, in thick clumps the wild teosinte still pushed up tasseled tops against the high sun. . . .

So it will go, unless here and there a few men still linger. For if man cannot prosper without the wheat and the corn, still less can they prosper without man.

Although George and Maurine kept track of the months and the days of the months (or thought they did), all the rest went more by the position of the sun and the state of the vegetation. Ish took pride in being able to estimate the time of the year, and when he compared notes with George's calendar, he was generally pleased to see that he was not more than a week or so wrong—if indeed he might not be right and George wrong, for Ish had no strong faith in George's accuracy.

In any case, a week or two made no difference when it came to planting the corn. Obviously the season was too far advanced. The cold weather would arrive before the corn was more than well sprouted. Next year they would try it.

In the next few days, however, Ish spent some time scouting about in the vicinity, trying to locate a good spot for the cornpatch. He took Joey along with him, and the two were soon talking learnedly about exposures, soil, and possibilities for keeping the wild cattle out. Actually, Ish realized, their particular region was about the worst place in the United States for corn-growing. A variety which was adapted to the dry and hot Rio Grande valley might not even mature at all in the chilly and fog-blanketed summers near San Francisco Bay. Moreover, he himself was not a farmer, and had never even had a green thumb for gardening. His knowledge of plants and soils was mostly theoretical, gained from his studies in geography. He remembered how podzols and chernozems were formed and he thought he might even recognize them when he saw them, but that did not make him a farmer. No one else in The Tribe had been one either, although Maurine had grown up on a farm. This accident, so you might call it, that they had no one who was close to the soil, had already been of much importance in determining their communal outlook on life.

One day—more than a week had passed, and the memory of Charlie and the oak-tree had faded somewhat—Ish and Joey came back to the house after having located what seemed the most favorable site they had yet seen. Em came out on the porch to meet them, and Ish knew immediately that something had happened.

"What's the matter?" he asked quickly.

"Oh, nothing much," she said, "I hope anyway. Bob seems to be sick, a little."

Ish stopped dead on the porch, and looked at her.

"No, I don't think so," she said. "I'm no doctor, but I don't think it's anything like that. I don't even see how it *could* be. Come and take a look at him. He says he's felt a little bad for the last few days."

During the years Ish had usually taken the responsibility of doctoring. He had developed some skill at treating cuts and bruises and sprains, and had once set a broken arm. But he had gained practically no experience with disease, because there were only the two that seemed to exist in The Tribe.

"Bob hasn't just got a case of that sore throat?" he asked. "I can fix that soon enough!"

"No," she said, as he had known she would—she would not be so obviously worrying about the sore throat. "No," she repeated, "he hasn't got a sore throat at all. He just seems laid out, flat."

"Sulfa will probably do the job anyway," said Ish, cheerfully. "As long as there are thousands of pills in the drugstores, and still good, we're lucky! And if sulfa won't work, I'll take a chance with penicillin."

He went upstairs quickly. Bob was lying in bed, lying very still with his face turned away from the light.

"Oh, I'm *all right!*" he said, irritably. "Mother gets excited!"

Proof enough to the contrary, thought Ish, lay in his taking to bed. A sixteen-year-old did not go to bed, before he was too sick to stand.

Ish looked around and saw Joey, peering curiously at his brother.

"Joey, get out of here!" he snapped.

"I'd like to see. I want to know about being sick!"

"No, you keep your nose out of *this*. When you get bigger and stronger, I'll show you, and teach you. But we don't want you getting sick too. The first thing to learn about sickness is that it may go from one person to another."

Joey backed out reluctantly, his curiosity stronger than any theoretical fear of being sick. The Tribe had had so little experience with disease that the children had no respect for it.

Bob complained of a headache, and a general sense of unlocalized discomfort. He kept very still in bed, obviously prostrated. Ish took his temperature and found it just under 101, not too good or too bad. He prescribed two sulfa pills and a full glass of water. Bob gagged over the pills; he was not used to swallowing such things.

Telling Bob to get some sleep, Ish went out, and closed the door.

"What is it?" Em asked him.

He shrugged his shoulders. "Nothing that sulfa won't cure, I guess."

"I don't like it, though. So soon . . ."

"Yes. There's such a thing, however, as coincidence, you remember."

"I know *that*. But you're the one that will be worrying."

"I'll give the pills every four hours, overnight at least, before I begin."

"That's fine, if it's so!" she said as a last word, and went off.

And Ish, before even he had got all the way downstairs, knew that her skepticism was justified. After all, why should a man not worry? In the Old Times when you had lived with all the protection of doctors and public-health services, even then the mysterious and sudden onset of disease was terrifying. How much more so, now!

Now, just as a man lacked the all-embracing power of a nation around him, so also he felt himself bare and exposed and helpless for lack of that age-old tradition of medical skill.

"It's my fault!" he thought. "All these years of grace! I should have been studying the medical books. I should have made myself into a doctor."

Yet the study of medicine had never appealed to him, even far back in the Old Times when he had been thinking about a profession. And a man couldn't be a universal genius! Besides, there had been no pressure, when nearly all the diseases seemed to have died out.

That fact, when he thought of it, sometimes even made the Great Disaster seem beneficent—a magnificent wiping off of the slate which allowed man as a species to escape from most of the aches and pains he had been accumulating for so many centuries, and start anew. Originally each little isolated tribe must have developed and maintained its own special infections. If the evidence had been available, the anthropologists would probably have said that the Neanderthal men could be identified as well by their own special parasites as by their own special ways of chipping flint. In archeology, when you found one culture just on top of another one, you assumed that Tribe B had wiped out Tribe A. So doubtless it had. But its weapons had probably been stronger parasites more often than longer spears.

As he thought, he grew more alarmed. Although less than half an hour had passed, he went upstairs, and looked in at Bob. Evening had come, and Bob lay quietly in the half-dark room. Ish did not want to disturb him, and so went downstairs again.

He sat in a big chair and smoked. He would have liked to talk the matter over with someone, but Em did not have the background, and Joey was still too inexperienced. So he thought to himself.

The Tribe—they themselves, that is—had preserved measles and some kind of sore throat. Someone, he himself perhaps, had been the carrier, or else the germs were maintained by some animal with which they were in contact—the dogs, or the cattle, or any one of a hundred smaller ones. But the people in Los Angeles might be free of measles, and have preserved mumps and whooping-cough. And those on the Rio Grande would probably have kept dysentery.

And now Charlie! Even if he had not had those particular diseases of which he boasted, he might well have been a carrier of whatever happened to be prevalent around Los Angeles. That had not been such a fine idea—sending the boys off to explore! Suddenly Ish began to feel an unreasoning fear of any stranger. Give them two-hundred-yards law, that was the idea, and then look at them over the sights of a good rifle!

A fly buzzed in front of his nose, and the over-emphatic way he struck at it showed that his nerves were tense. Josey called for him to come in to dinner.

Unlike the human lice, the house-fly—not having irrevocably linked its destiny with man's—had suffered nothing that approached annihilation. Like the house rat, the house mouse, the human flea, and the cockroach, this other intimate household companion had suffered only a considerable reverse. Where formerly it had buzzed by hundreds and thousands, now it was reduced to its twenties or tens. Nevertheless, it survived.

For, like that lord whom Prince Hamlet calls a "water-fly," the house-fly also was secure in "the possession of dirt," though for it dirt must mean, not lands and estates, but the word in its dysphemistic sense, as when the Bible of King James declares primly that Ehud struck King Eglon in the belly, "and the dirt came out." Thus, even though man should be reduced to the vanishing point or disappear altogether, the house-fly was secure as long as the larger animals still lived and continued to leave droppings behind them. The eggs of the fly, thus deposited, soon hatched out, and the larvae found themselves embowered in rich and succulent food on which to feast, as snakes upon rats, woodpeckers upon grubs, and men on the flesh of dead animals.

Still, with man eclipsed, times were hard. No longer did barnyards offer sites as rich as the ancient gift of the Nile, no longer was the countryside studded with beneficently unscreened privies, no longer did innumerable slums offer their choice piles of garbage and filth. Only here and there some few accumulations of nourishing excrement permitted the house-fly to lay numerous eggs and breed up well-fostered larvae and send forth vigorous and busily traveling adults.

A week later the epidemic was in full course. Dick, Bob's companion on the expedition, had been the next to go down. But now Ezra and five of the children lay stricken. In proportion to its numbers, the community was in the grip of a devastating outbreak of what must be—Ish felt certain—typhoid fever.

Some of the adults had been inoculated in the Old Times, but their immunity must long since have lapsed. All the children were totally unguarded. Even with all the old-time medical skill typhoid had been combatted chiefly by prevention. Once the disease was established, there was no remedy but to let it run its long and sinister course.

Easy enough now, thought Ish, to do some second thinking! Easy enough, he thought bitterly, to know that Charlie, no matter what other diseases he might have had or thought he had, was really carrying the germs from an attack of typhoid fever! Perhaps he had been sick years before; perhaps he had been sick recently, for quite possibly the disease had made the passage in the area where he had lived. They would never know. And now, what did it matter?

What they knew for certain was that Charlie, obviously unclean in personal habits, had eaten with the two boys for more than a week. In addition, the not too carefully constructed outhouses and the flies offered an obvious route of general infection.

They began to boil all drinking-water. They burned the old latrines and filled the old pits. They kept the new ones so well sprayed with DDT that no fly could alight and live. All such precautions were obviously too late. Already every individual must have been exposed to infection. Those who had not yet succumbed must either by good luck possess natural immunity, or else the disease was still lying dormant in them, building up strength through its period of incubation.

Day by day, one or more took to bed. Bob, now in his second week, lay tossing in delirium, a grim indication of the long road all the others must follow before they could grow better. Already those still on their feet were being worn down by the strain of nursing.

They had scarcely time to give any thought to fear, and yet fear lay all around them, daily drawing its circle closer. There had been no deaths as yet, but neither had anyone passed the crisis of the fever. As in earlier years each birth had seemed to force back the circle of darkness, so now with each newly stricken one the darkness moved a step inward, bringing annihilation with it. Even if they did not all die in the epidemic, the loss of any large number might break, it seemed, the communal will to live.

George and Maurine and Molly had taken to prayer, and some of the younger ones had joined with them. They were afraid that God was exacting retribution upon them for the death of Charlie. Ralph was just on the point of taking his family, as yet not stricken, and fleeing off somewhere. Ish dissuaded him, for the moment at least, arguing that any of them might already be infected and that to be taken sick as a small and isolated group would be much more dangerous than to share with the whole community.

"We are close to panic!" thought Ish, and then the next morning he himself awoke—depressed, feverish, and half-prostrated. He forced himself to his feet, made light of Em's inquiries, and avoided her glances. Bob was very bad, and took most of Em's time. Ish tended Joey and Josey, who were both in the early stages. Walt, they had sent off to help in one of the other houses.

In the afternoon, leaning over Joey's bed, Ish felt himself collapsing. With his last effort he managed to get to his own bed, and fall upon it.

Hours later, it seemed, he came to himself. Em was looking down at him. She had managed to undress him and get him into bed.

He looked up at her, feeling small. He gazed as a child might have gazed—above all, fearing that he would see fear. If she was afraid, all was lost!

But in her face he saw no fear.

The dark, wide-set eyes looked calmly at him. Oh, Mother of Nations! And then he slept.

In his days and nights of delirium, he knew little of what happened. Through his fever the great vague dream-shapes moved in and pressed upon him from the dark outside— horrible, inchoate as fog, not to be combatted. Then sometimes he called out for someone to bring him his hammer, and he called the name of Joey sometimes, and again (worst

254

of all) the name of Charlie. But also in his terrors he called sometimes on the name of Em, and then it might be that he awoke at the pressure of her hand and looked up. Always he looked for fear, but there was no fear.

Then there was a week when he lay quieter but so prostrated that at times his life seemed to him to be fluttering weakly to take flight and go—and he cared little. Only, when he looked up and saw Em, he felt courage and strength move out from her, and he held his lips hard together, for he thought life itself pressed close behind his lips and that if he opened its mouth it would escape like a butterfly. But as long as he looked up at Em, he knew that he would have strength to hold that little, faintly struggling thing within him.

Only, when she had gone, he said to himself, now that he could think a little, "She will break! Some time she must break! She may not get the fever. We may hope for that good luck! But she cannot carry the burden for all of us."

Now he realized more of what was happening. There had been deaths, he knew, but not who or how many. He dared not ask.

Once he heard Jeanie come, wailing hysterically at the death of a child. Em said little, but strangely the spirit moved out from her, and Jeanie went away with courage to fight on. George came, unwashed and filth-smeared, a terror-stricken old man—Maurine had suffered a relapse, and their grandchild lay gasping. Em said nothing about God, but again a spirit went out from her, and George walked away with head high, and saying the words, "Yea, though He slay me. . . ." Thus even when the shadows drew in most closely and the little candle seemed flickering and smoky, she knew no despair and sustained them all.

"It is strange," thought Ish. "She has none of those things on which I used to count so much—not education, not even high intelligence. She supplies no ideas. Yet she has a greatness within her and the final affirmation. Without her, in these last few weeks, we would have despaired and lost hold of life and gone under." And he felt himself humble beside her.

At last one day he saw her sitting near him, and on her face was such great weariness as he had never seen on a face before. He was appalled. Then suddenly he was happy, for he knew that she would never have sat there and let her weariness show unless the future was safe. Yet it was such a weariness as he scarcely thought could exist. Suddenly he knew that behind such weariness must also lie great grief.

At that moment too he realized that he himself was now

on the road to convalescence, probably less weary than she, able to share the load.

He looked at her and smiled, and even in her weariness she smiled back.

"Tell me," he said gently.

She hesitated, and he was thinking wildly. *Walt?*—no, Walt was not sick. He brought me a glass of water today. Jack?—no, I am sure that I have heard his voice; he was very strong. Josey would it be? Or Mary? It might be more than one.

"Share it with me," he said to her. "I am well enough now." And still he was thinking wildly. It must not be *that one*. He was not strong, but the weakest often endure illness the best. *No, not he!*

"Five—up and down the street—five are dead."

"Which ones?" he said, bracing himself.

"They are all children."

"What—about ours?" he said, knowing that she was sheltering him still, his fear suddenly dominating.

"Yes, five days ago," she said.

Then he saw her lips start to form the word, and he knew, even before he heard the sounds: "Joey."

What is the good of anything? (So he thought, and he asked nothing more.) The Chosen One! The rest might have followed; he only could carry the light. The Child of the Promise! Then he closed his eyes, and lay still.

Chapter 9

The weeks of his convalescence dragged along. Very slowly, his physical strength came back to him. Yet, even behind his physical strength, his mental vigor lagged. Looking in a mirror, he saw his hair now showing streaks of gray. "Am I old already?" he thought. "No, not really old!" At least he knew that in some ways he would never be the same. Some fine youthful courage and confidence had faded.

Always he had prided himself on being able to think honestly, to face intellectually whatever must be faced. Now he found his mind swerving off when his thoughts drew near to certain subjects. Well, he was still weak; after a while, he would go ahead once more.

Sometimes (and this frightened him) he found himself refusing to admit the actuality, making plans as if Joey were still there, escaping into the happiness of fantasy. He realized that he had always had something of this tendency. At times it had been an advantage, as when it had enabled him to readjust imaginatively when he had first been left alone. But now he was escaping because the reality seemed too bleak to be faced. Repeatedly a line of poetry, from the wide reading of all those years, came into his head when he tried to breast reality:

Never glad confident morning again!

No, never again! Joey was gone, and Charlie's shadow lay over them, and the all-necessary State had arisen, with death in its hands. And everything that he had tried to do so hopefully in that glad morning had failed. He questioned why. Then often in mere despair he fled into fantasy.

When he could think more calmly, the irony of all things impressed him more and more. What you were preparing against—that never happened! All the best-laid plans could not prevent the disaster against which no plans had been laid.

Most of the time he had to be alone. Some of the others still needed care, and what strength remained in Em had to be devoted to them. He would have liked to talk to Ezra, but Ezra too was not yet out of bed. Except for Em and Ezra, now that Joey was gone, there was no one to whom his heart really went out.

One afternoon he awoke from a nap, and saw Em sitting near his bed. With only half-opened eyes, he looked at her. She had not yet noticed that he was awake. She was still weary-looking, but no longer with the terrible weariness that he had seen before. There was grief too, but a calm covered it. There was no despair. As for fear, he no longer even thought of searching for that!

She looked at him, and noticed his opened eyes, and smiled quickly. Suddenly he knew that this was the time when he must face it.

"I must talk with you," he said, though his voice was scarcely more than a whisper, as if he were still asleep. Then he paused.

"Yes," she said quietly, "I am here. . . . Go on. . . . I am here."

"I must talk with you," he repeated, still afraid really to begin. He felt himself humble before her, the child who must ask questions of the grown-up, the frightened child trying to drive fear away and renew confidence. Yet, not being really a child, he feared that even she could make no answer that would bring that security.

"I want to ask you some questions," he went on. "How is it. . . ." he began bravely, and then paused again.

She only smiled at him, realizing his weakness, but she did not tell him to wait till another time.

"This is it!" he said desperately. "Is this the way of it? I know what George is thinking, and the others perhaps too! I heard something, even through my fever. Is it . . . is it a punishment?"

Then he looked at her, and for the first time in all those terrible weeks he saw in her face something which was fear, or might be. Even I have failed her, he thought in panic. Yet he knew that now he must go on, or else a wall of doubt and dishonesty would arise between them forever.

So he blurted on: "You know what I mean! Is it because we killed Charlie? Did something—did God—strike back at us? An eye for an eye and a tooth for a tooth! Is this why they all—why, Joey?—died? Did—what it was—*He*—use the disease that Charlie was carrying—so that we should all be sure how it was meant?"

Then, as he paused, he saw that her face was contorted with horror.

"No, *no!*" she cried. "Not you too! I faced the others so often alone when you were sick! I knew no arguments, but I knew that it could not be so. I could give them no arguments. All I could give them was my courage!"

She paused, as if the sudden vehemence had exhausted her.

"Yes," she went on, "I felt courage flow out from me—like blood! It flowed out to them all, and I grew weaker as it flowed, and I wondered 'Will there be enough? *Will there be enough?*' And you were talking of Charlie through your fever."

She was silent again, but he could say nothing.

"Oh," she cried, "do not ask me for more courage! I do not know the arguments. I never went to college. All I know is that we did what we thought best. If there is a God who made us and we did wrong before His eyes—as George says —at least we did wrong only because we were as God made us, and I do not think that He should set traps. Oh, you should know better than George! Let us not bring all that back into the world again—the angry God, the mean God— the one who does not tell us the rules of the game, and then strikes us when we break them. Let us not bring *Him* back! Not you too!"

Then she stopped, and he saw that her face was between

her hands, so that he could not tell whether or not there was fear in it. But he knew that she was crying.

And again he felt small and very humble before her. (Once more she had not failed him.) But most of all he felt calm and peaceful and reassured. Yes, he should have known. He, among them all, should not have doubted.

Reaching out, he took one of her hands.

"Do not be afraid," he found himself saying, though for him to be saying so to her was ironic. "You are right; you are right! I shall not think such things again. I know the arguments. But when there is death and a man has been very sick, he is weak. Yes, you must remember, I am still—not quite myself."

Then suddenly she was kissing him through warm tears, and had gone from the room. Again, he knew, she was strong. Again courage could flow outward from her. Oh, Mother of Nations!

He also, as he lay there still weak—he also felt courage again, whether he had drawn it from her store or whether her words had merely caused him to build up his own.

Yes, he thought—and did not flee from the thought—yes, Joey is gone. Joey is *dead*. He will not be back. He will not—ever again—come running to see what is happening. Yet, there will be a future. Though I am gray-haired now, yet still there is Em—and the others—and I may even be happy. It will be nothing like the future I planned—now that Joey is dead. Still, I shall do what I can.

Again he felt small and humble. He felt all the great forces of the world at work against him, against the only man still alive who could think and plan for the future. He had tried to face them head-on, and they had rolled over him. Yes, they might well have been too much, even if Joey had lived. He must plan more shrewdly now, work more subtly, select smaller and more practical objectives, be the fox and not the lion.

But first he must regain physical strength. Two or three weeks more, it would take him. Even so, well before the end of the year, he would be able to do something.

Immediately he felt his mind turn over and start to work. A good mind! He found himself appraising his own brain, as if it were a trusty instrument or machine—old, but still functioning smoothly.

Yet he was very weak, and before he had done much thinking, he slept again.

Perhaps there were too many people, too many old ways of thinking, too many books. Perhaps the ruts of thinking had grown too deep and the refuse of the past lay too heavy around us, like piles of garbage and old clothes? Why should not the philosopher welcome the wiping-out of it all and a new start and men playing the game with fresh rules? There would be, perhaps, more gain than loss.

During the weeks of the epidemic, the few who remained well had been able to give only hasty burial to those who died. After the convalescents were again on their feet, George and Maurine and Molly raised the question of a funeral service.

Ish, and Em with him, would have been glad to let the situation rest as it was. He realized, however, that the others would be happier if a service should be performed. A service might also be of some practical value, to mark a definite end to this period of emergency and fear and death, and signalize a return to a normal and forward-looking life. Although he dreaded the renewal of grief for Joey that such a service might bring to him personally, still he felt that after it he could move on toward whatever more modest plans for the future he could finally work out.

So he made the suggestion that the services should be held and that on the day following them all normal activities should be resumed. Although he had not given any special thought to the resumption of school, he found that the others naturally assumed it, and he could only acquiesce.

By common consent Ezra was placed in charge of the services. He chose to hold them very early in the morning.

As in any community where artificial light was inadequate, rising-with-the-sun was a habit, and they did not have to get out of bed much earlier than usual to be standing at the little row of mounds before the light was yet full. The sky was clear, but the western slope of the hills was all in shade. Some tall pine trees standing by the graves did not yet cast shadows.

The season was too late for wild flowers, but the older children, at Ezra's direction, had cut green pine-boughs and covered the mounds. Although there were only five graves, this loss represented a major catastrophe. In comparison with the small numbers of The Tribe, five deaths were more than a hundred thousand would have been in a city of a million people.

The survivors were all there—babies in their mothers' arms, little boys or girls holding their fathers' hands.

Ish stood, feeling the weight of the hammer in his right hand. It dragged him solidly down to the earth. He had started without it, but Josey had reminded him, assuming that he was merely forgetful. The hammer, in the minds of all the younger ones, marked a formal occasion. A few months ago, Ish would not have yielded, and he would have made a point of talking to Josey about superstition. But today he had brought the hammer. Actually, he was forced to admit, he himself was drawing comfort from it. He was humbler now, after all that had happened. If The Tribe needed a symbol of strength and unity, if they were happier with the hammer as a rallying-point—who was he to enforce rationalism? Perhaps rationalism—like so much else—had only been one of the luxuries which men could afford under civilization.

They had now all arranged themselves in an irregular half-circle, facing the graves, each family grouped together. From his position in the center Ish looked first the one way and then the other. George was wearing a conservative-looking dark-gray suit, the very one probably that he used to wear to funerals when he had been a deacon in the Old Times—or, if not the same one, its twin. Maurine stood beside him in solid black, with a veil. At least while those two lived, the ancient proprieties would survive. But all the others were clothed in the haphazard but comfortable leavings of civilization. The men and boys wore blue jeans and sport shirts, with light wind-breaker jackets over their shirts against the early morning chill. A few of the smaller girls were almost indistinguishable from the boys, except for their longer hair, but the women and most of the girls declared their femininity with skirts, and lent color by means of red or green or blue shawls or scarfs.

Ezra was walking forward to the center, getting ready to begin. The light of the sun behind the hill was brighter gold now; the hush was deeper. Ish felt his throat full. He was moved, even though he felt the ceremony to be meaningless, and talk in the presence of death to be almost an impertinence. Yet also he felt himself close to something very ancient in humanity, perhaps something also very significant for the future. Suddenly he was imagining himself an anthropologist of thousands of years in the future, one who was investigating the life of people just subsequent to the Great Disaster. "Little is known of their culture," he would write. "From the discovery of certain graves, however, it is known that they practiced inhumation."

When Ezra began to talk, Ish became a little fearful; there were many things that might be said wrong on the occasion. But as soon as Ezra was well started, Ish knew that he should have had more trust. Ezra had not looked up old funeral services. He did not mouth traditional words. He did not speak of a hope beyond the grave. Of all who stood there, only George and Maurine, and perhaps Molly, would have found comfort in such words. You found it hard to think of such a thing when across the tradition of the past lay the broad black mark of the Great Disaster.

So Ezra, who knew people, talked a little of each of the children. He told some small pleasing story of each of them, something which he remembered and which the others might like to remember.

Last of all, he began to talk of Joey, and Ish felt himself suddenly weak. But Ezra did not talk of any remarkable thing that Joey had done and did not even mention that a year had been named for him. Instead, he began to tell of some little incident of play, as with the others.

As Ezra talked of Joey, Ish saw some of the children begin to cast quick sidelong glances at him. They knew the special bond that had connected Joey and his father. Were they wondering whether he, Ish, would step forward at the last moment? He, the Old One, the American, who knew all that strange knowledge—would he step forward at the last moment, and hold his hammer before him stiffly, and declare that Joey was not gone, that Joey still lived, that Joey would come back to them? Would the earth of that little mound begin to stir?

But Ish noticed only their quick glances, sidelong and furtive. They said nothing. And whatever they thought, he knew that he could work no miracle.

When Erza finished talking of Joey, he continued speaking more in general. Why did he not stop? Ish felt something wrong. This service should not drag on!

Then abruptly Ezra brought himself to a close, and at the same moment Ish became conscious of another change. All the world was suddenly brighter. The first edge of the sun had risen above the ridge-line!

Ish suddenly did not know whether to be pleased or dismayed. "Well planned!" he thought. "But a stage-trick!" Then, looking around, he saw that the others were happy. He too relaxed, and even though he recognized the theatrical touch, he was comforted.

The return of the sun! That age-old symbol! Ezra had been too honest to promise immortality, but he had chosen his timing, and had the luck of a clear morning. Whether you thought of personal resurrection or merely of the continuance of the race, the symbol was there.

Now the lanes of yellow sunlight stretched out between the long shadows of the tall dark trees.

In this also we are men, that we think of the dead. Once it was not so, and when one of us died, he lay where he lay by the cave-mouth and we ran in and out there, not standing quite upright as we ran. Now we stand upright, and now also we think of the dead.

So, when the comrade lies there, we do not let him lie where he died. And we do not take him by the legs carelessly, and drag him into the forest for the foxes and woodrats to gnaw on. We do not cast him into the river carelessly for the stream to float him away.

No, but rather we lay him where the ground is hollowed out a little and there cover him with leaves and branches. So he shall return to the earth, whence all things came.

Or else we lay him to rest among the tree-branches, and give him to the air. Then, if the black birds come streaming from far to pluck at him, that too is right, for they are the creatures of the air.

Or else we give him to the bright and hot cleanliness of fire.

Then we go about our life as before, and soon we forget, like the beasts. But this at least we have done, and when we shall no longer do it, then we shall no longer be men.

After the ceremony at the graves was over, they all walked back to the houses through the early sunshine. Ish began to wish that he could be alone. He did not feel it right, however, to leave Em at this time. Before long she must have sensed how he was feeling, and she took the initiative.

"Go on," she said. "It will be better for you to take a walk, and be by yourself for a while."

He decided to go. As he had feared, the funeral service had stirred him deeply. Some people sought company in time of grief, but he was one who rather should be alone. He did not worry about Em; she was stronger than he..

He took no lunch with him, because he did not feel hungry.

In any case he could always step into a store, and pick out some cans. He did not strap his pistol-belt around him, though it was routine not to go far from the houses without some kind of weapon. At the last moment, however, he hesitated uncertainly, and then took the hammer from the mantelpiece.

The very fact that he took it troubled him a little. Why was it coming to loom so large in his thoughts? It was by no means his oldest possession, because scattered throughout the house were things which he had owned and could remember even from the time of his small boyhood. But still none of them was like the hammer. Perhaps it was because he associated it particularly with his survival in the first days. And yet he did not believe what the children seemed to believe about the hammer.

He walked away from the house, not caring in what direction he wandered, so long as he could be by himself. The hammer dangling from one hand was a nuisance. He began to feel an irritation against it. Was it really coming to be a superstition in his mind too, as it was in the minds of the children?

Well, why did he not simply lay the hammer down, and pick it up on his way home? Or pick it up tomorrow? Yet, he did not lay it down.

He realized that not merely the temporary inconvenience of the hammer was irritating him against it, but rather his feeling that it was coming to be a fixation with him. He made a sudden resolve to be done with it. He would not let his mind be imposed upon. As he had once before imagined himself doing, he would walk down to the Bay, and out on the old wharf, then he would throw the hammer violently, far out into the waves. It would sink through them deep into the soft mud beneath, and that would be the end. He walked on. Then the memory of Joey flooded over him again, and as he walked, he thought no more of the hammer.

After a while he came out of his sorrow, and realized that he was actually walking and carrying the hammer. Then he knew that he was not heading toward the Bay, in spite of his decision. He was walking south, not west.

"It would be a long walk to the Bay, and I am still not strong," he said to himself. "There is no use walking so far just to get rid of this old hammer. I can throw it into any gully among the bushes, and I shall soon forget where I threw it."

Then he knew again that his mind was trying to deceive

him and that even if he threw the hammer into a gully he would not forget where he had thrown it and would not lose it in that way. He quit his pretense, for he knew that he did not want to be separated from the hammer and that it had come to mean a great deal to him in some strange way. At the same time he realized why he was walking south and where subconsciously his mind was already directing his feet.

He was following the broad street which led toward the University campus. He had not been there for a long time. As he walked, his sorrow was still with him, but in some way now it had ceased to be so overwhelming, as if his decision about the hammer had made some change.

Now, as so often before, he loooked around him, and the mere pageant of the years seized his interest, and took his mind away from his grief. This particular section had suffered badly in the earthquake. There was a gully all the way across the old concrete pavement; some crack of the earthquake had made the break; rain and running water had widened and deepened it, and now trees and bushes were standing up from the line of the gully all the way across the wide street. Swinging the hammer to give him momentum, he jumped the four-foot gap from one edge of the pavement to the other, and was pleased that his legs, in spite of his illness, were not too weak.

As he walked along, he saw the houses on both sides of the street, fallen into ruin now, what with the earthquake and the mere passage of time. Vines climbed high upon them. Encroaching trees had thrown porches out of line.

Everywhere he observed the struggle between the native plants which were moving back into the gardens, and the exotics which once had been planted there and carefully tended.

He looked closely at these overgrown gardens, thus to take his mind off worse things. He tried to discover what plants were no longer in existence. He saw no wisteria or camellia or coprosma though they had once been common. But the tall climbing rose-vines were still vigorous. A large and handsome evergreen tree he recognized as a deodar, native to the Himalayas. It was still growing vigorously, but looking beneath it, he found no seedlings. Apparently it could live there, but would not reproduce. On the other hand beneath a eucalyptus tree, a species native to Australia, he found seedlings which had sprouted up through the litter of leaves in which nothing else would grow.

Coming to the campus, he passed first through a grove of

Italian stone-pines. Here, everything looked less confused than it had in the gardens along the street, because the pines had spread and formed a canopy beneath which little grass grew. The effect was still park-like.

Near one of the trees he saw a large rattlesnake lying in the sunshine. It seemed torpid, not yet quite revived from the chill of the night. He could easily kill it. He hesitated a moment, but went on.

No—he had once been bitten and still remembered something of that horror. But he held no enmity to the whole tribe of rattlesnakes. In fact, that bite had possibly saved his life. Perhaps, rather than being hostile, he should be grateful, and form a rattlesnake clan around that totem. No, not that either. He would be neutral.

Then he realized that this attitude of his applied to more than just rattlesnakes. He had noticed it in the younger people also. In the times of civilization men had really felt themselves as the masters of creation. Everything had been good or bad in relation to man. So you killed rattlesnakes. But now nature had become so overwhelming that any attempt at its control was merely outside anyone's circle of thought. You lived as part of it, not as its dominating power. To bother with killing one rattlesnake was foolish, because you had no chance of exterminating them or even of appreciably changing their number. If one of them came near the houses, you killed it of course, to protect the children. But you did not go crusading against rattlesnakes, any more than you did against mountain-lions.

He passed on, went down an almost overgrown stone stairway, and crossed a wooden bridge. He felt it shaky with rot beneath his feet. It had been an old bridge, he remembered, even when he was a boy. Along the stream the thicket was dense, and he had to push his way through, although underfoot he felt that he was still on an asphalt walk.

He heard a rustle somewhere in the thicket, and for a moment was nervous to be without a weapon. It might be a mountain-lion. Wolves or wild dogs also were likely to haunt these thickety stream-courses.

But as he burst through into the open again, he saw only some deer loping off through the trees.

High on his left, now, rose up one of the University buildings. He could not remember what department had been housed there. The shrubbery, which once had been kept neatly trimmed, had now grown up high and shaggy, masking the lower windows.

He went on toward his goal. It was only a little way ahead, now. He burst through another thicket, and saw the great Library building.

He looked. This building also was half masked by the shrubbery. One window was broken, apparently because the branch of a pine tree had grown out across it, and then slapped back and forth in some high wind. That accident had happened since he had last been here, several years back. He kept the University Library as a reserve for the future. He had even taught the children to respect it. Yes, he had even, he was afraid, put a kind of taboo upon it. In fact, not only here but everywhere, he had always tried to impress the children with an almost mystical value of books. Still he kept the symbol of the burning of the books as one of the worst things that men could do.

He circled the Library, here and there having difficulty in breaking his way through bushes. Once he had to crawl over the fallen trunk of a pine tree. The building, as far as he could see, was still in sound condition. He came at last to the window which he had broken many years before, and then boarded up. With the hammer he began to knock off a board. He was careful not to break the board, so that he could replace it. After all, he realized with pleasure, there had been a rational background for his bringing the hammer along with him.

Having knocked off the board, he was able to climb through into the building. Now he recalled the first time that he had gained entrance through the window. He had come when Em had told him she was going to have a baby, and he had been hunting for books on obstetrics. All that had seemed a tremendous problem at the time, and yet it had solved itself without difficulty. Why could he never learn to worry less about problems? Problems not infrequently solved themselves.

He went on through the hall, and found the old door into the stacks. Things were not as clean as they might be. In spite of his precautions, bats had apparently found their way into the building, perhaps through the recently broken window. There was also the litter of some kind of rodent. But the droppings had done no damage to the books. He put out a finger, rubbed the tops of some books, and brought it away dusty. That was natural, and there was not even a very surprising amount of dust.

Yes, they were all still there—well over a million volumes, almost all the accumulated learning of the world still safe within these four walls. He felt a sudden sense of security and safety and hope. He gloated, like a miser.

He went down one flight of the little circular stairway, and headed toward the part of the library, the geography section, which as a graduate student he had known best. He came to the familiar alcoves, and in spite of all the years he felt a sense of having come home. Looking at the shelves, he began to spot books which he had read and studied.

One, in particular, caught his attention, a well-worn volume, rebound in red buckram. He stretched out a hand, took it from the shelf, and blew the dust from its top. Looking at his find, he saw the name *Brooks* and the title, *Climate through the Ages*. He remembered the book. Opening it, he saw the card, and noticed that the last borrower of the book —the date only a month before the Great Disaster—had been someone named with the unusual name of Isherwood Williams. Only after a few seconds did he realize that he himself was Isherwood Williams. Nobody had called him by his full name for many years. Now he could actually remember that he had been reading this book during his last semester. It was a good book and interesting, although largely superseded, he curiously found himself remembering, by the later studies of—well, someone with a German name— Zeimer, perhaps.

He laid the hammer down, so as to have both hands for the book. Then he went to where light shone in through a dusty window, and looked curiously through the pages. Actually, this book was not of the slightest value to human progress. Climatic change was not a practical problem. In any case, this book had been superseded. He could just as well throw it away or tear it to pieces, but he did not. He went back, and put it almost reverently into its place.

He walked away, and then suddenly everything was dust and ashes in his mind again. What would be the use of all these books now? Why worry about one of them? Why worry about all the millions of them? There was no one left, now, to carry on. Books themselves, mere wood-pulp and lamp-black, were nothing—without a mind to use them.

Sorrowfully he went away, and he was just starting to climb the circular stairway when he realized that something was missing. He no longer had the hammer. He was suddenly frightened, and returned rapidly to the alcove from which he had taken the book. He had a great feeling of relief when he saw the hammer still resting where he had laid it on the floor when he wanted both hands for the book. He took it up, and retraced his steps.

He climbed out through the broken window, and automatically started to replace the board. Then, he stopped. The great feeling of desolation came over him again. Why replace the board? It would make no difference. No one was left who would come here, in the future, to read. He paused, swinging the hammer idly.

At last, slowly, without enthusiasm, he picked up the board, and with the hammer pounded the nails in again. There was no enthusiasm. There was no hope. Yet this was merely part of his life. Just as George would always work at his carpentry, just as Ezra would always be good with people, so he, Ish, would keep some illusion of books, and the future.

After that he went around and sat down to rest on the granite steps at the front of the Library. Everything was overgrown and half ruinous. He thought of an old picture which he remembered. Who was it—Caesar? Hannibal?—someone, sitting in the ruins of Carthage? He pounded idly with his hammer at the edge of one of the granite steps. It was sheer vandalism. He did not ordinarily do such a thing. The edge of the step chipped off. Still, wantonly, he pounded harder. A three-inch flake loosened and fell. The fresh edge of the broken granite looked out roughly at him.

As he sat there still pounding gently with the hammer, he felt himself for the first time remember Joey without merely dissolving into sorrow. How would it have been anyway? Joey might not have been able to do anything. He was only a bright little boy. He could not have changed things. He could not have stood against all the pressing current of this altered world. He would only have struggled and struggled, and in the end he would not have succeeded. He would have been unhappy.

"Joey," he thought, and he put the thoughts into words. "Joey was too much like me. I always struggle. I can never merely be happy."

He concentrated on a small chip of granite, and vindictively pounded it into bits.

"Relax, relax!" he again thought in words. "It's time to relax."

Thoreau and Gauguin—we remember them. But should we forget the tens of thousands of others? They neither wrote books nor painted pictures, but equally they renounced. And what of those others, the millions who turned their backs on imagination?

You have heard them speak, and seen their eyes. . . . "It was fine there, where we camped on our fishing-trip—sometimes I wished—of course I had to get back for the sales-conference." . . . "Do you ever think, George, of a desert island?" . . . "Just a cabin, in the woods, no telephone." . . . "The sand-spit by the lagoon, I like to fancy—but, you know, there's Maud, and the children."

What a strange thing then is this great civilization, that no sooner have men attained it than they seek to flee from it!

The Chaldeans told that Oannes the fish-god came up from the sea and taught men these new ways. But was he god or demon?

Why do the legends look back toward some golden day of simplicity?

Must we not think then that this great civilization grew up, not by men's desires, but rather by Forces and Pressures. Step by step, as villages grew larger, men must give up the free wandering life of berry-picking and seed-gathering and tie themselves to the security (and drudgery) of agriculture. Step by step, as villages grew more numerous, men must renounce the excitement of the hunt for the security (and drudgery) of cattle-keeping.

Then at last it was like Frankenstein's vast monster. They had not willed it, but it ruled them all. And so by a thousand little surreptitious paths they tried to escape.

How then, once overthrown, shall this great civilization, except by renewed Forces and Pressures, ever come again?

And then suddenly he knew that he was old. In years he was only in his forties, but he was the youngest of the older group, and beneath him a long gap opened before you came to the oldest of the younger ones. It was a long gap in years, and an immensely longer gap in culture and tradition. Never had there been—never could there possibly have been—such another gap between the older and the younger generations.

Sitting there, on the Library steps, pounding the chip of granite into smaller and smaller grains, he began now to have what seemed a little clearer vision of the future. It was all tied up in that same old question. How much did man strike outward to affect all his surroundings and how much did the surroundings press in upon him? Did the Napoleonic age produce Napoleon or did *he* produce *it*? So, even if Joey had lived, the welter of circumstances, the circumstances that made Jack and Roger and Ralph, would probably have affected Joey too, and one small boy was not much to set up against all of that. Yes, even if Joey had lived, things would probably have continued to move in the way they already seemed to be moving. Now that Joey was dead, it was certain —certain, that is, as far as anyone could reasonably expect, granting always some unforeseeable accident.

The stars in their courses! (The chip of granite was nothing but powder under the blows of the hammer.) *The stars in their courses!* No, he did not believe in astrology, and yet the shifting of the stars showed that the solar system too was changing, and that the earth itself was becoming a more or a less habitable place for man. Thus, at some profounder depth of reality, astrology might be right, and the changes in the sky could be taken as symbol of all the grinding wheels of circumstance. *The stars in their courses!* What was man, little man, to withstand them?

Yes, the future was certain. The Tribe was not going to restore civilization. It did not want civilization. For a while the scavenging would go on—this opening of cans, this expending of cartridges and matches stored up from the past, all this uncreative but happy manner of life. Then at last, sooner or later, there would be more and more people, and the supplies would fail. There would perhaps be no quick catastrophe because many cattle could be had for the taking, and life would go on.

So, he thought, and then a new idea came to him with a sudden impact. Even though cattle were left, though there was much food, what would happen when the ammunition for the rifles was exhausted? When the matches were gone? In fact, one might not even have to wait until the ammunition was exhausted. Powder deteriorated with time. Three or four generations, and all who were left might be merely some groveling primitives who had lost civilization and yet, on the other hand, had not learned all those thousand basic skills which enabled savages to live with some degree of stability and comfort! Possibly, indeed—and perhaps this would be best—in three or four generations the race would not be able to survive at all, would not be able to make the transition between the scavenging, uncreative life, and some new level of life at which they could remain permanently, or from which they could once more begin a slow advance.

Again he pounded heavily on the edge of the step. Another chunk of the granite fell off. He looked at it gloomily. He had just decided not to worry, and here he was, hard at it again.

What could he know about what would be happening three or four generations from now?

He got up and started to walk home. He was quieter now.

"Yes," he thought, again shaping words, "a leopard can't change its spots, and I'll always be a worrier, even though I've lived with Em for twenty-two years. I look before and after. Relax! Yes, I should relax a little. What I have been trying to do—that has failed. I'll admit it. Just the same, I'm certain I'll never stop trying a little. Now, perhaps, if I try for something less, I may in the end attain something more."

Chapter 10

By the time he had finished the long walk up the hill to the houses, his vague plans had shaped themselves, but he would have to wait until morning to begin.

That night, however, an autumn storm began, and he awoke in the morning to a world of low-lying cloud and steady dropping. He felt surprise, for with all the recent troubles he had failed to realize that time was slipping away. Now, however, when he thought of the matter, he remembered that the sun had been setting well toward the south and that the month, if one could still think in such terms, would be November. The rain interfered with the immediate fulfillment of his plans, but there was plenty of time, and he could mature his ideas with thought.

So completely had his attitudes changed within the last day that the sounds of the assembling children, that morning, came to him as a shock. "Of course!" he thought. "They are expecting to have school again."

He went downstairs to meet with them. They were all there—all except Joey, and two younger ones. He looked into their faces, as they sat on chairs wriggling, or squatted more comfortably on the floor. They were looking back at him, he imagined, with more alertness than usual. Joey was gone, and they must be wondering how this would affect school. Yet the change, he knew, must be only temporary, and behind this alertness must lurk still that basic lack of interest against which he had already struggled.

He let his glance run over the little group, pausing individually upon each face. They were fine children, not really stupid, but they lacked the flair. No, there was not one!

He made his decision, and he felt no pain in it.

"School is dismissed," he said.

There was a momentary look almost as of consternation in all the faces, and then he saw that they were suddenly pleased, although they were making some effort not to show their pleasure.

"School is dismissed!" he repeated, feeling that he was being dramatic about it in spite of himself. "There will be no more school—ever!"

Again he saw a look of consternation come into the faces, and this time no pleasure showed afterwards. They stirred uneasily in their seats. Some of them got up to go. But they knew that something had happened, something deeper than their minds could grasp.

They went out slowly and quietly. During as much as a minute after they had gone out into the dripping of the rain, there was silence. Then he heard them suddenly shout, and they were children again. School had been a passing incident. Probably they would never think of it again; certainly they would never regret it. For a moment Ish felt a heaviness within him. "Joey, Joey!" he thought. But he had no regret for what he had just done, and he knew that he had made the right decision. "School is dismissed!" he thought. "School dismissed!" And he remembered suddenly that he had sat in this same room many years before, and watched the electric lights fade out.

Three days of rain gave him plenty of time to think things over and mature all his plans. At last a morning dawned with blue sky and a chilly wind from the north. The sun came out, the vegetation dried. Now was the time.

He hunted through the deserted and overgrown gardens. This had never been an area where citrus fruits were grown commercially, but lemons had produced well enough, and here and there someone had nursed a lemon tree in his garden. That wood, he remembered, was suitable. Of course he could have read any number of books, but his approach had changed. He would read no books on this matter. He could do well enough by himself.

Two blocks up the street there had once been a large and showy garden. There he found a lemon tree. It was still living, although nearly crowded out by the growth of two pines. Moreover, it had suffered badly in a frost of some years previous. Never having been pruned after the frost, the tree was only a wreck of itself. Long suckers had shot up from its base after the frost, and some of these again had died.

Avoiding the long thorns, Ish pressed his way into the tangle, found a suitable shoot, and took out his pocket-knife.

The shoot at its base was nearly as big as his thumb. The dead lemon wood was almost as hard as bone, but after a while he whittled it through with his knife and pulled it out from the tangle. The shoot was seven feet long, straight for four feet before other branches had begun to interfere and it had grown crooked. At his shaking, it was stiff, but when he leaned against it, it bent and straightened sharply as he released the pressure. It would suffice.

"Yes," he thought a little bitterly, "it will be good enough for all my needs."

He carried the lemon-shoot back to the house, and sat on the porch, in the sun, whittling. First he cut off the crooked end of the shoot so that he had four feet of straight wood remaining.

Then he stripped off the dead bark, and began to taper the shoot at both ends. The work was very slow, and he paused frequently to sharpen the knife on a whetstone. The white tough-grained wood seemed to turn the edge after only a few strokes.

Walt and Josey had been off playing with the other children, but at lunch-time they came back.

"What are you doing?" Josey asked him.

"I'm getting ready to play a game," Ish answered her. He would not make the mistake, he had decided, of trying to tie this up with anything practical, as he had with the school. Here he would try to harness that love of play which seemed so deep-seated in the human race.

After lunch the children must have carried the word around. In the afternoon George came over.

"Why don't you come to my place," George said, "and use a vise and my spoke-shave? You could work a lot faster."

Ish thanked him, but continued to work with the knife, even though his hand was getting sore. Nevertheless he thought that he would do all this work with the simplest implements.

By the end of the afternoon his hand was beginning to blister where he held the knife, but he judged that the work was done. A four-foot length of the lemon-shoot was now symmetrically tapered toward both ends. He set one end of it against the ground, pressed it to a half circle, and felt it spring back sharply into straightness. Satisfied, he cut notches close to each end, and gladly put the knife away.

The next morning he continued the work. There was plenty of stout string available, and he considered taking some nylon fish line and braiding it into the proper size.

"No," he thought, "I'll work from things they can always get for themselves."

He found the skin of a recently killed calf. From it he cut a long thong of rawhide. The work went slowly, but he had plenty of time. He shaved the hair from the strip, and shaved the strip itself until it was no larger than a small cord. Then he braided three strips together to make a heavy cord, and estimating the proper length, he tied each end into a little loop.

He held the lemon-shoot in one hand and the braided thong in the other, and looked at them. Either by itself amounted to little. Then, bending the shoot, he hooked the loops of the thong into the notches at the ends of the shoot, and the two became one. Since the thong was shorter, the tapered shoot now bent in a clean symmetrical arc. The thong itself cut straight across between the points of the arc. Stick and cord, joined, had suddenly become something new.

He looked at the bow, and knew that creative force had again returned to the world. He could have gone to any sporting-goods store, and picked out a much better bow—a six-foot toy for archery. But he had not done so. He had made himself a bow from the wood itself carved with the simplest of implements, and a string from the hide of a new-killed calf.

He plucked at the thong. It scarcely twanged, but it gave forth a satisfactory dull throbbing vibration. He considered that his work for the day was finished. He unstrung the bow.

The next day, for an arrow, he cut himself a straight branch of a pine tree. The soft green wood cut easily, and he had shaped the arrow and notched it in half an hour. When he had finished it, he called for the children. Walt and Josey came, and Weston with them.

"Let's see how she works," Ish said.

He drew the arrow back, and loosed it. Unfeathered, it flew with a wobbly flight, but he had pointed it at a high angle, and it covered fifty feet before it struck, by chance, pointing upward from the ground.

Instantly he knew that he had won success. The three children had never seen anything like this before, and they stood wide-eyed for a moment. Then with shouts they broke into a run, and went to retrieve the arrow. Ish shot it for them, again and again.

At last came the inevitable request for which Ish had been waiting.

"Let me try it, Daddy," said Walt.

Walt's first shot wobbled a bare twenty feet, but he was pleased. Then Josey tried it, and then Weston.

Before dinner-time, every child in The Tribe was busy at work whittling on a bow of his own.

Everything worked even better than Ish had dared to hope. Within a week the air around the houses seemed to be full of badly shot arrows. Mothers began to worry about lost eyesight, and two children came in crying after having received arrows in various parts of their anatomies. But since the arrows were headless and shot from weak bows, no real harm resulted.

Rules had to be established. "You mustn't shoot in the direction of anyone." "You mustn't shoot close to the houses."

Competition developed. Having learned the trick from the older boys who shot from rifles, children began to hold contests against a mark. They experimented with different lengths and types of bows. When Josey complained that Walt always beat her at shooting, Ish subtly made the suggestion that she might try fixing some quail pinions to the butt-end of her arrow. She did so, and beat Walt, and then suddenly all the arrows had quail pinions at one end, and they were flying farther and truer. Even the older boys became interested, and some of them made bows although they were allowed to use rifles. But archery still continued to flourish chiefly among the ones who were too young for rifles.

Ish bided his time. The early rains had sprouted the grass seed, and now the land was green. At evening the sun set behind the hills to the south of the Golden Gate.

Walt and Weston, the twelve-year-olds, were now deep in some kind of boyish plot. They worked hard with bows and arrows, shaping and perfecting them. They were gone long hours during the day.

Then one day toward evening Ish heard the sound of excited boys' feet running up the steps outside. Walt and Weston burst into the room.

"Look, Daddy," Walt cried, and he held up for Ish the pathetic-looking body of a big rabbit pierced through the side with a headless wooden arrow.

"Look!" Walt cried again. "I hid behind a bush, and waited till he hopped up close to me, and then I shot him right through."

Ish, as he looked, felt a sympathy and pity for the poor dangling body, even though he knew that it was a symbol of his own triumph. Too bad, he thought, that even creation must make use of death also.

"That's fine!" he said. "That's fine, Walt! That was a good shot!"

Chapter 11

Day after day still, the sun set in the cloudless sky farther to the south. Now it was very close to its turning. The clear weather still held.

One day, so suddenly that you might almost say just at that particular moment it happened, the children became tired of playing with bows and arrows, and went off on some new enthusiasm. Ish did not worry. He knew that after the ways of children they would come back again, perhaps at the same time of year. The making of bows and the shooting of arrows would not be forgotten. During twenty years, during one hundred years if need were, the bow might remain a children's plaything. In the end, after the ammunition had failed, it would still be there. It was the greatest weapon that primitive man had ever known and the most difficult to invent. If he had saved that for the future, he had saved much. After the rifles were useless, his great-grandchildren would not have to meet the bear's rush empty-handed or starve in the midst of the cattle herds. His great-grandchildren would never know civilization, but at least they would not be groveling half-apes, but would walk erect as freemen, bow in hand. Even if they should no longer have metal knives, they could still scrape out bows with sharp stones.

He planned one more experiment, but he was in no hurry. Now that they had bows he could make a bow-drill and teach the children its use. Then after the matches were exhausted, The Tribe would still know how to kindle fire.

Yet, as with the children, his own enthusiasm too grew cool through the passing of the weeks. He thought less upon his own triumph in inventing the bow and tricking the children into enjoying it. He thought rather upon all the disasters of the year. Joey was gone, and that loss could never be redeemed. Also a kind of fresh innocence had faded from the world when the four of them had written that word upon their ballots. And also a great confidence and trust had gone from himself when he had realized at last that he must give up his dream of re-establishing the ways of civilization.

Now the sun was so near the limit of its southern course that a day or two would bring its turning. Everyone was

277

making ready for the holiday, and the carving of the number in the rock and the naming of the year. This was their great holiday of all, combining as it did, both Christmas and New Years of the Old Times, and yet including along with those two something of their individual own. Like so much else the holidays had suffered strange transitions in the passage of one world to the other. They still observed Thanksgiving Day with a big dinner, but the Fourth of July and all the other patriotic holidays had lapsed. George, who was a traditionalist and had been a good union man, always knocked off whatever he was doing and wore his best clothes when he judged it should be Labor Day. But no one else celebrated it with him. Curiously, or perhaps rather it was natural enough, the old folk-holidays survived better than those established by law. The children still celebrated April Fool's Day and Hallowe'en with great enthusiasm and with much of the traditional ceremony, although they had had to learn such things from their fathers and mothers. Also six weeks after the winter solstice, they talked about Ground-squirrel Day and whether the squirrel could see his shadow, for there were no ground-hogs in this area and they had substituted the ground-squirrel instead. Yet all these were nothing, compared with their own great festival when they cut the number in the rock and named the year.

Now Ish began to hear the children discussing the matter and speculating upon what the name would be. The younger ones were saying that it should be called the Year of the Bow and Arrow. But the slightly older ones, who could remember more vividly the whole year, said that rather it should be called the Year of the Journey. But those who were still older thought of other things also, and often they grew quiet and seemed embarrassed, and Ish knew that they were thinking of Charlie and of all the other deaths. Ish himself thought first of all about Joey, and then of all the changes of attitude which he himself had had to make during the year.

Then finally, as they looked out one evening, they saw that the sun set in the same place or perhaps a little to the north from where it had set the night before, and the older ones said, to the great excitement of the children, that tomorrow would be the day.

So again, at the end of the twenty-second year, they gathered at the rock, and Ish with his hammer and cold-chisel cut 22 into the surface of the rock just below 21. They were all there at the rock, because the day was fair, and warm for winter, and the mothers had brought even the youngest babies. Then after the numeral had been cut, all those who were old enough to talk called out Happy New Year as it had been in the Old Times, and as it was still at this time.

But when Ish asked, following the ritual set in the last years, what should be the name of the year, there came only sudden silence.

At last the one to speak was Ezra, the good helper, who knew the ways of men:

"Too much has happened this year, and whatever name we give the year will have a bad sound to us. People find comfort in numbers, and no bad thoughts. Let us give this year no name, but remember it only as the Year 22."

Here ends Part II. The second inter-chapter called Quick Years *follows, without time-interval.*

Quick Years

Once again the years flowed quickly, and now no longer he struggled and threshed, but instead, floated easily with the current.

In these years they grew a little corn, not much, but enough to harvest a small crop and to keep the seeds alive. Every autumn—as if the falling of the first rain gave a signal—the children played with bows and arrows for a while before they tired of the game. Now and then all the adults drew together to a conference, like a town-meeting, and what was decided there, each one knew, was binding upon them all.

"These things at least!" Ish thought. "These things at least, I have assured for the future." Yet in the meetings, more and more with every year, those who spoke and took action were young men. Ish, to be sure, presided. He sat facing all the others, and those wishing to speak rose and addressed him respectfully. He sat there, holding his hammer or balancing it beside him. When argument between two of the young men became too heated, Ish pounded with the hammer, and the young men were suddenly quiet and deferential. But if he himself spoke, though they listened intently, often they paid no attention to his ideas afterward.

So the years flowed—The year 23 "Of the Mad Wolf," the year 24 "Of the Blackberries," the year 25 "Of the Long Rain."

Then came the year 26, and old George was with them no more. He had been painting on a ladder. Whether his heart stopped and he fell, or whether he fell accidentally and killed himself by falling, no one ever knew. But he was gone, and after his death the roofs were never in such good repair, and the trim was never painted. Maurine lived on, for a while, in the neat house where the pink-fringed bridge-lamps would not light and the console radio would not play and the scarves were crumpled on the tables. But she too was old, and she died before the year was out. So they called it the Year when George and Maurine Died.

And still they ran on—27, 28, 29, 30. It was hard to remember now the names, and how they came. Was the Good-Corn Year, before the Red-Sunset Year, and did that come after the Year When Evie Died?

Poor Evie! They buried her next to the others, and in her

grave at least she was no different. All those years she had lived with them, and whether she had been happy no one knew, and whether they had done well to keep her living. Only once in all those years had she mattered much, and yet for that little time, when Charlie had come, she had seemed very important. Now that she was gone, the young people scarcely missed her; nevertheless the older ones remembered that her going marked still another broken link with the Old Times.

With Evie gone, only five of the original ones remained. Jean and Ish were the youngest of these five, and age showed least in them, although Ish limped more and more from his old wound. Molly complained of vague illnesses and wept often. Ezra coughed with his dry cough. Even Em walked with a less sure and regal grace. Yet actually they all enjoyed amazingly good health for people of their years, and their various decrepitudes sprang chiefly from approaching old age.

The Year 34—that was an important one! They had known for some time that there was another but smaller group of people living across north of the Bay, but in this year the surprise was that the other people sent a messenger with the proposal of a union. Ish made the young man keep distance, for he wanted no repetition of that business of Charlie. Having got all the information he could from the messenger, he called a meeting.

Ish sat with his hammer, for it was a time of great state. There was a hot argument. Reinforcing the fear of disease was a prejudice against strangers and all their strange ways. On the other hand, a kind of fascination in the very strangeness combatted the prejudice. Besides, there was the strong desire to strengthen the numbers of The Tribe, and particularly to obtain wives. For, in late years, fewer girls than boys had been born and some of the young men had nowhere to look. To Ish also there was the argument that the in-breeding of The Tribe might be dangerous, for now blood-relationship was universal and everyone had to marry his cousin.

But Ish himself, along with Ezra, opposed the union, in overwhelming fear of disease, and Jack and Ralph and Roger, the oldest of the younger men, remembered the Year 22, and supported Ish and Ezra. But the still younger men, especially the unmarried ones, clamored for the union, and Ish could see that the thought of the girls of that other tribe excited them.

Then Em spoke. Her hair was wholly gray now, but her calm voice held them. "I have said it before," she said. "Life is not lived by denying life. Our sons and grandsons will need wives. Perhaps death will come also, but that too we must face."

Not so much by what she said as by the spirit that flowed out from her, they all had courage. They voted without dissent to admit the others.

This time luck was with them, for the only epidemic was that The Others contracted measles, and soon were well again.

After that time there was always a division within The Tribe, as of two clans—The First Ones and The Others. When they intermarried, the children were of their father's clan, although Ish had wondered whether mother-lineage might not prevail, as with many primitive people. But the old tradition of the Americans was too strong.

Then in the next year Ish realized more than ever that Em walked no longer with that regal grace; suddenly when he looked at her, he saw strange lines in her face, not the lines of old age, but the lines of pain. Behind the darkness of the cheeks there was not the glow of red but an ashy gray. Deep within him he felt chill and fear, and he knew that this also had come close to its end.

Sometimes, in those grim months that followed, he thought to himself, "This may be merely appendicitis. The pain is in that place. Why can I not operate? I can read the books. I could find out how it is done. One of the boys could manage the ether. At worst, I would only end the pain."

But always he realized that it could not be—for his hands were no longer young and sure, and his courage too perhaps had grown weak, so that he dared not draw the knife-edge across the side of her whom he loved. So he knew that Em must face the future alone.

Before long, too, he knew that this was not appendicitis. As the sun swung southward again, she weakened and walked no more. He hunted in the ruinous drug-stores, and found powders and syrups, so that at least she suffered little. After she had taken the medicine, she would sleep or lie quietly, smiling. Then after a while, when the pain again began to make her toss, he would think: "Perhaps I should make the dose larger still, and bring a finish to all pain."

But he did not. For she, he knew, had always reached out toward life, and her courage would not fail.

282

So he sat long hours by the bed, holding her hand, and now and then they talked.

As it always had been, she was the one who comforted him, although she was the one who lay in pain and was going. Yes, he realized, she had been mother as well as wife.

"Don't worry," she said once, "about the children, I mean —and the grandchildren and all those that will come after. They will be happy, I think. At least, they may be as happy as they would have been otherwise. Don't care too much about that civilization. They will go on!"

Had she known all along? He wondered. Had she known that he would fail? Had she sensed how it would be? Perhaps because she was a woman? Perhaps because within her veins ran a different strain of blood? And again he puzzled over what made greatness—either in man or woman.

Josey cared for the house now, and for her mother—Josey, herself a mother, straight and full-breasted and walking with easy grace. Of them all, she had grown to be most like Em.

The others came also to the the bedside—the tall sons and the strong daughters and the grandchildren. Already the oldest grandsons were shooting up tall and on bodies of the granddaughters the fullness of their womanhood was showing.

Looking at them, as they passed the bedside, Ish knew that Em was right. "They will go on!" he thought. "The simple ones are also the strong ones. They will go on!"

At last one day he sat, again holding her hand. She was very weak, and then suddenly he knew that a third and dark presence was there beside them. She spoke no more and only once he felt a light flutter of her fingers within his hand.

"Oh, Mother of Nations!" he thought. "Her sons shall praise, and her daughters call her blessed!"

Then, where there had been three, now there was only one, for Death had gone and she too. He sat there bowed and dry-eyed. That too was finished. They would bury her, Mother of Nations, and place no marker, for that was their custom. And, as it was in the beginning, since love first and sorrow with it came to the world, he sat with his dead. And he knew that greatness had passed from them.

Yet still the years flowed, and the sun swung from north of the mountain, south past the Golden Gate, and back again. More years were carved into the rock.

One spring Molly died suddenly of what they took to be heart-failure. That same year a great tumor grew within Jean —swiftly, like a nightmare growth. There was no one who knew how to help her, and when she had died by her own hand, there was no one who blamed her.

"We are going, we are going!" thought Ish. "We Americans are old, and are dropping like last spring's leaves." So sometimes he was sad. Yet, as he walked along the hillside, he saw many children playing busily, and young men shouting to one another, and mothers nursing their babies—and little sadness, and much merriment.

One day Ezra came to him, saying: "You should take another wife." Ish looked at him with questioning eyes. "No," said Ezra, "*I* am too old. *You* are younger. There is a young woman of The Others, and no man to marry her. Except for an old man, it is better not to be alone. And there should be more children."

He felt no love, but he took her. She comforted him in the long nights, for he was still a man in his strength. She bore him children, though the children seemed always a little strange to him—scarcely his, because they were not also Em's.

More years were carved in the rock. Except for Ish and Ezra, all the Americans now were gone, and Ezra was a little dried-up wrinkled man who coughed and grew thinner and thinner. Ish himself was wholly gray-haired now. Though he was not heavy, his paunch stuck out, and he was thin-legged in the manner of old men. His side hurt him where the mountain-lion had clawed him years back; so he walked little. Yet still his young wife bore him a child in the year 42. He was not greatly interested in that child, and also now he had great-grandchildren.

On the day when the year 43 had ended, Ish did not feel like walking as far as the flat rock where they carved the numerals, and Ezra was too frail. So they put off carving the date in the rock or giving a name. They said to each other now and then that really they must do it, or else arrange with some of the younger men to carve the numerals, and sometimes also the younger men and even the children talked of it. But in a way that such things go, once it had been put off, still it was put off again. "Today is rainy," or "It is too cold," or "We are going fishing, and shall do it later." So the numerals were not carved, and the name was not given, and life went on with no one caring greatly. After that, no one knew how many years passed.

Now no more children were born to Ish's young wife. Then one day she came to him with a younger man, and the

284

two asked, respectfully, that Ish should give her to that one.

Then at last Ish realized that in this his curious life, he had now come close to the last stage of all. More and more often, after that, he and Ezra sat together as two old men.

There was nothing strange that two old men should sit together and talk, but what was strange here was that there were no other old people at all. Elsewhere everything was youth, at least by comparison. There were births and there were deaths, but always there were more births than deaths, and because everyone was youthful, there was much laughter.

As the quick years passed and the two old men sat on the hillside in the sun, they began to talk more and more about what had happened long ago. There was little that anyone— they, at least—could talk about as far as these years now were concerned. Some years were called good years and some were called bad years, but there was not much difference. So chiefly the two old men talked about things of long ago, and occasionally they speculated about life.

Often, when they talked, Ish realized that there was still wisdom and help in Ezra.

"A tribe is like a child," he said once, in that thin piping old-man's voice, which every day seemed more like a bird's—and then he coughed. When he recovered, he spoke again. "Yes, a tribe is like a child. You can show it the way by which it should grow up, and perhaps you can direct it a little, but in the end the child will go his own way, and so will the tribe."

"Yes," he said again on some other day, "time makes all things clear. Everything seems plainer to me now than it once did, and if I should live for a hundred years more, perhaps everything that has happened so far would seem very plain and simple."

Often they talked of the other Americans, those who now were gone. They laughed, remembering good old George, and Maurine with her fine radio that would never play. They smiled when they recalled Jean, and her refusal to go to church.

"Yes," said Ezra, "it is all clearer now with time. Why each of them survived the Great Disaster—that I still do not know. But I think I can see why each of them survived the shock that came afterwards, when so many went under. George and Maurine, and perhaps Molly too, they lived on and did not go crazy because they were stolid and

285

had no imagination. And Jean survived because she had her temper and fought back at life; and I, because I went out from myself and shared the lives of other people. And you and Em . . ."

But here Ezra paused, so that Ish himself could speak.

"Yes," said Ish, "you are right, I think. . . . And I, I could live because I stood at one side and watched what was happening. And as for Em . . ."

There he too paused, and Ezra spoke again.

"Well, as *we* were, so The Tribe will be. It will not be brilliant because we were not like that. Perhaps the brilliant ones were not suited to survive. . . . But as for Em, there is no need to explain, for we know that she was the strongest of us all. Yes, we needed many things. We needed George and his carpentry, and we needed your foresight, and perhaps we needed my knack of making one person work better with another, even though I did little by myself. But most of all, I think, we needed Em, for she gave us courage, and without courage there is only a slow dying, not life."

Almost while they sat there, it seemed to Ish, a fast-growing tree sprang up on the hillside below them, and grew until it cut off the view across the Bay, where the rust-red towers of the great bridge still stood high. And then after a while the tree seemed to sicken and die and fall. Again, from where he liked to sit in the sun on the hillside, he could look out and see the bridge. And once, as he looked, there was great fire raging in the ruinous city beyond the Bay, and he remembered that far, far back—even before he had been born—that city had burned before. Now it burned for a week, with the dry north wind driving the flames; there was no one to put it out, and no one even to care whether it burned. When the flames died down, nothing was left to burn.

There came a time when even talking seemed a labor. So mostly now Ish merely sat comfortably in the sun, and beside him sat an even older man who coughed and grew thinner. It was hard to tell just how the days passed and how they ran into weeks, and even the years seemed to flow with a man's scarcely noticing them. Yet Ezra remained, and sometimes Ish thought to himself, "Though he coughs and coughs and grows thinner, yet he will outlive me."

But now, since even talking was a labor, the mind turned inward on itself, and Ish thought of all this strange life. What was the difference in the end? Even if there had been no

286

Great Disaster, he would now be a very old man. Now doubtless, if it had not happened otherwise, he would be Professor Emeritus, puttering around, taking some books out of the Library and intending to do some research, a little of a nuisance to the younger men in their fifties and sixties who now ran the Department—though they might say loyally to the graduate students, "That's Professor Williams—a great scholar, once. We're very proud of him."

Now the Old Times were deeper buried than Nineveh or Mohenjodaro. He himself had seen everything crash and go under. Yet curiously, too, all that crash had not been able to destroy his personality. He was still the same person he would have been as Professor Emeritus, even though now the shadows were closing in on his mind while he sat on a lonely hillside as the dying patriarch of a primitive tribe.

At some time in those years something else strange began to happen. The younger men had always come to Ish for advice, but now—even though the shadows were closing in on his mind—they began to come in a different way. Whether he sat on the hillside in the sun, or whether, during rain and fog, he sat in the house, still they began to come to him bearing little gifts—a handful of ripe berries of which he was fond, or a bright stone or piece of colored glass to flash in the sun. Ish did not care for the glass or stones, even though the stones were sometimes sapphires or emeralds taken from a jewelry store, but he appreciated the gifts because he realized that the young men were giving him things by which they themselves would be pleased.

Having given him something, they would formally ask a question, while he sat holding his hammer. Sometimes they asked about the weather, and then Ish was glad to answer. He could still look at his father's barometer, and so he could often say—what the young men could not know—whether the low clouds would soon vanish before the sun's heat or whether they indicated an approaching storm.

But sometimes they asked him other questions—as, for instance, in which direction they should go for good hunting. Then Ish did not wish to answer, for he knew nothing of such matters. But when he did not answer, the young men were displeased, and then they would pinch him roughly. Because he was in pain he answered them, even though he knew nothing. He would cry out, "Go south!" or "Go beyond the hills!" Then the young men were pleased and went off. Ish sometimes feared that they would come back and pinch

287

him because they had not found good hunting, but they never did.

During those years, there were days when he thought clearly, and other days when a fog seemed to hang in all the corners of his brain. But one day when they came to ask him a question and he was clear-minded, he realized that he must have become a god, or at the least an oracle by which a god spoke. Then he remembered that time long ago when the children had been afraid to carry the hammer and when they had nodded knowingly at his saying he was an American. Yet he had never wished to be a god.

One day Ish sat on the hillside in the sun, and after a while he looked at his left side, and saw that no one sat there. Then he realized that at last Ezra, the good helper, was gone, and that no one would ever sit there beside him on the hillside again. At that thought he gripped the handle of the hammer, which in these days was very heavy for him to lift, even with both hands.

"It is called a single-jack," he thought, "but now it is too heavy for my one hand. Yet now it has become the symbol of a tribal god, and it is still with me, though all the others, even Ezra, have gone."

Then, because the shock of that sudden knowledge about Ezra had made him think and see more clearly, he looked alertly about him, and observed that he was sitting on the slope of the hill where many years before there had been a neat garden and was now only a trampled place of tall grass in the midst of overgrown bushes and high trees, with a half-ruined house standing up from among the tangle.

Then he looked at the sun, and saw that it was in the east, not in the west, as he had thought it would be. Also, it was far to the north, so that the season must be nearly mid-summer, whereas he had thought it should be early spring. Yes, in all those years, as he had sat on the hillside, he had lost hold of time itself, so that the swinging of the sun from east to west with the passing of the day seemed much the same as the swinging of the sun from north to south with the passing of the seasons, and he had lost track of them both. This thought made him feel very old and very sad.

Perhaps that sadness brought back to him the thought of other sadness also, and he thought:

"Yes, Em is gone, and Joey, and even Ezra, my helper, is gone now."

288

When he thus recalled all that had happened, and his lone-liness. he began to cry gently, for he was an old man, and he could not control what he did. And he thought to him-self, "Yes, they are all gone! I am the last American!"

End of the second inter-chapter called Quick Years.

The Last American

'Tis merry, 'tis merry in good greenwood.
—Old Song

Chapter 1

Perhaps it was that same day or perhaps it was only that same summer or perhaps even it was another year. . . . When Ish looked up, he saw, very clearly, a young man standing in front of him. The young man wore a neat-enough pair of blue jeans with copper rivets shining brightly, and yet over his shoulders he wore a tawny hide with sharp claws dangling from it. In his hand he held a strong bow, and over his shoulder was a quiver with the feathered ends of arrows sticking from it.

Ish blinked, for in his old eyes the sunshine was strong.

"Who are you?" said Ish.

The young man answered respectfully, "I am Jack, Ish, as indeed you yourself well know."

The way he said "Ish" did not indicate that he was trying to be unduly familiar with an old man, thus calling him by a nickname, but rather it carried something of great respect and even of awe, and as if "Ish" stood for much more than merely the name of an old man.

But Ish himself was confused, and he squinted, peering more carefully, because at short distances he no longer saw clearly. But he was sure that Jack should have dark hair, or perhaps turned somewhat gray by now, and this one who called himself Jack had long wavy yellow hair.

"You should not make jokes with an old man," said Ish. "Jack is my oldest son, and I would recognize him. He has dark hair, and he is older than you."

The young man laughed, but politely, and said, "You are talking, Ish, of my grandfather, as indeed you yourself well know." Again the way in which he said "Ish" had a certain strange sound to it, and now Ish noticed also the strangeness of his other repeated words, "as indeed you yourself well know."

"Are you of the First Ones?" Ish asked. "Or of the Others?"

"Of the First Ones," he said.

Then, as Ish still looked, he was puzzled that the young man, who was certainly not a child, was carrying a bow instead of a rifle.

"Why do you not have a rifle?" he asked.

"Rifles are good for playthings!" the young man said, and he laughed, a little scornfully perhaps. "You cannot be sure of a rifle, as indeed you yourself, Ish, well know. Sometimes the rifle works, and it makes the big noise, but other times you pull the trigger, and it only goes 'click'." Here he snapped his fingers. "So you cannot use the rifles for real hunting, although the older men say that this was not so in the long past years. But now we use the arrow because it is sure, and never refuses to fly and besides," here the young man held himself proudly, "besides, it is a matter of strength and skill to shoot with the bow—but anyone, they say, could shoot with a rifle, as you yourself, Ish, well know."

"Let me see an arrow," said Ish.

The young man took an arrow from the quiver, and looked at it, and then handed it across.

"That is a good arrow," he said. "I made it myself."

Ish looked at the arrow and felt the weight of it. This was no plaything for a child. The shaft was nearly a yard long, split cleanly from a billet of flawless straight-grained wood, and then rounded and smoothed. It was well feathered, with pinions of some kind, although Ish could not see well enough to know what bird had yielded the feathers. By feeling, however, he could tell that they were arranged carefully so that the arrow in flight would spin like a rifle-bullet, and thus keep its true course and carry farther.

Then he observed the arrowhead, again more by feel than by sight. The arrowhead was very sharp both at the point and along the edges. Ish nearly pricked his thumb. It had the bumpy yet slick feel which told him that it was of hammered metal. Though he could not see very clearly, he made the color out as silvery-white.

"What is *that* made of?" he asked.

"It is from one of the little round things. They have faces on them. The old men have a name for them, but I do not remember exactly. It is something like *corns*."

The young man paused, as if to be told the right word, but when he had no reply, he went on again, being obviously eager to show off his knowledge about arrowheads.

"We find these little round things in the old buildings. Often there are many—many—of them in the boxes and drawers. Sometimes they are rolled up together in bundles like short round sticks, but heavier than sticks. Some are red and some are white, like this one, and there are two kinds of the white. The one kind of white—the one that has the picture of the hump-backed bull—we do not use those because they are harder to pound."

Ish considered, and thought that he understood.

"And this white one here?" he asked. "Was there a relief—a picture—on this one?"

The young man took the arrow from Ish, and looked at it, and then handed it back.

"They all have pictures," he said. "But I was looking to see if I could still make out what picture was on this one. It has not quite all gone because of the hammering. This was one of the littlest ones, and it had the picture of the woman with the wings growing out of her head. Some of them have pictures of hawks—but not real hawks." The young man was talking very happily. "Others have men; at least, they look like men—one with a beard, and one with long hair hanging behind him and another with a strong-looking face, without a beard and with short hair, and heavy-jawed."

"And who—who do you think—were all these men?"

The young man glanced both ways, as if a little nervous.

"These—oh, these—yes! These, we think—as you yourself, Ish, well know—these were the Old Ones that were before our Old Ones!"

When there was no thunder from heaven and when the young man could see that Ish was not displeased, he went on:

"Yes, that must be it—as you yourself, Ish, well know. These men, and the hawks, and the bull! Perhaps the woman with the wings growing from her head sprang from the marriage of a hawk and a woman. But, however it is, they do not seem to mind our taking their pictures and hammering them up for arrowheads. I have wondered about it. Perhaps they are too great to care about little things, or perhaps they did their work a long time ago and have now grown old and weak."

He stopped talking, but Ish could see that he was pleased with himself, and liked to talk, and was thinking quickly of something more to say. He, at least, had imagination.

"Yes," the young man continued, "I have an idea. Our Old Ones—they were the Americans—made the houses and the bridges and the little round things that we hammer out for arrowheads. But those others—the Old Ones of the Old Ones—perhaps they made the hills and the sun, and the Americans themselves."

Then, though it was a cheap trick to play on the young man, Ish could not resist talking in double meaning.

"Yes," he said, "I have heard it said that those older Old

Ones produced the Americans—but I rather doubt that they made the hills and the sun."

Though he could not have understood, perhaps the young man caught the irony in the tone, and so said nothing.

"But, go on," Ish continued then. "Tell me more about the arrowheads themselves. I am not interested in your cosmogony." He used the last word in good-humored malice, knowing that the other would not understand it, but would be impressed by its length and strange sound.

"Yes, about the arrowheads," the young man said, hesitating a moment, and then regaining confidence. "We use both the red and white. The red are good for shooting cattle and lions. The white are for deer and other game."

"Why is that?" Ish asked sharply, for he felt his old-time rationalism stirring at the thought of all such magic and hocus-pocus. The question, however, seemed only to surprise and confuse the young man.

"Why?" he asked. "Why? How would anyone know *why?* Except you yourself, Ish! This matter of the red and white arrowheads is merely something that *is*. It is like—" He hesitated, and then the sunlight seemed to catch his attention. "Yes, it is like the sun that keeps on going round the earth, but naturally no one knows why, or asks why. *Why* should there be a *why?*"

Having said these last words, the young man was obviously very pleased with himself as if he had propounded some great philosophical dictum, although undoubtedly he had spoken only in great simplicity. But when Ish turned the matter over in his mind, he was not sure. Perhaps even in this simplicity there was a depth. Was there ever an answer to "why"? Did not things just exist in the present?

Yet, Ish was certain, a fallacy lurked somewhere in the argument. A sense of cause-and-effect was necessary for life at the human level, and this matter of the different-colored arrowheads was a proof of it, not the contrary. Only, the sense of causation here was faulty and irrational. The young man was maintaining an absurdity—that cattle and lions could be better killed with copper arrowheads hammered from pennies, whereas deer were better killed with silver ones hammered from dimes or quarters. Yet there could obviously not be enough difference in hardness or sharpness to matter. Only, in these primitive minds, the secondary matter of color had in some way come to be considered—this was rank superstition!—the determining factor.

Deep within him, Ish again felt his old hatred of loose thinking boil up. Though he was an old man, still he might do something.

"*No!*" he said, so sharply that the young man started. "*No!* That is not right. The white arrowheads and the red! One just as well as. . . ."

Then, slowly his voice trailed off. No, he thought, that was not the way it was destined to be. He heard a rich contralto voice saying to him, "Relax!" Perhaps he might persuade this young man named Jack, who was undoubtedly a remarkably intelligent and imaginative young man, possibly even somewhat like that little one named Joey. But what would it accomplish? Only, perhaps to make the young man confused and ill at ease among all the others. And what was really the difference? At least, copper arrowheads were not *less* effective against lions, and if the bowman thought them *more* effective, the thought gave him courage and steadied his hand.

So Ish said nothing more about the matter, and smiled at the young man reassuringly, and looked again at the arrow.

Another thought came to him, and he asked:

"Can you always find plenty of those little round things?"

The young man laughed merrily, as if this were a strange question.

"Oh, yes," he said. "There are so many that if all of us spent all our time pounding out arrowheads, still we should never run short."

Ish considered. Yes, that was probably true. Even if there were a hundred men in The Tribe by now, there must be thousands and thousands of coins readily to be found in tills and cash-boxes, even in this one corner of the city. And if the coins should be exhausted, there would be thousands of miles of copper telephone wire. When he had first made an arrow, he recollected, he had imagined that The Tribe would revert to stone arrowheads. Instead they had taken a short-cut, and were already fashioning metal. So perhaps The Tribe, his own descendants, had already passed the turning-point, were no longer forgetting more old things than they were learning new things, and were no longer sinking toward savagery, but were maintaining a stable level or perhaps gradually beginning to win new security. By showing them how to make bows, he had helped, and he felt greatly comforted.

Then, having finished looking at the arrow, Ish handed it

296

back. "It seems to be a very good arrow," he said, although he did not really know much about arrows.

Nevertheless the young man smiled with great happiness at this praise of his arrow, and Ish noted that he made a mark on it before he put it back into the quiver, as if he wished to know it and distinguish it from other arrows after what had happened. Then, as he still looked at the young man, Ish felt a sudden great love for him, and he had not been so moved for a long time since he had been sitting as an old man on the hillside. This Jack, who was of the First Ones, must be Ish's great-grandson in the male line, and he was also Em's great-grandson. So, as Ish looked, his heart yearned outwards, and he asked a strange question:

"Young man," he said, "are you happy?" The young man named Jack looked startled at this question, and he glanced in both directions before answering, and then he spoke.

"Yes, I am happy. Things are as they are, and I am part of them."

Ish began to think of what this might mean and to wonder again whether the words had been spoken only in simplicity or whether there was some deep philosophy behind them, but he could not decide. At his trying to think, the fog seemed again to move in at the corners of his brain. But still he recollected vaguely that the words—strange as they were—had a ring of familiarity about them. He had not perhaps ever heard those exact words before, but they were words that someone whom he had once known might well have spoken. For in his words the young man had not questioned, but had accepted. Ish could not recall this person exactly, but he remembered softness and warmth, and warm feelings flowed through him.

When he came out of his reverie and looked up again, no one was standing in front of him. In fact, Ish would have been unable to say surely whether the young man named Jack had been there that same day, or whether this was now some other day, or perhaps even another summer.

Chapter 2

He awoke so early, one morning, that the room was still in half-darkness. He lay quiet for a moment, wondering where he was, and for a moment he thought that he was a small boy again and had crawled into his mother's bed for comfort in the early morning. Then he realized that it could not be so, and he thought that if he stretched out his hand he would find Em lying there beside him. But that was not so, either. Then he thought of his young wife. But no, she would not be there either, for long ago he had given her to a younger man because it is right that a woman should bear children so that the tribe will increase and the darkness draw farther back. So then at last he realized that he was a very old man, and was lying in the bed by himself. Nevertheless, it was the same bed and the same room.

There was a strange dryness in his throat. After a minute he slowly got out of bed, and uncertainly on his old stiff legs he walked to the bathroom for a drink of water. As he went into the bathroom, he stretched out his right hand, and flipped the electric-light switch. It made the familiar click, and suddenly the room was brilliant to his eyes. Then after a moment he found himself in the half-darkness of dawn again, and he realized that the electric light had not flashed on. It had not so flashed for years, and would never again—and the familiar click had merely fooled his old brain, so that for a moment the room had seemed light. All this did not bother him, because it had thus happened before.

Also, when he turned the stiff faucet-handle at the washbowl, no water gushed out merrily. Then he remembered that years ago the water had ceased to run.

He could not get his drink of water, but he was not so much thirsty as merely bothered by that dryness in the throat. After he had swallowed a few times, he felt better. When he stood by the bedside again, he hesitated, sniffing. He could remember many changes of smells through the years. Far back there had been the smell of a great city. That had given way to the clean smell of green things and growth. But that also had yielded, and now there was about the old house a smell of age and decay. That smell, however, was familiar and was not bothering him. What he was trying to assay was a kind of dry smokiness. That dryness, he considered, had made him wake up so early. But he felt no fear, and crawled into bed again.

A steady wind was blowing from the north. It tossed the pine trees that now grew closely around the house, and the branches swished and knocked against the windows and against the walls of the house.

The noise kept him awake, and he lay there listening. He wished that he knew the time, but he no longer kept a clock wound. Time in its old sense of appointments to be kept and things to be done—all that had long since ceased to exist, both because the way of life had changed and because he himself was so old as to be almost out of life. In certain ways he had already, as it seemed, passed from time to eternity.

Now he lay by himself in the old and half-ruined house. The others slept in other houses, or in good weather lay in the open. Perhaps they felt that ghosts walked in this old house. Well, perhaps! To Ish himself the thoughts of those who had been long dead were often more immediately present than the bodies of those now living.

Though he had no clock, the half-light told him that the time could not be much before sunrise. Perhaps he had slept as long as an old man needed to sleep. He would lie there, turning himself over occasionally, until the sun had risen, and someone—he hoped it would be the young man called Jack—came to bring him his breakfast. There would be a well-braised beef bone on which he could suck, and some corn-meal boiled into a mush. The Tribe took good care of him, an old man. They let him have corn-meal, though that was something of a rarity with them. They sent someone to carry his hammer and help him outdoors, so that he could sit on the hillside when there was sunshine. Often the one who came to help him was Jack. Yes, they took very good care of him, even though he was a useless old man. Sometimes they grew angry with him and pinched him, but that was only because they thought he was a god.

The wind still blew, and the branches brushed and slapped against the house. But he had apparently not slept as much as he needed to sleep, and after a while he drowsed off, in spite of the noises.

The cuts in the hills and the long embankments for the roads—they will still show as narrow valleys and ridges even after ten thousand years have passed. The great masses of concrete that were the dams—they will remain like the dikes of the granite itself.

But the steel and the wood will pass quickly. The three fires will take them.

Slowest of all is the fire of rust that burns at the steel. Yet give it some short centuries, and the high trestle that spans the canyon will be only a line of red soil on the slopes below.

Faster by far is the fire of decay that feeds on the wood. But fastest of all is the fire of the flames.

Then suddenly someone was shaking him hard. He awoke with a great shock. As he focused his old eyes, he saw that the person who was shaking him was the young man named Jack, and that Jack's face was tense with fear.

"Get up! Get up quick!" Jack was saying. With the shock of the sudden awakening, Ish's mind seemed clearer than before, and both his body and his mind reacted faster. He moved quickly, pulling on some clothes. Jack helped him. Smoke was heavy in the room now, no longer a mere smell. Ish coughed, and his eyes watered. He heard a crackle and a dull roar. They went downstairs quickly, and out the front door, and down the steps toward the street. Only when he was out of the house did Ish realize how strongly the wind was blowing. Smoke rolled before it, and bits of burning leaves and bark swirled along.

Ish was not surprised. He had known always that this must happen some time. Every year the oat-grass grew tall, and then ripened and dried where it stood. Every year the bushes of the deserted gardens had grown more thick, and the dead leaves had fallen among them. It was only a question of time, he had always known, until some hunter's campfire would escape from him, and with a strong wind driving it, the fire would make a clean sweep on this side of the Bay, as it had on the other.

Just as they reached the sidewalk, the thick clump of underbrush around the next house to the north suddenly went up in a roar of flame so that Ish shrank away from the heat. Jack began to hurry him along the sidewalk away from the approaching fire, and just at that moment Ish realized that he had forgotten something although he could not remember just what.

They came to two other young men who were standing there looking at the approaching flames. Then Ish remembered.

"My hammer!" he cried out. "Where is my hammer?"

As soon as he had cried out, he was ashamed of himself to have made so much fuss about a trifle in a time of emergency. After all, the hammer was of no importance. Then he was amazed to see what a tremendous impression his words had made upon the three young men. They looked at each other as if they were panic-stricken. Suddenly, Jack dashed back toward the house, even though the bushes in the garden itself were now beginning to smoke.

"Come back! Come back!" Ish called after him, but his

voice was not very strong, and he was half choking on account of the smoke.

This was a terrible thing, Ish was thinking to himself, that Jack should be burned in the fire about such a small matter as a hammer.

But then Jack came running out. His lion-skin cloak was singed, and he himself was rubbing at some burns where sparks had fallen on him. But otherwise he was not hurt. The other young men seemed strangely relieved that he was carrying the hammer in his hand.

Obviously, they could not stay where they were very long because the flames were bearing down upon them.

"Where shall we go, Ish?" one of them asked. Ish felt that this was a strange question for anyone to ask of him, who was only an old man and would scarcely know what to do as well as the young ones would. Then he remembered that they sometimes asked him which direction they should take for their hunting. When he did not answer, they pinched him. He did not like to be pinched, and so he thought hard now, as to which way they should go. The young men themselves, he realized, could outrun the fire, but he himself would not be strong enough. So he thought more intensely than he had thought for a long time, both because he wished to save his own life and the lives of the young men, and also because he was afraid that they would pinch him. Thinking so intently, he remembered the bare flat rock where they had carved the numerals of the years in the time long ago. Round this flat rock were other high rocks where nothing grew, and in the spaces among these rocks they could find shelter because nothing was there to burn.

"Let us go to the rocks!" he said then, being sure that they would know what rocks he meant.

Even though the young men helped him, Ish was very tired when they got to the safety of the rocks. Once they were there, however, he lay quietly, panting and recovering his strength. The fire was soon burning all around, but among the rocks they were not in danger. There was an overhang to the one rock, and another tall rock close by, so that they were almost in a cave.

As he lay there, Ish dozed off with his weariness, or perhaps it was more as if he had fainted, because his old heart was pounding wildly after the dash ahead of the flames. But after a while he came to himself, and lay there quietly, and his mind seemed clearer than it had been for a long time.

Yes, he thought, it is now the dry autumn, and the time of bad fires because of dry north winds. And this is the autumn following that summer when I first came to know Jack, and talked to him about the arrowheads. Since then Jack has been the one who has chiefly taken care of me, as The Tribe at its meeting has undoubtedly ordered him to do. After all, I am very important. I am a god. No, I am not a god. But perhaps I am the mouth-piece of a god. No, I know that I am not that either. But at least they give me care, and I have comfort, because I am the last American.

Then again, since he was exhausted from his flight in front of the flames, he fell asleep, or perhaps fainted.

After a while he came to himself once more. He could not have been unconscious for very long, for he heard the flames still crackling. When he opened his eyes, all he could see was the grayness of the rock-overhang above him, and he realized that he must be lying on his back. He heard little noises of scuffling and the playful growls of a dog.

But now with this return to consciousness his mind seemed even clearer than before, so clear indeed that he was startled at first, and then a little frightened. For he seemed to know all the past and all the future too, as well as what was actually present.

"This second world—it has gone too." The thoughts flickered through his mind. "I saw the great world go. Now this little world, my second world, is going. It is going by fire. This fire that we have known so long—fire that warms us; fire that destroys us. They used to say that because of the bombs we would go back and live in caves. Well, here is a cave—but we have not marched by the road that anyone imagined. I survived the loss of that, my great world, but I shall not outlast the destruction of this, my little world. I am an old man now, and also my mind is too clear. I know. This is near the end. From the cave we came, and to the cave we return."

Just as his mind had grown clearer, so also his sight seemed clearer than usual. After a while, feeling stronger, he sat up, and then he could see all the others. At first he was surprised because there were not only three young men but also two dogs. He did not remember having seen the dogs before. They were ordinary dogs of the kind used for hunting —not large, long haired, mostly black with some white on them, a kind of sheep dog, he supposed they would have been called in the Old Times. They were intelligent dogs, and even well-mannered. They lay quietly now in the cave-like

302

overhang of the rocks, and did not make any excitement of barking.

Then Ish looked at the young men. Since now, all at once, he seemed to see the past and the future as well as the present, he could look more clearly at the young men for the mixture of past, present and future that they really were. Their clothing was like Jack's. They had soft, well-fashioned moccasin-like footgear of deer-hide; they also wore blue jeans with bright copper rivets in them. Above their waists they had only the tawny lion-skins with the dangling paws and the claws still attached. Each one of them had his bow and quiver of arrows, and each wore a knife at his belt, although they could not make knives. One of them had a spear with a shaft as tall as himself, and extending above the shaft, a spear-head. When Ish looked at it more carefully, he saw that it was really an old butcher-knife with an eighteen-inch blade. The blade had been socketed into the end of the spear-shaft, and since the blade was very sharp-pointed, this was a formidable weapon for close fighting.

Then at last Ish looked at the faces of the young men, and he saw that they were different from the faces of the men of long ago. These faces were young, but also they were calm, and they seemed to bear on them few lines of strain and worry and fear.

"See!" said one of them, and he was nodding in the direction of Ish. "See—he is better now! He is looking around." Ish realized that the voice was kindly, and he felt a great love for the young man even though a little while ago he had been afraid that that particular one would be the first to pinch him.

Something else that was strange also, Ish thought now, was that after all these years the young men still talked a language which people had once called English.

Only, as he considered more carefully, he realized that the language too had changed. When the young man had said the word "see," the sound was not quite as it should be. Instead, it sounded more as if it were "tsee," or perhaps, "tchee."

Some smoke was drifting in between the rocks now, so that they coughed a little. Outside, there was a great crackle of flame; a clump of trees or a near-by house must be burning. The dogs whined a little. Yet the air remained cool enough, so that Ish was not afraid.

He wondered what had become of all the others. There must be several hundred people in The Tribe now. The labor of asking questions seemed too much, and he could tell from the calmness of the young men that there could have been no disaster. Most likely, he thought, the others had left at the first threat of fire, and perhaps only at the last moment Jack had remembered the old man—who was also a god—who was sleeping alone in the house.

Yes, now it was easier merely to sit and look and think, without asking questions. So he looked at the faces again.

Now one of the young men was playing with a dog. He put out his hand, and then jerked it away quickly, and the dog snapped playfully and growled. The dog and the young man seemed almost to meet at the same level, and both seemed happy. One of the others was carving a piece of wood. The sharp knife bit deeply into the soft wood, and a figure took shape as Ish watched. Ish smiled quietly to himself, for he saw that the figure had wide hips and generous breasts, and he realized that young men had not changed altogether. Though he did not even know their names, except for Jack, yet they must all be his grandsons or great-grandsons. Here they sat in the cave-like gap between two high rocks, and they played with a dog or carved lusty little images while outside the fire crackled. Civilization had gone years ago, and now the last of the city was burning around them, and yet the young men were happy.

Was it all for the best? From the cave we come and to the cave we go! If that other one had lived, if there had been others like him, it might have been different. Again he thought of Joey—Joey! And yet would that have been better? He wished suddenly that he could live for a long time still—for a hundred years more, or even a hundred after that. All his life now he had observed the ways of the peoples on the earth, and he wished that he could still observe in the future. The next century and the next millennium would be interesting.

And then for a while, in the way of very old men, he merely sat quietly, not sleeping, and yet not quite thinking either.

Again, in that day each little tribe will live by itself and to itself and go its own way, and their differences will soon be more than they were even in the first days of Man, according to the accidents of survival and of place. . . .

Here they live always in awe of the Other-world, and scarcely dare make water without a prayer. They have skill with boats among tidal channels. To eat, they catch fish and dig clams, and gather seeds of wild-grasses. . . .

Here they are darker-skinned and talk another language, and worship a dark-skinned mother and child. They keep horses and turkeys, and grow corn in the flat by the river. They catch rabbits in snares, but have no bows. . . .

Here they are still darker. They speak English, but say no r's, and their speech is thick. They keep pigs and chickens, and raise corn. Also they raise cotton, but make no use of it, except to offer a little to their god, knowing it from of old to be a thing of power. Their god has the form of an alligator, and they call him Olsaytn. . . .

Here they shoot with the bow, skillfully, and their hunting-dogs are trained to give tongue. They love assembly and debate. Their womenfolk walk proudly. The symbol of their god is a hammer, but they pay him no great reverence. . . .

Many others there are too, each differing. In the distant years after these first years, the tribes will grow more numerous and come together, and cross-fertilize in body and in mind. Then, doubtless, blindly and of no one's planning, will come new civilizations and the new wars.

After a while they grew hungry and very thirsty. Since the fire had now died down in places, one of the young men sallied out. When he came back, he was carrying an old aluminum tea-kettle. Ish recognized it as the one which had been kept at the near-by spring. The young man offered it first to Ish, and he took a long drink of the cool water. Then the others drank.

Afterwards the same young man pulled a flat tin can out of the hip-pocket of his blue jeans. The label had long since fallen away from the can, and the metal was well rusted. The three discussed vigorously among themselves whether they should eat whatever might be in the can. Some people had died, one of them argued, from eating out of cans. They argued vigorously, but did not ask Ish's advice. If there was a picture of a fish or some fruit on the outside of the can, then you knew that that kind of food was inside. But even, one of them declared, a rusty can might be dangerous when you knew what was in it, for in some way, if the rust went clear through the can, then what was inside might be spoiled.

As Ish, who was not in the argument, could have told them, the obvious thing to do was to open the can and see in what condition the food inside might be. But being a very old man and having gained some wisdom with life, he realized that they were arguing merely for the fun of it, and that eventually they would get around to a decision.

After a while, indeed, they hacked the can open with one of the knives, and inside was some reddish brown material. To Ish it was obviously a can of salmon. They smelled at it inquisitively, and decided that it was not spoiled. Also they inspected the inside of the can, and found that no rust had penetrated through it. They divided the salmon, and gave a share to Ish.

Ish had not seen or eaten any canned salmon for a long time. The meat looked much darker to him than it should look, and it was lacking in flavor. But its taste—or lack of taste—he decided, might be partly the result of his own dullness of palate at his age. If it had not been so much trouble to talk, he would have liked to deliver a lecture to the young men about all the miracles that lay behind their eating this little snack of salmon. The fish must have been caught many years before, probably off the coast of Alaska, a thousand miles and more from the place where they were now eating it. But even if it had not been so much trouble to talk, still he recollected he could not even have made the young men understand what he was talking about. They had seen the ocean, perhaps, because it was not very far from where they lived, but they would have no conception of a great ship sailing the ocean, and they would have not known what he meant when he talked of a thousand miles.

So he ate quietly, and let his eyes rove from one of the young men to another. More and more often, however, his eyes came to rest upon that particular one who was called Jack. Life could not have been altogether easy for Jack. He had a scar on his right arm, and, unless Ish's eyes deceived him, the left hand had suffered some kind of accident and was a little twisted. Yes, Jack must have suffered, and yet his face, like those of the others, was clear of lines and free in all its movements.

Again Ish felt his heart yearn toward the young man, for in spite of the scar and the twisted hand the young man seemed child-like and innocent, and Ish was afraid that at some time the world would strike back hard against him and find him unprepared. Once Ish recollected that he had asked a question of this young man named Jack. He had asked him, "Are you happy?" And the young man had answered in such a strange way that Ish had doubted whether he had understood what the words meant. That was the way the things happened over all these years; though the language itself had not changed more than a little, yet there were ideas and differences that had gone out of people's thought. No longer perhaps did they make that sharp distinction between pleasure and sorrow that people had once made in the times of civilization. Perhaps other distinctions too had faded out.

So Jack may not even have understood the question exactly when he had replied then: "Yes, I am happy. Things are as they are, and I am part of them."

But at least merriment had not gone out of the world. As Ish rested beneath the rock-overhang, he saw the others playing with their dogs or joking with one another. They laughed easily and often. And, as that one still carved at his wooden figurine, he whistled a tune. It was a gay tune, and Ish remembered its lilt but not its name or the words to sing with it. Yet it brought to him a feeling of small bells, and snow, and little glowing red and green lights, and festivity. Yes, that must have been a gay song even in the Old Days, and now it sounded gayer than ever. Gaiety—that had survived the Great Disaster!

The Great Disaster! Ish had not thought of those words for a long time. Now they seemed to have lost meaning. Those people who had died then would now be dead anyway, from mere passage of time. Now it seemed to make little difference whether they had all died in one year, or slowly over many years. And as for the loss of civilization—about that too he had long doubted.

The young man still whistled gaily, and Ish thought that he could remember the words "Oh, what fun it is . . ." He could ask the young man about the words. As he sat there in the deep cleft between the two rocks, however, Ish still found himself too tired to bother asking questions. Nevertheless his mind was clear. It was frighteningly clear, and he could not remember when before he had been able to think so deeply in behind the surface of things.

"What is all this?" he thought to himself. "Why is my mind so keen today?" He thought that perhaps it might be from the shock of being pulled out of bed so roughly and forced to leave the burning house. But he was not sure. All he knew was that he thought more clearly than he had been able to do since he could remember.

Still he wondered at the faces of the young men and their confidence, when outside everything was burning. Though Ish could not solve that problem, yet he thought much about it, and had various ideas. Perhaps, he thought, the difference lay somewhere in the difference between civilization and the times in which they now were living. In civilization, he thought, these young men would have all been considering one another as rivals, because in the days of civilization there were many men. They did not think much about the world outside of them because man seemed to be greatly stronger than all that outside world. So they thought mostly about how they could get the better of other people, and so they were likely not to trust each other altogether, not even brother and brother. But now, he thought, when men are very few, each of these young men wanders freely with his bow in hand and his dog at heel, but needs his comrade close at call. Nevertheless Ish did not know, and though his mind thought very clearly and very deeply in those hours, still he was not sure.

By mid-afternoon the fire had swept past them, and was burning far off to the south. They left the shelter of the rocks; avoiding places where the fire was still smouldering and where embers lay hot, they made their way southward down the slope of the hill gradually, without much difficulty. Evidently the young men knew what they were doing. Ish did not bother to ask questions because he needed all his strength merely to keep moving. They waited for him patiently, and often they helped him, letting him rest his arms across their shoulders. Toward evening, when his strength was failing, they made camp near a stream. Because of some freak of the wind and also because of the greener growth there, the fire had left a small spot unburned.

A little water was running in the stream-bed. The larger game all seemed to have run before the flames, but many quail and rabbits had taken shelter along the stream-bed, and the young men, scattering with their bows, soon came back with plenty of food.

One of them, apparently out of mere habit, began to make a fire with a bow-drill. But the others laughed at him, and soon gathered together some still glowing and smouldering sticks from where the fire had swept through.

After he had eaten a little and felt stronger, Ish looked around, and saw by the gutted ruins of a great building that they had camped on what had long ago been the campus of the University. Though he was still tired, he stood up curiously, and made out the shape of the Library a hundred yards or so distant. The trees around it had burned, but the building itself was still intact. Nearly all of its volumes, the whole record of mankind, would probably be still available. *Available for whom?* Ish did not try to anwer the question that rose so spontaneously in his mind. In some way, the rules of the game had changed. He would not say whether they had changed for better or for worse. In any case, the Library—its preservation or its destruction—seemed to make very little difference in his thoughts now. Perhaps, this was the wisdom of old age. Perhaps, it was only despair and resignation.

"This will be a strange place for me to sleep tonight," Ish thought. "Will the ghosts of my old professors move before me after all these years? Will I dream of a million books passing in endless procession, looking reproachfully upon me because after so long I have begun to have doubts in them and all they stood for?"

That night, however, though he often woke and was cold and envied the young men sleeping soundly, yet between times of waking he slept well and had no dreams, because he was very tired from all that had happened during the day.

Chapter 3

In the dawn, when he awoke finally, he was weak but clear-headed.

"This is very strange," he thought, "because in the last few years I know that frequently I have not been wholly conscious of what was happening, and that is the way a very old man often is. But now, as it was yesterday, I see everything very clearly. I wonder what this can mean?"

He watched the young men making breakfast ready. That same one was whistling gaily at the same tune, and again it brought to Ish the thought of little bells and happiness, although he could not remember its name. But still his mind was clear—"clear as a bell," the old words came to him, since the idea of bells was already with him.

"I have heard," he thought, putting the thoughts into silent sentences, as he had always had a habit of doing, and now as an old man was more prone than ever to do. "Yes, I have heard, or more likely I have read it in one of all those books—at least, from somewhere I have got the idea that a man's mind becomes clear just before he is to die. Well, I am very old, and it is likely enough, and nothing certainly to be unhappy about. If I were a Catholic now and if things were different, I should wish to confess."

Then by the little stream, with the smell of smoke still in his nostrils and with the old University buildings looming up around him, he thought for a moment of his life, and considered what he had piled up of sins and of virtues. For he realized that a man should make peace with himself, even though all conditions changed, and that a man should face the question of whether in his life he had satisfied the ideas which he had built up within himself as to what he should be, and that all this was not a matter of priests and religion but of a man himself.

After he had considered his life, he did not feel perturbed. He had made mistakes, but also he had sometimes done the right thing, as always—or at least in general— he had tried to do. The Great Disaster had placed him in a position for which he had no training; still he had accomplished certain things, and had lived, he trusted, not altogether ignobly.

Just then one of them brought him a morsel of something that had been roasted on a stick before the fire.

"This is for you," said the young man. "It is the breast of a quail, as you yourself, Ish, well know."

Ish thanked him politely, and chewed at the meat, being glad that he had teeth left. The smoky tang of the open fire was in the meat, and the taste was delicious.

"Why should I consider dying?" he thought. "Life is still good, and I am the last American."

But he did not bother to comment on anything that was happening or to ask questions as to what they would do that day. He felt in some strange way as if he had partially withdrawn from the world, although he was still so fully conscious of it.

After breakfast there came a shouting from farther down the stream, and soon a newcomer arrived. There was a long talk then, but Ish did not pay much attention. He gathered, in general, that the whole tribe was moving toward a place where there were some lakes and where the fire had not swept. It was very good country, according to what the newcomer said. The three young men who had been with Ish were at first inclined to argue about this, because they had not been consulted in the decision. But the other explained that the whole question had been put up before the assembly of The Tribe, and so decided. The three then yielded, granting that what The Tribe had decided was binding upon them also.

Though this was doubtless a very small incident, Ish found it particualrly gratifying. That was something which he had taught them long ago. But the thought, though it was pleasant, also brought him sorrow and even embarrassment when he remembered Charlie.

Soon they made preparations to begin the march, but Ish was so weak that he could hardly walk at all. The young men then decided that they would carry him pickaback by turns, and so they started. Carrying him, they managed to move more rapidly than they had moved on the preceding day when he had walked. They made jokes, one with another, about how light an old man grew to be—happy jokes with a lusty vein running through them, as to why an old man was so light. But Ish at least was glad that he was no great burden upon them; in fact, one of them said that to carry the hammer was as heavy a load as to carry Ish himself.

Once they were moving in this fashion, perhaps the joggling of being carried pickaback affected Ish, and he found the fog again creeping in upon his brain. He did not even know just where they were going or in what direction they were moving. Only, now and then, some incident stood out clearly before him.

After a while they passed out of the burned area, and came to a part of the city past which the fire had swept, leaving it uninjured. From the dampness in the air which made him shiver a little Ish realized that the wind had changed and that this area must be close to the Bay. There were ruins of factory buildings in this section. Once he noticed the paralled rust lines of a railroad track. Everything was much grown up with bushes and some tall trees, but the long dry summers had prevented the country from returning to forest, and so there was always a good deal of grassy expanse through which the young men had no difficulty in finding a way. Often, moreover, they followed the actual lines of streets where the asphalt still showed in places, in spite of the weeds growing up through its cracks and the grass encroaching upon its sides where the blown dust of all these years had supplied a skim of soil to the surface. But generally the young men seemed to steer more by the position of the sun or by some distant landmark than to make their way along the lines of streets.

As they were passing a thicket, something caught Ish's eye, and he reached out his hand and cried for it, suddenly, as a child might. The young men saw what he was doing. They stopped, laughing merrily, to humor him. One of them went to get the thing for which he had cried out. When they brought it, Ish was delighted, and now they laughed at him as if he really were a child, good-naturedly.

Ish did not mind. He had what he wanted. It was a scarlet flower—a geranium, which had adapted itself to the new life and lived through these years. It was not the flower but the color, Ish realized, that had given him that sudden pang and made him cry out. There was not enough red in the world any more. Being old, he could remember a world in which dyes and lights flamed with scarlet and vermilion. But now the world had sunk back into a quiet harmony of blues and greens and browns—and reds no longer blazed everywhere.

But as he jogged along pickaback, he lost the sense of what was happening, and when he came to himself again, they were all seated on the ground taking a rest, and somewhere he had dropped the flower. Now, as he looked up, his eyes saw something a little distance away, and when he focused, he saw that it was a road-marker. It was shield-shaped, and he read U.S. and CALIFORNIA, and in large numerals, 4 and 0. He was so unused to seeing numerals that it was a moment before he could put the two together and form on his tongue the word "Forty."

"This, then," he thought, "this road which I can hardly make out because of all the things growing on it, this is old U.S. 40—the East Shore Highway. It used to be six lanes wide. We must be heading toward the Bay Bridge." And then again he did not remember clearly anything more.

There was still another incident of that morning's march which came to him clearly out of the dimness of the fog pressing in around him. Again they had halted, but this time they were not sitting. The young man called Jack was carrying him at this moment, and as Ish looked out over Jack's left shoulder, he saw the one with the spear right in front of them; one on each side, stood the two other young men, each with his bow half-drawn and an arrow nocked ready on the string. The two dogs crouched at heel, and they were growling deeply. Then, looking farther on, Ish saw a huge mountain-lion in the path.

The lion crouched, threatening, on one side. And on the other side, the men and dogs stood their ground. Thus they remained for perhaps a dozen breaths.

Then the one with the spear said, "He is not going to spring." He spoke quietly and in a matter-of-fact voice.

"Shall I shoot?" said one of the others.

"Don't be a fool!" said the one with the spear, calmly.

They all went back a little way, and made a detour off to the right, making the dogs keep close at heel, so that they would not rush off and alarm or disturb the lion. In this way they went around the lion, leaving him possession of the direct way, but avoiding trouble. Ish wondered greatly about all this. As far as he could see the men were not afraid of the beast but were merely avoiding trouble, and on the other hand the beast did not seem to be afraid of the men. Perhaps it was because there were no more rifles being used, or perhaps it was because there were so few men that a lion rarely saw one and could not realize how dangerous these not very dangerous-looking creatures could be. Or perhaps, if the young men had not been encumbered with a helpless old one, they might have attacked.

Yet certainly he could not help thinking that the men had lost that old dominance and the arrogance with which they had once viewed the animals, and were now acting more or less as equals with them. He felt that this was too bad, and yet the young men were going along just as unconcerned as ever, cracking their little jokes and not feeling that they had been at all humiliated by having to detour the lion, any more than if they had had to detour around a fallen tree-trunk or a ruined building.

When he next began to pay attention, they were approaching the bridge. Ish became interested, and again he wished that he could tell the young men something of the Old Times, of what the bridge used to be like when traffic was pouring across it in both directions and all six lanes were so full of whizzing cars that you could not have run from one side to the other and remained alive.

Now, however, as they slowly walked up the long approach and came to the first span on the East Bay side, Ish could see that the bridge as a whole, though rust-covered, was still intact. The pavement, however, was badly gone to pieces, and whole sections of the highway sagged a little, and some of the towers were noticeably out of line.

At one place they had to walk for a few feet across a single girder which offered the only passageway. Looking down from the young man's back, Ish could see clear down to where the waves were slushing back and forth, and he noticed that the metal of the bridge, where salt-water had splashed on it for all these years, was deeply corroded, and sagging and breaking.

This is the road that no man finishes traveling. This is the river so long that no voyager finds the sea. This is the path winding among the hills, and still winding. This is the bridge that no man crosses wholly—lucky is he who through the mists and rain-clouds sees, or even believes he dimly sees, the farther shore.

After that, Ish was not sure of anything again until at last he realized that he was sitting on something hard and leaning against something hard, and that his feet were very cold. Next he knew that somebody was chafing his hands, and then slowly he came into consciousness.

He found that he was sitting on the pavement at the edge of the bridge, propped against the railing. The first thing that he really noticed was his hammer on the pavement in front of him, the handle pointing stiffly in the air. On each side of him, a young man was chafing one of his hands, as if trying to get some blood back into them. The other two young men were near also, and they all seemed greatly disturbed.

Ish realized that his feet and even his lower legs were cold, or perhaps they had really lost all feeling in a kind of cold that might be called deathly. He knew then, his mind again becoming clearer, that he had not been merely passing through one of his lapses of old age but that he must actually have suffered some kind of seizure—a stroke or a heart attack—and that the others were frightened.

He saw Jack moving his lips as if he were talking, and yet making no noise. A strange thing to do! The lips moved more and more vigorously, as if Jack were shouting. Then Ish realized that he himself was not hearing. This thought did not pain him, but rather pleased him, because he knew that he would now not have the world press in upon him, as it must always upon a man who can hear.

The others began talking, that is, moving their lips in the same way, and Ish saw that they were trying definitely, even desperately, to tell him something. He shook his head, puzzled. Then he tried to tell them that he could not hear, but he realized that he did not have control over his speech. This disturbed him, for he realized that it would be a nuisance to live in the world when he could not communicate by talking and when nobody could understand what he wrote.

The young men had been very respectful and friendly all day. But now they became irritated. They gesticulated, and Ish could see they were insistent that he should do something, and were even frightened that he might not be able to do it. They made gestures toward the hammer, but Ish did not feel it worthwhile to try very hard to understand.

Soon, however, the young men were even more insistent, and then they began to pinch him. Ish felt the pain because his body was still sensitive, and he cried out, and tears even came to his eyes, though he was ashamed of that, and felt that it was not fitting for the last American.

"It is a strange thing," he thought, "to be an old god. They worship you, and yet they mistreat you. If you do not want to do what they wish, they make you. It is not fair."

Then, by thinking hard and by watching their gestures, he thought that they wanted him to indicate one of them to whom the hammer should be given. The hammer had been Ish's own for a long time, and no one had ever suggested that he should give it to anyone else, but he did not care, and besides he wished them to stop pinching him. He could still move his arms, and so with a gesture he indicated that the young man called Jack should have the hammer.

Jack picked up the hammer, and stood with it dangling from his right hand. The other three then drew off a little, and Ish felt within himself a strange pang of sorrow for the young man to whom the hammer had descended.

But at least they all seemed to be relieved, now that the inheritance of the hammer was settled, and they did not bother Ish any more.

He rested there quietly then, as if he had done all in this world that he needed to do, and had made his peace. He was dying on the bridge, and he knew it now. Many others, he remembered, had died on that bridge. He might have died there many years before in some mere crash of automobiles. Now he had lived clear out of his own world, and still he was dying there. One way or another, he now was contented. He half-remembered a line which he had read in some book at some time during all those years when he had read so many books. "Men go and come . . ." But that was trite and meaningless without its other half.

He looked now at the others, although there was a little mist before his eyes and he could not see very well. Yet he noticed the two dogs lying quietly, and the four young men—

three of them apart from the other one now—who squatted on the bridge in a half circle around him, watching. They were very young in age, at least by comparison with him, and in the cycle of mankind they were many thousands of years younger than he. He was the last of the old; they were the first of the new. But whether the new would follow the course which the old had followed, that he did not know, and now at last he was almost certain that he did not even desire that the cycle should be repeated. He suddenly thought of all that had gone to build civilization—of slavery and conquest and war and oppression.

But now he looked beyond the young men, toward the bridge itself. Now that he would soon be dead, he felt himself more a companion of the bridge than of the men. It too had been part of civilization.

A little distance off, he was surprised to see a car standing, or what was left of a car. Then he remembered the little coupé which had been parked there during all those years. Now the paint had weathered off almost entirely; not only were the tires flat but also the springs had grown weak, so that the whole car had settled downwards. All its upper parts were white with bird-droppings. Curiously, although it was a matter of no importance, he could still remember that the owner of the car had been James Robson (with a middle initial which was E. or T. or P., or something like that) and that he had lived on one of the numbered streets in Oakland.

But Ish let his gaze rest upon the little coupé only for a moment. Then his eyes moved higher, and he saw the tall towers and the great cables, still dipping in perfect curves. This part of the bridge seemed to be in a good state of preservation. It would apparently stand for a long time still, perhaps during the lives of many generations of men. The railings, the towers, and the cables—all were rusted red. But he knew that that rust must be superficial. The tops of the towers, however, were not red, but were shining white with the droppings of generations of seagulls.

Yet though the bridge might last still for many years, the rust would eat deeper and deeper. The earthquake would shake the foundations, and then on some stormy day a span would go down. Like the man, so the creation of man would not last forever.

He shut his eyes for a moment, and imagined the whole sweep of the hills around the bay, though he could not turn his head to see them. They had not changed their profile since the destruction of civilization; as measured by man's time, they would not change. As far as the b y and the hills went, he was still dying in the same world to which he had been born.

Opening his eyes, he now looked and was able to see the two pointed peaks at the crest of the ridge. "Twin Breasts" they had once been called, and the sight of them m..de him think of Em, and even further back, of his own mother. The earth and Em and the mother all mingled in his dying mind, and he felt glad to return.

"But, no," he thought, after a moment, "I must die as I have lived—by the light of my own mind, by what light it gives me. Those hills, though they may take the shape of breasts, they are not like Em or like my mother. They will receive me—they will receive my body—but they will not love me. They do not care. And also I am one who has studied the ways of the earth, and I know that the hills themselves, though men call them eternal—they too are changing always."

Yet as a weary and dying old man, he needed something toward which he could look and from which he could expect no change. He was cold now around the waist, and his fingers were numb. His sight was fading.

He fixed his eyes on the distant hills. He had tried very hard. He had struggled. He had looked to the p st and to the future. What did it matter? What had he accomplished?

Now certainly it made no difference. He would rest, and he would return to the hills. And they—in comparison at least with the passing of man's generations—remained without changing. And if the shape of the hills was like the shape of a woman's breasts, perhaps that too was not without its meaning and comfort.

Then, though his sight was now very dim, he looked again at the young men. "They will commit me to the earth," he thought. "Yet I also commit them to the earth. There is nothing else by which men live. *Men go and come, but earth abides.*"